MAGIC

FOR

LIARS

ALSO BY SARAH GAILEY

American Hippo: River of Teeth, Taste of Marrow, and New Stories

MAGIC

FOR

LIARS

SARAH GAILEY

A TOM DOHERTY ASSOCIATES BOOK  TOR NEW YORK

MAGIC FOR LIARS

Copyright © 2019 by Sarah Gailey

A Tor Book
Published by Tom Doherty Associates
175 Fifth Avenue
New York, NY 10010

www.tor-forge.com

Tor® is a registered trademark of Macmillan Publishing Group, LLC.

The Library of Congress Cataloging-in-Publication Data
is available upon request.

ISBN 978-1-250-17461-1 (hardcover)
ISBN 978-1-250-17460-4 (ebook)

Our books may be purchased in bulk for promotional, educational, or business use. Please contact your local bookseller or the Macmillan Corporate and Premium Sales Department at 1-800-221-7945, extension 5442, or by email at MacmillanSpecialMarkets@macmillan.com.

First Edition: June 2019

Printed in the United States of America

0 9 8 7 6 5 4 3 2 1

For the people who knew before I did

MAGIC

FOR

LIARS

PROLOGUE

THE LIBRARY AT OSTHORNE ACADEMY for Young Mages was silent save for the whisper of the books in the Theoretical Magic section. Honeyed sun poured through two tall windows onto rows of empty study tables, which still gleamed with the freshness of summer cleaning. It was a small library—each section took up only a row or two of tall metal shelves—but it was big enough to hide in. Sunlight from the windows along one wall of the library spilled between the shelves, casting long shadows. None of the students had come to linger, not in the first week of school—they'd dashed in and then out again, looking for friends or for classes they'd never been to before. Now they were all downstairs at the welcome-back dinner, an all-staff-all-students meal that marked the end of the first week of classes. They'd joke there about house-elves and pumpkin juice—or at least the freshmen would. By the time they were sophomores, that vein of humor was worn beyond use.

Mrs. Webb was not at the welcome-back dinner, and neither was Dylan DeCambray. One was hunting the other, a familiar pastime for both of them. Dylan was hiding in the stacks—specifically, in the Poison and Theoretical Poison section. He had tucked himself into the shadow of a returns cart, his legs cramping as he listened to Mrs. Webb's measured footfalls in the next section over: Electricity, Theoretical Electricity, Electrical Manipulations.

"Mr. DeCambray, let's not have another year like this. You're a senior now. I'd have expected you to be more mature than you were as a freshman." Her voice was thick with age. The condemnation of *immaturity* might have moved another student to self-immolation, but Dylan had a higher purpose. He would never let an authority figure stand in the way of that purpose, no matter the depths of their misunderstanding.

The Prophecy.

Mrs. Webb rounded the shelves into the Poison section. She moved slowly, deliberately—she'd often told students that hurrying was a fool's errand. *If you need to hurry,* her oft-repeated saying went, *you're already too late.* The early-evening shadows cast by the drooping sun should have deepened Mrs. Webb's wrinkles, but, as she turned, the golden haze that made it into the stacks hit her profile just right, illuminating the young woman she once had been. In that moment, only white hair, sculpted as always into a perfect bouffant, belied her eighty-six years. A few more steps, and her face was in shadow once more. Mrs. Webb was just a short distance from the returns cart, close enough for Dylan to inhale the faint powdery smell of her perfume.

Dylan took a deep breath, then cupped his hands and blew into them. He waved them in front of himself, a mime smearing grease across the inside of his invisible box. Mrs. Webb walked a few feet in front of him. Her sensible black clogs brushed across the industrial gray carpet tiles with a steady, rhythmic *shush-shush-shush*. She peered around the returns cart over the top of her red horn-rimmed glasses, looking straight into Dylan's face. He could have counted the black freckles that dotted her dark brown skin. She hardly had to stoop to be at eye level with seventeen-year-old Dylan; when he stood at his full six-foot height, he towered over the tiny woman.

He held his breath as she straightened and continued stalking between the shelves of the Poison section. His concealment charm had held. Mrs. Webb had looked right at Dylan, and she had not seen a pale, stretched-out seventeen-year-old with unruly brown hair and the hollow, hungry face of summer growth spurts. She had seen nothing but a few cobwebs and a row of books about the uses of arsenic.

"Mr. DeCambray, honestly," she called out again, her voice weary with exasperation. "I don't know what you're thinking you're going to find in here, but I can assure you that there are no mysteries to be solved, no conspiracies to be unraveled. Whether or not you're the—oh, *hush*," she snapped at the books in the restricted Theoretical Magic section. But their whispering didn't stop—if anything, it increased, the books murmuring to each other like a scandalized congregation of origami Presbyterians.

Mrs. Webb paused at the end of the Poison section, looking toward the Theoretical Magic section again. "Mr. DeCambray, please. Just come down to dinner. This is foolishness." She rounded the end of the shelves, and the murmurs of the books grew loud enough that Dylan couldn't quite make out what she was saying anymore. But that didn't matter. The only thing that mattered was that she was no longer between him and the library exit.

Dylan rose and made for the door, victorious: he had dodged her. He could make his way back to the dinner, and when she came to the dining hall to admit defeat, he could say he'd been there all along. It was a good way to start the year. This was going to be *his* year, Dylan thought. He eased the library door open, slipping his narrow frame through and closing it without so much as a silencing charm to cover the *snuck* sound of the latch. *Triumph.*

Dylan's shoes squeaked on the linoleum of the hallway as he ran. His too-long legs tangled, and he was about to catch himself midstride, about to make it to the end of the hall and the stairs that led down to the mess—but he skidded to a stop.

A scream echoed through the corridor.

Crap. His heart was pounding wildly—was this it? Was it finally time? Dylan DeCambray was torn between terror and elation. *It's happening, it's really happening*—he pelted back toward the library, toward the sound of Mrs. Webb screaming over and over again. He knocked over a chair or two on his way to the section where the screaming was coming from—the chairs weren't really in his way, but the moment felt so urgent that it seemed wrong to leave things undisturbed. A small voice inside him whispered, *Now, now, it's happening now.*

He pulled up short at the Theoretical Magic section, gasping for breath, his hands braced on the shelves at the end of the row. His foot crunched a sheet of copy paper that read "Reorganization in Progress: Do Not Enter Without Protective Equipment." The wards were down. The books, which had been whispering so insistently when Dylan left the library, had gone silent. They seemed to stare at the tableau in the center of the section.

Dylan stared too. Then his brain caught up to what his eyes were seeing. He turned, still clutching one of the shelves, and vomited. When he thought he could stand it, he tried to straighten—but then he saw what was in the aisle, and his empty stomach clenched, and he heaved again.

In the middle of the section, Mrs. Webb stood with the sun at her back. One hand clutched her cardigan closed over her throat; the other held an old, crooked birch wand high over her head, amplifying the sound of her screams to an inhuman volume. Her voice didn't break or cease—the screaming filled the school like a strobing siren.

She took a step backward, mouth open, still screaming, when she saw Dylan. Her shoes sank with a sick sucking sound into the soaked industrial carpet, which had turned so red as to look nearly black. Every time Dylan allowed his eyes to fall below her knees, he tasted fear-bitter bile rising in the back of his throat.

It was next to her feet.

At first Dylan had taken it to be two very slim bodies, facing away from each other. There were two fanning sprays of white-blond hair; there were two wide, pale green eyes staring up at the shelves out of two familiar profiles. But, as Dylan had noticed just before his stomach had twisted for the second time, there were only two long-fingered hands. Two *total*.

The woman on the floor had been cut in half, right down the middle, and laid out like a book with a broken spine. Her blood had soaked into the carpet and spread far enough to touch both bookshelves, a moat between Mrs. Webb and Dylan DeCambray.

As Mrs. Webb's voice finally began to crack with the strain of screaming, the books in the middle of the Theoretical Magic section of the library at Osthorne Academy for Young Mages began to whisper once more.

CHAPTER
ONE

I T MIGHT TAKE A LITTLE while to get there, but I'll tell you every-thing, and I'll tell you the truth. As best I can. I used to lie, but when I tell you the story, you'll understand why I had to lie. You'll understand that I didn't have a choice.

I just wanted to do my job.

No, I said I would tell you the truth. Of course I had a choice. We all have choices, don't we? And if I tell myself that I didn't have a choice, I'm no better than an adulterer who misses his daughter's dance recital because he's shacking up in some shitty hotel with his wife's sister. He tells himself that he doesn't have a choice too. But we know better than that. He has choices. He chooses to tell the first lie, and then he chooses to tell every other lie that comes after that. He chooses to buy a burner phone to send pictures of his cock to his mistress, and he chooses to tell his wife that he has a business trip, and he chooses to pull cash out of an ATM to pay for the room. He tells himself that all of his choices are in-evitable, and he tells himself that he isn't lying.

But when I hand his wife an envelope full of photographs and an invoice for services rendered, her world is turned upside down, because he chose. If I try to pretend I didn't have a choice, I'm not any different from the liars whose lives I ruin, and that's not who I am. I'm nothing like them. My job is to pursue the truth.

So, the truth: it's not that I didn't have a choice. I did. I had a thousand choices.

I was so close to making the right one.

The man who stood between me and the door to my office was trembling-thin, his restless eyes sunken with desperation, holding a knife out like an offering. It was warm for January, but he was shaking in the morning air. He wasn't going to follow through, I thought. Too scared. But then he licked his dry lips with a dry tongue, and I knew that his fear and my fear were not the same kind of fear. He'd do what he thought he needed to do.

Nobody decides to become the kind of person who will stab a stranger in order to get at what's inside her pockets. That's a choice life makes for you.

"Okay," I said, reaching into my tote. I hated my hand for shaking. "Alright, I'll give you what I've got." I rummaged past my wallet, past my camera, past the telephoto lens in its padded case. I pulled out a slim money clip, peeled off the cash, handed it to him.

He could have demanded more. He could have taken my whole bag. But instead, he took the cash, finally looking me in the eyes.

"Sorry," he said, and then he made to run past me, up the stairs that led from my basement-level office to the sidewalk. He was close enough that I could smell his breath. It was oddly sweet, fruity. Like the gum me and my sister Tabitha used to steal from the drugstore when we were kids—the kind that always lost its flavor after ten seconds of chewing. Looking back, I can't figure out why we ever thought it was even worth taking.

The man pelted up the stairs. One of his feet kicked out behind him, and he slipped. "Shit shit shit," I said, rearing back, trying to dodge him before he fell into me. He flailed and caught himself on my shoulder with a closed fist, knocking the wind out of me.

"Jesus fucking Christ, just *go*." I said it with more fear than venom, but it worked. He bolted, dropping his knife behind him with a clatter. I listened to him running down the sidewalk upstairs, his irregular footfalls echoing between the warehouses. I listened until I was sure that he was gone.

CHAPTER

TWO

BAD THINGS JUST HAPPEN SOMETIMES. That's what I've always told myself, and it's what I told myself then: I could have
bled out right there in the stairs leading down to my office, and
not a soul would have known why it happened because there was
no "why." No use dwelling on it: it would have been the end of
me, sudden and senseless. I clenched my jaw and pushed away the
thought of how long it would have taken before someone found
me—before someone wondered what had happened to me. I
pushed away the question of who would have noticed I was gone.

I didn't have time for an existential crisis. It didn't have to be a
big deal. People get mugged all the time. I wasn't special just
because it was my morning to lose some cash. I didn't have time
to be freaked out about it. I had shit to do.

I just wanted to go to work.

I made my way down the remainder of the steps toward the
door that hid in the shadowy alcove at the bottom of the stairs. I
nudged a Gatorade bottle with my toe. The man had been sleeping in my doorway. He couldn't have seen it by the dim light of

the streetlamps at night, but my name was written across the solid metal of the door in flaking black letters:

IVY GAMBLE, PRIVATE INVESTIGATOR
MEETINGS BY APPOINTMENT ONLY

I hadn't gotten the words touched up since I'd first rented the place. I always figured I'd let them fall away until nothing was left but a shadow of the letters. I didn't think I needed to be easy to find—if someone didn't know where my office was, that meant they weren't a client yet. Besides, walk-ins weren't exactly my bread and butter then. The dead bolt locked automatically when the reinforced steel swung shut. That door was made to withstand even the most determined of visitors.

I didn't run my fingers across the letters. If I'd known what would change before the next time I walked down those stairs, though? Well, I wouldn't have run my fingers across the letters then, either. I probably wouldn't have given them a second glance. I've never been good at recognizing what moments are important. What things I should hang on to while I've got them.

I stood on my toes to tap at the lightbulb that hung above the door with a still-shaking hand. The filaments rattled. Dead. On nights when that bulb was lit, nobody slept outside the door, which meant that nobody got surprised coming down the stairs in the morning.

I bit my lip and tapped at the lightbulb again. I took a deep breath, tried to find something in me to focus on. *Imagine you're a candle, and your wick is made of glass.* I gave the bulb a hard stare. I tapped it one more time.

It flickered to life. My heart skipped a beat—but then the bulb died again with a sound like a fly smacking into a set of venetian blinds and went dead, a trace of smoke graying the inside of the glass.

I shook my head, angry at myself for hoping. It hadn't been worth a shot. I thought I had outgrown kid stuff like that. Stupid. I stooped to pick up the little knife from where it lay just in front of the door, squinting at what looked like blood on the blade.

"Shit," I said for the fourth time in as many minutes. As I opened the heavy steel door, a white arc of pain lanced through my shoulder. I looked down, letting the door swing shut behind me. There was a fresh vent in my sleeve. Blood was welling up under it fast—he must have had the knife in his hand when he caught himself on me. I pulled off my ruined jacket, dropping it—and the bloodstained knife—on the empty desk in the waiting area of the office. It fell with a heavy thump, and I remembered my phone in the pocket, the call I was already late for. Sure enough, there were already two pissy texts from the client. I dialed his number with one hand, leaving streaks of stairway grime on the screen, then clamped the phone between my ear and my good shoulder as I headed for the bathroom.

I listened to the ringing on the other end of the line and turned on the hot water tap as far as it would go, attempting to scald the god-knows-what off my palms, trying not to think about the water bill. Or any of the other bills. The cheap pink liquid soap I stocked in the office wasn't doing anything to cut the shit on my hands, which was somehow slippery and sticky at the same time. My shoulder bled freely as I lathered again and again.

"Sorry I'm late, Glen," I said when he picked up. My voice probably shook with leftover adrenaline, probably betrayed how much my shoulder was starting to hurt. Fortunately, Glen wasn't the kind of person who would give a shit whether or not I was okay. He immediately started railing about his brother, who he was sure was stealing from their aunt and who I had found was, in fact, just visiting her on the regular like a good nephew. I put Glen on speaker so he could rant while I peeled off my shirt with wet hands, wincing at the burning in my shoulder. I stood there in my camisole, wadded up the shirt and pressed it to the wound. The bleeding was slow but the pain was a steady strobe.

"I hope you don't think I'm going to pay for this shit," Glen was saying, and I closed my eyes for a couple of seconds. I allowed myself just a few heartbeats of bitterness at how unfair it was, that I had to deal with Glen and look for my long-neglected first aid kit at the same time. I was going to take just a moment of self-pity before going into my patient *I've provided you a service and you were well aware of my fee schedule* routine—but then I heard the unmistakable sound of the front door to my office opening.

I froze for a gut-clenched second before hanging up on Glen. I let my blood-soaked shirt drop to the floor, shoved my phone into my bra so it wouldn't vibrate against the sink when he called back. I heard the office door close, and a fresh flood of adrenaline burned through me.

Someone was in the office with me.

No one had an appointment. No one should have been able to get inside at all. That door locked automatically when it closed, and I knew it had closed. I *knew* it, I had heard it click shut behind me. This wouldn't be the first break-in attempt, but it was the first time someone had tried it while I was in the office. I pressed my ear to the door, carefully gripped the knob without letting it rattle in my fingers. The lock on the door was busted, but at least I could try to hold it shut if they decided to look around.

"I'm here to see Ms. Gamble." A woman's voice, clear and steady. *What the fuck?* I could hear her footsteps as she walked across the little waiting area. I winced, remembering my jacket and the bloodstained knife on the abandoned admin desk. She murmured something that sounded like "Oh dear." My phone buzzed against my armpit, but Glen and his yelling would just have to wait.

"Once you've finished treating your wound, you can come out of the bathroom, Ms. Gamble. I don't care that you're in your camisole. We have business to discuss."

I straightened so fast that something in my back gave a pop. My head throbbed. I stared at the white-painted wood of the door as I realized who was waiting for me out there. This was not good.

This was not good at all.

The shitty waiting-room couch creaked. She was serious—she was going to wait for me. I rushed through cleaning up the slice in my shoulder, wadding up wet paper towels and scrubbing blood off my arm, half ignoring and half savoring how much it hurt. The bandage I hastily taped over the wound soaked through with blood within a few seconds. I would say I considered getting stitches, but it'd be a lie. I'd let my arm fall off before setting foot inside a fucking hospital.

I checked myself in the mirror—not a welcome sight. I pulled my phone out of my bra, ran a hand through my hair. There was only so much I could do to make myself look less like a wreck, and I kept the once-over as brief as possible. I like mirrors about as much as I like hospitals.

I opened the door and strode out with much more confidence than a person who has just been caught hiding in a bathroom should have been able to muster. I've always been good at faking that much, at least. The short, dark-haired woman standing in the front office regarded me coolly.

"Good morning, Ms. Gamble."

"You can call me Ivy, Miss . . . ?" The woman's handshake was firm, but not crushing. It was the handshake of a woman who felt no need to prove herself.

"Marion Torres," she replied. The woman peered at my face, then nodded, having seen there whatever it was she was searching for. I could guess what it was. It was a face I couldn't seem to get away from. *Shit.*

"Ms. Torres," I replied in my most authoritative, this-is-my-house voice. "Would you like to step into my office?" I led Torres to the narrow door just beyond the empty admin desk, flipping the light on as I entered. I opened a top drawer of my desk, sweeping a stack of photographs into it—fresh shots of a client's wife and her tennis instructor making choices together. Nothing anyone should see, especially not as a first impression. Although, I thought, if this woman was who I thought she was, I didn't want to impress her anyway.

Torres sat straight-backed in the client chair. It was a battered green armchair with a low back, chosen to make clients feel comfortable but not in charge. I remember being proud of myself for the strategy I put into picking that chair. That was a big thing

I solved, the question of what kind of chair I should make desperate people sit in before they asked for my help.

Light streamed into the office through a narrow, wire-reinforced casement window behind my desk. The sunlight caught the threads of silver in Torres's pin-straight black bob. I felt the sliver of camaraderie that I always experienced in the presence of other salt-and-pepper women, but it evaporated fast enough. Torres stared intently at the fine motes of dust that danced in the sunlight. As I watched, the dust motes shifted to form a face that was an awful lot like mine.

I swallowed around rising irritation. I would not yell at this woman.

"You don't look exactly like her," Torres said. "I thought you would. The face is the same, but—"

"We're not that kind of twins," I replied. I crossed behind my desk and pulled the shutters over the window closed, rendering the dust motes—and the familiar face—invisible. "Is she okay?"

"She's fine," Torres said. "She's one of our best teachers, you know."

I settled into my swivel chair, folding my hands on top of my desk blotter. *All business.* "So you're from the academy."

Torres smiled, a warm, toothy grin that immediately made me feel welcome. *Damn, she's good,* I thought—*making me feel welcome in my own office.* I pushed the comfort away and held it at arm's length. No thanks, not interested.

"I am indeed," she said. "I'm the headmaster at Osthorne Academy."

"Not headmistress?" I asked before I could stop myself. I cringed internally as Torres's smile cooled by a few degrees.

"Yes. Please do not attempt to be cute about my title. There are more interesting things to be done with words. We spend most of our students' freshman year teaching them that words have power, and we don't waste that power if we can help it."

I felt a familiar principal's-office twist in my stomach, and had to remind myself again that this was *my* office. "Understood."

We sat in silence for a moment; Torres seemed content to wait for me to ask why she was there. I couldn't think of a good way to ask without being rude, and this woman didn't strike me as someone who would brook poor manners. Distant shouts sounded from outside—friendly but loud, almost certainly kids skipping school to smoke weed behind the warehouses. They'd sit with their backs against the cement walls, scraping out the insides of cheap cigars and leaving behind piles of tobacco and Tootsie Pop wrappers.

Torres cleared her throat. I decided to accept defeat.

"What can I do for you, Ms. Torres?"

Torres reached into her handbag and pulled out a photograph. It was a staff photo, taken in front of a mottled blue backdrop; the kind of photo I might have seen in the front few pages of my own high school yearbook. A twenty-five-cent word sprang unbidden into my mind: "noctilucent." The word described the glow of a cat's eyes at night, but it also seemed right for the woman in the photograph. She was a moonbeam turned flesh, pale with white-blond hair and wide-set light green eyes. Beautiful was not an appropriate word; she looked otherworldly. She looked impossible.

"That," Torres said after allowing me to stare for an embarrassingly long time, "is Sylvia Capley. She taught health and wellness at Osthorne. Five months ago, she was murdered in the library. I need you to find out who killed her."

Direct. More direct than I was prepared for. I blinked down at the photo. "I'm so sorry for your loss." The words came automatically. "But isn't this a matter for the police? You—um. Mages. Don't you have police?"

Torres pursed her lips, looking up at the shuttered window. "We do. But they—hm." She hesitated.

I didn't push her for more. I knew from experience that it was far more effective to let a client sit with the silence—to let them decide for themselves to fill it. I've always been good at letting silence put down roots.

"I don't agree with their findings," Torres finally finished. "I'd like a second opinion."

"My opinion?" I said, flashing Torres the skepticals. "I don't do murder investigations." I said it as if it were a choice, rather than a simple fact of the law and my poor marketing. I was sure that there were some people out there who were still hiring PIs to solve murders, but none of them had ever come knocking at my basement door. I wanted her to think it was a choice, though.

"You come highly recommended," Torres replied, dry as kindling. "And you know about us. You've got the right eye, to see the things that the investigators missed because they were too busy looking for obvious answers to see this for what it was. This was murder."

"And what are the obvious answers?"

Torres pulled a business card from the space between naught and nothing. I bit back annoyance again. She wasn't doing it to antagonize me. Probably. She handed me the card, and, to my credit, I only hesitated for a couple of seconds before letting the paper touch my skin. A breathtakingly high number was written on the back in a headmaster's irreproachable penmanship. "That's the amount of retainer I'm willing to pay. Up front, in cash."

It's not that there was a catch in her voice, not exactly. But I could hear her keeping herself steady. I kept my eyes on her business card, counting zeroes. "Why are you so invested in this? If the magic-cops said it wasn't murder—"

"It was murder," she interrupted, her voice clapping the conversation shut like a jewelry box I wasn't supposed to reach for. I looked up at her, startled, and she pursed her lips before continuing in a calmer tone. "Sylvia was a dear friend of mine. I knew her well, and I am *certain* that she didn't die the way they say she did. Courier a contract to the address on the front of the card if you're willing to take the job. I'd like to see you in my office on Friday morning."

And before I could ask anything else—before I could come up with the next question or the sly rebuttal or the little joke that would keep her there, talking, explaining everything, telling me what the "obvious answers" were supposed to be—Marion Torres had vanished. I sat heavily in my chair, staring at the place where she had been, trying to swallow the old anger. It was just like these people to drop a line like that and then *poof*. If they would only stay vanished, my life would be a hell of a lot simpler.

I reread the number Torres had written down. I ran my thumb over the grooves her pen had left in the thick paper. I listened to my cell phone vibrating—Glen calling again to yell at me. I breathed deep, tasting the dust in the air. The dust that Torres had rearranged into the shape of my sister's face. It was the first time

I'd seen that face in years. It was a face I hadn't thought I'd ever see again.

I pressed one corner of the business card into the meat of my palm, deciding whether or not to take the case. I stared at the way the paper dented my skin, and I pretended that I had a choice.

CHAPTER

THREE

I NEVER WANTED TO BE magic.

That was Tabitha's thing, not mine, and sometimes you just have to be fine with things the way they are. And I was fine with it.

"Liquid lunch?" The bartender cocked an eyebrow at me as he placed a dark, sweating bottle in front of me next to a chilled glass.

"Part of a balanced breakfast," I replied mildly, decanting my beer into the glass. He gave me an easy smile, a you're-funny smile that he probably used on everyone. Affirmation and illusion, bound up tighter than two snakes in the same egg.

But then, maybe he didn't give that smile to everyone. Maybe he actually thought I was okay, for a lunchtime customer. Maybe I was just being a cynical asshole.

"I'm actually having kind of a terrible day, if I'm honest." I said it quietly, half hoping he wouldn't hear. Giving him a chance to ignore me. I leaned my elbows against the long reclaimed-wood bar. This wasn't my usual bar—the place was new in the neighborhood, eminently forgettable in the grand scheme of gentrification. This bartender didn't know my face, wouldn't recognize me. Didn't have to be nice to me now, or ever again. I'd come here telling myself I just wanted to exist while I drank my breakfast and digested everything that had come with the morning. I'd wanted to hide. But then the bartender gave me that you're-clever smile, and I realized I had to tell someone. Just to have it all out in the world, somewhere other than my own head.

The bartender didn't say anything. Maybe he hadn't heard me at all. I studied the decor as if I didn't care either way. Tiny pots with tinier succulents, weird art accents hanging above the bottles behind the bar. I couldn't tell if I'd been there for happy hour before, or if I'd just been to a thousand places exactly like it. Places like that were springing up around Oakland by the score back then, every one a marker of the way the city was changing. It felt all-at-once, even though it had been brewing for years. Decades. Across the bay, San Francisco bled money like an unzipped artery. Those who had been privileged enough to have their buckets out to catch the spray drove back over the water to Oakland— from The City to The Town. They bumped aside people who had been living in these neighborhoods for generations, and they tore down storefronts, and they built brunch pubs with wood reclaimed from the houses they were remodeling.

It was shitty and it was destructive and it was perfect, because I could slip onto a barstool and pretend I had a place to go. Just for a few hours at a time. Something familiar. Bars with driftwood behind the bottles instead of mirrors.

"Tell me about it?" The bartender was in front of me again, holding a bucket of limes. He started slicing them, looking back and forth between me and the knife.

"Shouldn't your barback be doing that?" I asked, watching him slowly quarter a lime.

"He's too hungover to function," the bartender said, rolling his eyes. "So what's up with your day?"

I took a pull of my stout—it was thick as a milkshake, and it hit my belly like a hug. "Well," I said. "I got mugged."

"Sucks," he replied, and I tipped my drink toward him in a cheers-to-sucks gesture.

"And then this woman came into my office. She wants to hire me for a case. A big one. It'll mean hiring someone to handle all the other active cases I've got going." The other active cases were small potatoes—two disability claims, three cheating spouses, one spouse who wasn't cheating after all but whose husband couldn't believe that she had really taken up pottery. She was pretty good at it too. This wouldn't be the first time I'd had to hire help; when the workload got too intense, I occasionally sub-contracted to other, less-established outfits in the area. I'd return the favor for them someday, if they ever needed someone to do a little heavy lifting. My remote assistant would arrange the logistics—the subcontractors, the paperwork, the payments, the letters to clients. No problem.

"Sure," the bartender said, and bless him, he didn't care enough to ask a single clarifying question. He didn't want to know who I was, where I worked. He just wanted some noise to make the limes less boring. It was perfect.

"So, the woman who was in the office this morning. She's the headmaster at the school where my sister teaches."

"Headmaster? Shit."

"It's a private school. Some kids board there, some don't. It's down by Sunol, in the hills. The Osthorne Academy for Young Mages."

He nodded, didn't flinch at the word "mages." I tapped my fingers on the table, one-two-three-four. This guy wasn't half listening to me. I wasn't anybody to him—just some freelancer drinking beer in the middle of the day and watching him cut a few dozen limes.

So I told him. I told him everything that I knew about the case, and about Osthorne. Halfway through the story, he looked up at me, opened his mouth to say something. Closed it again and went back to the limes, but a stillness had entered his movements—he was listening now, trying to decide if I was crazy. I took a long, slow sip of my beer, made a project of setting my glass down exactly within the condensation ring it'd left on the table.

"But magic isn't *real*," he said after a moment.

"Isn't it?"

"It—of course not. I would have heard of it. Everyone would have heard of it." His eyes were laughing now, waiting for the punch line. He had paused with the tip of the knife in the rind of a runty lime, and he waited for me to answer before pushing it the rest of the way through.

I tried to feel like I was talking to a friend, like this was a real conversation that wouldn't just turn into a weird story he told at the end of his shift. I tried not to feel temporary. Just for a few seconds. But trying not to feel something isn't the same as not feeling it, and I knew it was just a matter of time before I was alone again.

That's how life goes. People don't stick.

"*Haven't* you heard of it, though?"

He shook his head, used the knife's edge to scrape lime pulp off the edge of his cutting board. "But that's different. That's like . . . fiction. Or magicians. Illusionists. Or whatever."

"It's not quite like that." I needed him to believe me. Not that it mattered. I would never see him again. Let him think I was crazy. It didn't matter. "But it is *real*. There are people—a lot of people—who can do magic. Real magic. My sister is one of them. So's that woman who was in my office this morning. They're mages. They do magic." I looked at him, tried to beam understanding into his brain. "They *are* magic." I wasn't sure what I was saying anymore—the look on his face was making me lose track of things. He didn't believe me. This was it: he was going to give me a tight smile and walk away and later he would tell his friends about the lunatic who came into his bar to talk about magic.

But then he didn't walk away. He looked at me, and he didn't say anything, and I realized that he was waiting.

I took another drink, tried to get my thoughts in order. *Forward.* "So. There was a death on campus, in the school library."

"Your sister's school."

"Yeah. It's—she works there. We don't talk."

He nodded, and I couldn't tell if he believed me or had decided to just go with it. I couldn't tell which would be better. "And she's a . . . a witch?"

"A mage," I answered. "We don't call them witches. Or wizards—they hate that."

"Are you one too?"

"Nope. Not me."

"Why not?"

It wasn't like a punch to the gut, not anymore. Not after so many years. More like a sneeze the day after too many sit-ups, or the seat belt tightening after a too-fast stop, or a sudden wave of nausea at the tail end of a hangover.

I shrugged. "Who knows?" I took a long, hard pull of my drink. When I set the glass down it clinked against the table too loudly. "I'm not magic. I'm just . . . not. And she is. She went to a magic school and I went to . . . to regular school."

He wiped his hands on a towel—he was already halfway through the limes—and opened a fresh beer, the same one I'd been drinking. He set it in front of me, and I didn't pretend to hesitate before taking a sip right from the bottle. "She went to Oxthorne?"

"Osthorne, and no," I answered, grateful to get away from the why-not-you. "She went to a place called Headley. It was a boarding school up near Portland. Prestigious as hell. I think she was glad to get away from home." Home had been Woodland, near Sacramento, small and hot and stucco, strip malls and air-conditioned minivans. We had both hated it in that way some kids are just required to hate their hometowns, spent all of our time fantasizing about how we'd get out of there. And then she did. And then, a couple of years later, so did I.

"So you guys aren't close?"

I frowned. "I don't talk to her if I can help it. And most of the time I can help it."

"Okay," he said, and I could see him deciding to give me a reprieve. "So how does it work? Magic."

I shook my head, relieved. "Fuck if I know. I guess you have to be magic to understand it. Every time I tried to ask Tabitha when we were kids, she would make an analogy that's like . . . 'imagine if your heartbeat was a cloud and you could make it rain whenever you had a nightmare,' or 'imagine you're a candle, and your wick is made of glass,' or something. I'm no good at koans."

"Well, what's it look like?" He was in a groove, having fun, getting me to spin him a story. He wanted me to tell him about this. Not that it mattered if a bartender wanted to talk to me—just, it was nice, realizing that he might be disappointed if I left.

"Anything." I pointed at one of the lime slices. "If I was a mage, I could probably make that blossom, or like . . . turn orange, or grow a fish tail."

"Who's magic?"

"What do you mean? Lots of people are—"

"Who that I've heard of? Who's the most famous magic person in history?"

"Winston Churchill." I didn't miss a beat, and felt oddly proud of myself for it.

"No, really."

"Really," I answered over the top of my beer bottle. "He was a racist murderous fuck, but he was magic as all get-out."

The bartender gave me a skeptical eyebrow. "But if he was magic, why didn't he—I don't know. Strike Hitler with lightning or something?"

"Reasons, probably?" I shrugged. "Tabitha could tell you, but the explanation would involve a whole set of theories and committees and treaties you've never heard of, and by the end of the explanation you'd be so bored you'd be gouging your own eyes out to stay awake. Trust me, it's not interesting."

"Okay." He chewed on his lip. He was trying to think of a way to keep this thing from losing steam. "Okay. So. How do you know if you're magic, then?"

I thought about it, picking at the label on my beer bottle. "I guess you just . . . you do magic, and then you know. Lots of kids keep their magic a secret, because they know they're not *supposed* to be able to do things. Like, Tabitha found out when she was little, because she kept changing another girl's markers into butter."

He squinted at the lime in his hand. "What?"

"Yeah," I laughed. "I mean, there were other things too, but this was the first obvious one. She didn't like this other girl because I guess the other girl wouldn't share stickers? So she turned all the girl's markers into *butter*." I shook my head. "The teacher figured out what was going on and sent a note home, and my parents came into the school, and the teacher said that Tabitha was magic. She said that Tabby had probably been doing stuff like this for years, but that most magic kids don't get caught until they have a mage for a teacher. So anyway, she gave my mom and dad a pamphlet and the number of a special tutor who could help Tabitha out. And then . . ." I fluttered my fingers. "That was that. So I guess that's how you find out. You just do magic, and then someone tells you that you're magic."

"So your parents know about it."

Again, that little snag in my gut. "Dad does. Mom did, before she died. It's okay," I said, preemptively answering the oh-god-what-land-mine-have-I-stepped-on panic in his face. "I mean, it's not okay, but it's fine. It was a long time ago."

The bartender looked at me with way too much sincerity. "I'm sorry," he said, and I wanted to spit because I hate that. I hate it when people say that.

"It's fine, really. It happened when I was in high school. Tabitha was at Headley and I was at home." I anticipated the questions he was waiting to ask, the questions everyone always asks. The questions that I stopped wanting to answer the moment they became questions I *could* answer. The questions that made me into a person who didn't ever talk about my past. "It was cancer. In her stomach. Or at least, I guess that's where it started."

That's all he needed to know.

He didn't need to know about how we hadn't realized anything was wrong for a while, when she was just tired. And then she started to have pain in her neck, and she went to the doctor and they found cancer. It was everywhere by then. It was fast. She was sick for a month, and then she stopped treatment, and then she died a month later. He didn't need to know that part. "It was sad, or whatever. But it was a long time ago. I'm okay. Everyone's okay."

Well. Sort of okay. I had almost failed out of high school—graduated by the grace of an iron-fisted guidance counselor who just wanted to get a diploma in my hands and get me *out,* for Mom's sake. For the sake of her memory. The day top-of-her-class Tabitha had come home from Headley for the funeral, her eyes de-puffed with the help of some charm she'd learned in the dorms there, I'd said hello without hugging her. After that, the only time I hugged her was for Dad and his camera, and even then, the camera hadn't been pointed at us for five years or so. And Dad didn't notice the time passing because he'd lost the person he had planned his entire life around.

But other than that, everyone was okay.

The bartender sliced the last lime, grabbed the empty bucket. "I'll be right back, okay?" He pointed at me and smiled. "I've got lemons to do, too."

I smiled back and gave him a thumbs-up. As soon as he was out of sight, I downed what was left of my beer and slid off the barstool. I tucked a few bills under the empty bottle—enough to cover the bill, plus a decent tip. I walked out fast, furious at myself. I'd said too much. He'd gotten that look on his face, that pity look. I was supposed to disappear in that bar. Another round, and he'd be asking my name, giving me advice. Acting like he knew me.

I walked back to my office, just off the edge of sober and just past angry. Just drunk enough to dig into my pocket for my phone, open a social media app I never used. In my dad's profile picture, he was standing on a beach with his arm around a woman I didn't recognize.

I scrolled back through his pictures, through a few rounds of barbecues and birthday dinners with friends I'd never met. I kept going, back through years of posts until I found a photo with Tabitha and me both in it. In the photo, Tabitha had her arms wrapped around me. We were smiling in front of a Christmas tree—it was a for-the-camera smile, a for-Dad smile. He took a picture of us every year, because when we were little Mom had taken a picture every year. Until one year she wasn't there any-more, and we were all looking at each other in front of the Christmas tree, wondering how we were supposed to celebrate her favorite holiday.

In the picture we wore coordinating sweaters, reindeer and

snowflakes and little knit *x*'s. It was from a few years before we stopped talking altogether—Tabitha's bangs attested to that—but in the shot, my short black hair was already threaded with premature strands of gray. My scattering of freckles was cut through with the first few fine lines, laughter around the eyes and frown between the brows. We shared a sharp nose—nothing you'd call "aquiline," but certainly nothing you'd call "pert," either. She was a little slimmer than me. You could already see the wages of a PI's life on my body and in the lines of my face: too much booze, too many late-night stakeouts with fast-food wrappers littering the floor of the car. No cigarettes—I'd quit the second I left home, since I'd only been smoking them to piss Dad off—but I looked like a smoker. I looked tired.

Tabitha shone in the photo, like she did in every photo. Her long hair—used to be plain old "dark brown," but after she came back from school it was something else, something richer like chestnut or umber or ocher—hung in soft waves, and her large brown eyes were the same as mine but *more* somehow, more sparkling, more alive. Better. Not a freckle on her, and the only lines were laugh lines, and there were exactly the right amount of them. She was using all the tricks that used to drive me to it's-not-fair shouting back when we were teenagers. Back when the worst thing in my life was Tabitha, and the fact that she had come home from magic school knowing how to erase the hated freckles—but wouldn't do mine.

And now I was going to try to solve a murder at a place that was full of kids like that. Kids who were just like the person my sister had become while she was gone. I was going to take the case—I'd been trying to tell myself that I was conflicted about it, but really I was just getting ready to swallow a lot of bad medicine in order to do the job.

Because I had to do this job. It was good money, but more than that, it was a murder case. It was *real* detective work, something more than just some paunchy forty-nine-year-old accountant revving his secretary's engine in the Ramada near the freeway. I'd been following paunchy accountants for the better part of fourteen years. It's what I was good at.

But this? A real murder case? This was the kind of thing that private detectives didn't do anymore. It was what had made me get my PI license in the first place—the possibility that I might get to do something big and real, something nobody else could do. I didn't know the first thing about solving a murder, but this was my chance to find out if I could really do it. If I could be a *real* detective, instead of a halfway-there failure. If this part of my life could be different from all the other parts, all the parts where I was only ever *almost* enough.

I won't try to pinpoint the first lie I told myself over the course of this case. That's not a useful thread to pull on. The point is, I really thought I was going to do things right this time. I wasn't going to fuck it up and lose everything. That's what I told myself as I stared at the old picture of me and Tabitha.

This time was going to be different. This time was going to be better. This time, I was going to be enough.

CHAPTER

FOUR

THE DRIVE THROUGH THE SUNOL hills was as beautiful as the novocaine that comes before the drill. Once I got off the high-walled freeways, the pockmarked city streets gave way to land that screamed *green*. Tall, gnarled oaks leaned over the narrow, winding road, casting it into dappled shade and obscuring signage that warned me to watch out for leaping deer. Tiny offshoots from the road appeared at intervals, marked with signs for Hollow Stone Ranch or Crystalbrook Farm. I'd gotten intentionally lost down there a few times before, and knew that if I followed any of those signs in search of roaming horses with warm-velvet noses I could stroke, I'd quickly encounter gates informing me that I was on private property and would be shot should I choose to venture any farther.

Osthorne was no different—the sign by the road read OSTHORNE ACADEMY in dark debossed wood with white edging, and after I turned off the road, I started to see signs warning me of the dangers of trespassing. After nearly a mile of driveway featuring increasingly threatening signage, the rooftop of oaks thinned, then parted. The campus spread before me like a dream. As I pulled into a parking space, I peeked in my rearview at the wall of ancient, sprawling oaks behind me. Their branches twisted together, completely obscuring the school from view of the road. I wondered if the school had chosen this location for the camouflage, or if the mages who built the school had engineered the Sunol hills to suit their need for privacy.

I wove through the cars in the tiny visitors' parking lot, trying to look around without being too obvious a tourist. The mist was just thin enough for me to see the grounds in soft-focus. The drought-impossible velvety green lawn that surrounded the school looked like frosting waiting to have a finger run through it. The school itself was a long, low spread of brick and glass windows. It struck me as out of place, unfamiliar: there's not a lot of brick in Northern California, not for a little more than a century. Lots of brick facades in San Francisco, but they're different— glossy, and too even in color, and somehow thin-looking. It's not too hard to tell when a building is trying to pretend that it survived the 1906 quake. Not Osthorne, though. This place was the real deal, pocked and resealed dozens of times. Even from the parking lot, I could see the waver in each windowpane, a testament to the age and survival of the glass. There was no flagpole, no clock tower, no football field with blazing white lights. It was a dignified building, a serious place.

I had a moment of double vision. If things had been different for me—if I'd been born with whatever thing Tabitha had that I never got any of—I might have walked across that grass as a kid, with friends and a future all laid out for me. I might have been handed a totally different life. This place might have been the setting for my teen memories. Not the bleachers at my underfunded public school, not the parking lot at the abandoned bowling alley in the wee hours of the morning. Not the hospice bed in my parents' living room.

I shook it off. That wasn't the way things happened. There had never been any profit in wondering what might have been. People like me didn't get to want things like Osthorne. And besides, I *didn't* want it.

I didn't want it.

I rolled my neck, stretched just enough to let the wound on my shoulder hit my brain with a bright flash of clarifying pain. I had a job to do.

It was time to go to work.

———

"Ms. Torres should only be a few more minutes," the school secretary rasped. Her voice was a sharp, painful wheeze. The nameplate on her desk read MRS. WEBB. I had a sense that I should not ask for a first name. She was one of those tiny, ancient women whose papery skin is stretched over steel scaffolding. She watched me with the cool eyes of the unimpressed. I tried not to fidget. I tried to summon the courage I imagined I'd have if this was a place I belonged. It didn't help.

The door to Torres's office opened with a bang, and a tall boy with wild, dark-brown hair stormed out. His dark-blue school uniform was ill-fitting in the way of so many teenage boys—too short in the wrists, baggy through the shoulders. His blazer was wrinkled, and the angle of his gray-striped tie spoke to constant tugging. The teen paused, his eyes landing on me. He hit me with a long, intense stare, his protruding adam's apple working up and down. I was startled by the frankness of his gaze. Then he heaved an enormous, head-shaking sigh before continuing on his way out of the office, leaving me feeling like Ophelia in her closet.

It was totally beyond me, how a kid who's been handed a winning lottery ticket could look so damn broke. I watched him through the safety-glass window that separated the office from the main hallway. He'd already pulled out his phone. His fingers moved over the screen with unnatural speed, and they didn't slow down when he looked up from his phone to brood at me.

"Is that a spell?" I asked. From just over my shoulder came a deep laugh.

"Is what a spell? The texting? No—they're all that fast."

I turned around to find Marion Torres smiling at me. She was wearing jeans and a nice-but-not-too-nice blouse, and I felt simultaneously over- and underdressed. I'd spent hours over the weekend figuring out what to wear to a place like Osthorne. What would establish me as a professional, as someone who could solve a murder? What would keep me from sticking out like a splinter? I'd wound up digging out the clothes I'd worn to the only court case I'd ever been asked to testify in—an adultery job where the husband had followed up my findings by stabbing the wife with an ice pick. He'd cried more when I told him she was cheating than he did at the sentencing.

Next to Torres, in my court clothes, I felt like a kid playing dress-up. A great start.

We greeted each other: did-you-find-the-place-okay, so-glad-

you-can-help-us, did-you-get-the-contract. She handed me a sat-
isfyingly fat envelope of cash, which I didn't count, so she'd feel
like we had a good relationship from the start. I glanced back at
Mrs. Webb. She was watching us with the same flat, unimpressed
stare with which she'd greeted me. I was already dreading interviewing her.

"I'm going to show Ivy the Theoretical Magic section," Torres
said. "Would you like to accompany us?"

Mrs. Webb shook her head with a look of regret that did not
extend to the uneasy creases around her mouth. "I'm afraid I've
just got far too much to do here," she said in that grating voice.
"Perhaps another time."

Torres led the way out of the office. Her heels clicked on the
gray linoleum tiles that floored the hallway. As we passed, I
glanced back into the office through the safety-glass window.
Mrs. Webb didn't see me—her eyes were on the blank pages of a
ruled notebook. She stared at the paper intently. As I watched, she
lifted two fingers and pinched herself hard on the arm, hard
enough to bruise. Hard enough that I winced to watch her. The
older woman's face remained still as sea glass as she squeezed at
her skin. I shivered, and a whisper twined its way through my
thoughts. *Wake up.*

"Is she ill?" I asked, jogging to catch up with Torres's brisk
pace.

"Hm?"

"Mrs. Webb, your secretary," I said. "I just noticed that her
voice is kind of . . . ?"

"Oh," Torres said with a grimace. "No, she's not ill. She used a
spell to alert the school of an emergency, when she found the body

in the library. That spell is . . ." She paused. "It's fallen out of favor. The impact it has on the caster's body is significant."

"And permanent?" I asked.

"Yes and no," she said. "For many people, it is. But Mrs. Webb is working on it. She already sounds much better than she did in November. In a few more months, she'll probably sound normal again." She stooped to pick up a crumpled ball of notebook paper, then tossed it into a big gray trash can that stood watch over the hallway. It looked like every trash can I'd ever tipped over at Andrew Jackson Memorial during my reign of apathy.

The trash cans weren't the only thing about Osthorne that were familiar: it all felt like a place I'd seen a thousand times before. There were the scuffed gray linoleum floors lined with lockers, and the walls were frosted with paint that went on fresh every other summer. "Assthorne Asscademy" was scratched into several surfaces with what I'd bet was ballpoint pen. Bulletin boards hung thick with notices—auditions for *The Tempest,* lacrosse tryouts rescheduled due to weather, take-a-number to call Brea Teymourni for tutoring in math/economics/magic theory, lost my phone $50 reward call Arthur PLEASE PLEASE PLEASE.

There it was again. That feeling like maybe, in another life, I could have fit in here. I could have auditioned for *The Tempest.* I could have tried out for lacrosse. It was a feeling like nostalgia, but for something I'd never done. Something I'd never had.

"Ms. Gamble?" I looked up. Torres was halfway down the hall in front of me, waiting. Her face was set to "patient," but something in her posture made me hurry to catch up.

Classes were in session, and I swiveled my head like a small-town tourist in the big city for the first time. I don't know what I expected to see—mostly, I was shocked by how familiar it all seemed. How *recent*. The sights of posters hanging on classroom walls took me back to my own note-passing, sneaking-chips-in-my-backpack days. Most of the classrooms featured wide windows into the hallway, the glass crisscrossed with wire, and I peeked in at each one to look at the students doodling in their margins. I lingered just long enough to be seen: let the students wonder who the visitor was, let them whisper at lunch, let the word spread that someone was asking questions about the murder. I had never investigated a murder before, but this part was no different from any other case—let people know that there are questions being asked, and they'll line up to give you their version of answers.

"They look so young," I murmured, staring in at a classroom full of baby-faced teenagers hunched over tests. The sea of dark-blue blazers and starched white dress shirts was broken up by crests of brightly dyed hair and islands of eyeliner. The kids were filling in Scantron bubbles with number-two pencils and flipping back and forth between the pages of a packet.

"Freshmen," Torres intoned with crisp amusement in her voice. "They're always younger than you remember. It's easy to forget that fourteen is so close to twelve, isn't it?"

I fell into step next to Torres for a few paces, but stopped short before we rounded the corner. I was frozen in place, hypnotized by the lurid orange graffiti that sprawled across a row of sky-blue lockers: SAMANTHA IS A SLUT. The letters didn't look sprayed on—someone had been at this with a fine brush and a steady hand.

Torres paused next to me, regarding the graffiti. "It's more ordinary here than you expected."

It wasn't a question, but it hung in the air between us all the same. "I'm not sure. I guess I thought there would be more . . . I don't know. I thought it would be different."

"More cobblestones and gabled windows and moving stairways?" Torres's laugh said she had caught my embarrassed grimace. "I know. I get it. But at the end of the day, we're just a high school, Ms. Gamble. We're a very *nice* high school"—she gestured out a nearby window to the velvety green of the grounds—"but we're still a high school. That means gum, graffiti, cell phones, sex-ed, stupid pranks, students smoking weed behind the bleachers." She tipped me a wink. "If it makes you feel any better, here, I'll show you something magical." She pulled an impressive folding knife from the pocket of her jeans. "I confiscated this from a student earlier today. It's not the magical thing, it's just a knife. But watch this."

Torres flicked it open—the blade was long, with a wicked curve at the tip. She dragged it across poor Samantha's name. Paint peeled from the locker in little blue curls. Torres flicked the knife closed. I ran my fingers across the locker—I could feel the groove in the blue paint, but the screaming orange letters remained unscathed.

My jaw clenched. "How?"

"I'm not sure. Our graffiti artist used a spell that I've never encountered before. It's probably something they came up with themselves. Our groundskeeper—Francis Snead," she added as I took out my notebook. "He's tried a hundred different ways to remove it or paint over it, but nothing's worked so far. He's been working with the head of the Physical Magic department for weeks now."

"Can I talk to him? Snead?"

"Of course," she said. "He's the one who'll set you up in staff housing."

I blinked at her. "In what?"

The headmaster cocked her head at me as though I were posing a riddle. "Staff housing. We have a small apartment available for you to stay in while you're here. Unless you wanted to make the drive down from Oakland every day . . . ?"

It made perfect sense; there was no reason to say no. I aimed those thoughts at the twist in my gut, willing it to listen to logic: there was no reason not to stay here. Just for a little while. Just for the case.

"Thank you," I said. "Thanks, yes. I really appreciate that."

"Ivy—I can call you Ivy, right? I want you to have unfettered access to whatever you need." A tendon stood out in her neck as she spoke in a low, urgent voice. "Nowhere on this campus is off-limits to you, so long as you don't endanger any students. Talk to whomever you want to talk to. Talk to students, teachers, staff—I don't care." Torres's eyes shone hard and bright as she stared at me like I had the answers. She took a long, deep breath and let it out slow. "I have a responsibility here, to make sure that things get set right. The investigators who said that this was a suicide—they let Sylvia down. Do you understand? One of my staff members died on my watch, and those investigators barely lifted a finger to get her justice."

"I'll do my best," I said, and I tried to make her hear the thing I couldn't say because it's the kind of thing you just can't say:

I can't bring her back. I failed, though. I could see it in her face: she thought I was nervous, thought I was uncertain. But she didn't understand yet that I couldn't give her the thing she really wanted. I can never give any of them what they really want: I can't fix a marriage, and I can't undo a lie, and I can't raise the dead.

And I can never tell them, because they think they just want answers.

"Yes, you will," Torres said. "You will do better than they did." She took another deep breath, and this time I counted—five seconds in, eight seconds out. It was a familiar exercise. I took a mental note: Torres had been through anger management. "Anyway, yes, you can talk to our groundskeeper after he gives you the key to your apartment. And you should also talk to the head of the Physical Magic department. His name is Rahul Chaudhary. I'm sure he'll be able to answer any questions you might have about this particular incident." She waved her hands at the word "SLUT," which was still glowing radioactive on the lockers.

I ran my fingers over the orange paint again. I had never seen magic done by anyone but my sister. Something in me ached at the knowledge that a child had used their incredible, impossible magic for this: to make sure that after the world had ended, when alien archaeologists were digging up the thing that Earth used to be, they'd know that Samantha had been a slut. It hurt even more than the idea that someone had used their magic to murder Sylvia Capley. The idea of some teenager getting stoned and then etching the word "SLUT" into history—it burned in my throat like a swallowed sword.

Why them? *Why do they get the opportunity to waste this?*

I let my fingers linger on Samantha's name a moment too long, and something under my fingers popped, stinging. I snapped my hand away, startled.

"Ah, yes—I should have warned you about that," Torres said. "Sorry."

I stuck my sore finger in my mouth, glaring at Samantha's name. *Samantha*, I thought with unexpected venom. Then I realized: that was the whole point. Even if you didn't think Samantha was a slut, you'd remember that she'd stung you.

CHAPTER

FIVE

THE LIBRARY WAS JUST AS familiar as the halls had been. The checkout counter was unmanned; half of the lights were off, leaving the room lit mostly by morning sun. Tall rows of bookshelves flanked several banks of long, worn study tables. A poster encouraged kids to return overdue books to avoid fines. I was biting down on thickening disappointment—*Is this all there is?*—when a steel returns cart rolled past me, unattended. As I watched, it bellied up to a shelf, and books began nudging their way back into place between their fellows. I wanted to feel a sense of affection for the cart, or at least a sense of satisfaction at the understated practicality of the magic on display. But it wasn't enough to cut through the bitter ordinariness of the room.

There were four girls clustered around a study table, bees all trying to nose into the same flower. At the sound of Torres's voice, all four of them sat back in their chairs. The cell phone they'd been looking at had vanished, and I couldn't tell if it was teenage sleight of hand or real magic that had made flash cards appear in front of each of them.

"Hello, ladies," Torres said, her voice edged with a warning. "What are we studying today?"

"Theoretical Magic, Miss Torres," answered a girl with a long, rich fall of thick black hair. Her shirt was long-sleeved and high-necked but fit her closely enough that I could see her ribs—she was brittle-thin. Under the table, her feet were tangled with those of the girl sitting across from her. "We're doing a unit on electrical manipulations."

"Thank you, Brea. And how is the study session going? Fruitful, I trust?" Torres asked with just the barest brush of sarcasm. A click in my brain: Brea Teymourni, the tutor from the bulletin board. I've always had a good memory for names. Someone once told me at a conference that's all it really takes to be a private detective: *a good memory for names and faces, an eyeball for details, and a halfway decent invoicing system.*

I looked Brea over, searching for details, and found just enough *overachiever* signposts to satisfy my assessment of her from the flyer: textbook bristling with sticky-note flags, clear pencil case stuffed with a rainbow of highlighters, nervous twitch under one eye.

"It's going fine." This from the girl sitting next to Brea—pale, tall, broad-shouldered. Her brunette hair was held up in a falling-apart bun by a pencil and a paintbrush; her white uniform shirt was baggy and conspicuously paint-stained. Everything about her was screaming *artist* at top volume. I was flooded with memories of sitting in my bedroom, agonizing over what my fashion choices *meant,* what people would think when they saw me. It all used to be so important.

More than a hint of sarcasm from Torres now, and all four girls bristled. "Oh, good, Courtney. I'm so glad to hear it. I can expect your grade in the class to improve, then?" The square-jawed Asian girl whose feet were tangled up with Brea's—no makeup, low ponytail, basketball shorts—glared at Torres with her arms crossed. A half sleeve of ballpoint doodles crawled up her left arm. "And Miranda. Is this a new school uniform I was unaware of, or are you on your way to practice? Last I checked, the basketball team doesn't meet in the library."

"Um, excuse me?" This from the fourth girl at the table, a Renoir blonde with skin that told me her parents had money. She didn't sound affronted so much as politely confused. "Do you mind if we get back to studying? We have a big test on Friday." She aimed a you-understand-how-it-is smile at Torres, and pushed a wave of silken hair behind one ear. As her eyes flicked between me and Torres, my knees went watery. I felt like I was floating in a sea of everything's-fine-don't-worry-it's-all-under-control. I wanted more than anything to move along.

"Of course," Torres said, sounding slightly dazed. "Stick to studying while you're in here, ladies. Keep up the good work."

Torres turned to leave, and I trailed after her, feeling as though I'd missed something important. I felt the weight of four pairs of eyes as the girls began to whisper to each other. The moment I was out of sight of them, that move-along feeling dissipated. *What the hell?* I opened my mouth to ask Torres about it, and realized that I didn't really know what to ask. Was that normal, what just happened? Torres hadn't seemed to notice it.

The shelves of the library were marked with endcap labels that pointed to either side, Dewey decimal numbers and subject matter. I followed Torres past Math and Mathematical Magics;

Economics; Fictional Magic and Applications of Magical Fiction; Electricity, Theoretical Electricity, Electricity Manipulations. She paused at Poisons and Theoretical Poisons. The next row over—Theoretical Magic—was roped off. A sign hung on the rope: NO UNSUPERVISED ENTRY. Behind the rope, the aisle seemed to blur—when I tried to look at it, my eyes crossed, and I could feel the first prickles of a headache creeping into my temples. I looked away just in time to see Torres flick her wrist, pulling a thick file from midair. She handed it to me.

"This is all the information about the case. All the information I have access to, at least. Photos, mostly. And copies of everything the investigators could legally give me." I flipped the folder open. There was a stack of photos inside. I looked away before I could process what I was seeing, but I had a fleeting impression of blood matting white-blond hair.

"Right. I'll look over these tonight." *With a drink on hand.* "Shall we take a look at the scene?" *The scene of the murder,* I thought, fighting dizziness. *The murder-scene. I'm going to investigate a murder-scene.*

A flicker of hesitation. Then Torres unclipped the rope from the end of the shelves. I went to step past her, but she stopped me with a raised hand.

"Hang on. The rope is kind of a formality, and a warning. There's a ward. You'll get bounced out if you don't have a pass." From the same spot of air from which she'd drawn the file, she produced a lanyard with a laminated tag on the end that read "Theoretical Magic ACCESS." It was cut crooked along the bottom, like a teacher's assistant had gone at it with a pair of budget-cut scissors.

I looped the pass around my neck. "Why the ward? Is it dangerous in there?"

Torres rolled her eyes. "Meddlers. Students who think they can find the killer. This section has always been closed off—used to just be a simple no-access ward, to keep kids from getting into magic they weren't ready for. They couldn't walk between the shelves without a staff member present, and nobody could remove a book from the aisle, not even staff. If anyone wanted to look in a book, there would be a staff member standing right next to them to make sure they didn't try anything stupid. But after the murder, I asked Ms. Gamble—er, Tabitha, that is—to ramp things up a bit." The first mention of my sister. I didn't let myself blink at it. *It's fine, I'm fine. I don't care.* "Now, you can't see or hear anything that happens in there, and if you try to get in without a pass *and* a staff member, you bounce right back out." She eyed me. "We've had more than a few bruised behinds in the front office since we set this up—students who thought they would find hot clues, thought they would solve the murder themselves."

"Kids here do that?"

"One kid in particular," Torres replied, looping a second pass around her own neck. "Dylan DeCambray. You met him earlier this morning."

"Tall, brooding, hair that he spent a good few hours messing up?"

"That's the one," Torres said. "He was in my office trying yet *again* to convince me that Dark Forces are at work at Osthorne. Something about a Great Evil that's Bending the Will of Students." She spoke with great sweeping flourishes and heightened letters that lit up the absurdity of Dylan's accusations.

I cleared my throat, fighting the flush that was already rising in my cheeks. "Um . . . are, are they? At work? Dark forces, I mean?"

Torres laughed. She had a good laugh. "Ms. Gamble. Dark forces are at work everywhere. Turn on the news. But this kid . . . he wants to find a mystery. A conspiracy. *Anything.*" She shook her head. "He's what I would politely call 'troubled.' Don't worry— I'm sure you'll have a chance to talk to him."

"I'm sure I will," I said.

I pulled out my cell phone as soon as I stepped between the shelves, taking pictures of the broad swath of stained carpet that took up the middle third of the aisle. The stain was dark, closer to cocoa than rust; the blood had seeped through the carpet, saturated it. It was a Rorschach test, shaped like a distorted butterfly. The photos I took were for my reference, not for a client's use in court, so I didn't need to lug around my fancy, heavy camera with the zoom lens. I just needed to be able to remember later what everything had looked like. I wished, not for the first time, that I could capture the way things were beyond just how they looked—the way things *felt*. The old-things smell of the library, the tension in the air, the feeling that the books in this row were watching me. I crouched down and touched the edge of the stain with my middle finger.

"You haven't had this cleaned out?" I said quietly.

"We're going to have it replaced," Torres replied, only a bit defensive.

"Sensible," I said, glancing over my shoulder. "No wonder you're in charge." Torres softened a bit at that, although her smile said that she knew when she was being buttered up. "Do you mind walking me through what happened? I'm sure it's all in the file, but it'd help me to hear you tell it."

Torres stood at the end of the aisle, her narration gathering speed as I snapped photos. She explained about the welcome dinner, at the end of the first week, well after the boarding students had found their bedrooms and gotten unpacked and reviewed their schedules and evaluated the way everyone had changed over the summer. She explained about Mrs. Webb's discovery, about Dylan DeCambray, about the screams that had echoed through the halls all the way down to the cafeteria.

"I left the dinner immediately to investigate, along with a couple of other teachers. When we arrived," Torres continued, "we found Dylan over there, being ill." She pointed to a stained section of carpet near the end of the shelves, then indicated the butterfly stain in the center of the aisle. "Mrs. Webb was standing there."

"Where was the body, exactly?" I asked. The bloodstains could have told any number of stories, and making assumptions this early on wouldn't make the job any less impossible.

"The—I'm sorry, it's still so hard to think of her as 'the body.'" The headmaster kneaded her forehead with her fingertips.

"You two were close?" I ventured.

She rolled one shoulder in an aborted shrug. "I'm sure I thought of us as closer than we were. You have to understand . . . I keep most of the staff at arm's length. I'm at the top of the ladder here. It's crucial that I'm beyond reproach." I nodded, having no idea what she was talking about. Being beyond reproach wasn't the important part. *Get there, Torres.* "But Sylvia brought joy to a role that can occasionally be on the thankless side. She asked me how I was doing, and remembered my birthday, and—I don't know. I suppose this sounds silly to you."

"Not at all," I said, not putting my hand on her arm but wishing I could. "She was kind to you even though you were her boss. She treated you like a person, right?"

She smiled past the bloodstains on the carpet. "She treated everyone like a person. It's rarer than you'd think." She drew a breath. "Her body was there, and there." Torres indicated each of the butterfly wings of the stain.

"Wait. You mean . . . the body—er, Sylvia's body—it was in *both* places?"

Torres swallowed, looking away from the stain. "Yes. Both."

"I'm not sure I understand," I said.

Torres was quiet, then murmured, "I'm not sure I do either."

A chime sounded, and the headmaster looked at her watch before clicking her tongue. "The day is getting away from me. I'm going to be late for a parent meeting. I'm so sorry, Ivy," she said, not sounding sorry at all. "I'm going to have to leave you. Mr. Snead will be waiting for you in front of the school—he can show you to your apartment in staff housing, and you and I can touch base a little later." She gave me a sharp nod, and I didn't mean to blink, but of course I did, because she was gone.

I glanced at the folder in my hand. It looked so innocuous— bland, even—but the corner of a matte photograph stuck out of one side, as red and waiting as an open mouth. I looked down at the dark bloodstains and considered the fact that I was now standing in the place where a woman had lost her life. The folder in my hand contained the images of her death, and I was responsible for uncovering the truth. I wondered what I had gotten myself into.

I wondered what Sylvia Capley had gotten herself into.

Frances Snead was nothing like what I expected. I'd never met a groundskeeper before, and I had some idea, probably cobbled together from various reruns of *Scooby Doo,* that a groundskeeper should be a wizened old man shaking his cane at meddling kids who run on grass. But Mr. Snead, waiting for me in front of the school, was something altogether different—a tiny, waspish man with deep-set eyes and a cap of slick black hair. He wore a crisp white button-down, the collar of which was dark with water, and the smell of Ivory soap wafted off him like cologne. The fragrance brought into sharp relief old memories of my father leaving for work in the gray light of early morning, brushing past me as I stumbled into the house in a cigarette-smoke fog.

"You're Ivy Gamble?" The groundskeeper's voice was soft. His eyes didn't meet mine as he shook my hand. Calluses, and a firm enough grip, but fingers as light as a pickpocket's.

"That's me," I said, trying for friendly. He nodded once, sharp, then wheeled around and began striding across the vast green lawn that surrounded the campus. It took me a moment to realize that I was meant to follow.

"You'll be in staff housing." He said it as though to himself, his eyes trained on the sloping ground ten feet in front of him.

"This isn't a hotel, you understand? No one will be cleaning up after you."

"Good," I said, feeling loud and clumsy next to Snead. "I prefer not to have anyone in my space."

"You'll have that," he murmured. "No one going in there anytime soon, that's for sure."

We crested the little hill we'd been climbing, and I couldn't stop myself from coming up short. In the dip on the other side of the hill was a nest of townhouses. I thought of my drive up to the campus—of the shape of the road, and of what I had expected to find when the trees parted—and I tried to reconcile the size of this colony of homes with the surrounding geography.

It didn't work. None of it worked. There shouldn't have been a huge school with ample staff housing and sprawling lawns, not here. There wasn't room for all this sprawl, not in the cramped, rippling Sunol hills.

But, in a display of complete disregard for how space is supposed to function . . . there was the sprawl. There was the school, and there were the homes. It wasn't possible, but it was laid out before me as sure as anything.

Fucking magic.

I won't pretend that I didn't have a choice. I always have choices. We all make choices.

And in that moment—I had to choose.

I could have decided to be disoriented. I could have chosen to struggle with the things I was seeing, as plain as they were. As much as I knew that this was only the beginning—and as much as I knew the *impossible* would only get worse—I could have decided that it was already *too much*.

Or I could pretend that everything was normal. I could decide that this was a world where I belonged. I could accept the impossible.

I could stand with my toes hanging over the edge of the cliff, and I could just stare at the way the pebbles fell while my heart tried to fall out of my throat.

Or I could jump.

The empty eyes of the surrounding homes did not watch my descent. I staggered a little as I followed Snead down the hillside toward my apartment. Nobody saw me choose a path.

Nobody saw me choose. But I chose.

Snead handed me the keys and showed me the light switches. "No fire or electrical spells in here," he said with a grim frown. "If you want to do those, arrange with the science department to use the lab. Garbage goes outside your door on Thursday nights. Separate your recycling."

He was gone before I could say another word. He didn't vanish the way Torres did when she left my office, but the speed and silence with which he slipped out of the room told me that he didn't want to be here. Frances Snead didn't want to be in this apartment, or he didn't want to be near me.

It was a cute setup. There was no other word for it—cute was the thing that came to mind, and cute is what stuck. The front door opened right into the living room, which was separated from a galley kitchen by a low island with an empty bookshelf set into one side. Stainless steel appliances, granite countertop. New-looking, but there was a chip in the granite near the refrigerator and a decent-sized scuff across the front of the dishwasher. Past the kitchen, a carpeted hallway led to a bedroom and a bathroom.

Small.

Simple.

Cute.

So why didn't he want to be there for longer than he had to?

I felt foolish the moment I realized. It was the most obvious thing in the world. Why would there be an empty apartment in staff housing? "No one's going in there anytime soon, that's for sure," he'd said.

Because it was Sylvia's apartment.

I was going to be living in a dead woman's home.

I stood in the bedroom, staring at the two nightstands that flanked the bed, and I breathed it all in. I let my fingertips trail across the cheap duvet. It was slippery in that unwashed new-fabric way. I knew that if I buried my face in the sheets, they'd smell like big-box-store plastic.

"No fire or electrical spells," Snead had said. As if I belonged in that fresh-out-of-the-box home he'd made up for me. As if I were someone who might do the wrong kind of magic and light the place up. As if I could be the kind of woman who could live in a place like this. Who could die in a place like this.

It all stuck in my throat. I closed my eyes and gripped that shiny new duvet in both fists, and tried not to choke.

CHAPTER

SIX

B Y THE TIME I had emerged from my new home at Osthorne Academy for Young Mages the next morning, mist was draped across the school grounds like a headache clinging to the temples of a mildly concussed and half-hungover private investigator.

I swallowed an extra-strength Tylenol with a last swill of cold coffee left over from the night before. I cursed last-night-Ivy for her woeful judgment regarding gin—but the curse didn't have much firepower behind it. I couldn't blame past-Ivy, even if I wished she would have at least added water into the beverage rotation. The photos in the folder had merited a late-night trip to a neon-windowed liquor store in the nearest town.

I didn't spend much time looking at dead bodies. It was usually petty, shameful shit that I saw. This case was a whole new level for me. The headache was probably worth the lack of the complete nervous breakdown that should have come with looking through that folder. Looking at those photos.

They were high-quality matte prints, littered with scale rulers and yellow crime-scene markers and obscure annotations. In each of them, Sylvia Capley lay on the dull gray carpet of the Theoretical Magic section of the library. She looked like an optical illusion, like a crappy trick at a third-rate magician's afternoon show at an off-Strip casino in Vegas.

She'd been bisected, split down the middle; a clean line from the top of her head, through her nose, down the cupid's bow of her top lip, between her collarbones, all the way to her bellybutton and beyond. She'd fallen open like a split log; the two halves of her faced away from each other, staring at opposite bookshelves.

Subsequent photos of the carpet showed only bloodstains. I'd started leaving the tonic out of my gin upon realizing that, sometime between the photos of the corpse and the photos of the carpet, some poor bastard had to figure out a way to scoop Sylvia off the floor without leaving anything behind. I had wondered if there was a spell for that—to keep everything inside her, given her state—or if maybe they'd slid a sheet of cardboard under her. And then I had put the folder away and taken my drink to bed with me. I couldn't deal with it anymore. I'd fallen asleep before I could finish the last few fingers of gin, which was probably the thing that saved me from a debilitating hangover. I'd dreamed of Tabitha and a hall of mirrors that night; when I woke up, I felt mushy, staticky. Somehow pushed off to the left of center.

A spell gone wrong.

That's what the file said. I wanted to believe it—I wanted a reason to think that maybe this kind of thing just happened to people who got magic handed to them at birth, or whenever these things get handed out. It would have felt a little like justice. I'm not proud of thinking that, given that I was standing on a campus full of children who had two fistfuls of magic already and were reaching for more.

But then, this isn't a story about things I'm proud of.

The folder Torres had given me didn't just contain photos of horror beyond my wildest imagining. There was also a copy of a report with the logo of the National Mage Investigative Service stamped across the top: a spray of leaves, probably alder or something with a similar symbolic weight, over a barbed crescent moon that cupped a spread-fingered hand. I'd stared at the logo for a long time, studying the seven stars that were nested in the palm of the hand and wondering about the significance. Wondering if this was the kind of thing you know when you spend your school years in a place like Osthorne.

When I finally read the report, I found it even less satisfying than the emblem had been. It reported Sylvia's cause of death as "a miscast version of a theoretical spell intended to facilitate instantaneous physical translation."

I spent too long in a too-hot shower that morning, trying to cut through the fog in my brain and figure out what that meant; in the end, I decided that it probably meant she tried to teleport and failed. Or maybe it meant she was trying to transform herself and wound up split in half. I wasn't sure it really mattered either way. Sylvia Capley, it seemed, had tried to do something impossible because she thought that the rules of existence didn't apply to her. And she paid the price. It was, as the report wanted me to believe, that simple.

I took the long way from staff housing to the school grounds, trying to get a little fresh air to circulate where the last of the gin fumes might be lingering. I told myself that it was also to give me a chance to scope out the grounds—to see if there was anyone skulking around where they shouldn't be, scrawling "I am the murderer" on a wall somewhere. I scratched absently at the tape that held fresh gauze on my still-stinging shoulder. It itched like hell, and the only thing keeping me from reopening the wound was the bandage covering it. The air was crisp and cloud-smelling, but rather than clearing my head, the breeze grated against my headache like sand between my teeth. I kept taking deep breaths, telling myself that this was fine. It was all fine.

As I cut across the grass in a wide arc, a tone like a crystal glass being struck rang out through the morning, the sound bright in the thick silence. The immediate explosion of chaos and sound was only barely muffled by the walls of the school as students decamped from the first class of the day. Given the headache that lingered at the base of my skull, I was glad to be a safe distance from the banging of lockers, the squeak of shoes on linoleum, the blinding flashes of bright adolescence.

By the time I made it inside, a second clear tone had sounded, and most of the students were once again safely stowed in class-rooms. I walked through the halls toward Torres's office, feeling truant. Waiting for someone to ask me where I was supposed to be. I thought I remembered how to get to the front office, but my head was throbbing. I took a wrong turn. Then I got flustered and took several more wrong turns, tangling myself up in my own leash. I finally rounded a corner and things looked familiar again, and I thought maybe I was on the right track, but no. I wasn't at the front office; I'd found myself at the same bank of lockers I'd lingered over yesterday.

And I wasn't alone.

The boy I'd seen in Torres's office stood where I'd been the day before, his fingers tracing the *m* in "Samantha" from an inch above the metal, just far enough to avoid the shock. His hair was still unkempt in that hours-in-front-of-a-mirror way. He was rangy, but not hunched—there was something in his posture that suggested purpose. He had that too-many-bones look that teenage boys get, but I could almost see the shadow of the man he would become in six or seven years. He looked perched on the cusp of something. Or maybe he was at the edge of something, looking down.

Here we go, I thought. *Time to get to work.*

"Do you know who did it?" I asked. The kid—*Dylan,* I suddenly remembered, *that's right, Dylan the troubled*—jumped about a mile at the sound of my voice. He looked around to see if a teacher was going to make him go to class, if someone was going to yell at him.

"No," he answered. His face had gone still. The lie was as obvious as if it were a tarantula perched astride his wide, thin-lipped mouth. It struck me that he might not be sure if I was talking about the graffiti or the murder. I let his lie—and his uncertainty— linger for a moment before brushing it to the floor to scurry back into the shadows for another time.

"Okay." I clocked the twitch of surprise between his eyebrows; he couldn't tell if he was getting away with the lie or not. Good. Let him wonder. When someone thinks they're getting away with something, they're easier to manipulate. They stop looking closely at the things that might make it feel like their lie is unraveling, and they reveal things they didn't mean to. "It's supposed to be some really advanced stuff, isn't it? This spell." I gestured to the graffiti, watching his face closely, but he didn't look proud so much as irritated.

He nodded, twisted his mouth up. "Yeah. I mean, I haven't even been able to figure it out, and I'm supposed to be—" He stopped himself, looked down at his shoes. "I'm supposed to be smart."

"Remind me of your name?"

"Dylan DeCambray." He shoved his hands into his pockets, glowering. I beamed at him, bright enough that he surely knew I wasn't missing his glare so much as willfully ignoring it.

"Great, Dylan, it's nice to meet you. I'm Ivy Gamble, PI." His face rearranged itself when I dropped those two letters after my name: I'd piqued his interest. I handed him a card. "I'd love to talk to you sometime—smart kid like you, I could use your help." A spark of pride—that was good. It meant he was at least a little bit gullible. "Meantime, though, can you show me the way to the main office? I promise not to rat you out for skipping class." He nodded and fell into step beside me. "So. Are you?"

"Am I what?"

"Are you smart?"

He seemed to chew on this for a minute. "I have to be."

"Says who?"

He gave me the kind of shrug that probably made his mother's ears shoot steam. "It's complicated."

"Oh, I see. Too hard to explain." I said it mildly, trying not to be too obvious about pushing the big flashing red insecurity button. It was like stealing candy from a big bowl of free candy surrounded by helpful multilingual signposts.

"It's in a *Prophecy*," he huffed, leading me through a set of double doors. He said "Prophecy" with a capital P. "My family Prophecy. It's a *huge deal*. It's been passed down for like, centuries. It got smuggled out of Dalmatia, okay? It got saved from the Prophecy purges in the sixties, too, back when people decided that prognostication was a False Magic. So you know it's one of the really important Prophecies." He took a deep breath. "My generation is supposed to have a Chosen One."

Jesus, this kid speaks in a lot of Proper Nouns. "And that's you?"

"Well, nobody else is right for it. My half sister Alexandria and I are the only ones who were born at the right time, and all she cares about is eyeliner and who's friends with who and *popularity*." This was a sore point too, then—or maybe he was just broody by default. "So it's not like *she* could be the most powerful mage of our time."

"And what's the Chosen One supposed to do?" I asked.

Dylan pulled up short; we'd reached the main office, and he'd stopped just out of sight of the windows that looked in on Mrs. Webb. When I glanced back at him, his eyes were intense; sixteen-year-old me would probably have described them to her diary as "burning."

"I'm supposed to change the world," he said.

The door to the office opened behind me. I startled as a student walked out—a girl, holding a pink hall pass and a small white pharmacy bag. I turned back to ask Dylan how he was supposed to change the world, but he was already gone.

I bit back the old, familiar anger. *Get it together, Ivy,* I reminded myself. *These people love to disappear.*

———

I sat in Torres's office and we reviewed the facts in the file: Sylvia Capley, thirty-five years old, health and wellness teacher. Split down the middle by . . . what?

When I mentioned the spell-gone-wrong theory, Torres closed her eyes, fighting some internal battle I couldn't identify. She took a slow anger-management breath.

"I'm not qualified to comment on it. As the 'miz reminded me several times."

"The—sorry, the 'miz?"

"Oh, yes—the National Mage Investigative Service. Nobody wants to say 'NMIS,' so it usually gets shortened to 'MIS,' or—"

I nodded. "Right, got it. So, what's your unofficial opinion, then?"

She picked up a letter opener, twisted the point of it against the pad of one thumb. It wasn't sharp enough to draw blood, but I watched the place where her skin dented with a wary eye. My shoulder prickled.

"My *very unofficial* opinion, which I am not even giving, which we are not discussing, which you are not writing down or recording: Sylvia didn't screw around with theoretical magic. She was too smart and too . . . wary."

"Wary?"

Torres leaned back in her chair, still pressing the top of the letter opener against her thumb. "Sylvia was a cautious person. And reliable—until the week of her death, she hadn't taken so much as a sick day."

"What happened the week of her death?"

Torres shrugged. "She took a sick day. Three, actually. Right before she died. Normally I would have been angry at a staff member taking days off during the first week of school, but there was a rash of food poisoning that week—five teachers and a student got sick. And besides, even if Sylvia had been the only one out, I wouldn't have held it against her. Like I said, she was easily my most reliable staff member. She wasn't the type to play with fire. It just doesn't make sense."

"'Fire' meaning theoretical magic."

"Right." She pursed her lips. "You've never taken a TM class, so you may not understand—but it's a very dangerous field even at the entry levels. It's a lot like sticking your hand into a black box that may or may not have cobras in it."

I blinked. "That's the most coherent explanation of magic I've ever heard."

"Ah, yes, well." The corners of her lips pinched in an ironic almost-smile. "I imagine the only person who's ever explained magic to you is Tabitha? And she's . . . well. She lives in the black box."

"That's apt. I'll have to ask if she's a cobra or not." I couldn't help watching Torres's face for a sign of something, anything, that might allow me to avoid stepping into the black box alongside my maybe-snake sister. Anything to keep from having to go in there alongside her. But Torres just laughed.

"I'll learn what I can from Tabitha," I continued, "although I don't know how germane theoretical magic is to my investigation—I really just need to rule it out. I'm honestly more interested in the people." Torres was kind enough not to comment on the obvious lie. Of course I needed to learn about theoretical magic for this investigation. But I wasn't ready to face talking to Tabitha. Not yet. I flipped through the folder, past the photographs, and landed on a list of names I'd compiled while reading the NMIS report. "I'll want to interview the people who were spoken with last time, if you don't mind. Is that okay with you? It looks like there's a lot of staff on this list."

Torres flinched. "Of course. Officially speaking, there was nothing suspicious about Sylvia's death, and Osthorne is and shall remain a safe haven for students and staff alike." Her words had the practiced rhythm of a letter sent to worried, angry, tuition-paying parents. "But unofficially . . . do whatever you need to do. Talk to whomever you need to. Solve this case."

"I'll do my best," I said, then looked at her narrowing eyes and revised. "I'll solve the case. I will." I shouldn't have made a promise—that's a rookie mistake if ever there was one—but I couldn't help it. Marion Torres needed to hear a promise.

She nodded, then put on a pair of reading glasses and began tackling a pile of papers that was waiting on her desk blotter. I knew a dismissal when I saw one. I stood, let my hand rest on the doorknob. Then I turned back as though I were just remembering something—something small, unimportant, oh-by-the-way.

"I almost forgot to ask—where's Sylvia's medical record?" I asked. Torres looked over the top of her glasses at me.

"It's in the file, isn't it?"

"No," I said. "It's funny—the coroner's report is in there, and it refers to 'attached medical records.'" I pulled out the report and read her a short section. "'No anomalies found excepting sagittal bisection. Anomalies noted in medical records, Appendix B, not found.'" I held up the report for her to see—two pages, no appendices. "So, where's Appendix B?"

"I gave you everything I had," she said. "Maybe they didn't send it over?"

I thumbed the staple on the report. There was a tiny shred of paper stuck to the backside of the staple—the top corner of a sheet of paper. "Maybe," I said, watching Torres closely. "Can you give the 'miz a call and see if we can get a copy?"

She nodded absently as she looked back down at her paperwork. I watched her for a few more seconds, then accepted the dismissal. I closed the door behind me as softly as I could, and went in search of a box with a cobra in it.

Tabitha stood at the front of her classroom. Her stance was commanding; behind her on a whiteboard, a series of diagrams showed—well, I have no idea what they showed. Arcs and angles and a few symbols that I thought I recognized from the five or six calculus classes I'd actually showed up for, back when I was doing my best to flunk out of high school. I stood in the doorway, watching my sister speak about a theorem I'd never heard of, and tried to recognize the girl I remembered in the woman she'd become.

She looked exactly the same as I remembered, but I still wouldn't have recognized her if I'd passed her on the street. So much was different—the line of her back, the timbre of her voice. She commanded attention, respect, authority. You'd never believe that she'd cried for hours over a squashed frog in our parents' backyard. I couldn't connect the woman I was seeing with the girl I'd been so angry at for so long. The double vision that had been plaguing me since my arrival at Osthorne returned—I could see the Tabitha that was, and a Tabitha that might have been. Someone I could get drinks with after work. Someone I could make eye contact with at holidays. Someone I could trust.

But that wasn't this Tabitha. Not by a long shot.

My head throbbed. A sound like a whipcrack filled the room, and electricity arced between her palms. All of the students in the classroom jumped—it took me a moment to be sure my heart hadn't stopped. Tabitha spread her hands wider—the electricity fizzed between them, too bright to watch. I couldn't see her face, but I was willing to bet that the sparks were lighting her from below, ghost-story shadows making her eyes look hollow.

Then she closed her fists, and the light was gone.

"Alright, everyone. You've got the concept—now, pair up and try it for yourselves. Take notes! I'll expect your lab report on Monday!" Her voice rose as students started to rustle and fidget, eager to pair off with their preferred partners before they wound up stuck with *that other kid*. "One person at a time—you try, and your partner will have a Suresh Stick to disrupt the arc as needed. Then switch. I want to see everyone take a turn." She clapped her hands, and the kids flitted to each other.

The room brimmed with the scraping of chairs and murmuring of *Do you want to be my partner?* and *Okay um who goes first?* Tabitha turned to walk back to her desk; when she spotted me standing in the doorway, she smiled. It was a broad smile, one that would greet a stranger; I could see the exact instant when her mind processed me. Ivy Gamble, her sister. Standing here, in this context, where I had no business at all.

"Ivy? Oh my gosh, what on earth are you doing here?"

I returned her fixed smile. Surely Torres would have told her that I was going to be here. Surely. "I'm on a case. I'm supposed to come talk to you about"—I waved my hand around her classroom, gesturing toward the kids who were sending anemic sparks flying between their palms—"this, I guess. Theoretical magic."

Tabitha cocked her head to one side. Her eyes were even brighter than I remembered, like shards of glass under a streetlight. "What are you—? You know what, this isn't a great time." She blinked at me hard—she couldn't reconcile seeing me here, now, in this place where I didn't belong. "Maybe we should get drinks after work? This isn't a great time. I know a nice cocktail bar downtown. It's hipstery, but usually pretty mellow. We'll be able to hear each other."

"Wh— Drinks?" My head throbbed again, reminding me that drinks were a bad idea I'd had the night before. I also didn't relish the idea of getting into a situation where I had to linger with Tabitha long enough to settle a bill. But I knew that if I didn't rule out her involvement that night, I'd just have to do it some other time. I didn't have a choice, not really. "Okay, drinks," I said, edging toward the door. "Come find me after the last period of the day?"

"Sure," she said, watching me. "Sure, that's fine. I normally wouldn't go out, but tomorrow's Saturday, so . . ." She trailed off. Tabitha had never liked saying things that she thought were obvious. "You'll be here all day, then?"

"Yeah, I'm going to be doing some interviews. Well. Not really interviews, just meeting some people." I was holding the doorframe like it could keep me steady. "And I'm going to be here all day . . . every day, I guess. I'm kind of staying on campus, in the empty apartment?"

She cocked her head. "Empty apartment?"

"Yeah, in staff housing? Torres is putting me in it so I can be here doing the investigation." There I went, overexplaining. Tabitha would have just said *yes* and left me to wonder whatever she didn't happen to disclose.

"An empty—oh. *Oh,*" she said, some understanding dawning across her face. "Okay."

"Yeah," I said, "I guess it's kind of spooky, right? But I don't get haunted vibes or anything." I tried a smile, but she didn't return it.

"Drinks tonight," she said, closing off so suddenly that I wondered if I'd imagined that weighty *oh*. "I'll text you the address of the place, you'll meet me there. Yeah?"

I was about to suggest that we just open a bottle of wine at my place or hers—that we catch up, linger. I was caught in that double vision. It felt like there was a second Tabitha there, a possible-Tabitha, and if I just reached for her, I could slip into the world where that sister lived. The world where we were friends. The world where I wasn't alone.

But then there was a smell like burning hair and one of the girls in the classroom shrieked. Tabitha whipped around just as the girl's partner whacked her hands with a rubber rod, disrupting the stream of electricity. My sister turned her back to me as though I had never been there at all. The emergency was over, but she was gone—talking to the class about safety measures and how to properly protect each other. Midway through a sentence I didn't understand, she looked over her shoulder. Her eyes glanced off me like I was furniture, and I realized that to her, I wasn't there anymore. Plans for the evening had been made. I'd been contained.

I eased out of the room as quietly as I'd left Torres's office, and when I shut the door, there weren't two Tabithas on the other side. There was only the real Tabitha, my real sister. And she was a stranger.

CHAPTER

SEVEN

WHEN THE FIRST STUDENT FOUND me, I was camped out at one of the long study tables in the library. The table I'd picked was tucked to one side, but had a clear view of the window to the hallway. I had feathered my nest with file folders, nonspecific glossy photographs of blurred figures, sticky notes. A legal pad covered in vague notes with circles around randomly chosen words, arrows pointing to question marks. Detective stuff.

Between the diorama I'd set up and the students who had seen a stranger wandering their halls, I hoped to become hot gossip. I figured that those kids would see my setup and latch on to me like stray cats following a fishmonger. They wouldn't be able to resist the lure of a real live detective. A real mystery. They wouldn't be able to resist the story, because they were all trying desperately to find the Thing, the elusive Something that would make every adult's prediction come true: *These are the best years of your life.*

I couldn't blame the kids for searching so hard. I remembered what it was like, walking through my high school and feeling like everyone else's lives had already started. There was the girl who was an amazing singer and played guitar outside at lunch, the academic kid who won an award at the national level for some kind of algae farm, the young artists who sat and moodily sketched their friends. I remembered looking at them, and then looking at myself, and wondering when the hell my *thing* would turn up.

My friends and I, we had all been looking for it. What would make us crystallize? Anything could be the Thing that started it all, that started our stories. But the only stories we had to work with—the only stories these kids at Osthorne had to work with—were the ones we'd seen a million times already. It was why prom was so huge. It all fit into a story we knew by heart. Nervous proposal, careful planning, once-in-a-lifetime dress, incredible night, everything changes. It was why prom was so disappointing: because afterward, everything would be the same.

I wanted these kids to see me with the same hopeful glow I remember seeing my peers wearing in the weeks leading up to the prom that I had skipped. I wanted them wondering: *What if this is it? What if this is the big change that shakes everything into place? What if this is the turning point?* I wanted them to come to me and tell me what they knew, and I wanted them to feel like if they didn't tell me what they knew, they'd be missing out on their one chance to change their lives. So I presented them with a familiar narrative, something they'd seen on TV and in movies a million times. A Private Investigator is on the case, stirring things up, anything could happen, who's the killer, who's a witness, who's important, who has the biggest secrets? I gave them a story to slip into, to try out. Maybe this time things could be different.

Maybe this time, something would *happen*.

It wasn't all for show—I truly was working at that gum-bottomed lab table. Strictly speaking, the official NMIS report was a write-off: a lot of we-did-the-legwork-and-found-nothing-of-consequence. Still, there was a dense thicket of starting points for me to work through. The report listed five staff members and four students as "persons of interest." All of them had verified alibis and all of them sounded perfectly innocent, which meant that the report was a sham. I was willing to wager that none of these people had actually been interviewed for more than a minute or two each. I'd seen it before with burglaries—that kind of thing happens when the investigating officers think they already know all the answers. The NMIS officers had clearly decided early on that the death was an accident, and had gone through the motions to ensure that their conclusion wouldn't be questioned.

But even a sham report has clues in it if you know where to look. If there aren't clues, there are at least a couple of footholds. I took notes on each person mentioned in the file, including pertinent details from the perfunctory interview transcriptions appended to the report. I was in the middle of reading about Rahul Chaudhary (Osthorne staff member, teacher of physical magic, well-documented passion for theoretical magic) when I noticed a blond shimmer in my peripheral vision.

I was being watched.

I didn't look up. I had a feeling I knew who this was going to turn out to be, and I knew I had to play my cards right if I wanted to really get the Osthorne gossip machine churning. I started flipping through photographs, tapping my lower lip with my pen; shook my head, flipped to a fresh page on my legal pad. Every movement designed to signify that I was doing a whole lot of very important *detective work*. Clever Ivy.

"You're that detective, right?"

It was the girl from the day before—the blonde with the study group. The in-charge girl who had managed to make Torres back off without so much as a curl of her high-gloss lip. She didn't wait for an answer before she seated herself in the chair across from me. She crossed her legs, tossed her hair back over one shoulder as she glanced around to make sure we were alone. I wasn't the only one performing.

I gave her the long, suspicious look she wanted. "Maybe I am. Who's asking?"

She looked over her shoulders again, arching her neck. I took mental notes: long blond hair with a pyrite glint to it, cheekbones that Hollywood hopefuls would have paid for with six months' rent money. No makeup other than the lip gloss—or if there was, I was meant to *think* there was none. Her uniform didn't show the look-at-me hallmarks that I would have expected: no rolled-up skirt, no unbuttoned blouse. It struck me that this girl looked exactly like she was *supposed* to, which meant that she knew what people were looking for, what people would latch on to as weakness. She didn't want anyone thinking she needed their attention, their approval. *Don't underestimate this one,* I thought.

When she looked back at me, I could see her taking her own mental notes, but her face was too still to reveal what she took my measure to be.

"I'm Alexandria DeCambray."

"Shouldn't you be in fourth period, Alexandria?"

She smiled. "I got a hall pass for a bathroom trip. I just thought

I'd drop by on my way. Are you with the 'miz?" A twinkle in her eyes—*Aren't I clever?*

I put my hand out for her. "I work for myself. Ivy Gamble, PI." She didn't jump at the two letters the way I'd hoped, but I thought I saw a sheen of interest in her shark eyes. "DeCambray. You're related to Dylan, then?"

Wrong question. She rolled her eyes, sat back in her chair. "He's my half brother or whatever. We have the same dad. Where did you go to school?"

A small-talk opener from the kind of kid whose family throws galas—the what-do-you-do of the wealthy academic elite. She was trying to take my measure. I raised an eyebrow and dodged the question. "Half brother? Your moms must be . . . different. He's a few muffins short of a basket, huh?"

I saw her register my evasion, but the bait was too juicy. She pounced, her eyes glinting. "Um, *yeah,* our moms are pretty much opposites? His mom totally ran off when he was like three or whatever? And I guess our dad had to raise him totally solo, which sounds crazy, because our dad can be like . . . really intense." Something shifted in her face, a flinch—she'd said too much. She veered back on course with all the skill of a speed skater recovering her lead. "He's a *total loser freak.* I mean, I don't want to talk bad about him?" Another elaborate look around to make sure we were alone. "But he's like, *totally weird.*"

I nodded, took a note, made sure to let her see me underlining Dylan's name. "You've really got your finger on the pulse here, Alex. What can you tell me about Sylvia Capley?"

Something dark and animal slid across her face. "It's Alexandria."

"What? What did I say?"

"You called me Alex. That's not my name. My name is Alexandria."

She bit off the five syllables of her name. I ducked my head, apologetic, my mistake, so sorry, won't happen again. "Of course. Sorry about that."

And just like that, the noir dame was back—the girl who'd snuck across enemy lines to get me information, all-cooperative, ready to trust me with what she knew. "It's fine. Who were you asking about?"

I slid the staff photo of Sylvia across the table to her and threw some chum on the water. "Sylvia? Ms. Capley, your health and wellness teacher. You know. The one who was mur—er, who died."

I saw her catch my slip of the tongue, saw her do the math. She'd come to find out why I was here and how I could become part of her story, and there it was: *murder.*

"Ohmygod yeah, Ms. Capley. It's so sad, what happened to her." Gears turning; something clicked into place in her mind. "I mean. She was an *amazing* teacher. I considered her a mentor." Calculated tears. Just enough to make her eyes glitter, not enough to spill over and make her eyes puffy.

"You two were close?" I had a feeling I'd be asking that question a lot.

"I mean, not like . . . inappropriately close."

I raised an eyebrow. "Was she ever inappropriately close with anyone else?"

I watched as Alexandria weighed it for a half second—the rumors she could launch, the investigations she could kick off—before discarding it. "No, never. I mean she was totally a lesbian? Not that it matters," she added quickly. "I mean, like, I don't care or anything. Brea and Miranda are totally lesbians too. But it was whatever, she was dating someone anyway."

"That wasn't in the 'miz report," I said, scribbling faster than necessary on my notepad. "The dating-someone part, I mean. Not the lesbian part." Although that hadn't been in the report either. Obviously. *Get it together, Ivy.* "Do you know who she was dating?"

Footsteps in the hallway; Alexandria slid up out of the chair. "Yeah, I do. But I have to go before someone sees me." She picked up one of my business cards from the table, suddenly overcome by the need to be a responsible member of the Osthorne student body. She whispered urgently. "It was supposed to be some big secret who she was dating. I don't want to say here. Can I come to your office?"

I whispered back, spooling out the intrigue. "My office? No—no, you might be seen coming to Oakland. I'll tell you what—I'm staying on campus. You know where the good places are to meet without being noticed, right? We can have a cup of coffee, talk somewhere private." It didn't make a goddamn lick of sense. The chances of her being spotted on or near campus were about a billion times higher than the chances of anyone seeing her in Oakland. But she must have figured that the odds worked in her favor, because she grabbed the chance to be in charge of our meeting.

"I'll text you," she said, tucking the card into her blazer pocket.

"Wait—" I caught her attention, letting a thin thread of urgency into the conversation. "Before you go. Is there anything else I need to know about Ms. Capley?"

She looked me up and down with a devastatingly quick flick of her eyes. In a millimeter of pupil movement, I'd been evaluated, quantified, categorized, and dismissed. "She was weak," she whispered in a voice devoid of cruelty. She left without a glance back to make sure I was watching her go.

I took some of the notes I hadn't wanted her to see me taking—notes on her, what she really knew, what I thought she was lying about. I caught myself before I could finish writing "shark eyes." I stayed in the library, let myself be seen during the passing period. Then, when the tardy bell for fifth period had rung and the hallways had emptied again, I tucked the notepad into my jacket, leaving the rest of my set decoration behind, and went to see if there was free coffee in the teachers' lounge.

I found it without too much trouble—it was in the same hallway as the library, thank God. Tall tables lined with stools, a few couches in front of a decent-sized wall-mounted television. Two big refrigerators. A wall of mailbox cubbies. A true teachers' lounge, not the lounge-slash-copy-room-slash-mail-room of my public high school. A tall guy sat on the couch. I could only see the back of his head, thick dark hair and headphones. I heard the shuffle of papers, the quick scratch of a pen. Grading papers, then.

The coffeemaker stood in the corner, one of those fancy space-age deals with the pods. It looked straightforward from a distance, but after a few minutes pressing buttons and tugging on levers, I still hadn't figured out how to get the top to open so I could put the pod in. Ivy Gamble, Ace Detective.

Just when I was about to give up and go back to the library in a dire state of caffeine deprivation, a throat cleared behind me.

"Can I give you a hand with that?"

It was the guy from the couch. I looked up at him. And up, and up. He just seemed to keep *going*. "Oh, god, please yes." I bit the inside of my cheek. "I really need the caffeine."

He nodded at my visitor's badge as he popped the machine open by pulling a lever I could swear I'd pulled on nine or ten times already. "You're the detective, right? Ivy? The staff got a note that you'd be around. You're here about what happened to Sylvia."

"That's me," I answered. "How did you get that open? I was trying for ages, and—"

"Oh," he said, "it's easy—you just have to cast an unsealing charm while you pull on this lever. We have to keep it locked, or the kids will sneak in here to steal coffee before first period." He popped my pod into the machine and pressed a button that made the whole thing purr like a saber-tooth tiger. Double vision: an Ivy who knew what he was talking about, and an Ivy who didn't.

Another threshold, right then, and I decided which Ivy to be. I made a choice, one I made in case I needed more credibility, in case I needed him to trust me in ways that he might not otherwise.

It was a professional decision. This was a job, and I had a deliverable to pursue. By any means necessary.

"Oh, right," I said. "An unsealing charm. Of course." I laughed, and my laugh wasn't awkward, and it wasn't hesitant. It was self-deprecating and charming and easy, so easy. "It's been a while since I've been in a school. It didn't even occur to me that I might need to use one of those on the *coffeemaker*." He grinned at me— *what a strange world us teachers inhabit, of course*—and I smiled back, leaning against the counter as the coffeemaker hummed. "Are you a teacher here?"

"I teach physical magic," he answered.

"Oh! You're . . ." I reached into the depths of my memory, bumping against that lingering headache on the way. I could remember his alibi—he'd been in urgent care for dehydration resulting from some kind of food poisoning. He'd been one of the five teachers absent from school grounds on the day of the murder, and he'd even provided his insurance paperwork as evidence. His interview answers in the transcript had been direct, if a touch impatient. His name finally floated to the surface of my memory after an embarrassingly long time. "Rahul, right? Sha . . . crap, I swear I knew your last name."

"Chaudhary," he laughed. "But please call me Rahul? I always feel weird when an adult calls me the same thing that my fourteen-year-old students do."

Is this guy flirting with me? I wasn't used to being around friendly men—most of the guys I met were jealous of their wives, or were angry that I'd exposed their fraud, or were trying to dodge a bill. I didn't like this, the way I felt slow and clumsy. I reminded myself what I was there to do. But if he was flirting with me, he would probably slip up and tell me things, right? It couldn't hurt to go with it.

I added half a packet of fake sugar to my coffee and decided to press the advantage. "Mind if I join you here for a few minutes? I need to get out of that library. It's like a peach pit in there."

He gestured grandly to the couch. "Of course. And I know what you mean about the library."

I blinked at him. I hadn't even known what I meant. I shifted his stack of graded papers to the little coffee table in front of the couch. The top one was marked by a blue "B+" with a smiley face next to it. "Really?" I asked, trying not to sound too incredulous.

"Yeah," he said as he folded his mile-long legs to sit next to me. "Totally. Ever since Sylvia's body was found, it's kind of hard to get kids to go in there. Well, except Dylan." He rolled his eyes. "But nobody wants to go in there for educational purposes. They think it's haunted, what with the books and all. You've heard the books, right?"

I suppressed a shudder. "Yeah, I've heard the books. But, about the students—I saw a group of girls in there just the other day."

Rahul shook his head. "Was it Alexandria DeCambray and her group?"

"Yeah," I said. "Why?"

"They were in there on a bet. They took a video of themselves walking through the stacks and posted it online this morning."

I crinkled my nose. "A bet? That doesn't really seem like Alexandria's style."

"No? This morning, the entire prom committee stepped down and was replaced by those four girls," he said. "When Alexandria plays, she plays to win."

"Wow. You've got the inside scoop, huh?"

"I only know about it because I'm the staff facilitator for prom this year. Prom was kind of Sylvia's thing. After she died, no one else wanted to take it on. But I thought the kids kind of needed it, you know? They need that normal thing."

"Yeah, yikes." We shared the awkward silence that comes from small talk gone sad. It was a silence I experienced whenever a new person found out that my mother was dead. "So," I said in too-bright voice, trying to rescue us both, "physical magic, huh?"

"That's my jam," he said.

"What made you decide on that?" I pretended that I wasn't pretending. I pretended that I knew what physical magic was, that I knew how it worked, that I had a reason to ask my question. And whoever I was pretending to be . . . Rahul liked her. His face lit up, his warm brown eyes crinkling.

"Well, it's just so . . . awesome, right? I mean, for most kids, the first time they do magic, it's physical magic. Like, maybe they accidentally turned their hair blue, or they grew their poodle three sizes. So they're already pumped about it, and then I get to teach them that there's so much *more*."

I nodded like I knew *exactly* what he was talking about. I remembered another one of Tabitha's first times doing accidental magic, which was nothing like what he was describing. She'd turned all the water in our community swimming pool into sparks. *So much more, indeed.*

"It's such a trustworthy kind of magic, too, you know?" He leaned toward me, bright with enthusiasm. "It's not like metaphysical, where you're turning something into something else. It's just . . . making things a little different. Like—can I show you my favorite thing?"

I nodded without having a clue what he was going to do. He reached forward and touched a scar on my arm, a half-inch-long one that I'd had since an unfortunate tangle with my first training-wheel-free bike. Under his fingertip, it shivered silver like a thread of mercury. My breath caught. I'd never let Tabitha try to do anything like that to me—I'd screamed at her like a banshee the one time she came for my hair with a detangling spell.

"Wow," I breathed, then realized how wide-eyed that sounded. "Wow, I forgot I even had that scar." It was a bad cover, but when I looked up, it didn't seem like he'd noticed.

I couldn't tell if I liked what he'd done or not—my heart was pounding with some combination of excitement and disgust and shame and heat. He sat back with a smile, and my scar went back to its normal pale pink.

"See what I mean? It's not metaphysical. It's exactly what it is. But it's also *more*. I guess I just like things to be more of what they are," he said, rubbing the back of his neck and giving me a bashful half smile. "More or less."

I got back to the library five minutes before the final bell. It was just enough time to gather my props, which were in abject disarray: someone had been investigating me. I started sweeping my scattered business cards into a pile, ignoring my phone buzzing in my pocket. It would be Tabitha, sending me the address of the bar I was supposed to meet her at. Part of me had wanted to invite her back to my bare little apartment in staff housing—me and her and a bottle of wine. I imagined us with our feet tucked up on the couch, leaning toward each other, smiling, laughing about things we'd forgotten. But it was a best-friend tableau I'd never actually experienced. Not with a real best friend, and certainly not with Tabitha. I hadn't been alone with my sister since high school. I couldn't begin to imagine what it would be like to be *friends* with her. I tried to imagine it: Drinks after work, dinners on the weekends. Visiting our mother's grave together.

But we didn't have that. We had silent Christmases and smiles that were just for photographs. We had the crushing weight of things that had gone unsaid for so long that they'd calcified between us. Walls too high to ever turn into bridges. An actual friendship with her would be—

The tracks evaporated from under my train of thought. I froze in the middle of stacking glossy photos. There was a something tucked under the top page of my legal pad. I lifted the corner of the page—a piece of paper was hidden there, folded into an elaborate star.

I looked around without picking it up. I couldn't see anyone else in the library, although I thought I heard a sharp increase in the whispering from the roped-off Theoretical Magic section. I suppressed a shiver and swept everything from the study table into my bag. I needed to get the hell out of that place.

Once I'd made it to my car, I dug through the debris, letting the bogus photos crumple against each other. It was stuffy, hot, but I didn't want to turn on the air conditioning, not yet. It felt like the whispers from the library had woven through the pit of my stomach, and they wouldn't quiet until I'd unfolded that star, read the note I'd been left.

Tracing my fingers along the seams at the bottom of my bag, I finally found it.

It was made from lined paper, torn out of a notebook, the perforated edge carefully trimmed. Two sentences were written in a bubbly print in unsmudged pen, right in the heart of the star.

She's not who you think she is. Watch out.

As I read them the words ran like watercolors, the dark blue ink growing thin and spreading to the edges of the page. The pigment sank into the paper and then faded, taking the light notebook-paper lines with it. I stared at the wide stretch of white nothing on the page. I realized that I had no scale for how weird this actually was, in a world where scars can turn to silver and sparks can fly between the palms of a fourteen-year-old kid. I was in so far over my head that I didn't know which way was up anymore.

"Shit," I said, turning the car on without looking at the address Tabitha had sent. I didn't care if I drove twenty miles in the wrong direction—I needed to get off that campus, far from the library and the bloodstains and the graffiti that wouldn't scrape away. "Shit." I pulled out of the Osthorne parking lot with my eyes on my rearview mirror, unable to shake the feeling that someone was standing behind one of those leaded-glass windows, watching me go.

CHAPTER

EIGHT

TABITHA AND I FINISHED OUR first two rounds with the efficiency of people who drink when they don't know what to say. The bar she'd chosen for us was dimly lit and still had a musty jukebox in one corner and a condom vending machine in the ladies' room, but the menu revealed that there was a budding mixologist behind the bar and the drinks were strong, which was good enough for me. Tabitha was a half round ahead by the time I showed up. I was late, but at least I wasn't hearing phantom whispers anymore. She wasn't angry at me for my tardiness, but somewhere a score was being kept and I certainly wasn't in the lead.

Tabitha ordered spicy, smoky cocktails—habanero and mezcal. I favored lime and ginger and whatever clear liquor the bartender wanted to pour. We picked our way through the kind of conversation you're supposed to have with someone you haven't seen in a while and don't particularly understand. Lots of small talk and avoidance; the occasional reference to experiences we'd shared a long time ago, back when we still shared things. I kept wanting to explain that I was a different person than the Ivy she remembered, but then I'd catch myself thinking that she was the exact same Tabitha I remembered, and so I'd doubt myself. Maybe I hadn't changed. Maybe I wasn't different. Maybe I just liked to tell myself that I'd come a long way—a convenient fiction to make it easier to keep going home to the same empty apartment every night.

Finally, after we'd ordered a third round of drinks and a basket of popcorn to share ("sea salt and pink peppercorn," nine dollars a basket), we started to *really* talk. She leaned across the table with a sparkle in her eyes, and she laughed at something I said. A good laugh, a real one. I leaned forward too, trying not to let myself get too hungry, but caught in the pull of possibility.

The thing about me is, I let things go. I let people go. I don't know how to hang on to them—I try, but I hold too tight or not tight enough or something in between and they go. They always go. But all it took was three drinks, and there was the sparkle in Tabitha's eyes and we were leaning toward each other and she was laughing, and maybe, maybe, *maybe* this could be something that I could keep. We were sisters, after all. I thought of how it would feel to end our estrangement and patch things up, and my heart ached with a hope that I hadn't let myself feel for a long time.

Maybe this could work.

If I didn't manage to ruin it first.

"So, are you seeing anyone?" I asked. She looked surprised. "Well, I just remember Dad mentioned last Thanksgiving that you'd met some new girl, right? He seemed to think you were pretty excited about—"

She cut me off. "It didn't work out." She smiled like a door slamming, and frost spread across the surface of her drink.

That was a mistake. I shouldn't have reminded her of the way Dad gave us updates on each other. I shouldn't have reminded her that we traded off holidays so as not to have to sit across from each other. *Damn it, damn it, damn it.*

"Ivy," she said, stabbing her straw through the layer of ice in her glass with a savage crunch. "I appreciate what you're doing, but come on. We don't have to try to make this into something it's not. Let's just talk about what we need to talk about. It's not like we're here to become best friends, right?"

Oh.

My chair suddenly felt too small. "Sure, of course. I'll just be right back," I said, and walked to the restroom without waiting for her reply.

I shut myself in a stall and rested my forehead against the scarred door. Clenched my fists. Wished I was more drunk. Wished I was less drunk. I dug my nails into my palms and stared at my shoes—sensible boots with a professional-enough-looking toe that I could pass for a grown-up in the company of people who wore blazers. Had Tabitha noticed them? What did she think of them? What did she think of me, after all these years? *It's not like we're here to become best friends.*

I stood at the sink running my hands under the water until long after the watered-down liquid hand soap had rinsed away. It was the same kind that I kept at my office, just as ineffective. I didn't look at myself in the mirror. Fucking *Tabitha*. She still did that thing to her eyes, the thing that made them look bigger and more open, more alive. Not makeup, something else. Something fucking *magic*. I didn't like looking at myself, seeing my eyes, and knowing that she had them, the exact same ones, and had decided that they needed to be better.

I pushed my shoulders back as I walked to the table and tried to look like I hadn't just been giving myself a pep talk in a bathroom that had phone numbers written on the walls. I don't know why I bothered—Tabitha wasn't paying attention. She was playing with the cocktail napkin that had come with my third drink, flipping it between her fingers while condensation from my glass pooled on the table. She flicked it with her index finger once every second or so. As I got closer, I could see what she was doing: turning it into water, then tree bark, then clear plastic, then something that looked like bone.

When I sat down, she flicked the napkin one more time, and it reappeared under my glass, a neat square of copper mesh.

"That'll leave green spots on the table," I pointed out.

"You're thinking of brass," she replied, sipping her drink. I looked back down, and my copper napkin was a shade browner than it had been before. When I looked up at Tabitha again, the light from a streetlamp outside was falling across her hair at just exactly the right angle to make it glimmer.

I clenched my teeth together until I could hear them creaking.

"Sooo?" She stared at me over the top of her drink, her eyebrows arched. "You want to know about theoretical magic, right?"

I stared at the metal mesh under my glass. *No.* I didn't want to know about magic. I wanted to get up and walk away and continue pretending I didn't know anything about it. I rolled the words over my tongue like a butterscotch candy: *Never mind. I'm not taking the case. Goodbye.*

I pictured the relief that would settle over her face as she realized that she didn't actually have to try to teach me about magic. That she didn't actually have to talk to me at all. I pictured us finishing our drinks, paying the tab, and parting ways. I pictured returning the barely touched retainer to Torres and going back to taking pictures of adulterers and insurance scammers. I pictured myself burrowing back down into my cozy nest of petty fraud and adultery, and it was so tempting.

But then I watched the brass coaster under my glass as it turned green so fast that it couldn't have just been the water and the air doing it. A different picture clicked together in my mind. I envisioned the murder of Sylvia Capley spreading across Osthorne, oxidizing it, rotting it. I imagined my father at Christmas, watching Tabitha turn pine boughs into ice sculptures, and I pictured a glimmer of doubt in his eyes. His magical daughter couldn't fix everything, after all.

Two sides of a coin that I would only have one chance to flip. Learn about magic and solve this case, or run back to the comfort of my basement office. Talk to my sister, or give up the chance to solve a murder.

Stay or go.

I looked at Tabitha. "Yes," I said. "Tell me about magic."

———

Four hours, several more cocktails, and three more baskets of overpriced popcorn later, we were evicted from the closing bar. We wheedled two compostable potato-starch-foam takeout cups of water from the bartender and walked out into the damp night air. They locked the door behind us, flicking the switch on the neon OPEN sign and leaving the window dark and empty.

"I think I get it," I said, leaning against the wall outside the bar and watching a fine mist of almost-rain drift through the light of the streetlamps. "I think I really get it."

"No, you don't," Tabitha said, sitting down at my feet. "But that's okay. You're not supposed to. That's the whole point! It's *theory*."

I slid down the wall until I was sitting next to her, both of us tucked under the awning outside the bar. The canvas didn't keep the drizzle from getting to us, but it wasn't coming down hard enough to be a bother. Not really. I bumped Tabitha's foot with mine. "We haven't talked this long since grade school."

Her head lolled. "Not since I turned your strawberry barrette green. You were so mad at me." Her chin tucked in as she frowned. "You're still so mad at me."

I didn't say anything. The sound of the bartender and the waiter flirting drifted out to us—*what are you doing after this what are you doing tomorrow morning what about spending them both at my place.* Tabitha gave a wet sniffle, and I realized she was pretty drunk. I realized I was pretty drunk. Impulsively, I grabbed her hand.

"I'm sorry, Tabbie. I'm sorry I'm such a bitter asshole."

She gave another loud sniff. "When are you going to forgive me for being magic?"

I squeezed her hand, leaning my head back and thumping it against the bricks. "Probably never," I said.

She laughed lightly, squeezed my hand back. "When did you start? Hating me, I mean?"

It was the kind of question I would normally have dodged, but the mist was making the streetlamps into fairy lights and Tabitha was holding my hand and there was something between us that I would have called magic if I didn't know about *real* magic. "Six months after you left for Headley," I said.

"Really?"

"Yeah." I tapped her thumb with mine. "When you came home from spring break the first time."

"Was it the thing with my hair?" So she remembered that, too. We'd had a screaming fight about it—the way her hair was a different color. She'd offered to make mine "better" too, and I'd been furious that she wouldn't just change hers back.

"No. That wasn't it." I chewed on my lip. "It was the mirror."

"The—? . . . Oh."

I could hear it, the way she almost didn't remember. "Yeah. You gave me that mirror before you left for school, and you told me it was a magic mirror. Like I could leave you—"

"—magical voicemails," she breathed. It was coming back to her. "Oh my god, I did, I told you that, and then—"

"I didn't figure it out for months," I said. "I kept sending you messages and waiting to get one back, and I never did. It took me until Christmas to figure it out. And then you came home and I asked you about it, and you laughed at me."

"Jesus, Ivy, I was such a shit." She sounded sorry. I could have rubbed it in, could have told her more. About how I'd spent hours talking into that mirror, never once questioning that I was telling my sister about my life. About boys and girls and my first period and being scared of my math teacher and worried about her and missing her so, so much.

I could have told her about how I couldn't look in mirrors anymore without remembering the sound of her laughter when I asked her about it, the way she'd talked to me with a scorn I'd never heard in her voice before she left for Headley. *I can't believe you thought that was real, Ivy. We're not little kids anymore. Grow up.*

I could have ground it into her face, made her feel the kind of bewildered and hurt she'd made me feel. But then she was holding my hand.

"It's fine. It was a long time ago. I barely think about it anymore. And anyway, I was probably a shit to you, too."

She laughed. "Yeah, probably. I hardly remember."

It was more honest communication than we'd had in decades. I couldn't take much more. I felt like her laugh was wrapped around my rib cage, crushing the air out of my lungs. I didn't know what to do. I didn't know how to enjoy her company. I fought down a swell of something like panic.

"Ivy? I should tell you something—"

She said it in an almost-whisper, and I couldn't. I couldn't hear whatever it was, couldn't handle the possibility of intimacy. I should have, but I couldn't. It was too much too fast, and if she kept going I was going to have to admit how much I wanted it, how much I wanted her to be my sister again, how much it hurt that we had gone so long without talking—so instead, I pretended not to hear.

"So who's your favorite student?" I blurted, too fast, too eager.

She paused. When we were kids, she'd take that pause every now and then while we were playing, deciding whether she was going to let me make up a new rule or not. She almost never played along—but this time, she did.

"Probably Miranda Yao." She said it and I was almost convinced that I hadn't derailed her at all. I let myself believe it.

"That name's familiar." I thought back to the study group, tried to picture the girls who had crowded around that phone in the library.

She shrugged. "Runs with Alexandria DeCambray? You mentioned that you'd seen her, and seeing her without her posse is pretty rare." Tabitha leaned her head on my shoulder. "She's sporty. All-American type," she murmured, and I remembered the Chinese girl in the baggy basketball shorts, with her square jaw set in a scowl. "But she's stealth-brilliant. Gives Brea Teymourni a run for her money."

"Stealth-brilliant?"

"Yeah," she said. "She's smart but she keeps it on the down low." She had pitched her voice deep when she said "down low," and dissolved into a fit of giggles. They were contagious—I started giggling too, and it was strange, hearing our laughter together. We had the same laugh.

After a few minutes we caught our breath—both of us went "hooooo" at the same time, which got us laughing again—and I asked why Miranda would keep her intelligence a secret.

"Ah, well, Brea was there first," she said.

"Brea—what?" I wondered if maybe she was more drunk than I'd thought.

"Brea was there first," she repeated. "She was friends with Alexandria first, and she's the smart one. When she brought Miranda into the group, something had to give." She missed her straw a couple of times before successfully taking a long drink of water.

"I think I'm missing something," I said.

Tabitha set down her cup and scooted away from me by a few

inches. "See, check it out," she said, and I turned to find her staring at me, her eyes flashing under the streetlight. I'd forgotten how intense she could get. "Alexandria, she curates people. She puts together her group of friends, but—" she hiccupped, took another sip of water. "But they're only allowed to have one *thing*."

I laughed. "What does *that* mean? 'One thing'?"

Tabitha nodded. "Yeah. One thing each. See, right now, there's three of them." She counted them off on her fingers. "Brea, she's super-smart. Miranda is the sporty one. And then there's Courtney." She cleared her throat. "She's artsy."

"So what's Alexandria?"

"Powerful. In charge? She's the boss."

"Wait, no, this doesn't add up. Aren't two of them gay? But that's allowed, there's allowed to be two lesbians in the posse? They don't have to be different?"

She shook her head. "That's not really how it works? 'Being gay' isn't their *thing*. It's just who they are. Although it probably doesn't hurt that only Brea is gay. Miranda is, um." She waved her hands. "Whaddayacallit. All of it. Pansexual?"

I stared at her. "How on *earth* do you know that?"

She shrugged. "They're out. Miranda's pretty vocal about it. Brea, less so. They've been together since sophomore year. I think they're going to the same college, even. They're really good together."

"Huh." We shared a quiet minute, thinking about how things had changed and hadn't changed since we were kids.

"Yeah," she said after a long drink of water. "They're braver than I was at that age. I couldn't have committed to a girl that way back then."

I didn't mention that, as far as I knew, she'd still never really committed more than a few months at a time to any one girl. "So, wait," I said, "what happens if someone tries to be two things? Or tries to be something that's taken?"

Tabitha smiled then, rueful. "Ask Samantha Crabtree. One day, she was in the Arty Friend spot. Then she went out for track." Tabitha slid a finger across her throat; her fingernail left the ghost of a white line behind it. "Next thing you know, she's in the headmaster's office. Rumors of an inappropriate relationship with a teacher."

"Yeaugh, what?" I grimaced at her, but she waved me off, leaning her head back against the wall again and peering out of one half-open eye.

"Nah, there was nothing to the rumors. I mean . . . none of us would really put it past Toff? The English teacher?" She held a fist on top of her head. "Man bun, MFA, novel that's dead in the water. He's kinda . . . icky."

I snorted, raised an eyebrow. "'Icky'?"

She scowled. "I get a weird vibe off him. Sylvia *hated* him. Said he made a pass at her in the teachers' lounge. Apparently he told her that she was an eight, but that if she wore makeup she could be a nine?"

"Oh, god, he sounds gross," I said.

"Yeah. But we investigated pretty thoroughly and there wasn't anything gross going on with Toff and Samantha." She closed the half-mast eye, and I realized it was easier to look at her when her eyes were closed. Tiny beads of mist clung to her eyelashes, to the tiny hairs of her eyebrows. "The rumors were enough, though. Samantha was pretty emotionally wrecked for all of last year. She almost didn't come back this semester. Her parents said she's not all that stable these days. Sylvia kept an eye out for her, though. I think . . . she'll be okay," she added, "but not until after she graduates, I think. That whole deal really traumatized her." She poked me hard with an index finger. "And don't you think for a *minute* we didn't know where the rumors started."

She went quiet; I thought she'd dozed off. I drank my water and thought about Alexandria.

"The graffiti?" I said.

"Yep," she said, not opening her eyes. "I can't prove it and she won't admit it, but that's got Alexandria written all over it."

"And nobody can figure out what spell she used?"

"Nobody," she said, her voice trailing into the soft murmur that precedes sleep. "I looked into some theoretical possibilities, but it's beyond what I can even really grasp. So . . . see what I mean about her?"

I nodded. "Powerful." I nudged Tabitha's foot with mine again. "Hey, kiddo. Time to get you home, huh?"

She grabbed my hand as her eyes flew open. Her fingers were cold and damp. "Let's just stay here for a minute, Ivy. Just—a couple minutes. I dunwanna go back." She was slurring, half-drunk and half-sleepy. My sister, holding my hand. I didn't want to tell her no. I tried to find the anger I'd felt just a couple of hours before, the bitterness—but her hand was in mine, and her head was on my shoulder, and I couldn't break the spell just yet.

"Okay." We sat silently for a few minutes. My mind was ticking over everything she'd told me. Maybe there was an easy solution to this. Maybe I could walk away from Osthorne with a few days' worth of expenses, the balance of the retainer, and the memory of my sister's hand in mine. And then I'd have done it: I'd have solved a murder. *Can it be this easy?*

"Tabitha?" I whispered it, almost hoping she wouldn't hear me; but of course she did.

"Yeah?"

"I hate to even ask this, but you know I have to. Where were you that night?"

She stiffened beside me—that hesitation, *Am I going to play this game?* Then a shrug. "Home sick. Food poisoning. Lots of us got it."

I tried for a self-effacing laugh. It came out sounding canned. "Great! I guess I can cross you off the list, then, huh?"

She did a better laugh than I had as she stood, brushing sidewalk grime off her pants. She suddenly seemed very sober. "Yep. Need some proof? Or am I free to go?"

"Wait," I said, my voice breaking in the middle of the word. "Wait, no, I believe you. I'm sorry. I didn't mean to make this about work."

"It's fine," she said. "It was always about work, Ivy." She looked down at me with weary eyes, and the puddle of light from the streetlamp above her shivered as she gestured at me with two crooked fingers.

The next thing I knew, I was standing on the lawn at Osthorne, dew soaking the cuffs of my pants. I knew, the way you know when you're going to throw up, that I'd gotten into a cab and taken it home. But the last thing I could really *remember* between standing outside the bar and standing on the grass was the look Tabitha had given me—disappointed and satisfied, both at once. Like she'd seen it coming.

I walked into the apartment and looked around. It was barren in there, sterile. I filled a glass of water, then went down the hall into the bedroom. I stared at that huge bed and felt like I was going to scream. It was too big, too empty. It belonged to a dead woman. I grabbed the slippery duvet with both hands and pulled hard. The mattress shifted as the tucked-in blanket popped out from under the edges. I left it off-kilter, wrapping the duvet around my shoulders before stumbling back into the living room. I fell onto the couch, letting the fabric of the cushion imprint a weave onto my cheek.

As I fell asleep, I heard Tabitha's voice over and over again. *It was always about work, Ivy. It was always about work.*

CHAPTER

NINE

MONDAY MORNING CAME ON LIKE a head cold. I stumbled into the bathroom of the staff apartment, dragging the full weight of the week to come. I avoided looking into the bedroom, where the bare mattress stared back out like an accusation. I'd slept on the couch all weekend, shoving the duvet to one side during the days so I could sit up and review reports and reply to subcontractor emails and make a dent in the gin bottle.

I was making progress. It was fine.

I stood in front of the bathroom mirror and peeled back my shirt collar to look at the wound on my shoulder, which was . . . not fine. I'd left the gauze off all weekend, vaguely remembering something my mother had said about how it was important to "let it breathe." The cut itself was a livid white smile inside a wide ellipse of red. The skin around it was swollen, tender. I caught my own eye in the mirror as I prodded it, and I realized that the injury was the best-looking part of me: the bags under my eyes were definitely well past the carry-on limit, and it was painfully obvious that I hadn't actually showered or brushed my hair over the weekend. I ran my fingers through my tangles as though that would make a difference.

I looked like something that had been pulled out of a shower drain, but really, I was fine. I'd just had an intense weekend. I'd gotten wrapped up in reading background checks on all the staff. They were super clean, although some of them had heavy redactions that I would have wagered were redacted because they were magic. I got wrapped up in those reports. I got wrapped up in all of them—it wasn't that I had lingered over Tabitha's, I hadn't. There was nothing there that I didn't already know. Background reports don't go all that deep. They don't explore *why are you the way you are?* or *what would it take for me to understand you?*

Besides, there wasn't time to linger. If there was no time to shower, there certainly wasn't time to dwell on things I couldn't change.

I turned away from the mirror and started the process of making myself into a human being, someone who could walk into a meeting with Marion Torres without embarrassing herself. I'd shopped on Saturday morning, and the clothes and makeup I'd bought were all still packaged and tagged. As I tossed labels and stickers into the tiny bathroom trash can, I reflected that I could have just driven back up to Oakland. I could have gone to my empty apartment there and grabbed the things I needed to live here, in this other empty apartment.

But I had needed some new things anyway. I only bought the slightly nicer brands because I was flush with cash, not because I was trying to impress anyone at Osthorne. If the things I was wearing happened to look like the clothes the faculty at the school wore—well, they looked good, didn't they? There was nothing wrong with drawing style inspiration from people who look good in what they're wearing. There was nothing wrong with wanting to look as casually professional and put-together as they did.

I kept telling myself that as I showered and got dressed and tried to make myself look like someone who could walk between worlds. It was an outfit, not a costume.

This could be the real me.

On my way across the lawn to the school, I rubbed absently at my shoulder. It didn't hurt, per se, but it felt taut and soft at the same time, like overripe fruit. I gave it a poke and bit back a swear as a flash of blue pain bit through my vision. Okay, so maybe it *did* hurt, per se. Very fucking per se.

I was still massaging it with the heel of my hand when I got to the main office. I ran into a student on their way out—another girl holding a pink hall pass and a white pharmacy bag. I turned to look after her, pausing with my hand on the doorframe, my mouth half-open to ask a question I hadn't finished forming yet. The question vanished entirely at the sound of a throat clearing.

"Can I help you?" I turned to see Mrs. Webb, watching me with a flinty glare. I could deal with her. I was used to flinty glares. People don't like a PI nosing around: they think we'll create drama by turning over stones and revealing what's living in the soft damp dark underneath. They don't realize that the things live in the soft damp dark whether or not we expose them to the sunlight. "Did you have an appointment with Ms. Torres? I don't see you on her schedule," she rasped, not bothering to open the thick engagement calendar that sat on her desk.

"Actually," I said, clearing my throat, "I'm here to talk to you, Mrs. Webb. I'd like to get your perspective on what happened on the day of the murder. When you found the, um. Body." My I-can-handle-this petered out rapidly as Webb watched me, unblinking.

"I gave a full testimony to the NMIS under oath," she said.

"Yes, but I was just, uh, hoping to—"

"I have no interest in discussing it further," she said. "You can read the deposition transcripts in the file I composed for Ms. Torres to give you. It is a very thorough file, Ms. Gamble."

Mrs. Webb and I regarded each other. The way she was staring at me reminded me of the way she'd been pinching herself when I saw her last. I tried hard not to let my gaze fall to her arm, where there were surely bruises hidden under the cardigan. I knew I had to push for answers: *What did you see? What did it do to you?*

After a moment, she clicked her tongue. "Alright, then, let's see it."

I blinked at her, feeling like a cow faced with a differential equation. "What?"

"Take that ridiculous jacket off and let's see your shoulder," she rasped, bracing her arms on her desk and pushing herself out of her chair. My indignation was slow to set in.

"Ridiculous? This is a nice jacket, I got it from—hey, what are you doing?" With quick fingers, she'd somehow gotten my jacket halfway off before I'd even realized what she was doing. *Fucking mages.*

Mrs. Webb pressed on the red, swollen skin of my shoulder with her dry fingertips. They were so cool, so gentle—then, she pressed harder, and my shoulder lit up with white-hot pain. Then, "Ow, shit, no, hey, st—"

Then everything went very fuzzy around the edges, and my shoulder exploded.

CHAPTER

TEN

"YOU ARE NOT STUPID, MS. GAMBLE." Mrs. Webb's voice floated through the red haze of my vision, her throaty rasp echoing across the hiss of panic-static in my ears.

The red haze was not the metaphorical mist of rage that blinds a furious detective so they don't have to explain exactly how they wound up with a gun in their hand. It was a literal four-foot-wide spray of blood and tissue, floating in front of me like a hologram. Tiny sponges of bone hovered a few inches from my nose. I had an absurd urge to reach out and bite one.

"Are we sure I'm not stupid?" I whispered.

"In spite of all evidence to the contrary, yes," Mrs. Webb said crisply. "You are not stupid, or I wouldn't have suggested that Ms. Torres hire you to solve Sylvia's murder." My field of vision began to narrow, my periphery going gray. A dark brown finger pushed aside a strand of muscle fibers that hovered in front of my nose, and then pointed to a large blob of gray-yellow toward the middle of the shoulder-fog.

Something in my brain screamed, vomited, fainted. I didn't

blink. I didn't look down at the place where my shoulder should have been, because I didn't want to find out if it was still there. I suspected strongly that it wasn't.

"You're not stupid, and yet you did not take this infection to a medical professional. Would you care to explain?"

I gave a high-pitched squeak, then cleared my throat and mumbled something unconvincing about how I was dealing with it myself. I petered out halfway through my explanation as two hunks of muscle brushed against each other like kelp in a slow current. I heard the wet *shush* they made as they met, and I lost the ability to make words.

I could practically hear Mrs. Webb's mouth forming a thin line of disapproval. A slim piece of wood poked its way through the floating morass of shoulder parts, then prodded the yellow-gray blob. The blob shuddered, blackened, smoked, and disintegrated.

My arm felt like it was filled with bees, but the bees were made of fire and the fire was made of lightning and the lightning was— and then, just like that, the fog of blood and muscle was gone.

I sat down hard on the floor.

I looked up at Mrs. Webb. She was sitting behind her desk, not a hair out of place, staring at me over her glasses as though she hadn't moved an inch. My jacket was back on.

"Next time," she said, "you'll go to the doctor."

I nodded slowly. Then, before I could unstick my tongue from the roof of my mouth, the door to Torres's office opened.

"Ivy?" Torres peered at me with a small frown. "Are you alright?"

"Yes, I'm, uh." I reached up and grabbed my shoulder. There

was still flesh and bone filling out my apparently ridiculous jacket. My shoulder didn't hurt when I dug my fingers in, and I dug them in hard, just to make sure everything had been put back where it was supposed to be. I scrambled to my feet. "I'm fine."

"Did we have an appointment?" She looked between Mrs. Webb and me. "I don't recall—"

"Yes," Mrs. Webb said. "You have a ten-minute check-in this morning."

I looked at Mrs. Webb. She was offering me an exit. My internal debate about whether to take it was abominably short. On the one hand, I knew that I should really stay to interview her. I had the deposition transcripts, and I had the file, and I could go off those—but it would be unprofessional to skip an interview. On the other hand, she could explode me with a touch. And judging by the way she was looking at me, she'd be very happy to do so.

"Just a quick check-in," I said, forcing myself to smile. Torres held her door open and I followed her inside, lowering myself gingerly into the chair in front of her desk.

"Are you sure you're alright? You look pale." She looked me over with concern. "We don't have a school nurse anymore, Sylvia was the closest thing. But Mrs. Webb could take a look at you, if you're not feeling well."

I jumped. "Mrs. Webb?"

"Yes! Yes, Mrs. Webb used to be a professional healer. Top of her field. I can't think of anything she wouldn't be able to handle." She blinked. "Well. Within reason, obviously."

"I don't understand," I said, still a little out of breath. "What—why is she . . . ?"

Torres smiled ruefully. "Why is she here? I know, she's seriously out of our league. But she got bored during her second retirement, and her granddaughter had been a student here, and she decided that she'd get involved for a few months. That was, let's see . . . nine years ago? Now she more or less runs the place." She leaned in conspiratorially. "She's *way* overqualified to be filling in as school nurse, but I'm sure I could ask her to—"

"No, no, that's, no," I stammered a bit too fast. "I'm fine, really, I just. Need to get some coffee. In a few minutes." I rustled my papers to give my hands something to do.

"Alright," Torres said, settling back in her chair, still eyeing me. "How's the case going? Have you made any progress?"

I took a deep breath. In my mind, I took what had just happened to my shoulder, and I put it into a box. A box with a tight lid. I dropped the box into a deep brick-lined oubliette. It landed somewhere next to my mother's last words and my searing loneliness and everything else I needed to forget, and just like that, I was fine again.

"I've got a few good starting points," I said. "But I want to set expectations—this is probably going to be a slow process. It will take weeks for me to gather the evidence necessary to even approach a conclusion." I gave her the familiar spiel about keeping a reasonable outlook—a speech I could have given in my sleep. It was one that every client needed to hear: no case solves itself in a week of miraculous discoveries and confessions. I stopped myself before my usual last line: *I can't just pull answers out of thin air— I'm a PI, not a wizard.*

I flipped open my notepad and pretended to check my notes as if I hadn't memorized them over the weekend. "It would be great if I could get Sylvia's medical records—did you have any luck getting them from the 'miz?"

She looked uncomfortable. "They assured me that they'd sent a copy already. They said that the records were appended to the coroner's report."

I raised my eyebrows. "They were definitely gone by the time I got the report." I glanced around her office—there were locking cabinets in several corners. "Where did you store the file before you gave it to me?"

Her lips twitched. "I stored it on my desk." She rubbed her temples. "It didn't occur to me that anyone would try to tamper with it—that anyone would even *know* to tamper with it."

"Oh," I said. "That's . . . interesting." Someone was trying to hide something. In that moment, it hit home: *The killer is here. Right here on campus, and likely in this building.* "We can get another copy of the medical record, yes? Did you already ask for that, or . . . ?"

"They said they'd send it over sometime next week," Torres said with a grimace. "Bureaucracy, I'm afraid."

I waved a hand at her. "Don't worry about it. I'll see if I can hassle them into sending it sooner. Otherwise—I think I'm ready to start talking to people, to get an idea of who Sylvia was. It'll help me to understand her life. To get a picture of who was involved in her day-to-day, and who might have had a reason to, you know." I cleared my throat. "To kill her." Torres's lips pursed minutely. I made a mental note to practice discussing murder until it didn't make me stumble anymore. "I was hoping to formally interview a few students this week, and then staff members next week, if that's alright with you?"

"Formally interview students?" The temperature in the room dropped by a few degrees. Her eyes narrowed, and I suddenly wished I was back out in the main office with Mrs. Webb, looking at a cloud of my own blood.

"I just need to learn a bit more about Sylvia, that's all." I balanced my tone on the incredibly narrow ridge between placating and casual. I didn't read Torres as the kind of woman who would take kindly to blatant mollification. "Students usually know more about teachers than we give them credit for. You said it was alright for me to talk to them—I just want to move those conversations into a setting where they can be a little more candid."

Torres hesitated before nodding. "As I understand it, 'miz guidelines require that at least two adults be present for formal interviews. But you aren't from the 'miz, and our Department of Education leaves internal matters up to each school's headmaster." She looked at me with frank evaluation. "I can't spare staff to supervise these interviews, so I'd like you to be somewhere that feels a little more public than an administrative office. Will the library work? I noticed you working in there yesterday. If you're comfortable where you were, you're welcome to it."

I exhaled as slowly and evenly as I could, trying hard not to look like I'd been holding my breath. She'd just made two concessions, and now, I had to ask her for a third. "The library will be perfect," I said. "Under one condition."

"What's that?"

"We close it off during the interviews. Put a sign up, make an announcement. Make sure everyone knows *not* to go in there."

She pursed her lips at me, and I thought for sure I'd overplayed my hand. But then: "You can't close the library for two weeks. I doubt anyone would be spending any time there anyway—they steer clear these days. I think the whispering 'creeps them out.' But they need to have the *option* of going in there, yes?" She tapped the side of her pen against the edge of her desk. "I can give you a day. And it has to be open during lunch and after school."

I shook my head. "One week?"

"Two days. It's the best I can do."

"Sold."

She looked me over. Something about our conversation was sticking out—something that she didn't quite like. She drummed her fingers on her desk. "Do you usually do interviews? Is that normal?"

I chewed my lip. "Well. No," I answered truthfully. "I actually almost *never* do interviews. But then, I don't usually get murder cases across my desk, either. So I'm doing what seems like it'll work."

She nodded. "I suppose that's all I can ask for," she said. "Two days. Then the library's back open, and you'll need to find something else that 'seems like it'll work.'"

"Deal," I said, and stood to leave.

"Oh, hang on," she said, rummaging in a desk drawer. "I have this for you." She slid a pass to the restricted Theoretical Magic section across the table. "For the purposes of the ward on the section, you're now officially considered a member of the Osthorne staff. You shouldn't have any problem getting between the shelves so long as you have the pass."

"Thanks," I said, taking the pass and stuffing it into my bag. Torres gave me a thoughtful look. "What?"

"Oh, it's just—I was just thinking. As far as I know, you're the first nonmagical staff member at this school. We've never hired anyone without *any* powers before."

I smiled at her so I wouldn't scream. "You haven't mentioned that to the existing staff members, by any chance?"

Her brow, which had been furrowed for most of our meeting, cleared into a look of plain, blank surprise. I realized with a start that she was younger than I had guessed. "I haven't mentioned anything to anyone, other than that there's an investigator on campus and they should give you their full cooperation," she said. "Why? Should I make an announcement . . . ?"

"No, no, that won't be necessary," I said. "I'd like them to talk to me the same as they'd talk to anyone. I can look up anything I don't understand, right? I wouldn't want anyone to act differently just because I'm around."

I don't know if she believed that explanation. But I believed it, and that was enough for us both. I walked past Mrs. Webb's empty desk and into the hallway where I would never belong, and I looked down a row of lockers, waiting for the disorientation to hit me—that strange double vision that I knew would come over me if I let it.

I waited for the double vision, not because I couldn't work the case without it, but because I didn't want to. When it came, I looked at the school where a different version of me could have belonged, and I straightened the starch-stiff lapel of my jacket, and I smiled.

———

I set up my detective-at-work tableau again, in the same place as before—visible, but not obvious. Just tucked away enough that people would feel like they were figuring something out. I'd made myself into a prize.

I taped a small piece of paper to the door that said the library was closed. It may as well have been a neon sign. "Nothing to see here, move along." Throughout the morning, it seemed as if every single one of the two hundred students at Osthorne Academy for Young Mages stopped to peek in at the window while pretending to check their hair in the glass. I spent the first few periods of the day pretending not to watch them as I finished reviewing background checks and set up my interview list.

They *all* looked so much younger than I would have thought. Not just the freshmen—all of them. Somehow, I'd pictured Osthorne's students as preternaturally self-possessed, as having some little extra bit about them that made them into something more than high school students. Maybe it was because Tabitha was the only high school mage I'd ever met before—she had always seemed to float a decade or so above our shared age, as if she had access to some well of wisdom that I'd never thought to drop a bucket into.

But these mages were, for the most part, kids. Sure, some of them looked like they could have been teaching the classes that they were making themselves tardy for by peering in at my little window display. Some of them were only identifiable as "students" because they wore dark-blue Osthorne blazers over their white uniform button-downs. But they were all *kids*—all elbows and try-hard hairdos and sidelong glances at each other. They shouted in the halls and passed notes and cried and made out against the lockers, sometimes all at once. I kept waiting to see something amazing, something different. Something that would help me understand what made these kids different from me. Something unexpected.

That's not to say that there wasn't magic happening—but I wouldn't have called any of it surprising magic. Quite a lot of it was performed just within my range of vision, although the teenagers casting the spells assembled themselves into a statuary of nonchalance to make sure I knew that none of it was for my benefit. A sandwich levitated past the window; a paper airplane transformed into a flock of starlings; a tree burst out of a locker, heavy with ripe pink apples. Several varieties of penis-shaped clouds thundered loudly for about six minutes before Rahul burst out of his classroom to dispel them. He caught my eye as he worked his hands through the air to make the dick-clouds dissipate, and I dissolved into uncontrollable laughter at the look on his face.

So, yes, there was magic. But even the magic was distinctly *teenager* magic. There was something in the flavor of it that spoke to a desperate lostness, a struggle to self-define; an occasional lunge toward the juvenile that said, *We still get to be kids, right?* The more time I spent looking for a way that they were different— looking for something that gave them the right to be magic—the more absurd it all felt. I caught myself smiling wistfully at some of the more juvenile spellcraft, but it was a nostalgia that didn't belong to me. Every time I caught myself grinning at memories that weren't mine, the realization was a little more bitter: *This isn't for you. None of this is for you.*

As soon as the end-of-lunch tone rang through the halls, I visited Mrs. Webb to deliver the list of students I wanted to interview. I approached her warily, unsure whether or not she'd be exploding any of my other body parts. She took the page I offered and spoke to me while she looked it over.

"How's the shoulder, Ms. Gamble?"

I gave it an exploratory roll. "It's, uh. It's all better, I think. Ma'am." I didn't think, I knew. My shoulder was completely healed. The swelling was gone, the heat was gone. The cut was gone. The *gauze* was gone. There wasn't a scar—just an impossibly smooth stretch of skin. Even the freckles were the same as they'd been before.

Mrs. Webb still didn't look up from the list of names I'd given her. She didn't say anything. I shuffled my feet and took a breath to ask if we could have a quick chat, but startled when she raised her hand. My heart pounded, but she was just making a shooing motion.

"That's all," she murmured.

"Oh, okay. Thanks. Thank you," I stammered as I left. On the way past the window, I looked in at her. She wasn't pinching herself this time, but her hand hovered over her arm, one fingertip pressing at the place where I knew the bruise would be.

Forget it, I thought, and as I walked back to the library, I wondered if her oubliette was overflowing.

When I got back to the library, the lights were off; gray light from the overcast morning filtered in through the bank of windows, filling the room with shadows.

I wasn't alone.

Whispering echoed through the stacks—an extra layer of it, nested in among the constant whispers of the theoretical magic books. I closed the door behind me as quietly as I could, turning the knob slowly so it wouldn't make so much as a click. I tucked myself into the shadows of the stacks and began making my way between the shelves, toward the voices.

They were incredibly tantalizing. I could almost make out words—*howcouldyou whatwereyou whydidyou*—and I wondered if whatever weird magic was cast over that aisle to make the books whisper was intended to keep students out or to draw them in. I wondered why anyone would think it was a good idea to make them whisper in the first place. I pressed myself against the endcap between the two sections, straining to make out what the books were saying.

You never but I wish I could have and maybe then we would have did you do it but she can't know she can never know wait someone's here—

There was a crash. A book cart rocketed out of the Poison section and smashed into the wall in front of me. I smothered a shout of surprise. I rounded the corner, looked into the Theoretical Magic section—but I'd left my pass in my bag by the tableau and my head spun. Too late, I backtracked and watched as two shadows detached themselves from the darkness in the Poison section. They ran away from me, rounded the shelves; I chased them, but then they were gone, the library door slamming behind them. When I opened it and stared out into the hallway, nobody was there.

Too late.

The books in the Theoretical Magic section were silent. I realized that they had been silent all along.

I closed my eyes, tried to remember the last thing I'd heard them say.

Did you do it?

She can never know.

I stepped into the Poison section. There, on the floor, was a crumpled piece of notebook paper. I took it to the window to look at it in the light. The strange pattern of creases looked familiar. I pulled the note from Friday out of my pocket and compared the two.

They matched.

The ink on this note hadn't run the same way mine had, but it had been folded into the same elaborate star.

Meet me in the library, it said. *We need to talk. I know what you did, but I still love you. We can't let her come between us anymore.*

I stared at it, waiting for the words to dissolve, but they stayed. I read them over and over again until my first student interview arrived. The more crumbs I found, the more certain I was that the whole cake was still at Osthorne. Sylvia hadn't been murdered by just anyone. The killer was someone at the school. It *had* to be.

"Um, Miss Gamble?" Dylan DeCambray's voice broke over my name. "Hello?"

I shoved both notes into the pockets of my jacket, tearing the tiny seam of threads that had stitched the pockets closed while it was on the rack. "Yes, Dylan. Hi. You can turn the lights on." The fluorescents overhead buzzed to life, washing the shadowy room in thin, milky light. I glanced up at the flickering panels that checkered the ceiling and noticed a dark patch: the lights over the Theoretical Magic section were out. "Well, that's a bit precious, isn't it?" I muttered as I walked over to the desk I'd spread my files across. I shuffled a couple of papers before squinting at Dylan.

"Hi, uh. Miss Gamble." He held out a slip of paper. "Mrs. Webb said you wanted to see me? She pulled me out of physics, which—"

"Would you like to take a seat?" I sat without taking his hall pass.

"Sure," he said, not making eye contact with me. I couldn't tell if he was nervous or pissed.

"Physics, huh? Do you mean physical magic? With Mr. Chaudhary?" Not that I cared.

He rolled his eyes, slouched in his chair so thoroughly that it looked like his spine was melting. I suppose that solved the nervous/pissed mystery. "No, I mean *physics*. We're in lab today, and I really shouldn't be missing it." He stared at me like I gave a shit about his lab.

I let him simmer while I made a show of flipping to a fresh page in my notebook, of turning on a recording app on my phone and setting it on the table between us. He had the long, lean look of pulled taffy, and I wondered if he was done growing yet or if he had one more torturous season of outgrown pants to deal with. He looked almost-there, smudgy, like someone had pulled him off the press a moment before the ink had dried. His hair was messy, but I noticed that he didn't run his hands through it; instead, he occasionally ruffled it at the roots with his fingertips. This was a Look—he was channeling something. I flashed back to our Chosen One conversation, looked him over one more time.

Yes—he was definitely cultivating a persona. I had my angle. I took a deep breath, tugged at the cuffs of my jacket, and tried to slip myself into the game. Into his story.

"I'm sorry I had to make you miss your lab, Dylan. I know that's so important, and I'm sure your lab partner is missing you. It's just that . . . well. There are bigger things going on at Osthorne than physics class. I think you know what I'm talking about?" I raised my eyebrows significantly: can't say too much, you don't know who might be listening. "I need your help."

He stopped breathing for a couple of seconds, just long enough for me to see it catch in his mind. *Is it happening? Oh my god, someone is finally listening.*

"What can I do?" he said, leaning forward against the table. His elbows rested on a folder full of black-and-whites from an archived case.

Careful, Ivy. Not too fast now, I thought. I leaned forward too, mirroring him. "Let's start with what you know. Then we can discuss what I need you to do."

He frowned at me. "What I know?"

"I know you've been investigating too, Dylan," I said, going out on a limb. "I need to know what you've found. It may be the key to finding out who—or *what*—is behind the murder. So, can you help me catch the killer? Or not?"

He sat up as straight as if a snake had crawled up his pant leg to get warm. The hook was set. I'd picked the right tactic, playing on his desperate need for there to be a conspiracy, *dark forces at work,* something, anything bigger than what he already knew was going on. If he'd done anything wrong, he'd hang himself trying to get on the inside of the investigation. If he hadn't done anything wrong . . . he'd still have the rope. Maybe he'd lasso someone for me.

"Okay," he said, his voice pitching low. "I'll tell you everything I've found. But you can't record it, and you can't take notes." His eyes flicked to my phone, then to my notepad, where I'd written the date and his name along with a few illegible faux-notes to make him feel researched. "If anyone finds out what I have to tell you, my shit will be one hundred percent wrecked. You understand?"

I put my notebook down and reached out a deliberate finger to hit the big red STOP RECORDING button on my phone. I sat back in my chair, let him see that I wasn't hitting a secret button hidden under the table, wasn't signaling anyone hidden behind a one-way mirror. I spread my hands wide as I bumped my digital recorder with my foot. The little green LED blinked up at me from the floor.

"Okay, Dylan DeCambray," I said in a clear and carrying voice. "Tell me what you know about the murder of Sylvia Capley."

He took a deep breath.

And we're off.

CHAPTER

ELEVEN

YLAN HAD A LOT OF groundwork to lay. He spent the better part of an hour telling me the details of the Prophecy. He told me that it was important, and after my first few attempts to interrupt him, I decided to let out some line and see where this thing was going.

The Prophecy had been passed down through his family for generations. It was from a time when soothsaying wasn't considered a magical pseudoscience; his family had never let it go. It foretold that a child would be born into his generation, and that child would be the most powerful mage of the day and would forever change the world of magic ("and stuff," as Dylan helpfully added). There was some lace and fringe about the position of the planets and the weather when the child was born, and a long epilogue about the child changing the world of magic before they even came "of age."

He was sure it was him.

"I turn eighteen in March," he said, "so this is it. This has to be it. It's all my father and I have been working for this whole time.

I know that I can help, just tell me what to do. Do you need me to anchor a spell? Or pull together a working group? I'll do *anything*."

The weight he put behind the word "anything" carried a dark kind of desperation that I wanted to give a wide berth. This kid was ready to jump off a bridge if it meant fulfilling his destiny. I nodded slowly and leaned forward on my elbows. "What I really need right now," I said, in tones of great import and mystery, "is to know what *you* know about the murder."

"Right. Well." He looked over his shoulders, reminding me of a hunched-over version of Alexandria. "The school is trying to keep people out of the area where Ms. Capley died."

It took all my strength not to slam my head against the table. "Oh, I see. Very interesting. What else?"

"Well, they don't want anyone investigating. Asking questions. I almost got *suspended* for trying to cast an illumine charm over the stacks."

"An illumination charm?"

He raised his eyebrows back. "No, an illumine charm. I invented it. An illumination charm just casts sunlight. An illumine charm does that too, but it can also reveal *secrets* if you put the right twist on it." I could only just hear the difference, but I nodded as if I were impressed. As if I understood. "I cast it over the stacks and I was looking for clues, and then I got in trouble because I guess the light is bad for the books or whatever, but obviously it can't be bad for the books because then why would they have these big windows? Anyway, Ms. Gamble caught me and she totally ripped me a new assho— Um, I mean, she was really mad. And she took me to the office and said I was skipping classes—"

"Were you?"

"It was just Toff's class," he said, rolling his eyes. "I can afford to miss creeper-hour."

"Tell me about Toff," I said. "I've heard some weird stuff about him. What's the deal there?"

Dylan treated me to the kind of elaborately disinterested shrug that belies a wealth of care. "I don't know, he's just like . . . weird sometimes. With the girls. Whatever, it's not even a thing."

Oh, it was definitely a thing.

"You don't have to tell me anything you don't want to," I said carefully. "But if there's anything you think I should know about Toff, I want you to know that you can share it with me."

He looked away as though he hadn't heard me, as though there was something far more interesting happening in the gray patch of sky that was visible from his seat. I waited, debating whether I should prompt him further. After a long, uncomfortable silence, he spoke, still staring out the window.

"Okay, look," he started, then took another long pause. "All I know is, Alexandria and all her friends always talk about how gross he is. And how he makes them feel, I don't know. Weird, I guess. Capley and Torres were always on his case about it, but he never did anything bad enough to get fired, so I guess they backed off, and it's not like—"

"Hold on, Dylan, back up a second. Capley was on his case about it?"

"N— Um, no," he started, but I raised my eyebrows and he shifted in his seat. "No, I mean. They just had this big fight on the first day of school, but it was probably nothing. I don't know."

I was losing him, I could tell—the teenager was winning out

over the vigilante, and soon I'd just be left with a shrugging lump of nothing to interview.

"Never mind, Dylan, this is all very helpful. I'm sorry, I get distracted sometimes. So, when you were looking in the stacks under the illumination charm. Did you find anything, or . . . ?"

He suddenly looked extremely uncomfortable. This kid was no poker player. "Um. I, uh, no." He became very interested in something on the sleeve of his blazer. I became very interested in whatever it was that he didn't want to talk about.

"You're sure you didn't find anything? No clues at all?"

He looked up at me, his face resolute. "Nothing. Nothing at all." The kid was lying his ass off. He wasn't doing a good job at it, but he was committed. He was convinced that he had found something big. He was also convinced that he had to hide it from me. I debated calling him out for cowardice, seeing if that was a button I could push to make him talk.

But I studied the set of his jaw for a few more seconds, and I revised my assessment. He wasn't a chicken. He was being brave. Being brave means holding your fear in one hand and your responsibility in the other, and this kid was doing what he thought was right, even while he was pants-shittingly scared of whatever he'd found out.

"Okay, no worries," I said crisply. "That's fine. It's okay if you didn't find anything." I grabbed one of my business cards off the desk, held it out to him. "Give me a call if you think of anything, or if you find anything else. That's my cell number on there. Thanks for your time." I didn't bother looking at him, started flipping through a file folder. *Dismissed.*

"Wait, that's it?" He seemed startled. *Good.*

"Yep. That's it." I grabbed my pen, drew a star next to a random line in the file. "If you didn't find anything and you don't know anything, you're free to go back to your physics lab." I glanced up at him. I've never seen a kid so at war with himself.

"Wait," he said. I dropped my pen and looked at him sharply.

"Look, Dylan," I said in my best no-more-bullshit voice. "I know you want to help. But it sounds like you don't have anything for me. That's fine—maybe this isn't your thing. I'm sure you looked as hard as you could. But I have a murder to solve, and if you don't have anything that can help me, the best I can do for you is a certificate of participation. There's a *killer* at this school, and I can't waste any time. So go on back to class."

He went still, a rabbit in the instant before it bolts. For the second time that day, I was sure I'd pushed too hard. He was going to break and run. But then:

"Okay." He said it so quietly that at first I thought he'd let out a sob. He cleared his throat, stared at his hands. "Okay, I—I did find something."

I raised my eyebrows, looked up at him. "What do you mean?"

"I did find something. When I cast the illumine charm. I just didn't want to say because . . . it might get someone in trouble. Someone I care about."

I tapped my pen against the desk a few times. "Do you think this person you care about is the murderer?"

He looked up at me, and again I thought of how teenage-Ivy would have been knocked flat by the intensity in those eyes. Adult-Ivy knew he was doing it on purpose, that he was thinking to himself *blazing stare,* but still. I could catch the edges of it, how intimidating it must have been when he turned it on his peers. How convincing.

"I don't know."

I nodded. "I appreciate your honesty, Dylan. Why don't you tell me what you found? I'll put it together with whatever else I find before I make any decisions, and it'll stay between us until then. You have my word."

He let out a long, shaky breath and flexed his fingers a couple of times.

"Look, Ms. Capley was . . . like. She was different, you know? She wasn't like the other teachers. You could go to her for . . . stuff."

"What do you mean?"

He shifted in his seat, picked at the edge of a file folder. Wouldn't look at me. "Okay, look. I don't think she did anything *wrong,* okay?"

"Sure," I said, shrugging. So casual. Low stakes. *Come on, Dylan.* "Sure she didn't."

"I mean, she was just trying to help. I don't want anyone to get in trouble or anything. I want to help," he added hastily, looking at me as if I were about to push him out the door. "It's just that if this got out, you know, like . . . if people *knew*—"

The door burst open. Dylan froze in place, midsentence. He stared at the door. I turned to yell at the intruder—something more eloquent than "get the fuck out, we were just *finally getting somewhere.*"

But it wasn't an intruder. It was my next interviewee.

"Alexandria! I wasn't expecting you for"—I glanced at the time on my phone—"negative ten minutes." I gave her an apologetic look. "Dylan and I are just wrapping up, if you can wait outside for a min—" But Dylan was already on his feet, headed for the door. He was red-faced, staring so hard at the floor that he almost ran into Alexandria.

I allowed myself a small sigh. "Or we can get started now."

I couldn't be angry at Alexandria. It wasn't her fault she'd interrupted. But damn, there had been something *there*. Something that kid thought was really important. And now it was gone, and I didn't know if I could ever get it back.

But there was no sense in being so upset over that chance that I missed out on this one. I boxed up the lost opportunity and dropped it into the oubliette, and I turned my attention to Alexandria.

She sat in the same chair Dylan had been in. She folded her hands on the desk. I didn't rub my temples or close my eyes or pray for some merciful god to beam me a cup of coffee and a bottle of Tylenol. I looked her right in the eyes and swallowed my headache.

"So, Alexandria—"

She interrupted me in an urgent whisper. "I thought we were going to meet somewhere *else*? Coffee, somewhere private?" At the word "coffee," my brain perked up like a hopeful puppy. I squashed it down, ignoring the whimpers of caffeine deprivation.

"Yes, well, that was when it seemed like you were interested in being helpful—but you were holding out on me the other day, weren't you? I need to know what you know, Alexandria. I need you to be *honest* with me. And you haven't been, have you?"

She stared at me with a deer-in-the-headlights look that I knew best from the other side. It was disorienting to see it from this angle—I had only ever been the teenager in the position of trying to figure out which lie I'd been caught in, and never the adult panning for truth.

She opted for caution. "What do you mean?"

"I know you and your friends are hiding something," I said.

I knew no such thing. I was fishing, just like I had been with Dylan. I didn't know what I'd hook—something about Toff, maybe? Something about Osthorne? Whatever it was, *something* that Tabitha had told me about Alexandria's little gang was sticking in my craw. Something about the ruthlessness of the graffiti on the lockers and the way Miranda hid her intelligence. Something about the way Alexandria's lips had curled back from her teeth when I'd called her "Alex." There was something dark there, a big shadow under the surface of the water, and I needed to know if it was a log or a crocodile.

She sat back in her chair, not taking the bait. Her face was the surface of a skating pond, two feet deep with ice. The shadow stayed hidden beneath the frost. "I don't know what you're talking about."

"Okay," I said, flipping to a page in my notebook and angling it away from her so that all she could see was a few vague scribbles including her name. Her eyes flicked back and forth between the page and my face. "Then I guess that would make your friend Courtney a liar?"

"Courtney didn't talk to you," she said. It came out fast, sure. *She wouldn't dare.* I just nodded, eyebrows raised. I wanted Alexandria to ask what Courtney had said, to demand answers, but she wasn't having it. She was determined to call my bluff. *Damn again.*

I got casual, and fast. "Okay, sure. If you say so." I flipped the notebook closed again, so all she'd have in her memory would be the tantalizing glimpse of her own name in my notes, herself as a person of interest. She stared at the notebook hungrily, and I knew I'd laid good groundwork at least. The seed was planted. She was afraid that I knew about the lie, whatever it was.

But then, abruptly, her face smoothed over. As her features shifted, I realized with unease that she was mirroring me. I'd shifted into nonchalance, and she was doing the exact same thing. Casual, and fast. Her mouth tucked up at the corners in an achingly polite smile. "Did you go here?"

"What?" I was caught totally off-guard by her sudden transformation, and it took me a moment to parse the words into a meaningful sentence.

"For school," she said slowly, as though I might be a bit stupid. "Did you go here? I looked through all the old yearbooks over the weekend, but I couldn't find you. Or did you go to Headley? I remember Ms. Gamble told us once that she went there." She looked at me closely, her eyes flicking back and forth between mine. "You're sisters, aren't you?"

This had the flavor of a trap. She was being too polite, too casual. Too studied. But I couldn't figure out what I needed to be watching out for. Was this an invitation to lie? Or a bluff? What did it mean to her if I hadn't gone to Osthorne? Why was she bringing up Tabitha? Why was she looking for me in the yearbooks? It felt like the ground was shifting under me, rippling with the waves of a wake I couldn't identify.

I blinked. This wasn't a game I needed to play. I wasn't part of whatever competitive academic mage shit she was stuck in, and

I didn't need to impress her with my credentials. *Jesus, Ivy, where do you think you are?*

"We aren't here to talk about me, Alexandria," I said with a thank-you-for-condescending-to-ask-after-me smile. "And I don't want to waste your time on unimportant things. Let's talk about what you wanted to tell me the other day." I put the notebook aside, leaned across the table toward her. "About who Ms. Capley was dating."

The shift was instantaneous. Casual vanished faster than it had arrived. She went taut, looked back toward the door. "I told you, I can't talk about that here."

"Why not?"

"It's complicated."

"Try me."

The exchange was just cliché enough to hook her. She leaned in, mirroring me again, speaking low.

"Okay, here's the deal. She was seeing someone. They were serious. But it was a secret, okay? Not just a 'secret,' but like . . . a *total secret.*" She watched me to make sure I understood what she meant. And I did—I remembered. A "secret" is something that everyone knows but no one talks about, like the fact that your mom's cancer is why you're failing half your classes. A real *secret* is something that no one knows, like the fact that your mom has started refusing treatment for the cancer and is going to die within a couple of weeks.

"Got it," I said. "A *total secret.* So, do Brea and Courtney and Miranda know?"

She shook her head. "Only Courtney. And she hasn't told any-one." That certainty again, *she wouldn't dare.* I mentally highlighted *only Courtney*. "Ms. Capley and her girlfriend, they really didn't want anyone to know. I bet they could get fired. Like, when I found out? They both totally freaked out."

I knew bait when I saw it. I also knew when it was time to bite. "And how exactly did you find out?"

Her eyes glittered with the story. Alexandria had been *dying* to tell someone other than Courtney, but her respect for the *total secret*—or her fear of the wrath of this clandestine couple—had been enough to keep her mouth shut.

But now Alexandria's teacher was dead, and she could crack the seal on what she wasn't supposed to know. I was almost surprised that she hadn't told anyone before now, but then I remembered Tabitha's cautious assessment: *powerful*. I'd assumed she meant magically powerful, but maybe she'd also meant another, headier kind of power. Deeper power. The kind of power that comes from absolute discipline. I'd seen it in the way Alexandria curated which emotions she showed and which ones she hid, and now I was seeing it again in her willingness to wait until her information had ripened to *perfection* before inviting anyone to take a bite.

As she spun me the story, I could hear how she'd told it inside her head a thousand times, until it was as smooth as a stone polished by years of worry. Alexandria had every angle just right. She'd gone to Sylvia's office the previous May, she told me. It was one day after school: she'd gone to get a cramp-relief tincture because she was having an extra-bad period—this said with forthright woman-to-woman assuredness, none of the embarrassed lash-fluttering of a younger girl, no faux-gross-out hesitation. She'd knocked on the office door, but no one had answered. She thought she might just go in and get some of the tincture herself. Of course, she normally wouldn't dream of doing something like that, but she was in a lot of pain, I knew how that went, right? It wasn't like she was stealing or anything.

I nodded—of *course* breaking into a faculty member's office to take medication from their private cabinet wasn't stealing. Naturally.

Alexandria smiled, then continued her story. "The door was unlocked, and when I opened it . . ." She paused as though she were looking for a delicate way to describe what she'd seen. She had a fine-tuned sense of theater—she knew exactly what she wanted to say, but she preferred that I fill in the blanks with my imagination. "Well. There they were. It was pretty obvious what they'd been doing."

I reminded myself that going along with her was necessary, that I couldn't derail this whole thing by shouting "What, were they *fucking or something?*" Instead, I cleared my throat fussily, acting out my part. "And what was it that you saw, Alexandria?"

Her brows twitched up and she gave me a prissy little smirk. "Well. They were in a compromising position. Let's just say that Ms. Capley's skirt needed smoothing once they realized I was there."

I raised my eyebrows, unsmiling. *Let's just say. Compromising position.* She was getting too into her own story, slipping into a hallway-gossip rhythm, dropping in phrases that made her feel clever. She was forgetting that she was talking about a murder victim. To her credit, she seemed to realize her misstep immediately and backtracked gracefully, dropping her voice back into the helpful almost-adult register she'd been using a few minutes before.

"I mean, I didn't see *that* much, it's not like I was watching or anything, I just—you know. When you see something like that, even just for a second, you know what it is you're looking at. It was their private business, but—"

I nodded. "Of course. And then they freaked out, right?"

"They *totally* freaked out." She paused and looked at me like she'd forgotten her next line. I realized that she'd only rehearsed her story until the skirt-needed-smoothing part. A flicker of fear smoked across her face, almost fast enough to miss. This was big, important. As important as Dylan's *it might hurt someone I care about*. Alexandria had come up to the edge of telling me whatever this enormous secret was, and now she needed a little push.

No problem.

"Alexandria," I said, shooting her back a signal she'd recognize by looking over both my shoulders. I leaned forward, matched her low pitch. "I need you to tell me. It's important. The person Sylvia was with that day, when you walked in. Was it a student?"

She shook her head. Her eyes got wide, excited—she was ready, she was going to tell me who it was. She was going to give me my first real lead in this goddamned case. I thought I'd done it. I'd tugged the information right out of her gullet and she was going to unclench her teeth and give it up.

But I was wrong.

Too late, I realized that the look on her face wasn't just the excitement of getting to tell *someone*—it was the excitement of getting to tell *me*. Of getting to watch me find out what she knew. It was, I suddenly saw, the excitement of a cat with a spider caught under one paw. But it was too late to take back my line of questioning, before I could tell her that we were out of time for the day, sorry, back to class, Alexandria.

I hadn't tugged the information out of her, after all—she'd tricked me into putting my hand between her teeth.

Her unblinking eyes were still on me, hungry for my reaction. "It was your sister."

CHAPTER

TWELVE

I SAT IN THE LIBRARY as the school wound down for the day. I'd removed the sign from the door and locked it from the inside. Hopefully Torres wouldn't get pissed that I was denying the Osthorne student body access to what the poster behind the checkout desk called "The Magic of Learning." I turned off the fluorescents so the library was bathed only in the yellow-gray light of the indecisive sky outside. At a study table that was out of view of the windows in the hall, I rested my head on my arms, hoping the clouds would break into a white-noise rain so I wouldn't have to think anymore.

The tableau needed a break. The detective needed a break.

It had been hard work, getting Alexandria to leave. She had wanted to stick around to watch my reaction. Her eyes had glittered as she waited for me to show my underbelly. I'd tried to change the subject a few times, asking her about Toff in hopes that there would be a note of the salacious there that might grab her interest—but it didn't play. She kept saying that there was something *else* about Sylvia that I needed to know, something *big*. But she played too coy for too long, and I finally decided that whatever she knew couldn't possibly be worth getting my head fucked with. I told her that I needed some time to think about what she'd already told me. It seemed to satisfy her need for me to be reeling, and I sent her back to class nearly on time.

Tabitha and Sylvia.

Why hadn't Tabitha told me? We weren't exactly in the business of telling each other things, but couldn't she have dropped into conversation that she'd been dating—or at the very least, fucking—the woman whose grisly murder I'd been hired to solve? I thought back to the night we'd gotten drinks, when I'd worked up the courage to ask her something personal. When I'd gone with the safest option I could think of to get her to connect with me.

"Are you seeing anyone?"

"It didn't work out."

Didn't work out, indeed.

Every single book I'd ever read, every seminar I'd ever attended, every true-crime show I'd ever watched—they all rang through my head with the same crystal-bright tone as the Osthorne lunch bell. *It's always the spouse.* I drew spirals in my notebook as I thought about the timeline, not wanting to write it down.

Alexandria had found out about Tabitha and Sylvia in May. They'd been seeing each other since at least Thanksgiving of the year before, which is when my Dad gave me the annual Sibling Update. Tabitha wouldn't have mentioned to Dad that she was seeing someone if they hadn't been together for at least a month or two already.

I thought of Tabitha changing the coaster under my drink into copper, then brass. I thought of her eyes, of the sunbeams that hit her hair just right. I thought of my shoulder, exploding. I very carefully did *not* think about Sylvia, lying bisected on the floor of the library.

What had the books in the Theoretical Magic section seen? Had they seen my sister?

I drafted and deleted a few text messages to Tabitha, then put my head in my hands as the last bell rang and the halls filled with sound. My phone buzzed in my pocket three, four, five times. I watched the weak sunlight crawl across the study table toward me and wished for an eclipse.

Finally, after I-have-no-idea-how-long, something inside me snapped shut. I ran my fingers through my hair and rubbed them across my face, smashing my eyes under the heels of my hands. I let out my breath. I said "shit" because it felt good to swear. I said it a few times. I stood up, put on my jacket, and stalked out into the hallway. Texting wasn't going to work, this needed to happen in person. There was nothing else for it: I was going to go find Tabitha and hammer this out with her.

Fuck. If I talked to her and she was anything but beyond reproach, I'd have to drop the case. I'd have to return the retainer—which I no longer had—and I'd have to walk away. Part of me desperately wanted the opportunity to turn my back on Osthorne and never think about it again. But then, if that happened, how would I tell Torres why I couldn't follow through?

Could I implicate my own sister in a *murder*?

I opened the library door and went to pull my phone out of my pocket to see what all the buzzes were about. I stared at the little

maze of dots on my phone screen, a security measure that a soft-
ware update had exhorted me to set up a couple of weeks before.
I could never remember the sequence of dots I was supposed to
press in order to get my phone open. I tried two or three times, and
my phone buzzed angrily at me to let me know I'd gotten it wrong.
I finally remembered the code—a little spiral, counterclockwise—
and just as I got it right, I smacked headfirst into someone. I caught
a glimpse of thick black hair and crinkly eyes as I went down.

Rahul Chaudhary.

I fell flat on my ass, a perfect slapstick fall that sent a breath-
taking bolt of pain up my tailbone. My phone flew out of my hand,
skidded across the floor, and slid neatly under the nearest bank
of lockers. Rahul had been carrying a stack of papers; it flew into
the air and fluttered down around us like the feathers of some
massive exploded bird as he tumbled backward, skidding across
the linoleum floor.

Of course I would run into him. Of all the staff and students
at Osthorne, it would have to be him. At the exact instant when
I least wanted to see *anyone in the world,* of course I would see the
dreamboat physical magic teacher who had maybe been flirting
with me. *Classic.*

"Shit, fuck, damn it, ow," I said. My words seemed to echo
slightly, and I realized that Rahul had said the exact same thing
at the exact same time. Our eyes caught and we both burst out
laughing. The laugh slipped me sideways a little. Nonmagic Ivy
who was trying to decide if her sister was a murderer couldn't
have laughed just then if her life depended on it.

But the version of Ivy that lived on the other side of that double vision . . . she probably laughed all the time. She probably

laughed easily. She probably loved little moments like this one, probably laughed about them again later over wine with friends.

Meet-cute, her voice whispered.

Shut up, I thought. But I didn't think it very loudly.

"Here, let me—" I started gathering Rahul's papers, but he held out a hand to stop me.

"No, no, it's fine," he said, helping me up. I let myself smile at his hand in mine. His papers were spread snowily across the full length of the hallway—some had even slid under the lockers after my phone. They covered every part of the linoleum that wasn't occupied by my black boots or his brown loafers.

"This seems like a bit much," I said, surveying the sheer distribution of the papers.

"It's just this hallway that does it," he explained. "It's a charm someone cast back in October. If you knock someone's books or whatever out of their hands, they'll fly to opposite ends of the hall."

I swallowed down a flash of anger at the way these kids wasted their magic. They could do anything, and this is what they chose. I forced myself to give Rahul a wry smile. "That's not terribly . . . well. Charming."

He looked delighted. "It's clever as hell, though, isn't it? Fortunately, the staff knows the countercharm." He spread his hands wide, made a gesture that combined the wave with a game of one-sided patty-cake. I bit my lips to keep from laughing at him, and I let myself enjoy the feeling of having to hold back laughter.

"I know," he said with a one-sided smile. "The student who designed the charm constructed it so that undoing it makes the victim look as stupid as possible."

"Why don't you just . . . I don't know, get rid of it?"

He shook his head. "Can't. It's airtight—only the caster can undo it. To be honest, I'm kind of proud of whoever came up with this thing. It's really just . . ." He did a funny little wiggle that could have been part of the counterspell, but also could have been an expression of sheer joy. "It's really *neat magic*. Besides, it's kind of fun to watch the freshmen dance after they drop something." He did a complicated series of maneuvers that seemed to involve his hands passing directly through each other. When he laid his hands out flat in front of him, they were full of papers again.

I'd expected to see the papers come floating showily back, one by one, settling in his hands after a brief whirlwind of sparks. But no—it was suddenly as though they'd always been there, as though he'd never dropped them. The floor of the hallway was clear.

I could have stared in open-mouthed amazement. I could have asked him how that was possible. I could have said any number of things. But I was still a little warm with the feeling of laughing at a shared moment with a good-looking guy, and I didn't want to let it go. I didn't want to let the Ivy I could have been get swept away by the Ivy I was.

So I made a choice.

"Wow. I mean, that was really smoothly done. I haven't seen anything that clean in a while." My heartbeat only picked up a little. Rahul grinned at me, and I knew that he was grinning at the Ivy I was pretending to be, but I loved the way his smile felt. No part of me wondered if there was condescension there. No part of me flinched away. "I don't understand, though—if the kids can cast spells that you can't undo, how do you keep them from using magic to cheat?"

"We don't," he said with a shrug. "We usually just catch them after the fact, and then they get a failing grade. Did you have anything?" he asked as he tucked his huge stack of papers into the air in front of his chest. The papers vanished. "The countercharm only works on items the caster dropped. Which is nice, I suppose— keeps students from using it to steal from each other."

"I had my phone." I looked around, even though I'd seen it slide under the lockers. I didn't want him to see me scramble around on the floor, but no other viable options were presenting themselves.

"Do you want me to show you how to do the countercharm?"

"Oh, um, no, that's okay," I said. "I'll just, uh. I'll just grab it."

For the long minute during which I was on my hands and knees, reaching through the grime under the closest bank of lockers and feeling through the cobwebs and mystery-gunk to find my phone, I wanted to black out from embarrassment. I wondered how my ass looked in my new slacks. I wondered if the Ivy I was pretending to be would wonder how her ass looked in those same slacks. I wondered if I even wanted the attention of a guy who'd prioritize my ass over my apparently useless brain—even if he *was* tall and crinkly-eyed and filled out his own slacks very nicely. My hand brushed past at least one spider as I groped under the lockers—I felt its fat, sleek body wiggle out from under my palm. I was about to give up when my fingers closed over something slim, hard, rectangular. Something that my hand immediately recognized as "phone."

I pulled it out, and it snagged on something. There was a rustle, a ripping sound. I yanked my hand back fast, thinking of spiders and egg sacs. A small flood of fat white things erupted out after my hand. I screamed, scuttled backward on all fours like a crab, ran into Rahul's legs. He gripped my arm in one strong hand and hauled me up next to him. He didn't let go of my arm as we watched folded paper stars pour out from underneath the lockers.

"What the hell?" We said it at the same time again; this time, we weren't laughing.

"Can I see that?" he said, reaching. I was about to ask why, but Rahul didn't wait for my answer. I thought he was going to take my phone. Then I thought he was going to take my hand. He didn't want either: he reached between them with deft fingers and pulled something out—something that had gotten stuck to the backside of my phone. There was a piece of not-old-enough gum between the two. I made an oh-god-why noise as the gum stretched between the sheet of bright green in Rahul's hand and the phone in my hand.

Rahul wrinkled his nose. He twitched his hand at the long line of gum, as if he were flicking water at it. It hardened and crumbled, falling to the floor between us in a shower of greenish dust. He winked at me, saying, "That's one that comes in handy around here a lot too."

He was holding a piece of paper that looked like it had been ripped out of a notebook. Nothing was printed on the side that I could see, but there was something written in dark ink on the side that faced him. He read it for a moment, then showed it to me. "I wouldn't have expected to find one of these babies under there, would you?"

Another opportunity to choose. This was the moment for me to say "One of what?" or "What's that?" or anything, anything that might give him a hint. Anything that might come near the truth. "Why not? Doesn't seem so out of place."

"Well, I mean, it takes a certain amount of skill to put one together at all—much less to stash one where you can't see the target for it. That's probably how it wound up with gum on it, don't you think? Bad aim."

I took the sheet of bright green paper from him. It had a few words written on it, but they were . . . wrong. They looked like English words, but every time I looked away from the paper, they swam in my memory until I wasn't sure what they'd said at all.

"Hm," I said, trying to sound thoughtful. "So this was with all of those, then?" I gestured at the fifty or so folded paper stars scattered at our feet.

"Ooh," Rahul breathed, taking the paper back from me and looking it over with all the enthusiasm of a kid with a new action figure, "I bet they decided on the dimensional pleating because they don't know how to do the air-pocket-file yet! Man, do you remember how much energy it took to keep those things up? But if they didn't know the air-pocket-file or at *least* a basic safekeeping illusion, they'd think it would be the only way to—" He stopped suddenly, shaking his head. "But of course, your sister can tell you more about dimensional pleating than I can. I shouldn't speculate. Sorry. I get a bit carried away talking about theoretical magic sometimes. I'm kind of an enthusiast."

I made a mental note—*dimensional pleating, and oh god he's smart*—and then caught up with the rest of what he had said. "Oh, right. Tabitha will tell me. Sure." My voice caught on her name. No matter what version of myself I was pretending to be, I still had a sister to confront.

Rahul didn't say anything. He just waited, leaving me the space to tell him why I couldn't say my sister's name without choking on it. But I really didn't even know yet what I would say.

Instead, I stooped to collect the stars. Rahul hesitated for a second or two before folding his long legs and helping me.

There were seventy-three in all. They all looked exactly like the warning that had been left for me, like the one that was dropped in the library. Fat, seven-pointed things that seemed to have no proper edges.

"Aaah," he said, picking one up and turning it over. "I love these things."

"What do you mean?" I asked, trying and failing to figure out how to keep the notes from slipping out of my grip. I gave up, laying my brand-new jacket out on the floor with a wince and piling the stars in the middle of it.

"Oh, well, every class figures out a different version of this. They all think they're coming up with something brand-new, but it happens every year—someone comes up with a spell to fold notes and get them to the person they're intended for, and then spreads the spell around. In a way, they *are* brand-new. The shape is different every year. It's kind of a rite of passage."

"Huh," I said. "So, what year are these? Do you know?"

"Seniors," he answered. "I've been finding these stars around for almost four years now. Juniors are doing rabbits, sophomores are sailboats. Freshmen are doing something that I think might be a Pokémon."

"I don't get it—why don't they just text each other?" I asked as we piled the last few stars onto my jacket. I folded the jacket around them, tying the sleeves to make a bundle the size of a beach ball. He shrugged.

"Most of them do, after the novelty of the spell wears off about halfway through freshman year. After that, it usually ends up being a few hopeless romantics sending love notes, or random hate-mail shoved in lockers, or just rude drawings." He paused. "Hey, can I get one of your business cards? I don't think I got one from you when we talked the other day."

I set down my bundle of notes, sat back on my heels, and dug through my bag, finding the least-crumpled business card I could. "Here—that's my cell number on there, it's the best way to reach me. Rude drawings?" I asked as I handed him the card, even though I could imagine what he probably meant.

"Yeah. Usually, you know. Dicks." I laughed as he spread his hands about two feet apart. "Almost always dicks, with these kids. And then, of course, the occasional high-quality sketch of a hunky teacher with no shirt on." He winked at me.

It was out of my mouth before I could stop it. "Are you flirting with me?" I almost didn't recognize my own voice—there was invitation there, clear as anything. Whatever kind of Ivy I was pretending to be, she was bolder than me.

Rahul stood and gave me a lip-biting grin. I found myself easily able to imagine some rude drawings of my own as I got to my feet, clutching the bundle of secret notes to my chest.

"Huh. Yeah, maybe I am," he said. He turned on his heel and, with his hands in his pockets, walked down the hall, his shoulders tucked up around his ears. As he walked out the door, he stumbled, and in the moment before he caught himself, the lockers in the hallway glowed briefly, changing hue. It took me a moment, but I recognized the color. It was the same brown as my eyes.

Tabitha had already gone home for the day by the time I made it to her classroom. Her locked door felt like a reprieve from the universe: I had at least one more day before I had to confront her about her relationship with Sylvia. One more day before I had to make myself ask her if she knew anything about her girl-friend's death.

When I stepped out into the parking lot, most of the clouds that had been bruising the sky all day had clotted near the horizon, and there was just enough sun shining to make me squint. I found a reusable grocery bag in the trunk of my car—one that I'd bought in a fit of good intentions but had never actually used. I emptied my jacket into it, filling it to the brim with paper stars. I carefully folded the jacket so that the high school hallway grime was fac-ing in, and put it gingerly on top of the stars in the bag. I started toward home.

Not home. I didn't live there. This wasn't *home*. This was just a case. It wasn't my apartment. It wasn't my place.

But it was home for the time being. It was okay to think of it that way. Just for a little while.

I flickered between self-reproach and luxuriant basking as I walked. I should have told Rahul that I wasn't magic—but then, it was better for the case if nobody knew. They would talk to me

differently if they realized I was an outsider. It wasn't because I
wanted him to *like* me—it was just for the case. For the job.

Still. I'd asked if he was flirting, and he'd said *maybe I am* as if
it were a delightful surprise he'd uncovered. I tried not to let it
charm me, but I caught myself smiling. It was nice, being flirted
with. I bit my lip hard and tried to shake off the giddiness. It didn't
belong to me. It belonged to whoever he thought he was flirting
with, whoever I was letting him think I was.

I tried to shake it off. But I didn't try very hard.

As I approached my front door, my phone buzzed again. I
pulled it out of my pocket, brushing off some of the sub-locker
gunk, and unlocked it on the first try. There were four messages
from a subcontractor updating me on a case, and one from a number I didn't recognize. I ignored the subcontractor to open the
mystery text.

It was a photo. A candid shot, blurry with rain, taken from
across a decently lit street. Me and Tabitha. In the picture, we
were sitting outside the hipster bar, and she was looking right
at the camera. She looked angry. Not startled or curious—just
pissed, like the photographer had caught her at a bad time. I was
drinking my water, not looking at my sister.

I studied the picture. I should have been looking for clues as
to who took it, why, what they wanted when they sent it to me.
Instead, I studied the two of us. The way we leaned slightly away
from each other at the shoulders. The way we both sat with one
foot tucked under the other—her, right over left. Me, left over
right. Mirror images. I zoomed in a bit, and the photo got grainy,
but it was clear enough for me to see that her eyes looked different in the picture than they had in person.

They looked just like mine.

I went over that night in my head, but I couldn't remember a single second when she'd dropped whatever the spell was that made her look like *more* than me. I couldn't recall seeing it flicker. So when had she let it go? And why? Who was she doing it for?

Once I was inside with the door firmly locked behind me, I sent a response to the unknown number. *Who is this?*

I left my phone on the kitchen counter and headed for the bathroom. I splashed water on my face, ran wet hands through my hair. Considered filling the sink with water and dunking my head in. I braced myself on the sink, avoiding the mirror as I tried to get my head straight.

Truth matters. Truth has always been the thing I'm after, the most important thing. But sometimes, to get to the truth, detours through fiction are necessary. That's the job. Osthorne was a big case—a career-changing one with real consequences. I would do whatever it took to solve it.

I left the bathroom, my face still dripping. I stared into the empty bedroom. The stripped mattress was still off-center. I looked at the bare walls, which were painted a washed-out kind of tan.

I couldn't sleep in there. It was too hollow. It was too familiar. There was pretending to be someone I wasn't, and then there was sleeping alone in a bed that didn't belong to me, and the gap between the two was too wide for me to jump.

But just because I wasn't sleeping in there didn't mean the space couldn't be useful.

I left the doorway to get the bag of paper stars. When I returned and stepped inside, I was overwhelmed by the feeling that the room had been waiting for me. The whole apartment had been waiting for me. All day, while I'd been gone, it had been waiting to welcome me back.

I shut the bedroom door behind me, and I left my double vision behind. There was clarity in here. Something in the emptiness brought me back to myself. I upended the bag over the bed, scattering paper stars across the mattress. As I got to work, I felt myself fully exhale for the first time that day.

I was home.

CHAPTER

THIRTEEN

B Y ELEVEN O'CLOCK THAT NIGHT, I'd made my way through half a bottle of wine and opened all of the star-shaped notes. I took a photo of each one as soon as I opened it, but, fortunately, none of them dissolved the way that first one had. Apparently these were made to last.

They were love notes, for the most part. I tacked them up on the bedroom wall in no particular order. They were written in the same bubbling hand as the warning and the note from the library—when I noticed, I pulled a marker out of my bag and started circling handwriting flourishes in case I needed to spot them later. The way the letter *a* was written like typeface, the way the author didn't close their capital *B*s at the bottom, the weird and regular misspelling of "were" as "where." There was never a name mentioned anywhere—never a "Dear [Murderer's Name]" or a "Love, [I Know Who the Murderer Is]"—but there was a lot there. A lot of words. I resolved to read them in depth later, when I could focus. When there wasn't wine in between me and the letters.

The notes papered a full wall of the bedroom. I sat in the middle of the bare, off-center mattress, staring at the words. I let my eyes unfocus just enough that the written lines formed uneven, abstract shapes. Or were they abstract? The longer I looked at them, the more it seemed like there was something beneath the words, something shifting, something that was just beyond my grasp. If I could only look at it the right way, I could—

But I couldn't. It would always be just beyond me. The longer I stayed in that room, the farther the other possible Ivy seemed to drift. The more ridiculous it seemed that I was letting myself sink into that life. I wasn't magic, and I never would be. The best I could hope for was a passing glimpse of a world that would be polite to me but that would never want me.

I didn't want that world to want me. I just wanted to solve the case. I just wanted to be a good detective who could solve a murder, and the answers were there, they were all right there in front of me, if I could just be good enough to see them.

I slid from the mattress to the floor, leaned my back against the bed frame, slumped low enough that my spine ached. I let my eyes unfocus again, and I stared at the words on the wall. Lightning. River deltas. Continents. Marshland as viewed from the window of a plane. Rows and rows of books, so many books, and whispers just beyond the edge of my hearing, saying my name over and over again, *Gamble gamble gamble gamble*—

I startled awake as my wineglass started to tip out of my hand. "Fuck," I muttered—I'd drifted off, and I'd been dreaming, and there had been an answer on the periphery of the dream, but it was gone. And so was half my glass of wine, sacrificed to the thick nap of the carpet. "Fuck," I said again, louder this time as the situation came into focus.

I scrambled up and grabbed a towel out of the bathroom. By the time I was on my hands and knees pressing the towel into the spreading wine stain, I'd completely lost the thread of my dream. All I could remember was that it had been . . . important.

I lifted the towel to check on the carpet. Most of the stain was gone, but there was still a faint pink hue to the fibers. I refolded the towel and pressed down like I was performing CPR, trying to soak up the stain, hoping I wouldn't have to go out and buy some kind of carpet cleaner—and something caught my eye.

I don't know how I saw it. I shouldn't have been able to see it, not from my angle. I've thought about it a thousand times since—there's no way a shadow under the bed should have grabbed my attention. But it did, and I looked again. I bent, leaning my weight on my elbows on that poor wine-soaked towel, my heart fluttering in that looking-under-the-bed way that calls back to childhood certainty about where monsters and murderers will hide.

I shouldn't have been able to see it. I had to reach far enough that my fingertips only just caught the far end of the little book.

When I got it into the light, I forgot the spilled wine. It was a journal, bound in soft, mottled black leather. The surface was covered with the kind of pockmarks and scuffs that come with real age and not a factory stamp. I ruffled the uneven pages, which were swollen and creased with use. There were no initials on the inside cover, no "This book belongs to" inset. But the pages were filled, cover to cover, with tight scribbles. There were a few different pens, and as I leafed from the first page to the last, I saw that the dates of the entries were spread over nearly eight years.

I should say that my first thought was that this was a major clue. It had to be Sylvia's diary, or at the very least her datebook. I should say that my first thought was how the journal would give me insights about the dead woman whose apartment I was squatting in. But the truth is that the moment I saw the symbols written in that journal—some of which I recognized from high school chemistry classes, and some I couldn't begin to comprehend—I just . . . *wanted* it. I wanted it more than anything.

It didn't occur to me in that moment that it was hers. I'd found it, and in that moment, it was *mine*.

And then, when I noticed Sylvia's name on one of the back pages, my immediate possessiveness was justified. It was evidence. It was a clue. I couldn't give up a clue.

I tossed the towel through the open bedroom door and across the hall. It landed on the bathroom floor with a wet-fabric noise. I didn't bother looking at the carpet where it had been sitting. Instead, I leaned back against the mattress, and I opened the journal, and I began to read.

When I woke late the next morning, my skin was prickling. I was still slumped against the mattress, and my ass was half-numb from sitting on the floor for so long. The journal was still open to the page I'd been reading when I dozed off, an entry from a few years before. The top half of the page was nearly black with dense lines of symbols, arrows pointing between what looked like equations, cross-written numbers that could have meant anything. It all looked like the scribblings of a lunatic. But the bottom half of the page was devoted to a totally lucid journal entry. I read it as I made coffee, holding the journal in one hand and spilling water on the counter with the other.

The journal was strange. About halfway through reading it, I began to wonder who it was really about. Some entries were clearly that of a teacher at the school, referencing meetings and parent-teacher conferences and stress about grading. Mostly, though, the journal was full of an obsession over a single spell. The one that they were trying to work out at the top of that page, maybe. The entry had started out as a reflection on the process of putting the magic together—*I've tried looking at it as glass lightning, and that didn't work. I took a blood-as-sand approach, but the light levels wouldn't support it. I'm starting to think it would be better served by a sponge-made-of-slowly-growing-roots perspective—* but by the end of the page, their reflection had devolved into a case study of academic insecurity. *Sometimes it feels like I'm in a staring contest with failure, and if I blink, I'll die. If I stop for even a second to consider that I might not be as good as they think I am, the oxygen will get sucked out of the room and I'll suffocate.*

The pressure the author described sounded maddening. I was only about a quarter of the way into the journal, but I could already see them spiraling. Trying to be the good-enough, smart-enough, clever-enough kind of person who deserved to be at Osthorne. The kind of person who might experiment with theoretical magic they weren't ready for—the kind of person who might screw up and find themself split in half in the middle of the library. I wondered if the NMIS was really that far off-base about how Sylvia had lost her life.

My phone buzzed with a reminder—time to get to work, Ivy.

I downed the last of my coffee and, after a moment of indecision, put the journal in the bedroom.

I tilted my head, trying to see the pattern in the letters again, the one I'd half dreamed when I'd been staining the carpet with wine the night before. It was on the tip of my tongue, in the corner of my eye, like an overheard conversation where the sounds are clear but the words aren't, and if I could just—

My phone buzzed in my hand. A number I didn't recognize lit up the screen, and I almost didn't answer. Strange phone numbers had been too big a factor in the previous few days. But I caught myself before that brief flush of cowardice could make me let the call go to voicemail.

"Ivy Gamble?" The voice on the other end was loaded with the patient exhaustion of someone who worked in customer service. "I'm calling regarding your request for documentation in the matter of the death of Capley comma Sylvia."

The 'miz. "Yes, hi, thank you," I said brightly, hoping that if I sounded polite and optimistic enough, they might actually help me.

"At this time," they continued as though I hadn't spoken, "the locational data of the medical file requested has been erroneously allocated. We are taking steps to process a location analysis report and should have an update available to you within the next six to twelve weeks."

I digested the bureaucratic doublespeak for a minute, then swore. "You *lost* it?"

A long, stern pause. "We should have an update available to you within the next six to twelve weeks regarding the status of the location analysis report request. Have a nice—"

And before they could tell me what nice thing I was supposed to have, they'd hung up.

"They lost it," I breathed, staring at the *call ended* time stamp screen on my phone. "Great job, 'miz. This case is falling together like a fucking dream." I squinted at the letters pinned to the wall, glaring as if they were responsible for the missing file. I was angrier than I should have been. I was missing something.

I turned to leave the bedroom, with the bare mattress and the journal and the letters on the wall and the wine in the carpet. It was harder than it should have been, turning my back on those letters. I shut the door behind me, and as the latch clicked, I stepped back into the person I'd been the day before. The version of Ivy who laughed and flirted and belonged here.

The version of Ivy who could solve this case.

I walked through the empty halls as the Osthorne student body settled into their first-period classes. I peeked into classrooms, catching glimpses of the ordinary. I let myself slip deeper into a sense of nonexistent nostalgia: *Ah, yes, I remember what it was like.* A sense of fondness stole over me, and it was like drifting to the bottom of a cool, deep ocean.

As I walked through the hall to the library, I paused to look at the bank of lockers. I remembered them flashing brown as Rahul tripped over his own two feet, and a trail of warmth started to spread up my neck. But there had been something more important here—the notes.

I glanced around before getting down on my hands and knees

again to look underneath the lockers. This time, I pulled out my key chain and turned on the tiny flashlight I kept there, sweeping the beam back and forth. A few many-legged shapes scuttled out of the path of the light. They ran over coins, dust bunnies, a few pieces of gum. I wasn't sure what I was looking for—more notes? A signed confession? As I swept the flashlight back and forth, I started to notice movement following the light. At first I thought it was an enterprising spider. Then—

I moved the beam slowly, as slowly as I could, from left to right. Letters fleetingly fluoresced as the flashlight beam passed over them, fading again after a second or so. They were written on the wall behind the locker, near the place where my phone had caught on the paper that hid the flood of love notes. I read the letters several times to make sure I had it right. Then, I went into the library to set up my tableau and prepare to interview Osthorne staff. As I spread myself out, I tried the words out in my head.

"All that's gold does not glitter."

It seemed like the kind of thing that a kid would think was super-deep, would want to get tattooed on themselves. It was important enough to someone that they set up some kind of a spell to keep it near their love letters—but they went to all that trouble, and kept it hidden under a bank of lockers with the spiders and the gum.

I pushed aside the bitterness that, yet again, these kids used their magic for such trivial shit. I pushed it aside, because really, I was being shortsighted. It wasn't trivial to them. It was worth all the trouble.

My note-sender was someone who loved a good secret.

As I straightened, my phone buzzed. It was a multimedia

message from an unknown number. I had an urgent flush of adrenaline, wondering if it would be another melodramatic warning from my note-sender.

When I opened it, laughter bubbled up out of my belly uninvited. It was a selfie of Rahul, holding an empty pizza box and making an elaborate pouty-face. The text read *I was going to have leftovers for dinner, but my roommate ate them all.*

I laughed at the thought of him taking that picture at home and then saving it all morning so he could send it to me. I workshopped my response for an embarrassingly long time before I texted him back: *I guess you'll just have to cook?*

The response came immediately. *Actually, I was thinking of going out . . . but the place I wanted to try only accepts reservations for two.* A giggle bubbled out of me, taking me completely by surprise. I couldn't remember the last time I'd giggled. But it was easy, somehow, when I was pretending to be the kind of person who could feel that ocean-bottom fondness for a place like this.

I was trying to come up with a clever, flirty reply when a follow-up came through. *Unrelated question—would you happen to be free around seven-thirty tonight? For a thing?* Then, a few seconds later: *A date-thing?*

I walked into the library and sat down, rereading the exchange. I waited for my cheeks to cool before responding. I tried hard to think of a good response—something that would make me sound as smart and charming as the person he thought I was—but in the end, the only thing I could come up with was *yes*.

CHAPTER

FOURTEEN

I WAS DUE TO GET started on staff interviews, something I'd been dreading. The kids at this school were no picnic, but at least they mostly thought of me as holding some kind of intrinsic adult authority. The staff at Osthorne would be under no illusions about the amount of power I held over them, or the amount of cooperation they owed me.

My first interview of the day was with Stephen Toff, the infamous English teacher. I wished I'd left him for last the moment he walked into the library. Tabitha hadn't misrepresented him in the slightest—there was the man-bun she'd mentioned, plus a patchy, ill-advised goatee. He looked me up and down as he sauntered through the library, then sat down in the chair across from me. I caught a whiff of some kind of cologne that reminded me powerfully of ranch dressing. He was short, but he sprawled his legs out like a giraffe at a watering hole. I had an immediate fantasy of shoving him aside on the train so I could sit.

"You're Ivy, right?" he said with an upward twitch of his chin.

"That's me."

"Cool, cool. I'm Stephen Toff. You can call me Toff." He winked, looking pleased with himself.

We did small talk for a while—where are you from, where did you go to school, how do you like teaching at Osthorne. Inconsequential bullshit to get him comfortable answering questions. For the first few minutes, he didn't ask anything about me—not where I went to school or who I knew or whether I ever tried to arrange a spell using a sponge made of slowly growing roots as a framework. He answered my questions, and he talked about himself and his teaching and the book he was writing. It was easy.

I never even had to lie.

And when the small talk started to drift toward me, I shifted gears—I took it as a sign that it was time to get into the meat of the thing. I cut off his question about where I was from, flipping through my file to the background check on him. His expression stiffened when he saw his own photograph at the top of the page. Good.

"So, Stephen. I'm assuming you know why I'm here?"

He nodded, leaned across the table. He was trying to get a peek at the background check; I closed the file before he could get a good look.

"You're investigating Sylvia's death, right?" He said it in a respectful murmur, his face serious, and I wondered if I'd misread him at first.

"Just following up on a few loose ends," I said, trying to keep him from feeling too important.

"It's a damn shame she decided to play with fire like that." He shrugged. "Some people just aren't cut out for theoretical magic, you know?"

"What do you mean?"

"Well, you know. Sylvia was great and all. Really warm, totally sweet. Great when girls needed to talk to someone about, you know. Their changing bodies, and birth control and stuff." I swallowed bile as he winked at me again. "But . . . she taught *health class*. She was the school nurse. She wasn't exactly the brightest star in the Osthorne constellation." His eyes twinkled, and I was pretty sure I knew who he thought the brightest star was. I congratulated myself on not having misread him in the slightest.

"Did you say birth control?"

He wiggled his eyebrows at me. "Comprehensive. Osthorne provides clinic-level care for the kids. Nothing invasive or whatever, but we do STD and pregnancy testing and prevention." He said the last part like it was a line he'd memorized in a mandatory meeting. As he said it, he winked at me yet again. I wondered if perhaps he had an undiagnosed condition that rendered him incapable of keeping both eyes open for more than a few minutes at a stretch. "If you ever need condoms, just hit me up—I know where the cabinet is." It is a testament to my unparalleled self-control that I nodded politely at this, rather than telling him to sew himself into a burlap sack so I could throw him into the ocean.

I even smiled at him. A smile that would have made Alexandria DeCambray proud. "You teach . . . what, again? English, right? Is that a part of the nonmagical curriculum?"

He nodded. "I like to think of it as a kind of magic all its own, though. I teach the kids to create something out of nothing, using just the power of—"

"Did you two get along well?" I cut him off before he could get too hard about his ability to galvanize youths.

He leered at me, his lower lip buckling under his front teeth. "Uh, yeah. We got along *pret-ty* well."

I raised my eyebrows. "Were you two . . . involved?"

"No, no. Never officially. But we had, you know. A lot of chemistry."

I nodded, remembering Tabitha telling me how much Sylvia had hated him. Remembering the huge fight Dylan had ever-so-briefly mentioned. I decided to let him have a little more rope. "So you two were fucking, then? Sorry—" I gave an apologetic smile. "'Sleeping together,' rather."

He blinked a few times, startled by my candor. His eyes fell on my phone, which was lit up and recording. He shook his head as if to clear it. "Uh, no. We never did anything. Together."

I kept my face smooth as I scribbled on my notepad, keeping my satisfaction to myself. It felt good to throw him off his game. More importantly, if I had read him right, off-his-game was exactly where I needed him to be. I needed him scrambling to regain his certainty that he was a big dog.

"So, your big fight wasn't a lovers' quarrel, then?" I leaned forward in my chair just enough that he checked to see if I was showing cleavage.

"Our big fight?" He did a very convincing I-don't-know-what-you're-talking-about face, all pursed lips and furrowed brows. I flashed him a conspiratorial smile.

"Oh, sure. Your big fight on the first day of school. The one your students overheard? Sounds like it was a real whopper."

He laughed. "Oh, gosh, that! I had forgotten all about it. It was really nothing, I don't even—"

"Tell me about it anyway," I interrupted. I flashed the smile again. "So I can tell those kids there's nothing to worry about, when they bring it up."

"We just had a little misunderstanding," he said. I nodded, encouraging as I could muster, and he eased into a lopsided smile. He spread his hands, all charm and humility. "Sylvia could be a little uptight about things, I guess. Not to speak ill of the dead, of course."

"Of course," I said. "Some people think they know what's best for everyone, right?"

"Exactly." He smoothed down one eyebrow with the pad of his thumb. "Sylvia was a great little health teacher, but she was really wrapped up in inconsequential things."

"So what was she wrapped up in on the first day of school?"

Looking everywhere but at me. "I mean, it was really not a big deal. I guess she saw me having lunch with this girl I was seeing, and she didn't think it was 'appropriate' for me to kiss her goodbye."

"Wow." I quirked an eyebrow, looked around, lowered my voice. "You weren't kidding about uptight, huh? I mean, I had heard some things, but—"

"You heard right," Toff said.

"So, walk me through it." I drew tight spirals on my notepad, keeping my voice light and easy. "She sees you with your girlfriend—"

"Girl I was seeing," he cut in. "Not my girlfriend."

"Right, my mistake. She sees you with this bird and doesn't like it, and, what? Tears you a new asshole about bringing your arm candy to work? Like it's any of her business, right?" Tighter spirals, but I still didn't let the lines touch.

He rolled his eyes. "Sylvia just had a lot of outdated opinions about who it's appropriate for a teacher to date, I guess. The girl I was seeing used to be one of her students, or whatever, and it weirded her out, and she wasn't cool about it."

I stilled my pen. "She used to be one of *Sylvia's* students? Not one of yours?" Still light, still breezy. Just a small detail. And yet, I felt a thread of tension tighten between us. I made myself look up with a winky you-sly-dog kind of grin, and he smiled back, but the thread stayed taut.

"I mean, she was probably in my class at some point, who can remember? Anyway, she was already eighteen by then, and that's what matters. And who I date is—er, was. Who I date was none of Sylvia's business."

"So you and this girl you were seeing—"

"Woman," he corrected.

"Right, sorry. The woman you were seeing," I said, feeling like I was swallowing a mouthful of oil. "You broke up because of the fight?"

"Well, I stopped hanging out with her after that," he said. "Not worth the hassle. Not like I can't get what I want when I want it from other sources, anyway." He winked at me.

"I'm gonna grab some coffee," I said, standing up. I needed to get the hell out of there before I slapped him so hard his wink turned permanent. "Do you need anything? No? I'll be right back."

"Oh, actually, I probably should go," he said, glancing at the clock behind the returns desk. "My prep period is almost over." He stretched, his shirt riding up to reveal a large silver belt buckle. He grabbed one of my cards and stood close enough to me that I could smell that salad-bar cologne. "Can I call you sometime?" I opened my mouth to give him a vehement *no*, but he didn't let me get the word in edgewise. "For research. I don't know if I mentioned, but my novel is a murder mystery." He had indeed mentioned this. "I'd love to ask you some questions. It's about an adjunct professor who gets murdered by his psycho girlfriend when she doesn't pass his class. Really dark stuff. You'd probably be into it." He nodded, agreeing with himself.

"Mmmm," I said.

"Anyway, I'll call you about it. We can get a drink or something." He didn't wait to hear whether or not I accepted the invitation; he waved over his shoulder as he walked toward the door. I let him get halfway across the library, just far enough for him to wonder if I was checking out his ass, before I interrupted him.

"Oh, hey, *Toff,*" I called, and he turned around with his brows raised, every kind of expectant. "I almost forgot to ask, what were you doing that night?"

"What night?"

I took a few steps toward him, leaned my ass against a worktable. Casual. "The night Sylvia died," I said. "Were you on a date?"

"I was at the welcome dinner, same as everybody else," he said, already turning back toward the door. He waved over his shoulder, not waiting to hear if I had a follow-up question. "Ciao."

"Ciao, *Toff*," I muttered under my breath. I sank into my chair and rolled my neck, waiting to make sure he wasn't coming back.

I had a break between interviews, so I put my headphones in and started playing the interview back, taking notes on important parts. There was a lot of chaff to sort through. In the playback, Toff's attempts to steer me away from asking about the fight were more glaring. I added to my list of leads: find out the name of the poor kid he'd been dating, make sure Torres knew about it. Check with Webb to make sure he'd actually been at the welcome dinner. I was rewinding to the section of the conversation about the student, hoping there would be something I'd missed that might point to her identity, when I caught a flicker of motion in my peripheral vision.

I looked up and saw Brea Teymourni silhouetted in the doorway, her hand still holding the door ajar as though she could bolt at any moment. I smiled at her, but didn't move toward her. I kept my voice low, like I was trying to coax a cat out from under a car. "Hey, Brea. Did you want to come in?"

She hesitated, looked out into the hallway with something like regret. A hand appeared on her shoulder, and Miranda Yao appeared from around the corner, still wearing her off-uniform basketball shorts. She was murmuring something too low for me to hear, and her high, glossy ponytail fell over Brea's shoulder as they talked. Brea took a deep breath and nodded. Then she crossed the room and sat in the chair that had been occupied by Stephen Toff just a few minutes before. Her shoulders were hunched, and her warm brown eyes couldn't seem to land on any one thing. She pulled at her Osthorne blazer, fidgeting with the edges of the long sleeves she wore underneath. There were goosebumps on the backs of her brittle-looking wrists. Miranda hovered in the doorway, looking uncertain, until Brea looked back at her. Their eyes locked. Miranda jogged over to sit beside her.

It wasn't a show. That was the first thing that struck me. These two girls weren't putting anything on for me, weren't trying to make me think anything in particular. They were scared, is all. They were scared, and they were helping each other to be brave.

"Brea," I said, setting my pen down. "Is something wrong?"

She swallowed hard. "I was hoping maybe you wouldn't be here," she whispered, then cleared her throat. "I was, um. I thought I could just leave you a note or something." She sounded louder, more confident, but she was still looking everywhere I wasn't.

"A note?" My heart leapt. "Are you the one who left me a note the other day?"

She shook her head, looking confused. "No? I just . . . I don't want anyone to know I talked to you. Sorry, I hope that's not rude or anything."

Damn. "Okay," I said, putting my chin in my hand. I kept my voice low. "That's okay. Nobody has to know that we talked."

Miranda looked to the door. "Can you put up a vocal barrier or a distortion wall or something? Just in case?"

I shook my head, and the answer came out of me before I realized what I was saying. "Not in here. That requires a blood-as-sand approach, and you know the light levels won't support it." I sounded so confident, so clear. I sounded like the kind of person who could write a journal filled with arcane equations and reflections on my academic insecurity.

I sounded real.

Miranda's shoulders slumped. "Okay."

"Don't worry," I said, not pausing to digest what I'd just done. "No one will see you. And if they do, you can tell them that I called you in here but you didn't talk to me about anything, okay? Now, what's up?"

Brea was quiet for a long time, biting her lip. She looked over at Miranda, her wide eyes brimming with worry, watching her girlfriend like a claustrophobe watches elevator doors. I could tell that she was working up courage, and I gave her the space to do it.

Finally, she lifted one delicate hand and touched it to Miranda's square, clenched jaw. Brea nodded, then took a deep breath.

"I have to tell you something, but it's probably not a big deal." She turned to me, wary. I would have bet my PI license that what she wanted to tell me was *definitely* a big deal.

"Okay," I said. "Let's hear it."

She did some more fidgeting, fraying her sleeves. Eventually, Miranda reached out and grabbed her hand, squeezing it tight enough to turn both of their knuckles white. I wondered what story Brea thought she was in. Her eyes kept darting to the window. She was afraid that someone had followed her, that someone would be reporting back on her. I decided to try poking at that fear.

"Brea, if you don't tell me what it is, I can't tell you that it's not a big deal." I glanced out the window, then looked pointedly toward the door. "And the longer you're here, the more likely it is that someone will walk by that window and see you."

"You can do it, babe," Miranda murmured. She ran her thumb over Brea's knuckles.

Apparently, that was what she needed to hear. She straightened in her chair and got down to business, looking at me like I was a multiple-choice test that she was about to *slay.* "Okay, here's the deal. You know Alexandria, right?"

"Yeah, sure," I said, cool as anything. "What about her?"

"Okay, look," she said, leaning forward over the table. "Alexandria is my friend and I don't want her to get in trouble or anything. But . . ." She took a deep breath. "Isawherfighting-withMissCapleythedaybeforeshedied."

I took a moment to process the rush of words. "Okay," I said slowly. "What happened?"

She told the story in fits and starts, with Miranda periodically nudging her onward. Her story was peppered with "but it's to-tally not a big deal," and "but Alexandria would *never* do anything like what happened to Miss Capley." When she said the latter, she couldn't look at me, and I knew that I wasn't really the one she was trying to convince.

I could see why she'd waited to tell me the story. The way she told it, she had gone to Miss Capley's office to get weighed. When she explained that she had to go and get weighed every week, a flash of something crossed Miranda's face—frustration? worry?—and I wondered but didn't ask. When Brea had gotten to Capley's office, she'd heard voices inside. She said she recognized Alexan-dria's voice right away.

"She talks kind of different, when she's angry," Miranda inter-jected. She grimaced with some painful memory. "Her voice gets . . . bigger? Scarier. Not like shouting, but it just. It makes you feel like you'd do anything to make her stop being mad. Like you'd do whatever she wants, just to keep her happy." She bit her lip and glanced over at Brea, who nodded in agreement.

I spoke quietly, trying to make my voice the opposite of everything she was remembering. "What were they saying, Brea?"

"Um. They were saying—Miss Capley was saying, 'I can't, I can't, I could get fired,' and Alexandria was saying, um." She trailed off, looking like she'd come up to the edge of a swimming hole but couldn't tell whether the water was deep enough to jump in. I could have pushed her, but instead I waited. I let her decide that she was brave enough.

She took a deep breath and closed her eyes. "Alexandria said that—she said, 'If you don't do it, I'll tell *everyone* what I saw, and then you'll get fired anyway.' And then Miss Capley was quiet for a while, and I was going to maybe knock and pretend like I hadn't heard anything? But then I heard her say, um." She opened her eyes, and she looked exhausted. I wondered how heavy this had all been for her to carry. "I heard Miss Capley say 'I'll see what I can do,' and Alexandria said, 'You'd better, or you'll be sorry,' and then I left."

She let out a huge breath and slumped in her chair. Miranda leaned over and pressed a kiss to the top of her head.

"Hey," I said, "you did the right thing by telling me about this. I'm sure you're right and it's no big deal"—a blatant lie, but one that she needed to hear—"but I really appreciate you letting me know." I gave her a small, warm smile, and she returned an even smaller one.

"I couldn't keep it a secret anymore," she said. "Ms. Capley was,

I don't know, I just." Brea huffed out an almost-angry sigh. "She was one of the good teachers, you know? She didn't talk to us like we're stupid. She listened. None of them ever *listen*—" She stopped midsentence and looked up like a deer at the sound of a twig snapping. Footsteps echoed in the hall outside.

"Shit," she said, then looked at me. "Sorry. For swearing. I just—I have to—"

I waved my hands at her. "Go, go! I won't tell anyone you were here. Go on."

She blew into her hands like they were cold, then waved them in front of her face like a mime trying to find the latch on his box. Miranda threw me a final glance, mouthed the words "thank you," then did the same motion with her hands. One second, I was looking at them; the next, I couldn't seem to fix my eyes on the place where I knew they'd been. The door to the library opened and closed, and I couldn't put my finger on when I'd started being alone in there.

CHAPTER

FIFTEEN

S O, YOU WENT TO SCHOOL up in Portland, right?" Rahul
asked as he dropped his credit card on top of mine. The
waiter swept by and picked up the check without looking at us.

"Yeah," I said. It didn't feel like a lie. It just felt like a story we
were sharing. That's all. Under the table, his foot bumped against
mine. "Same school as Tabitha." I didn't feel even a little guilty.

"Wow," he said, his eyes widening. "Headley is really intense.
Was it weird to be competing against each other for ranking and
stuff?"

I laughed and shook my head. "Honestly, you've met Tabitha.
It was never a competition. I've never been on her level. Not aca-
demically, anyway."

It wasn't a lie. Tabitha was more brilliant than I'd ever be. The
world had given her magic and brains and she had pressed her advantage to the fullest extent of her ability. So it wasn't a lie when
I told Rahul that I'd never felt like I was competing with Tabitha's
intellect. I wasn't lying much at all—just the bare minimum, just

the smallest details to support his belief about who I was. And those were just little lies, just propping up the story.

The date was easily one of the best I'd ever been on. There had been almost no initial awkwardness to get through. Rahul asked all the right kinds of questions about my work. I coaxed a few funny Osthorne stories out of him, without the conversation turning to Sylvia or the investigation. I made him laugh so hard that he almost choked on a basil leaf. In retaliation, he turned one of my jalapeños into a ghost pepper.

It was easy. It was *fun*. And, somehow, I hadn't once had to stop being the version of Ivy who could flirt with a physical magic teacher without flinching. I hadn't once been irritated by the little magic things he did. I wasn't trying to pretend that he was normal. I was just . . . *being* with him, like he was anyone, like I was anyone, like there was no barrier between us. I'd cracked a window into another world, and I was sticking my head through it, breathing the sweet air on the other side.

"Anyway, me and Tabitha, we went really different routes. In the end I guess going to Headley mattered more to her than it does to me, you know?" I continued. Rahul's calf nudged mine under the table. A flock of starlings fluttered inside my chest. The waiter dropped our cards back off, and we both signed, peeking at each other's tips.

"I don't know that he really earned that much," Rahul said with his eyebrows raised.

"I know," I muttered, "but the pho was really good and I want to come back here sometime."

"Oh, right," Rahul said, quickly scratching a larger number

over the one he'd already written. We pushed our chairs back from the table with a loud scrape; before we'd finished standing up, the table was being cleared and wiped down.

"So," I said as we made for the door. Rahul held it open for me, and we stood outside on the sidewalk, uncertain and hopeful under the pinking sky.

"So," he said back. "Walk you home?" He held out his arm.

"You certainly may," I said, threading my fingers through his as we started walking together down the two-lane road. When we passed the Osthorne sign, Rahul's grip on my hand tightened a little. "So," he said again. "This is going to sound like a line."

"I'll gird my loins," I said.

"I had a really good time tonight—"

"That's not a line," I interrupted.

He glared at me. "Let me finish and then tell me it's not a line," he said. I rolled my hand in a go-on-let's-hear-it circle, and he cleared his throat. "I had a really good time tonight and I don't want the night to be over."

"I have a bottle of wine at my place," I said, bold as brass.

He flushed. "I swear it wasn't a line. What if we grab that bottle of wine and take it somewhere? I know a cute spot on campus. Not that I don't want to—"

"That sounds perfect," I said, remembering the state of the apartment. He smiled like I'd rescued him.

"Tell you what," he said, "why don't I go grab a blanket for us to sit on, and you grab the wine, and we'll meet back here?"

When we met up again, he was holding a big tartan throw. I had a bottle of screw-top cabernet under my arm. The sky was turning from pink to gray, and I was completely giddy. I told myself that it was the giddiness that comes with a crush. I told myself that it didn't feel the same way shoplifting had when I was a kid, told myself the adrenaline was different.

It was different.

Rahul led me through the clutch of apartments and townhouses that constituted staff housing. For a moment I was concerned that maybe he wanted to sit in a little courtyard we passed through, which featured a velvety expanse of lawn and a few battered chairs, and which was visible from at least six different townhouses. But he kept going, ducking down a space between a townhouse and a utility shed. I followed him around the utility shed, and there, between the shed and the beginning of an overgrown hedge, was a half-broken porch swing.

"Here we are," Rahul said, beaming at me. I looked at his smile, which clearly communicated that I should be excited about the pile of splintery wood in front of me.

"Um," I said, trying to smile back.

"Hang on," he said, holding out the blanket to me. "Trust me." He looked so excited, I had to find out what was next. I took the blanket and tucked it under my arm. He grabbed my free hand, and I felt warmth rush up my arm. I couldn't tell if he was casting a spell or if it was just the feeling of his rough palm against my skin, his strong fingers between mine.

Rahul reached out his other hand and touched the porch swing with his fingertips, running them lovingly across the top crossbar of the frame. As he slid them from one end of the frame to the other, the dust vanished; the wood of the swing smoothed and glowed in the dying sun. It went from looking like a death trap to looking brand-new. *I like things to be more of what they are,* he'd said.

Rahul turned to me with a boyish grin. Two deep dimples creased his cheeks. My head swam. "Ready?" he asked.

"What? Yes," I said, not knowing—or caring—what he meant. He grabbed the blanket from me and spread it over the slatted bench. He patted the seat next to him, and I sat down, leaving the wine bottle on the ground at our feet. He scooted toward me until our thighs were touching, then gave a theatric yawn, stretching his arms over his head. His arm draped across my shoulder, and I covered my face with both hands as I collapsed into the kinds of giggles that apparently overtook the person I was pretending to be.

I felt his fingers brush closed around my wrists. "Hey, open up," he laughed as he gently pulled my hands away from my face. When I uncovered my eyes, he was still smiling at me with those impossible dimples. I shook my head.

"What do you call that?" I asked.

"What do I call what?"

"Whatever spell it is you use to make your smile so . . ." I ran out of words, and he raised his eyebrows, still grinning. I shook my head as a blush climbed up behind my ears. "Forget it," I said, realizing how close I'd come to asking the wrong kind of question.

"No, no, Ivy Gamble," he said, laughter laced behind his low murmur. "To make my smile so what? Tell me about my smile." His fingers were lightly closed around my wrists, and his thumbs traced circles on the backs of my hands. I shook my head again. His eyes flicked to where I was biting my lip.

"You really shouldn't do that, you know," he said.

"Shouldn't what?" I replied, suddenly very aware of how close we were on the bench.

"Shouldn't bite your lip." He lifted one thumb and brushed my lower lip, pulling it free of my teeth.

"Don't tell me what to do," I murmured. Then I leaned forward, closing the two inches between us, and kissed him.

The kiss was light, tentative, close-lipped—but it was as if he'd been waiting for me to make the first move. The instant I broke off the kiss, his hand was cupping my jaw, pulling me back to him. My fingers found their way into his hair; his other hand moved to my waist, tugging me closer. He kissed my chin, my jaw—I gasped as I felt his teeth tugging on my earlobe. He paused, one hand on my hip and the other in my hair.

"Is this okay?" he whispered, his lips brushing the place where my jaw met my throat. I closed my fingers around the hair at the nape of his neck and gave the smallest of tugs; his head tilted back, and our eyes met.

"*Yes,*" I whispered back, as vehemently as possible.

Twenty minutes of "yes" later, my back was pressed against the outside of my front door. We'd abandoned the blanket and the wine and I'd forgotten all about the state of my little apartment because the only thing in my head was still *yes.* I gripped the belt loops on the side of Rahul's pants with one hand, yanking him toward me so I could feel exactly how badly he wanted me to get that door open. With the other hand, I fumbled for the doorknob. He had successfully unbuttoned the top third of my blouse and was nudging my collar aside with his nose by the time I finally succeeded in opening the door. We fell inside, stumbling, our legs tangling together. He caught me by the back of the waist and buried his hands in my hair, murmuring my name against my lips as I slid my hands up under his untucked shirt—

He froze. I opened my eyes. "What's wrong?" He looked like he'd seen a ghost. In a feat of superhuman willpower, I slowly pulled my hands out from underneath his shirt. He cleared his throat. I realized that he wasn't looking at me. He was looking over my shoulder. The state of the apartment came rushing back to me—the duvet on the couch, the half-empty takeout cartons, the empty bottles lined up on the kitchen counter.

But before that could sink in, a coherent thought—which had been totally unable to form when Rahul's hands had been gripping my ass—zipped to the front of my mind: *Why was the front door unlocked?*

I turned, slowly, waiting for the worst. Expecting to see that the place had been trashed, or robbed, or that someone was standing there waiting for me with a gun.

What I saw was worse.

"Tabitha?" I said. My voice came out huskier than I cared for. I cleared my throat and said her name again, but she didn't seem to hear me. She was sitting on my couch with her face in her hands, curled in on herself. She was sobbing so hard that she was choking. I couldn't believe that I hadn't heard her from outside.

Rahul was staring down at me with a solemn, uncertain expression. I shrugged and made an I-have-no-idea face. I looked back at Tabitha and walked slowly over to where she sat. I laid a hand on her shoulder. She startled, hiccupped. When she looked up, I could tell that she had been crying for a long time.

"Hey, Tabby," I said softly.

"Hey," she said, then choked on a sob. I straightened and ran my hands through my hair, then walked back over to Rahul.

"I'm sorry," I said, "I think I have to—"

"It's okay," he interrupted, "I totally understand. You have to . . . yeah."

I sighed and started buttoning the three shirt buttons he'd gotten to before we noticed Tabitha, mentally apologizing to each button for undoing his good work.

"Hey." Rahul's fingers were light on my arm, but I jumped as if he'd grabbed me. His face was totally calm as he whispered, quiet enough that Tabitha wouldn't be able to hear him over the sound of her own weeping. "Are you going to be okay? Do you want me to stay?"

God, yes. I wanted him to stay in so many ways—but he was Tabitha's coworker, and she was my sister, and I have never been one for the rules of dating, but the conversation Tabitha and I were about to have? Even I knew that it was definitely *not* something you should invite a guy to watch on the first date.

"No," I said, with a sigh. "No, that's okay—we'll be fine. I'll be fine. I think we just need to talk about some stuff."

His fingertips lingered on my arm for a moment, warm and steady and so, so temporary. I ached at the injustice of the fact that he would be leaving while Tabitha got to stay here. I gave him a reassuring smile, the kind that new-Ivy apparently knew how to give.

"Okay," he said after studying my face for a few seconds. He leaned forward, and I thought at first that he was going to whisper in my ear—but then his lips were pressed against my cheek, lingering and not at all chaste. "I'll see you," he murmured.

Then, before I could answer, he had slipped out of my front door and was gone.

It took a good twenty minutes to calm Tabitha down. I didn't have any tissues, so I brought her a roll of toilet paper from the bathroom to wipe her face and blow her nose. She went through about a third of it as I sat beside her on the sagging couch, the duvet crumpled on the floor. I rubbed her back in little circles. I made her drink a glass of water, mostly because I couldn't think of anything else to do. She continued hiccupping for a long time after she finally stopped crying.

"Tabby," I said in as gentle a voice as I could muster, "what are you doing here?"

Her eyes welled up again, and she answered in a very small voice that didn't sound like her at all. "I didn't know where else to go."

I didn't know what to say to that. Why would she come here, of all places? I realized that I was staring at her and looked down at my hands.

"I just. It's been a really hard few months, you know?" She sniffled next to me. "And I haven't really had anyone to talk to . . ." She trailed off.

"Since Sylvia died," I whispered. I could feel her go still, even without looking at her.

"Yes," she said softly. "Since Sylvia died." She stroked the arm of the couch with her fingertips and stared at the pattern woven into the upholstery.

The silence between us was thick, awkward. I was wondering how to start trying to talk to her about this huge thing, this secret she'd been sitting on for months. She was probably wondering how I knew, who else knew. Who told. How far her secret had traveled.

To her credit, she didn't ask any of those things. Instead, she asked the question that I hadn't even been willing to ask myself.

"Do you think I killed her?"

The question slammed me right in the gut, knocking the air from my lungs. I hadn't been willing to think it, not really. Not all the way through. Every time the thought had entered my mind, I'd shoved it away hard. *Did I think Tabitha was the killer?*

I looked up at my sister. She'd let her eyes get puffy and red. She hadn't done any magic to make them look pretty. They were bright with tears. I bit my cheek, took a deep breath, and decided to be honest with her—because if I couldn't be honest with her in that moment, when could I?

"I don't know."

She pressed the backs of her fingers to her flushed cheeks, then let out a short, sharp laugh. "Holy shit," she said, then covered her mouth and laughed again. "Holy shit," she repeated, the curse muffled by her fingers. "You think I did it? You think I could really do that to someone? To someone I loved?"

I felt my stomach tighten around a fist of anger that had been slowly clenching there since the day before. If I was honest with myself, that fist had been clenching since Tabitha came home from school for my mother's funeral.

"How would I know what it looks like when you love someone?" I spat.

"Come on, Ivy. That can't be what you think of me . . . ?"

"Are you seriously fucking asking me that?" I said it in a choked whisper. The room suddenly felt pudding-thick, too quiet. I could see the faint pulse of my heartbeat, blurring my vision twice every second. Tabitha looked at me, confused. "Are you *seriously* asking me *that fucking question* after what you let happen to Mom?"

Tabitha's brow knit, and I realized I was shaking. I stood up and walked into the kitchen and poured myself a glass of water, wishing it was whiskey. Just to give my hands something to do. Just so I wouldn't hit her.

"I don't know what you mean," she said.

I poured the water down the drain without drinking any of it. I couldn't have swallowed around the knot in my throat anyway. I walked back out into the living room and yanked the neck of my shirt to one side, exposing the unblemished skin of my shoulder.

"Seven fucking days ago," I said. "Seven fucking days ago this was sliced open by a knife that probably had *botulism* on it."

She kept looking at my shoulder. Her lost eyes infuriated me.

"I don't understand," she said in that same small voice. I sat in the chair across from her, leaning my elbows on my knees and gripping fistfuls of my hair. I stared at the wrinkles in the duvet so I wouldn't have to look at her sad, puffy eyes.

"The goddamned school secretary fixed it," I growled at her. "She blew up my shoulder and zapped the infection and made it better in *ten fucking seconds*. And yet, in four *months*, you couldn't find time to help Mom." She opened her mouth as if to say something, but I had finally taken the lid off seventeen years of anger and there was nothing she could do—nothing she could say—to stop me. "You knew how much pain she was in, Tabitha. You *knew* how much she was hurting, you knew she was fucking *dying*, and you didn't even come *home*, you just kept sending home emails about how *great* you were doing, how *awesome* the magic you were learning was. Emails about your fucking *grades.*" I knew I was shouting, but I couldn't figure out how to calm my voice. I couldn't remember getting to my feet. I was jabbing a finger at Tabitha. Silent tears streamed down her face as she watched me with wide, unblinking eyes.

"Do you know what happened to *my* grades?" I asked, undiluted venom in my voice. "I nearly failed junior year, while you were off learning *magic.* I only passed because the vice principal knew Mom, knew what was happening to her." I laughed cruelly. "She probably knew more about what was happening to Mom than you *ever* did." I sniffed hard—my nose had started running, was I crying? I couldn't tell. I couldn't stop. "Did you know she used to ask for you?" Tabitha let out a small sound, not quite a whimper. "That's right," I hissed. "She used to ask where you *were,* when the pain was so bad that she couldn't remember you'd gone off to magic school. She used to ask where you *were,* and I was the one who had to *lie to her* about it. Do you want to know what I told her?"

I waited, every muscle in my body coiled tight. When she finally answered, she didn't manage to make any sound—her mouth moved, wordlessly, her lips forming the word "What?"

"I said you were on the way," I answered.

Somehow, when I said that, all the anger slid out of me. I collapsed back onto the chair, feeling like the full weight of those seventeen years had settled onto my shoulders. "I told her you'd be there soon," I whispered, more to myself than to Tabitha. "She kept asking, right up until the end. And I kept lying to her. You made me a liar."

I closed my eyes as fat, hot tears rushed to blur my vision. I heard Tabitha stand up and go into the bathroom. She closed the door and was gone for a mercifully long time.

By the time she came back, I'd wrestled down the tears and the anger. I felt like I had vomited something poisonous. She looked like she had splashed water on her face—her eyes were clearer than they had been when I got home. She settled across from me, her hands in her lap, and looked at me steadily.

"I understand why you feel the way you do." She spoke carefully, as though the words were broken glass she had to pick her way around. "But there's a lot you don't understand." I curled my lip, ready to fling some snide barb at her, but she held up her hand. "Please, Ivy. Please let me explain." She looked right into my eyes as she asked, and something made me decide to listen to what she had to say. It wouldn't occur to me until much later to wonder what made me decide to listen—whether it was the look in her eyes, or something more. Something magic.

"What Mrs. Webb did for your shoulder . . . that was huge magic. She's one of the best healing mages in the *world*, Ivy. When Mom was sick, I was just a kid. I was doing a great job in school, but asking me to heal her would be like asking a first-year med student to perform a heart transplant." She swallowed hard, closed her eyes. "I'm telling you that now because it's what I told Dad, when he asked. Back when we first found out Mom was sick."

My fingers tightened on the arms of my chair. I hadn't known that Dad had asked Tabitha to heal Mom—couldn't imagine it. I couldn't imagine her, seventeen years old, having to tell him what Mom's doctor hadn't been willing to: *There's nothing I can do.*

"And even if I had been more advanced," she continued, "I still probably couldn't have helped her. That's not something we can just fix. The risks involved . . . they're enormous, Ivy. That type of healing, to that degree? I'd need to take her entire body apart and hold it that way for . . . for *days*." Another tear slipped down her cheek. She didn't seem to notice it. "And then I'd have to put her back together again, alive, all in the right order. Can you imagine how impossible that is?" She laughed bitterly. "I've been studying for half my life to try to figure it all out, and *I* can't even explain the risks."

I put my head in my hands. "God, Tabitha. I had no idea."

"I know." She said it gently—more gently than I deserved by a long shot. "That's probably my fault. I didn't tell you. I didn't know how to tell you."

When I looked up, the naked vulnerability on her face was too much for me to handle. I got up and sat on the couch next to her. I told myself to be brave, and I grabbed her hand. Her fingers felt impossibly small. "Can you tell me now?"

Tabitha swallowed hard again, more tears welling in her eyes. She nodded.

We talked for hours. The anger had seeped away out of the room, and with it, the fear that had been between us. We talked about all of the things we'd spent half a lifetime *not* talking about. Mom, and what it had been like to lose her. Dad, and what it had been like to see him wade through the depths of his grief. What it had been like to see him slowly, slowly claw his way out of it.

At some point, she leaned her head on my shoulder. We'd sat this way a hundred times before she'd left for the Headley Method Preparatory School—our feet propped on the coffee table, arms linked, shoulders touching. I wasn't sure when her voice started to fade, but at some point she stopped answering me. I looked down and saw that her eyes were closed. While I was talking about the summer Dad tried gardening (with disastrous results), she'd fallen asleep.

I eased myself out from under Tabitha's head and tucked a blanket around her shoulders. I did the good-person thing and left a glass of water on the coffee table, even though I could have left her to stumble around in the dark and find one for herself when she woke up, puffy-eyed and headachy. As I brought the half-full glass back from the kitchen, I stopped to look at her.

She was smaller asleep. There was a crooked crease between her eyebrows, like she was worrying. The line that never appeared when she was staring at a hard math problem, but that I had occasionally seen when she looked at Dad.

An ache gripped my chest, sudden and overwhelming. *That's my sister.* Even after everything—even with everything that was still between us, that would probably always be between us—she was my sister. I was born reaching for her.

I covered her with the duvet, feeling that strange tenderness that comes with putting a blanket over someone else when they're sleeping. She was going to get the couch, which meant I had to sleep in the bedroom. I hesitated before leaving her alone—in the end, I grabbed my laptop from the floor beside the couch. It wasn't that I thought she'd look through it. She'd never do something like that. It wasn't that.

It was just a matter of professional discretion. That's all.

I turned the living room lamp off and walked down the hall to the bedroom, feeling like a trespasser. I eased the door open.

The bare white mattress looked too big, too cold. I curled up in the center of it and tried not to look at the wall of letters just beyond the foot of the bed, but my ears still pricked, listening for whispers from the pages. I looked at my phone for the first time since before I'd sat down with Rahul, hoping for a distraction. The blue glow of the screen was blinding-bright. I squinted against the too-harsh light, sighing when I saw the time, which was well after midnight.

There were three text messages waiting for me. The first was a brunch invitation from a woman I'd been trying to become friends with. The second text was from Rahul; the third was from an unknown number.

I should have responded to the brunch invitation. I should have. But that was an invitation to leave this Ivy behind, this temporary, impossible Ivy I was losing myself in. And I've never been good at friends. People don't stick.

So I didn't reply.

And then, like ordering a third drink even though I knew I should stop at two, I opened the one from Rahul.

I think I'm supposed to wait for a day after the first date to send a text, it said, *but I can't stop smiling.*

Warmth spread up my neck as I remembered his strong, sure hands. I could still feel the warmth of his breath against my throat as he whispered "Is this okay?," waiting for my "yes" before pressing his mouth against my collarbone. Just the memory made my stomach jump, like I was in an elevator that had started a too-fast ascent.

Maybe after a few hours' sleep, I'd be able to string together a sentence without my heartbeat climbing up into my throat. As I started to close my eyes, I caught a blue flash: the notification LED on my phone, still blinking at me. For one wild second, I thought maybe Rahul—but then I remembered.

There had been a third text message.

It was a multimedia message from a blocked number; when I opened it, I realized that it was from the same person who had sent the photo of me and Tabitha sitting outside the bar. The new message was another photo. This one showed Tabitha standing outside my apartment, her hand on my doorknob. She was looking over her shoulder. The photo wasn't an amazing one, but I could make out her expression. She looked hunted.

As I studied the picture, another message came in from the same number. This one was a text message, a question, just three words long. It made my skin jump, but not the same way that the feathery brush of Rahul's eyelashes against my jawline had. I suddenly felt very cold and very small, as I realized I didn't know the answer to the question posed.

Are you safe?

CHAPTER

SIXTEEN

I WOKE UP TO MY phone buzzing. It was still in my hand from the night before. I opened one eye and peered at the screen—it was the same woman who wanted me to get brunch, probably calling to follow up on the three invitations she'd sent me. I watched the green ANSWER button pulse twice before thumbing the red REJECT button.

I put the phone down and closed my eyes, letting my cheek fall onto the bare mattress. She would stop trying soon enough.

"Good morning."

My eyes snapped open again, my heart pounding. She was standing at the foot of the bed with her back to me. Tabitha.

My sister, Tabitha.

"You're still here," I mumbled. She turned just enough that I could see her profile. She was smiling.

"I came in to see if you wanted some coffee and I got caught up in your crazy-wall."

I pushed myself up onto my elbows. "It's not a crazy-wall. It's evidence."

"Mmmm." She took a sip of coffee, turned back to the wall. "What is all this?"

Something was different. It wasn't like we'd become friends. I wasn't fooling myself on that score: a few shared tears hadn't undone everything that was between us. But something had moved. And she was still there.

My phone gave a short buzz, the sound of a waiting message. I dismissed the notification without listening to the voicemail.

Tabitha was still here.

"They're letters," I said. "I'm still figuring them out, but I think I've got them in the right order."

She sipped her coffee again without responding. I slipped out, splashed water on my face, got a cup of coffee from the pot Tabitha had brewed. As I poured it, I realized that she probably knew this apartment better than I did. She'd spent nights here before, woken up and brewed coffee, padded around barefoot in the quiet hours of the morning. When I returned to the bedroom, she was still standing there, reading the notes.

"This is just one side," she murmured.

"Yeah. They're all from one person," I said. "Although a few of them go back and forth." I pointed at the notes that had two different kinds of penmanship on them. The creases on those ones were deepest—they'd been folded and refolded, softened by pockets, passed back and forth throughout a day or two. "This is just half of the exchange, though. One person's stash, at least for this part of the correspondence." The notes spanned ten months or so: the first one mentioned the upcoming Winter Break, and they continued through the summer. The last one was dated shortly before Sylvia's murder.

"These are from students, right? Why wouldn't they just text each other?" Tabitha asked, tapping her fingernails against the side of her mug. "This seems like a lot of work."

I tapped the sixth note in the exchange. Most of it was about how someone—referred to only as "X" within the text—couldn't find out about the relationship because if she did, she'd freak out and ruin everything.

"So it was a secret," she said slowly, her eyes flicking over the text. "Can't risk cell phones. Can't risk getting caught."

"Exactly."

"Aren't you glad you aren't in high school anymore?" she muttered.

"You think that's drama? Wait'll you get a load of the next one."

The ghost of a smile creased one corner of her mouth as she skimmed the first letter in the next row down. "Valentine's Day?"

"That's the one. From what I'm piecing together, they couldn't be seen at the Valentine's Dance together, so they both played sick and spent the night together at . . . I'm not sure. I'm thinking her parents have a vacation home or something? Or maybe his do? It mentions 'the cabin' a few times."

She raised her eyebrows. "Okay, so, they sneak off and . . . what, have a bunch of teenage sex, right?"

"You know it. And then, they *keep* having a bunch of teenage sex."

"Yikes." She grimaced. "Since when do kids call it 'making love'?"

"These two've got it *bad*." I pointed out phrases with my free hand, feeling . . . impressive. I was showing my sister my job. I was showing off my research. And she looked fascinated. She was *listening* to me. "They've never felt this way before. And if you look down here, they start saying 'I love you' pretty soon after the cabin thing. They spend a lot of time together over the summer, sneaking away, talking about what they're going to do after senior year. Then, right around the middle of the summer—before they start talking about classes but after they've finished talking about how great summer's going to be—something changes." I pointed to a note that was low on the wall, late in the exchange. I didn't say anything, suddenly nervous. Had I been talking for too long?

Tabitha scanned the page. "Holy shit," she breathed.

"Yeah," I murmured. "That's what I said." It was a holy-shit kind of note. It was tear-stained, the ink smudged in places. There was terror between the lines—*I don't know what to do* was repeated several times, and the words *it was positive* had been traced over until they were thick and uneven. They screamed fear from the center of the page. *It was positive.*

"Shit," she said, drumming her nails faster against her mug. "Baby on board."

"I know, right? High drama."

"Huh. That's interesting."

I tore my eyes from *it was positive* and looked at Tabitha. She was staring at the note with the same intense focus she'd slipped into when we were kids trying to stay patient enough to finish a jigsaw puzzle. "What's interesting?"

"Well, it seems like she's scared of what X will say. She's scared of what will happen to her. But . . . she doesn't seem scared of what A will say. She doesn't seem worried that he'll freak out or leave her."

"Well spotted," I said. "Check out the last one. It's kind of amazing." The last note, all the way on the bottom corner of what Tabitha had called my crazy-wall, was crowded with both sets of handwriting. It was a few sentences at a time, probably passed back and forth in class. *I missed you* and *you look great* and *I can't even tell that you're . . . you know.* "Check out the bottom of the page," I murmured, and she looked. I felt giddy—I was sharing something with her, my sister, my twin sister Tabitha, the way I hadn't let myself imagine doing for years.

Her lips moved slightly as she read the lines at the bottom of the page, and I could hear her just barely breathing the words out loud. *Don't worry*, the note said. *I'll get into the library + find the spell if you can't get the potion from Capley.*

The response, in B's handwriting, was at the top of the next sheet. *What if we can't do anything about it?*

Then we'll get married, and we'll be the best parents in the world, the response assured.

She didn't say anything for a long time. Finally, I ventured commentary. "These two were pretty desperate. They had a big secret, and then they had an even *bigger* secret, and they thought Capley was the answer. I think they thought she could set them up with a solution." She still didn't say anything. Her face was as still as a held breath. I kept going, wanting to see her eyes flicker with interest again, holding too tight to the thing that had been there just a minute before. "So, I figure, what if A tried to get his hands on that potion, and Capley said no? I'd call that a motive. Crime of passion. So, who is A, and where was he the night of the murder?"

Tabitha remained quiet, staring at the letters on the wall. *It was positive* seemed to throb, heavy and immediate in the uneasy silence. The rest of the room faded into grayscale. All I could think was, *Look, look, look, it's right there, it's right in front of you, if you just look—*

"I have to get ready for work." Tabitha's voice was smooth, calm. Empty. She walked past me, brushing my shoulder with a hand. "It sounds like you're really on to something here, though. Thanks for showing me."

"Oh." Disappointment was a stone on my tongue. I did my best to talk around it. "Sure, yeah." *She has to get ready for work. You didn't do anything wrong, people just have to go to work, this is normal, it's fine.* But something was wrong. She'd turned distant. She'd turned nice.

"Hey, seriously, thank you," she said, pausing in the doorway. "And thank you for last night. It meant a lot."

I nodded. *See? Everything's fine. You were imagining that she cooled off.* But her face was still placid, and her eyes weren't meeting mine. "Coffee soon? Or drinks?"

"You know where to find me." She smiled, and the smile slid off me like rain beading up on oilcloth, and then she was gone. The sound of the front door closing felt like an indictment of something I'd done, or something I hadn't done, or something I'd missed.

I refilled my coffee and told myself to shake it off. We'd cried on each other, and she'd asked about my work. That was all. I was letting myself get distracted by her, by a thing that wasn't there between us. By something I missed from back before I was too young to understand how unimportant it was.

I looked at my mug and told myself that the thing with Tabitha didn't matter. Then I added a slug of rum to my coffee and went to get my laptop. No time to get wrapped up in her, in regret, in that aching loneliness that I couldn't afford to look at directly. No time for that shit, not now.

I had a job to do.

CHAPTER

SEVENTEEN

AFTER HOURS OF REVIEWING THE letters and the notes and comparing them to my own notes and staff files, I decided to take a lap around the outside of the school. I needed to get my head straight, and I needed to figure out how to deal with being in the same building as my sister, and Rahul, and almost certainly a murderer. And I needed to walk away from that bottle of gin before I got carried away with it—I was already starting to get the midafternoon headache that comes with too much of a bad coping mechanism.

I put my hands in my pockets and tried to stroll across the sprawling green lawns instead of walking with my usual sense of hungover purpose. The grass was impeccable, manicured in tidy, straight lines. Dandelion-free. My dad would have killed for a lawn like that one, and I wondered if it had ever occurred to my sister to tell him the secret that the Osthorne groundskeepers seemed to possess. Right on cue, I passed by one window and saw that the lawn just underneath it was dense with gardenias—my mother's favorite flower. When I peeked in the window, I saw the back of Tabitha's head, silhouetted against a huge orb of what looked like ball lightning.

I ducked away before she could turn and see me. Things had changed the night before, there could be no doubt about that. Something between us had been . . . not repaired, not exactly, but splinted. I didn't know how to put weight on it yet, but maybe with time—

"She said that you told her."

I froze before I rounded the corner, pressing my back against the mossy bricks. I'd reached a shadowy section of the Osthorne grounds, and from the sound of it, I wasn't alone.

"I didn't, I swear to God, Alexandria." I didn't recognize the second girl's voice, but it sounded terrified.

"Do you know what a risk I took for you? Do you have *any idea*? I haven't told anyone what we did, but you—"

"I *didn't*, though!" The second girl's voice rose above a whisper, and I could hear Alexandria shushing her.

"Look, Court. I get it, okay?" *Courtney, then.* Alexandria's voice had turned gentle, almost saccharine. "It's exciting, having a real live detective talk to you. I know you don't get much excitement in your life. Plus, you want to be useful, right? You want to help for once, instead of getting in everyone's way. I really, truly get it. But you can't tell *anyone* what happened. If you do?" Her voice dripped honey and acid. "I'll say you're a lying slut."

An oppressive shock wave of unwarranted terror shot through me, like the shiver before you realize someone is coming up behind you in a dark alley. Grass rustled as Alexandria stalked away. I stood there, trying not to breathe, as waves of a-tiger-is-chasing-you panic rippled across my skin, and listened to Courtney crying. I was trying to decide whether or not I should round the corner and ask her what was going on, but my palms were sweating. *What the fuck?* I took some deep breaths, pressed the back of my head against the bricks and squeezed my eyes shut as the fear ebbed. *What is going on? Why do I feel this way?*

I heard Courtney give a deep sniff and a sigh. There was a clack and a thud. I rounded the corner just in time to see a fire door swinging shut.

Well. I didn't know what had just happened—between Courtney and Alexandria, or with that sudden fear-bomb—but my gut was screaming at me that it was bad.

Really bad.

I found the person I was looking for in the teachers' lounge. I glanced around when I got in—Rahul wasn't there. I couldn't tell if I was relieved or disappointed. I was still shaken from whatever had happened outside, and I was a little wobbly from the morning of rum and obsessive study, and I didn't know if I'd be able to show him the person I wanted him to see.

It was for the best that he wasn't there. It was for the best that I hadn't texted him back yet. It would wait. It would keep.

The only person in the lounge was Mrs. Webb. I had half hoped that I wouldn't be able to find her, but I still had to follow up on Toff's alibi. And here she was, sitting with her head bent over a bowl of water. She was staring into it with intense, absolute focus.

"Mrs. Webb?" I said, hesitant. Her head snapped up. I jolted—

meeting a stare that was such a deep blue as to approach black. The whites of her eyes were completely occluded by liquid, shining darkness, as though her pupils had expanded to completely fill the spaces between her eyelids. They looked cold, standing in stark contrast to the warm brown of her skin.

Then she blinked a few times, and her eyes cleared. The water in the bowl between her hands went from clear to a faded blue-gray.

"Can I help you?" she asked, her voice less icy than usual.

"You, um, your, I." She waited patiently while I stammered. "Yes, I just had, uh. A few questions. If now is a bad time . . . ?" I was already edging toward the door. I closed it behind me before she could answer, and when I looked back into the teachers' lounge through the little window that was set into the door, her eyes had darkened again.

I watched for a while, unable to tear myself away. Every few minutes, she would blink over the bowl; I never saw the blackness fall away, but the water in the bowl got darker every time her eyes cleared.

"Ivy?" When I turned my head, Tabitha was walking down the hall. I put a finger to my lips, and she pulled up beside me with knit brows. When she looked through the window to the staff lounge, her brow cleared.

"Oh, dang. I guess I'll have to come back later. I wish she wouldn't do that in the teachers' lounge. I *really* wanted a coffee." She made an oh-well face. "What are you doing here?"

"Just, you know. Workin' the case," I said, not sure how to talk to my sister now that we seemed to be on speaking terms. Now that I had seen her broken.

"Oh, okay. Well." She looked as awkward as I felt. "I won't bother you, then. I mean. I won't interrupt, not that you're making me feel like a bother, just—I should go supervise my class anyway, I left the student aide in charge so I could caffeinate. I'll let you get back to it." She started to leave, but I put out a hand and she stopped midstride. She looked wary, like she could feel the fragility between us and was just as afraid to step on it as I was.

"Wait, sorry," I said. "I'm just wondering—what exactly is it that she's *doing* in there?"

Mrs. Webb was staring into the space above the bowl. The water in the bowl was still dark—but when I looked at Mrs. Webb's eyes, they were covered by a film of gray.

"Oh, that. It's a memory extraction," Tabitha said, standing beside me again to look at Mrs. Webb. "She's pulling out the things she's seen and washing them away. When she pours the water down the drain, she won't have to remember anymore. She's been doing it since she found . . . you know."

I blinked at Tabitha. "Really? Wait, really? Do people do that?"

"Nobody does that," she said, her voice pitched low. "It's extremely dangerous to mess with your own brain the way she does. It's really old-school—seriously, it's like . . . like using leeches to draw out the bad blood. Except, you know. What she's doing kind of works."

"I thought she was a really amazing healer?"

Tabitha shrugged. "Well, yeah. If I tried that I'd probably—" Her voice caught, and she cleared her throat. "I'd probably die in the process. She's the best healer of our lifetime, Ivy. But you know . . . she's old-school."

I shuddered as Mrs. Webb's eyes cleared, then began to fade to black again.

"So, does she save the memories after?"

Tabitha shook her head. "They're not really memories anymore once they're out of her head. It's not like you could use them again. They're waste, at this point. Like how the stuff inside of zits used to be white blood cells?" She wrinkled her nose. "She'll probably just wash them down the drain." A bell rang, and Tabitha swore under her breath. "That's the five-minute bell, I have to go get ready to dismiss my class," she said. "Can we get drinks tomorrow night, though?"

I nodded, and she grinned at me before she turned to walk away. It was an easy smile—the kind that you would share with a friend who you know you'll see again soon.

I'd never seen her smile like that before. It felt like a promise.

I turned to go, and ran straight into a lanky blur. I reached out a hand to steady myself and got a fistful of bony arm for my trouble.

"I really need to start watching where I'm going," I muttered, sick of running into people. I looked up to apologize to whoever I was clutching. Dylan DeCambray's architecturally intense face stared back at me—but it was blurred, almost foggy, and kept snapping in and out of view.

I blinked hard, let go of his arm. The instant I let go of him, he disappeared.

"What the fuck?" I blurted. There was a startled hiccup from a few feet in front of me. Dylan appeared again, waving his hands in front of his face like he was clearing away cobwebs. His face blazed pink.

"Sorry," he muttered, not making eye contact with me.

"What did you just—what was that? What did you just do?" I asked, then caught myself. Shit. I should know what it was that he did. "I mean, what are you doing?"

Mrs. Webb's voice rasped from behind me. "That was Mr. De-Cambray illustrating his ability to break school rules by casting a see-me-not illusion on Osthorne grounds during school hours. *And* by being in the halls without a pass during class time." She was looking at him with weary amusement. She brandished a white pharmacy bag with a pink hall pass attached to it. "I imagine that you're here for this, Mr. DeCambray?"

He went even pinker, his ears very nearly glowing, and nodded. "Thanks, ma'am," he said, taking the bag. He walked away, not making eye contact with either of us, and by the time he'd reached the end of the hallway he'd gone invisible again. Mrs. Webb shook her head at the seemingly empty halls.

"Did you need something, Ms. Gamble, or were you just going to watch me through the window all afternoon?" She was looking at me with the same weary amusement she'd given Dylan. I wondered if maybe weariness was just a baseline for her.

"What's in those bags?" I asked, still staring at the place in the hallway where Dylan had vanished.

Mrs. Webb opened the door to the teachers' lounge and walked in without waiting for me, but I had the feeling I was supposed to follow. As she made her way back to the little table she'd been sitting at before, I realized she was talking. I strained to catch her hoarse words.

". . . all depends on the student, of course. But for the most part, it's birth control." She shook her head as we sat at the table. I noticed that the bowl of blue-black memories was gone—in its place was a mug of steaming milky tea. The swirling steam filled the air with the smells of honey and cardamom. "These kids don't want to learn about the old magic that would let them deal with their bodies—they want pills and patches and condoms." I don't know what the look was that crossed my face upon hearing this, but whatever it was, it drew a genuine laugh out of Mrs. Webb, creasing her face like rumpling silk. "Oh, it's better this way, of course," she said. "If you do the magic wrong, it doesn't work, and then you wind up with all kinds of problems. But still—I miss the days when a girl had to understand herself well enough to learn an ovary-clamping charm."

I had absolutely no idea what to say to that. Another bell rang, and the hall outside began to fill with bodies and noise, with shouts and squeaking sneakers and slamming lockers.

"Now that young man?" She pointed a finger toward the hall, which was full of young men, but I knew she meant Dylan. "That young man right there has nothing to be embarrassed about. I keep telling him so, but he insists on using that damned illusion every time he comes to see me. He's one of the only ones who comes to me for something *other* than condoms."

"I know you probably can't tell me, but . . . what is he coming for?"

Mrs. Webb laughed again—not quite a cackle, but something that was a close cousin to it. Whenever she laughed, her freckles disappeared into the network of wrinkles laced across her cheeks. "I can tell you whatever I please, Ms. Gamble. He's getting a tincture for his girlfriend's cramps."

I looked toward the hallway as though I'd be able to see the invisible Dylan there amid the sea of teenagers. "Well, damn. That's pretty great for a teenage boy."

"I know," she said. "She's a lucky girl, whoever she is."

"It seems like you'd know everything that goes on around here," I ventured. "You really don't know who he's dating?"

"You have a limited number of breaths in this life, Ms. Gamble," she murmured. "Do you really want to waste any on trying to flatter me into telling you student gossip?"

Another bell rang, and the halls began to empty again. It seemed like such a short time that the kids had, to get from class to class. Such a short time in which to see each other, pass notes, trip each other, steal from each other, make enemies, find friends, make out. I wondered how they managed it all. I wondered how I'd ever managed it all.

Mrs. Webb stared steadily at me across the table, waiting for me to say something worth her time. I tried another tactic. "So you handle all of the . . . what, the clinic stuff, right? The stuff that Sylvia used to handle?" She nodded, sipping her tea, and I let myself take it as an encouraging sign. "Would that include taking care of pregnant girls?"

She eyed me over her mug. "Why do you ask? Is someone pregnant?"

I cocked my head. "I'm not sure. What if someone was, though?"

She suddenly gave me a penetrating look, and I felt a rich warmth spreading through my abdomen. I looked down and saw that it was faintly glowing, as though someone were shining a flashlight through my shirt. I yelped as I realized that the question I'd answered wasn't the one she'd been asking.

"No! Not me!" I resisted the urge to shield my stomach with both hands. The glow and the warmth both vanished.

"I'll say," she said. "Nothing of note in there. Although you're not getting any younger. Tick-tock, Ms. Gamble."

I cleared my throat, trying to regain my composure. She sipped her tea and watched me. She seemed to be enjoying herself. Well, at least one of us was.

"I meant, what if a *student* was pregnant? Would you be the one who would know about that?"

She set her tea down and wrapped her hands around it. When she spoke, her voice was marginally less raspy than it had been. "If they came to me for help, I would know about it, yes."

I pulled out my notebook in a manner that I hoped would be nonchalant, but her eyes zipped to it and stayed there as I uncapped my pen. "What kind of help?"

"Any kind of help," Mrs. Webb said. "But I think what you're really asking is what kind of help I would be able to *provide*, yes?"

I flashed back to my third-grade teacher: *I don't know, Ivy, can you go to the bathroom?* "Yes ma'am," I said evenly, "that is what I'm asking."

"Official policy says I can give them prenatal vitamins and a reference to a registered obstetrician in the mage community," she said, then pressed her lips into a thin line. Everything on her face said *this sentence is unfinished,* but her eyes were on my notebook and pen.

I set the pen down, closed the cover of the notebook. "What does unofficial policy say?"

She leaned across the table. "There are certain things that we don't do, Ms. Gamble. We don't do gynecological examinations, because this is a school and we aren't about to start making children take off their clothes in front of teachers. But handing out over-the-counter medications, prescribed medications, and potions graded below a level 4N by the Medical Mage Association? That's allowed." She leaned back and cleared her throat—her voice was starting to get raspy again. She took a sip from her tea, and I noticed that although she'd drunk quite a bit of it, the mug remained full. "Now, district policy states that we don't provide any medications or potions that might induce adverse effects in a fetus being carried by a student we know to be pregnant." She stared at me, unblinking, making sure I understood.

"But you might do that anyway?" I said slowly. She merely raised her eyebrows and took a drink. I folded my hands on the table and waited.

"You're a stubborn one," she said. I didn't respond. "If, hypothetically, a student came to me in the immediate aftermath of an *accident,* I could provide them with a potion that would prevent fetal implantation or induce a menstrual period. Either one would cause about thirty minutes of heavy bleeding followed by a bit of fatigue. If, hypothetically, a student came to me in the less-immediate aftermath of an accident—say, perhaps, anything earlier than nine weeks in—I could give her a pair of potions. She'd take the first one right away, and then spend the next three days bleeding and drinking the second one." Mrs. Webb was very still, speaking softly enough that I unconsciously leaned toward her. "She would have to drink the second one every hour, on the hour, even at night. She would have to take it continuously, do you understand? But there would be no pain, no risk of infection, no nausea even. She'd feel fine. But I would give the girl the full day off of her classes in case she has a hard time emotionally. *Hypothetically*," she said, her voice suddenly returning to full volume. "Not that I've ever provided a student with such a potion."

"Of course not," I answered. "After all, you haven't been doing this part of the job all along. Only since Sylvia died, right?"

"Five months," she said with a dark twinkle in her eye, "is certainly not long enough for anyone to get pregnant."

"Certainly not," I said. I didn't wink at her, even though I wanted to. She didn't feel like a woman one should wink at. "Now, let's say—hypothetically—that a student approached you who was not in the earliest stages of pregnancy?"

At this, she shook her head, the dark twinkle gone. "I have the expertise for it, but I wouldn't take that risk on school grounds. That's a surgical procedure."

"Really?" I was taken aback. "There's no potion for it? No magic?"

She rapped the table with her knuckles. "That's not what I said, girl. Listen better next time." Her voice was sharp. "I said that's *surgical*." She reached out a finger and jabbed it into my left shoulder; I felt a twinge of terror at the sudden memory that arced through me. My shoulder, dismantled and floating in front of my face. Her wand, zapping away the infection.

I swallowed hard as I understood. "So that's, uh, that's how it's done?"

Mrs. Webb nodded. "It's perfectly safe if it's done by a medical professional in a sterile environment. The girl gets a sedative so it's not too traumatic. She walks out when the sedative has worn off. Much less invasive than the nonmagical version of the procedure."

"Is it?" I asked before I could stop myself.

"Of course it is," she said. "No stirrups. No pain. Twenty minutes at the most." She sipped more tea, then tapped the side of the mug twice with her ring finger. Fresh steam swirled from inside the mug. "I performed hundreds of them, back when I was practicing. But never here."

We sat in silence for a minute or so as I digested this. Finally, she made a harrumphing sound. I looked up at her and saw that she was watching me, impatient.

"Can I ask one more thing?" I said, and was frustrated at the quaver in my voice.

"What is it?" she asked. Her face was still impatient, but her tone had gone gentle.

"What you did to my shoulder—what you used to do for the women in your clinic. Can you do that for other things?" She didn't answer, waiting for me to stop dancing around the real question. "I mean, if someone had cancer. Could you take it out?"

Her face went still and cold. "You've been talking to Tabitha, have you?"

"What? What do you mean?"

"I'll tell you what I told her: not cancer at that stage." Her voice was level, but the table trembled with the force of what I realized must have been a lifetime of frustration at the limitations of healing. "Theoretically? A healer can do anything," she said, "but realistically, it's just not possible to do that to someone. To take them apart for hours, and hold everything alive, and find everything in the bones that's wrong. And then to put them back together again." Her mouth twisted as though she were going to spit. "It can't be done. It's never been done. There's nothing we could have done."

She stood up and waved a hand over her mug of tea; when I looked down, it was empty and clean, although a faint smell of cardamom lingered in the air. She turned on her heel and made for the door. She let it swing shut behind her. I sat in the chair and stared at the place where she'd been sitting. I thought back to the night before—to Tabitha crying on my couch, telling me that she couldn't have helped Mom. That even if she'd wanted to, even if she'd known how to, she couldn't have saved our mother from the painful death that I had to watch her endure. I let out a shaky breath.

After a few minutes I walked out after her, taking deep breaths. A few students were milling in the hall, doing some class activity that involved sticking pieces of paper to each other and then turning them pink or blue with a snap of their fingers. I recognized Courtney—she was working with another girl, directing her partner to stick papers to the back of her baggy, paint-stained gym-class sweatshirt. She kept vacillating between turning them pink or blue, pink or blue, pink or blue.

Courtney caught me watching and lifted her hand in a wave, knocking one of the papers from her shirt. As it fell, it folded in the air, falling to the linoleum and bouncing high before falling a few feet away—an elaborate star. She laughed as she and her partner stooped to pick it up at the same time. Her partner tossed the folded paper back to her, and she caught the star easily.

She turned it over in her hands, and then looked back up at me.

She tried to smile again, but she wasn't fast enough to keep me from seeing the way that star broke her. She turned away before the tears could fall, but I saw them there, brimming already. And then she was gone, back into the classroom, her project partner abandoned.

Courtney dropped the star behind her as she walked away. It unfolded as it fell, but the light caught the contours of the folds in the paper, and I knew: in the shadows of those creases, there were answers.

EIGHTEEN

HERE'S THE TRUTH ABOUT MOST detective work: it's boring, grueling, and monotonous. It involves a lot of being in the right place at the wrong time. But if you spend enough hours being in the right place, eventually, it'll be the right time. You have to be able to recognize it.

I recognized it when I saw Courtney crying in that hallway.

I waited until she went into her classroom, then poked my head in. There were only fifteen or so kids in the class. All of them sat at desks that were littered with scraps of multicolored paper—white, blue, pink. Rahul stood at the front of the room, not noticing me. I took the liberty of watching him, feeling only a little creepy. He moved his hands a lot while he talked. I'd noticed it during our dinner, but it was more pronounced here, in front of the students. His fingers were blunt and callused, but incredibly agile. Rahul demonstrated a set of complicated gestures, explaining the principles that would allow his class of seniors to change the way light was absorbed by paper. I didn't understand a word of it, but I could have watched him all day.

It didn't take long for the students to start whispering and nudging each other and pointing at me. Rahul finally looked over. The look on his face was complicated—a combination of what-are-you-doing-here and excited-to-see-you and dear-god-not-in-front-of-the-students. I gave him a cool, professional nod-and-smile, and said, "Sorry to interrupt your class. I just needed to borrow one of your students for a minute, if that's alright?" I pointed to Courtney.

Relief and worry crowded his expression. He nodded, gesturing to Courtney without looking away from me. As I waited for her at the front of the room, I felt my right hand growing hot. I held the door open for her, taking the opportunity to discreetly peek at my palm: the place between my love line and my life line had reddened. It faded as I watched. I looked over my shoulder just before I closed the door, and Rahul was watching me with a small, tentative smile.

In the hall, Courtney crossed her arms and stared up at me from between hunched shoulders. Her cheeks were dry—freshly scrubbed with the sleeve of her sweatshirt, no doubt—but her eyes were still rimmed with pink. She wasn't wearing any makeup, at least none that I could see, and her hair was still in that twist, held up with a paintbrush and a pencil. She was doing everything she could to make sure that her defined role as "artist" came across loud and clear. I wondered if she even liked the aesthetic, or if she just felt like she was supposed to like it.

"Hey, Courtney," I said, trying to figure out how to start. Her eyes darted back and forth along the hallway.

"Hey, um, hi," she said, her voice soft. She didn't want to be seen, didn't want to be heard. I flashed back to the conversation

I'd overheard just an hour before—*if you tell anyone, I'll say you're a lying slut.*

She was afraid.

I handed her my card. "I know you can't talk here, but we need to have a chat." I looked over my shoulders, let her see that I was watching out for her. Let her feel clandestine. I stepped out onto the limb and tested whether or not it would hold my weight. "All that's gold doesn't glitter."

Her eyes snapped to mine. She looked hunted. "What did you just say?" *Bingo.*

"I know about you and Dylan," I whispered. She shook her head vehemently.

"I don't know what you're talking about," she hissed back.

I crinkled my nose at her, conspiratorial. "Come on, Courtney. I found the stash of notes."

"What stash?" She looked genuinely confused, and I had the panicked thought that somehow I'd totally miscalculated, but then I saw the flash of fear in her eyes. *He wasn't supposed to save them.*

"We shouldn't talk about it here," I said. "Meet me in the library after school. Theoretical Magic section. I'll get you a pass, and nobody will be able to see us in there. Or hear us. I promise." I ducked my head so our eyes were level. "This is important, Courtney."

She stared at my card with unseeing eyes. Pink blotches had spread across her chest and were climbing up her neck—an ugly blush, one she hadn't figured out how to magically control the way my sister had. After a long minute of silence, Courtney turned and walked back into Rahul's classroom without a word, my business card crumpled in her fist. As the door swung shut after her, I caught Rahul's eye. He looked uncertain. I waved at him, holding up my hand for a few seconds longer than necessary. A tiny lopsided smile tugged at the corners of his mouth.

Then the door clicked shut, and I was alone, and all I could do was wait.

⁓

I stood at the end of the Theoretical Magic section, holding the two passes that Torres had given me. Most of the school day had slid by with alarming speed. I'd slipped in two more fruitless teacher interviews, listening to a lot of hemming and hawing about small disagreements between Capley and the econ teacher about whether students should be given aspirin. A kindergartener could have told them that didn't come even close to constituting a motive, but instead I let them talk for hours. They turned into white noise, and I pretended to listen while I watched through those huge library windows as the clouds thinned, parted, and then merged together again.

The Theoretical Magic section was still dizzying to look at, and I could hear the books inside whispering. The sound was nothing like pages turning—it was more like the sound of a room full of people who have just realized that a celebrity is sitting among them wearing big dark glasses and a scarf. I kept trying to make out the words, but they all blended together into a steady patter of hushed scandal.

None of the other sections had talkative books. I'd asked Torres about it when I'd gotten the passes from her.

"If I had to guess?" she'd said. "The books whisper because they saw something so terrible and powerful happen. It's part of why I don't believe Sylvia had an 'unfortunate accident'—it would take something big to make those books talk."

"What are they saying?" I'd asked, hoping that there was an easy answer to be found.

"No idea," Torres had replied. "I had Tabitha working on it for a few weeks, but she said that it's a new book-language, beyond what we can even begin to translate."

I'd shaken my head, disappointed. "So you don't know what caused it and you don't know what it means." She'd nodded. "I guess magic isn't an exact science, huh?"

Her eyes had grown wide and she'd leaned back in her chair. "It's exactly like science, Ivy. We're making a lot of guesses, some of which are right, and we're trying our best to name phenomena we may never truly understand. So I'd say that it is absolutely science."

I chewed on the conversation as I waited for Courtney, who might not show up. Who might not have had anything to do with anything, but who was the closest thing I had to a lead in this case. If I was honest with myself, I had to admit that I still had no idea if I was handling the investigation the right way. I usually scraped out my living by following people who were in shitty situations—they were trapped and they were petty. I'd found a couple of missing people before, including one kid who'd run away from home and gotten on the right side of the wrong crowd by doing some things I hadn't known how to tell his parents about—but even the horrible things that boy had gotten involved with were pretty tame, if I compared them to this case. I felt like I was just barely keeping my head above water, swallow-ing brine with every new wave.

Finally, Courtney showed up and dropped a life preserver over my head. She walked right past me, looking down every row of shelves as she passed. At first, I thought maybe she'd forgotten where we were meeting—but then I realized she was checking to make sure no one would catch us. She blinked hard and shook her head when she passed the Theoretical Magic section, but she didn't actually acknowledge me. After she'd checked all of the other sections, she doubled back, stalking toward me with one hand held out for her pass. I stepped out of the shadow at the end of the row of books and slapped the slip of paper onto her palm, then unclipped the rope at the end of the shelves so we could cross the boundary that hid the bloodstains from the students. As we did, the whisper of books grew louder, like autumn-red trees rustled by an incoming wind.

She dropped her book bag at her feet and crossed her arms, her brown eyes narrowing as she looked everywhere but at me. Her baggy sweatshirt drooped off one broad shoulder. She bit her lip, tapped her fingers on her arm—this girl was ready to jump out of her skin.

"Hi Courtn—" I started, but she interrupted, as though she'd been waiting for a starter pistol to go off before she leapt into the conversation.

"You don't know *anything about me,*" she said in a harsh whis-per. "You don't know anything about me and you don't know anything about Dylan and I don't have anything to tell you any-way, and it's not like we did anything *wrong—*"

I didn't whisper like she had, but I kept my voice low. "I just want to ask you some questions. I don't think you did anything wrong."

She ran a hand through her brown waves, still not looking at me. "I don't care what you think," she said, and it was convincing. Which is not to say that I was convinced.

"Courtney, I really mean it. I don't think you did *anything* wrong. I think you did what you had to do."

Her eyes shone. "She told you?"

"Who told me what?" I asked, but she didn't seem to hear me.

"She said we couldn't tell anyone—but—"

A trickle of understanding crept down the back of my neck like an ant looking for a honey jar. I took a calculated risk, and guessed. "About the potion?"

There was a second of hesitation. Two seconds. Four. Then: "Yes. The potion."

The books fell silent for a beat, then began whispering more loudly than ever. I caught snatches of phrases, but it was like listening to a conversation through a wall—the words didn't come together to form anything other than a general impression of *angry* and *sad* and *tired*.

"Can you tell me about it in your own words?" I asked. "I'm not writing anything down, and I'm not recording." I was telling the truth this time, about not recording—I'd tested my recorder in the aisle before she arrived, and all it would pick up was the constant rustling of the books. "I just need to know if I'm headed in the right direction, okay?"

"I don't have to tell you anything," she hissed. "You're not even a cop."

Something in my chest shifted, then settled. *Enough.* "You're right," I said. "You're absolutely fucking right." She flinched when I swore. Good. "I'm not a cop, and I'm not a teacher, and I'm not your parents. I'm a private detective, and that means I get to decide what I tell people and what I don't. It means I get to decide if I help you cover your ass or if I throw you right under the god-damned bus. Right now I'm pretty low on leads, and you're the only one I can find who had a problem with your dead teacher. I'm giving you a chance to tell me why I shouldn't cut my losses, tell the authorities that you're the killer, and walk away from this shitshow of a case. So what's it gonna be, Courtney?"

She chewed her lip, wide-eyed. Cornered. She was out of options, and her tough-girl act was disintegrating. "Okay. I'll tell you." A dart of her eyes. "I'll tell you *if* you give me all the notes you found."

"Sure," I said, no hesitation. I would say that I considered mentioning that I had digital copies of all the notes, but it didn't cross my mind. I wasn't there to be scrupulous. I was there to solve a murder.

She scowled at the floor for a while before muttering, "I didn't have a problem with Capley."

"No?" I shot back, just a little aggressive.

"No," she said, her voice a bit stronger.

"So she just gave you the potion, no questions asked?"

Courtney chewed on the side of one thumb before answering. "I mean, she asked some questions. About how long it had been since I had my period and stuff. She wanted to know if the—um, if the father knew and was okay with everything. She asked if I was safe."

"Did Dylan know?"

She gave me a look that clearly communicated her complete and total disdain for my deathly idiocy. "Of *course* he knew."

"Did he pressure you? To get rid of the baby?"

Her eyes shifted from the shelves to the carpet to my knees, like she couldn't figure out where to look. "No, not really."

"What does that mean?"

"He told me that he would support me no matter what, and that it was my decision. And he totally meant it, okay? Like, if I said I wanted to keep it and get married, he would have. But . . . I couldn't do that to him. He's got a lot of responsibility, with the Prophecy and everything. He's the *Chosen One*, you know? You can't be the Chosen One if you have a baby before you even graduate high school."

I shook my head. "Of course you can."

She just rolled her eyes, *okay whatever, very inspirational.* "Anyway, I wouldn't have wanted to keep it even if he'd asked me to. My parents would . . ." Courtney trailed off, her eyes on the bloodstain in the carpet. She took a deep breath, forced her eyes back to me. "And I couldn't go to a clinic. I couldn't afford it, even if my dad didn't know every other doctor in the state. So I went to Miss Capley. She usually has—*had*—everything that anyone needed, in terms of like, birth control and stuff. So we figured she could probably help out with this, too. Dylan wanted to come with me to get the pills, but then Miss Capley said nobody could come in with me."

"Pills?"

She blinked. "What?"

"You said you went to get pills from Miss Capley. I thought it was a potion?"

"I didn't say pills," she said. "I said potions. Dylan wanted to come with me to get the potions."

I took a mental snapshot of the moment, then let it go. I leaned against a shelf and felt the rustle of a book against my sleeve. "Okay, so you got the potions from Capley. Then what?"

"I took the first one, like she said, and then I took the second one and I started . . . you know. Bleeding. I stayed home from school for a few days. It was like a really heavy period but then I felt dizzy and nauseous and I had strong cramps."

I raised an eyebrow. "'Strong cramps'?"

Courtney nodded. "But I took some Tylenol and that helped. And then it was over and I came back to school, and the next day Miss Capley was—um." Her eyes fell on the bloodstain that bridged the aisle. "The next day, she died," she whispered.

"So she gave you the potions on the first day of school, and then you missed a few days and came back for the welcome feast, and then she was dead?"

"Yeah," she said, her eyes still on the bloodstain.

"And she gave it to you without an argument or anything? Just handed it over."

"I mean, she wasn't excited about it, but it's not like it was a huge deal," Courtney said. "She probably did that kind of thing all the time."

"Okay," I said. "One last question." She huffed out a breath and shifted her weight, one hip jutting out. "Do your friends know about all this?"

Her face went still. "Only Alexandria," she murmured. "She figured out that I was—um, that I was pregnant. She didn't know it was Dylan's. Doesn't know." She didn't say *Don't tell her, please don't tell her, oh god anything but that.* But then, she didn't have to.

"Okay," I said. "I'll keep that in mind if I have to ask her more questions."

We stared at each other as Courtney tried to decide if I was threatening her or comforting her. She looked like a trapped cat that hasn't decided if it should try to dart between your feet or launch itself at your face. A bell rang—it was muffled behind the hiss of the books, but we both heard it. She picked up her book bag and threw it over one shoulder, giving me a hard look. "I have to get to class. You already made me miss algebra."

"Wait, Courtney. Just one more thing?" She stopped, one hand on her hip, and gave me an I'm-waiting look. "Do you ever feel afraid of Dylan?"

She blinked at me, thought it over. I wondered if there was a possible situation, in any universe, when someone having to stop and think about that sort of question would indicate a good answer.

"He's going to be the most powerful mage in the world," she said. "Of course I'm afraid sometimes. But he would never hurt me. At least, not on purpose."

She hiked her bag up on her shoulder and stalked out of the aisle without another word. I stared at the place where she'd been standing, six inches from the end of the dark brown bloodstain that marked the place where Sylvia Capley had died.

"Shit," I muttered, pulling out my phone. I didn't want to be right. That's the worst kind of hunch, the kind that comes with a knot of dread. A quick web search unspooled that knot of dread, and I closed my eyes for a moment, hoping that when I opened them, the text on the screen would be different.

But, of course, it wasn't different. It was right there on the Planned Parenthood website: what to expect after a medical abortion. It sounded exactly like the lines Courtney had fed me, down to the way she'd slipped up and said "pills" instead of "potions."

She was lying. And she wasn't just lying in the moment—she had that explanation handy. She had looked it up ahead of time, if not for me then for someone else. She'd found a plausible story, she'd memorized the symptoms that would fit, and she'd tried to get me to buy it.

"What are you hiding, Courtney?" I whispered it to myself, and the books seemed like they were trying to answer—but their answer was incomprehensible. I chewed the inside of my cheek and ran a finger along the cover of *What Plants Know: A Theory of Horticultural Alchemy*. I could feel the leather buzzing. "What did you do?"

CHAPTER

NINETEEN

I STAYED IN THE STACKS for a long time after Courtney left. I sat in the shadow of the shelves and stared at the carpet, letting everything sift through my brain. The books settled down so long as I stayed quiet—they whispered occasionally, the soft flutter of sleeping birds resettling their wings. It was nearly peaceful, if I didn't let my eyes wander too near that huge, dark bloodstain. I traced fingers along their spines, feeling them shiver as they talked to each other in that indecipherable static.

"What did you see?" I whispered. "What happened to you?"

For a few seconds, all of the books went dead silent. I caught my breath. I wondered if maybe, possibly, they were going to answer me. If maybe there was something about me that the books knew, something I didn't know, something that would make it so that I could be a recipient of their secrets. *Could it be that easy?*

But then they erupted into more noise, so loud that I flinched away from the shelf that I'd been unconsciously leaning my ear toward. I darted out from between the rows as quickly as

I could go without running, the books hissing louder and louder behind me.

GambleGambleGambleWeKnowYouGambleDidYouGambleAreYou

I paused by the end of the stacks and listened to the books seethe with my name. I pressed my hand to my navel and made myself take slow, deep breaths, feeling the way my belly pushed against my palm with each inhalation. I made myself breathe through the panic as I listened to the rise and fall of the whispers coming from the Theoretical Magic section. It was a trick I hadn't used in years—a trick my high school guidance counselor had taught me when I told her that I got so angry that I wanted to throw up. She'd taught me how to find my way through what I thought was anger. It took me years to realize that she was actually teaching me how to find my way through fear.

I headed for the hallway when I could breathe again. I hated that fear. I hadn't felt it in so long. I hadn't felt it when I'd moved out of my parents' house to live on my own for the first time with no job and no degree. I hadn't felt it when my first client had pulled a gun on me. I hadn't even felt it a few days before, when that mugger ran at me with his knife pointed at my throat—but here, in the presence of magic?

I was back to being seventeen again, hyperventilating because everything was just Too Much.

I had my hand on the doorknob and was trying to decide how I could get out of that place without talking to anyone when I heard footsteps behind me. I whipped around, my heart pounding again already.

"Wait!" Rahul staggered out from behind the returns desk,

peeking over the top of a tall stack of wilting magazines. "Can you hold the door?"

I propped the door open with my foot and shoved everything that had happened that day into the brick-lined oubliette where I'd been tossing the rest of my feelings about this case. It took a little work to press everything down into there, but I managed it. So I was able to stop myself from asking how long he'd been there, whether he'd seen my panic. I pulled it together, slipped into the skin I'd worn for him before, the Ivy that never was.

I became her, and she smiled at him.

"Doing some light reading?" I said, relieving him of the top half of the stack.

"Oh, god, thank you for taking those." Rahul sighed. I booted the door open and walked beside him as he headed for his classroom. "And, you sort of made a pun but you didn't know it. And I don't really know how to reverse-engineer a pun. But, yeah, 'light reading.' My seniors are working on color theory."

I wrinkled my nose. I couldn't remember another time in my life when I'd wrinkled my nose to show that I was confused, but there I was, making a cute face at Rahul. "Color theory? Isn't that kind of basic?"

He looked at me askance. "Uh, no. It's really advanced. You have to change the property of the interaction of light with the molecules in the—" I rolled my eyes at him, and he laughed. "Okay, fair enough. You don't need to hear the whole lecture. But no, it's not usually in the 101 courses here. Were you in advanced classes in high school or something?"

"Wait, so what do the magazines have to do with the

properties of light?" My dodge was graceless, but the redirect still worked beautifully.

"It's the properties of the *interaction* of light, you can't actually change the properties of light itself. Or, well. I don't think you can. Tabitha might tell you something different." He gave a little half shrug as he used one elbow to shove on the handle of his classroom door, then held it open by standing in the doorway so I could squeeze by. I stopped as I passed in front of him, and for those two heartbeats, I forgot all about the secrets I'd found in the library and the horror of those books hissing my name. We were so close that I could see the end-of-the-day stubble coming in on Rahul's jaw. I wondered how it would feel against the soft skin on the inside of my wrist. Then I wondered how it would feel against the soft skin on the inside of my thigh.

And then a third heartbeat, and I was past him. I dropped the magazines on his desk and shook out my arms.

"Okay, so the properties of the interaction with light, then," I said, flipping open a battered old copy of a car-enthusiast magazine so I didn't have to make eye contact.

Rahul dropped his stack of magazines beside mine and started sorting them into piles. "The assignment is to pick out an ad or a photo spread and make it into a color negative of itself." I caught on to how he was sorting the magazines—by the dominant colors on the cover—and started sorting my own stack into his piles. He paused, watching me, then nodded. He didn't say anything to confirm that I was doing it right; he just accepted that we were on the same page. He trusted that I knew enough to be there.

"What do you mean by 'a color negative'?" I asked. "Doesn't a negative have to be black and white?"

"That's the fun part," he said. "The kids have to figure out what the opposite colors are in the picture, and then they have to figure out how to reverse them. That means they have to understand color theory, and the physics of light, and abstract pigmentalia, and focused applications of all of that stuff. It's a whole project. It'll last them about a month, and we'll wrap right before Spring Break so they don't have time to get antsy." He opened a copy of a nature magazine to a photo spread featuring a huge owl. It was a classic, big spectacle eyes and tufty horn-looking things. In the photo, it was in flight, clutching a doomed rodent in one set of talons.

Rahul glanced at me, which I probably wasn't supposed to notice. Then he placed his finger in the center of the owl's forehead. Slowly, like ink bleeding into water, the colors on the page began to shift. After thirty seconds, it was completely different—the browns had turned blue, and the yellows were purple, and I should have felt like my eyes were bleeding but the effect was actually kind of pretty. I leaned in closer and saw that every feather was shaded a slightly different color; he'd even maintained the little drop of blood that welled up under the owl's talons.

"A color negative," I murmured, tracing a fingertip over the owl's wing. "Okay. Cool."

"Yeah," Rahul said. I looked up and realized I'd leaned so close to him that we were nearly cheek to cheek. I felt myself flush as he grinned at me, his eyes flicking across my face. I saw him notice me biting my lip. "It's really cool."

I opened my mouth to say something that was going to be clever and charming and was certainly not just going to be me saying "cool" again like a trained cockatiel. But before I could say anything, the door to his classroom burst open. We startled away from each other as though we'd been doing what I can safely say we'd both been thinking of doing—as though it had been more than just magazines spread across that huge desk of his.

Alexandria DeCambray was framed in the doorway, one arm bracing the door open. There was no sunlight in the hallway or in the classroom, but her sun-blond hair glimmered regardless. She glanced around the room, her eyes barely landing on either of us.

"Can I help you with something, Alex?" Rahul said.

"It's *Alexandria*," she snapped, and I flinched as a wave of shame and fear battered me. "And no, I was just looking for Dylan. Have either of you seen him?"

"Mmmmmno," Rahul said. "But if I see him, I'll tell him you're looking for him."

"Don't bother," Alexandria said, every line of her face taut with irritation. "I'll find them eventually." She finally looked at Rahul, and on the way to him, her eyes snagged on me.

"Who else are you looking for?" I asked. She gave me a tight little fuck-off curl of the lip and left without answering me.

"Jesus," I muttered. "What was that?"

"Yeah, she's intense. You have no idea," Rahul said. "Both of them are."

"What's the story there?" I asked, raising my eyebrows, but he just shook his head.

"No story. There never is a story with her. I mean—it always seems like there *could* be a story, but she does damage control better than anyone I've ever seen. The hurricane always just misses her." His brow furrowed. "Or maybe it's more accurate to say that she always seems to be right in the eye of the hurricane. Which I guess would make Dylan the hurricane."

"Oh, yeah?" I went back to sorting magazines and hoped our hands might brush together again. They did, enough times that I wondered if maybe he was going out of his way to grab magazines that were closest to me.

"You heard about the graffiti thing, right?"

"Yeah, poor Samantha," I said.

"I mean, yeah, poor Samantha, but that's not the part of it that's stuck with me." He shook his head again. "They wanted me to try to fix the lockers, so I got a close-up view of the magic involved there. It's some of the most advanced spellcraft I've seen in a long time. And there's no way to prove that Alexandria's the one who did it, but we all know that it was her. They had a falling-out. With *extreme* prejudice."

"Is that how she can do that, uh. That thing?" I realized I still wasn't sure how to describe the rush of emotion that came with being around her, that made me want to just . . . *bend* in whatever direction she told me to. That made me feel like if I didn't bend, I'd break.

I'd call it a personal rule to never ascribe powers of manipulation and mind-control to teen girls—it's a line of thinking that rings a little too Humbert Humbert for my liking. So I didn't say anything about the floods of fear and shame and regret that I felt whenever I made Alexandria DeCambray angry. I didn't say anything about what I'd overheard earlier. I left it vague, and Rahul shrugged as he flipped through *Hounds Quarterly*. He traced his finger across every instance of the word "bitch," and the words vanished at his touch. He saw me looking.

"It's so they can't cut the word out and paste it on each other.
I've done this project every year since I was hired here—you learn
to think ahead on these things." He flipped past a spread of blood-
hounds running through a British-looking field. "Anyway, yeah.
Alexandria. I have no idea if she did that graffiti herself or if she
had help. But I can guarantee you that it was her idea."

I tossed a copy of *Mariner's Magazine* onto the blue pile. "How
do you figure?"

"Well, like I said, the falling-out was epic. And the other girls
in her group aren't really that vindictive. But Alexandria—well.
She's, uh. She doesn't pull punches." He suddenly seemed very absorbed in an article about coat glossiness in Afghan hounds.

"What's with the 'Alex' thing?" I asked, rescuing him from
whatever discomfort he was failing to hide.

"Hmm?" Rahul looked up from the magazine, but his eyes
were still distant. A crease had formed between his brows. I resisted the urge to smooth it with a fingertip.

"The 'Alex' thing," I repeated. "She gets really pissed if anyone
calls her that."

"Oh," he said. "That. Well, when she got to this school, she
went by Alex. I had her in my Intro to Phys class that year.
She was really different then." He opened a copy of *Teen Style*
to a picture of a girl. Her teeth made me think she was probably
a Disney star. Rahul traced his fingers across the page, and the
starlet's features shifted until she looked a bit like Alexandria.
"When she got here, she looked like that."

I realized that I was looking at his exact recollection of
Alexandria from four years ago. Her hair was brown, with
mistake-bangs, and she had crooked eyeteeth. She was smiling

a wide, excited, can-I-sit-with-you smile. Her uniform shirt was misbuttoned. Her face was younger, that on-the-cusp face that girls get when they're one summer away from coltish. She was pretty, sweet-looking. Her eyes weren't shuttered yet.

"Okay," I said. "She looked like that, and she went by Alex. And then?"

"Then something changed. Like, overnight, she was practically a different person." He sounded bewildered, but I knew exactly what he meant. Every girl I'd ever known had gone through a change-everything phase. Rearrange the bedroom, do an at-home dye kit, maybe a haircut. Learn to do makeup, start wearing hoop earrings. The hope—that fervent, please-God-let-it-work hope—was always that it would be like it was in the movies, where a girl has a big montage that involves eyebrow waxing and bursting out of a changing room wearing different outfits while a close friend nods or frowns. The hope was that everything would be new, and easy, and fixed. Or that everything would still be broken, but at least it would all go together and make sense.

I had gone through it myself, right after Mom died. It didn't help anything make sense. But it helped, somehow. It made it feel okay that I wasn't going to college, that I wasn't likely to join the FBI like I'd planned. That I would never become any of the things Mom had wanted me to be. That she wouldn't be there to even see.

"Alex DeCambray came back from Spring Break that year and she was blond, and her bangs had suddenly grown out, and she had all this . . . I don't know. Charisma. And she wanted to be called 'Alexandria,'" Rahul continued. "We've all tried to remember not to call her 'Alex,' but honestly, it's such a natural abbreviation that it just slips out sometimes."

"I get it, though," I said. "I get wanting to be someone new."

"Oh, yeah? Were you ever not-Ivy?" he asked, the beginnings of a joke in his voice.

"Yeah," I said. I tried to say it light, easy, but it was too heavy. The weight of it pulled the conversation down. "I was not-Ivy for a long time."

I held my breath while the silence pulled itself out between us like taffy. Finally, Rahul bit his lip and closed the magazine. He didn't look at me.

"I was going to give her a B-minus last year. She didn't do well on this project." He tapped the piles of magazines. "I normally grade for effort as well as execution, because I'm a total softie. And I know she can do colors without even thinking about it. I mean . . . well. You've seen her hair, right?" I nodded. "Alexandria maintains that all day, every day, even when she's taking tests. So, she can handle color. I knew that she did poorly on the project because she hadn't wanted to put the effort in, and I told her so. I said I'd pass her effort with a D-plus. But this is a pretty big project, so the D-plus would have brought her cumulative grade down from an A-minus to a B-minus. And I don't grade on a curve, so—"

"Um, Rahul—?"

"Right, I know, that's not the important part. I just." He closed his eyes. "I just don't want to talk about the next part."

I put my hand on his and gave it a squeeze.

This isn't a story about things I'm proud of, and I said I would tell the truth. I didn't put my hand on his because I wanted to comfort him. It was because I could tell that he was about to give me something, and I wanted it. I wanted to know about Alexandria and the thing she'd done. I wanted to feel like I'd gotten the scoop, like I was doing *real detective* work. So I squeezed his big, callused hand, and I caught his eye, and I tried to look gentle and nonjudgmental and receptive.

And it worked.

Rahul took a big breath. He looked at me. Heat rose in my cheeks when his eyes caught mine, and I clenched my stomach like a fist around the first tremblings of guilt. I told myself that I wasn't actually manipulating him. *I'm just listening. I'm a good listener.*

"Okay," he said, more to himself than to me. "So, she showed up in my classroom at the end of the day. I think she actually watched for everyone to start leaving. She said she'd forgotten something and needed to look for it. Once everyone else had cleared out, she came up to me and said that if I didn't raise her grade, she'd go to Torres. She said that she'd tell Torres I was writing theory essays and selling them to my students."

He looked queasy. I squeezed his hand again, and this time, it was true.

"What did you do?" I whispered. He rubbed his thumb across my knuckle.

"I reported her. Immediately. I went to Torres and told her the whole thing. She believed me, thank God. Alexandria was called into the office and denied it, of course, but it was enough to scare her off. She didn't try to blackmail me again. She took the D-plus.

I thought it was over, you know? I figured we were even. But then, a few months later? I went out to my car after work and . . . and it had been smashed."

"The windows?"

Rahul cleared his throat. "The whole car. It had been turned into glass, and then shattered. Probably with a vibration-key spell."

"Holy shit," I said. "She can do that?"

He shrugged. "Someone can. And it didn't quite feel like a coincidence, you know? Vibration-key spells are . . . well, you know how rare they are. Whoever did that to my car was flexing, I think. Making sure I knew what they were capable of. And the craziest part is, she waited a few months so the administration couldn't directly tie it to the incident."

I didn't know what to say, so I settled for another hand squeeze. He sighed, then looked at me in that way people do when they want to be done sharing hard feelings.

"Anyway, that was the end of the school year last year, and when we came back this year? She had a different teacher for Advanced Phys, and she didn't so much as blink at me funny when she asked if I had a nice summer."

"Damn," I said.

"Yeah," he said. We were quiet for a few minutes, because "damn" and "yeah" pretty much encompassed the breadth of what we could say on the matter. The only sound was the rustle of magazine pages as we continued sorting. When all of the piles were settled, Rahul snapped his fingers; the stacks nudged themselves into neat, well-aligned rectangles of glossy color.

He cleared his throat and looked at me. "Just for the record," he said, "I didn't sell theory papers to any students."

"I figured."

"But like . . . I really didn't. Tabitha has charms that detect cheating. And. I wouldn't do that."

I laughed. "I *know*, dummy." He breathed a laugh, relief caught in the crinkles around his eyes.

He let go of my hand and ran his fingers nervously along the edges of the stack of green magazines. "So, hey, I was thinking. If you're not doing anything tonight, would you maybe want to have dinner again? Um, together?" Rahul flushed around the edges of his hairline, but soldiered bravely on. "I just got a huge batch of fresh scallops. I guess I must have . . . I must have accidentally asked for like, twice as many as I needed. And I have to use them within the next couple of days. I thought maybe I could cook them for the two of us. If you want."

I rode a brief but extreme emotional roller coaster as I imagined dinner at his place, and then breakfast at his place, and everything in between the two—and then as I remembered that Tabitha had already asked me to get drinks with her. I kicked myself hard for saying yes to my sister. "Oh, man," I said, "I would love to, but I have plans tonight."

"Tomorrow, maybe?"

I hesitated. A second date would make this into more than a fun, easy flirtation. I should have hesitated more. But it was right there: a second date with someone who thought I was enough. "Yeah. Tomorrow."

"Okay, great!" He was trying so hard not to look relieved that

I couldn't hold in a bubble of laughter. "I'll, uh, well. I was going to say that I'd text you my address, but you don't really need it, since we're neighbors and all."

I smiled. "I'll bring a bottle of wine. I can't wait."

Neither of us could figure out what to say, so we just stared at each other—*okay, we're doing this.* After a minute of this, we both decided to break the tension.

I broke it by laughing that other-Ivy laugh, bubbling and bright and strange.

He broke it by leaning across his desk to kiss me.

Magazines scattered as he braced himself against the surface, his careful piles sliding off the edge of the desk and onto the floor. A large stack fell onto my feet, slapping against my shins. Rahul put his hand on my waist and the corner of a magazine dug painfully into my hip as he pulled me across the desk. Our teeth bumped.

It was perfect. For a minute—just one, just long enough for me to close my teeth around his lower lip—I forgot about the whispers in the library and the lie of who he thought Ivy Gamble was and the bloodstain on the carpet and the students who may have committed murder. For that minute, the only thing making my heart pound was Rahul's breath, whispering its way over the top of my tongue.

For just that one minute, everything was okay.

CHAPTER

TWENTY

TABITHA PICKED THROUGH THE NEARLY empty popcorn basket on the table between us, sorting the half-popped kernels from unpopped ones. The bar was busier this time than it had been the Friday before, but Tabitha had imposed a pocket of quiet—an invisible bubble of calm that made it so we could hear the awkward silences that occasionally bloomed between us. The waiter was a hulking blond guy who looked like he commuted to the bar from his home in Valhalla. His forearms rippled with unnecessary muscles as he took our empty glasses and deposited full ones. Tabitha eyed her new drink skeptically. "Did we order these?"

"I don't think so," I said, "but it's possible." We were both just drunk enough that it was completely within the realm of possibility that we'd ordered the drinks and forgotten about them in the time it took the waiter to fetch them for us. Tabitha stuck a finger into her cocktail, turning the drink an offensively bright shade of pink.

"What'd you just do?" I asked around a mouthful of half-popped popcorn kernels.

"I turned it pink," she said.

"Why?"

She shrugged. "So it'll be pink."

I sipped my drink—which was not pink—and realized I couldn't taste the alcohol in it anymore. I tried to gauge internally how drunk I was, and compared it to how drunk I needed to be in order to get through the night without bursting into either tears or inappropriate laughter, or both. I calculated that I still had a long way to go.

"Hey, do you have a hangover cure?" I asked.

"Yeah, a big drippy cheeseburger and like . . . a liter of red Gatorade," Tabitha mumbled, licking the tip of her finger and using it to pick up popcorn crumbs. I rolled my eyes.

"No, come on, you know what I mean. I want a *magic* one."

She stuck her crumb-finger into her mouth, shaking her head. "S'different for everyone," she said. "I mean, are we talking about a whiskey hangover or a tequila hangover? Do you get headaches or nausea or . . . ?" She giggled in a very un-Tabitha way, then did a spooky-ghost voice. "Or *the poooops*?"

"Oh, god," I said. "I'm not answering that question."

"Then I can't help you," she said, smothering a laugh with a fistful of half-popped kernels.

We'd spent the last two hours like this—getting steadily, intently drunk as we felt our way through conversation about things we'd spent our lives *not* discussing. So far we'd covered politics (we felt the same), religion (we felt very differently), and sports (neither of us felt anything). I kept wanting to find some exact revelation that would make us sisters again, that would prove that everything was fixed. I wanted something to wrap up our lost years in a nice tidy packet and deposit them in a basket. It kept being not-quite right, though. It kept feeling like small talk.

"I don't get it," I said testily. "You have a way to make dick-clouds and go invisible and spot plagiarism on essays and, and . . . and *cure the common cold* probably, but you don't have a way to fix a hangover?"

Tabitha shrugged again, then knit her brow. "Wait, how do you know about the cheating thing?" She looked at me and burst into laughter, loud enough that Thor looked over at us from behind the bar. "Ivy, you're *magenta*."

"I am not!" I was.

Tabitha dipped her fingers into her water glass and flicked them at me. "How do you know about the cheating thing? Tell me, or I'll douse you." Her fingers hovered threateningly over her glass.

"Fine!" I said. *She was teasing me.* "Rahul told me."

"What? I can't hear you when you have your hands over your face like that."

I took a long sip of my drink, choked on it, coughed. Took a smaller sip. "Rahul told me," I said again, then bit my lip to keep from smiling. It was a real smile—not the smile that belonged to the Ivy I'd been pretending to be. A smile that belonged to the Ivy whose sister cared enough to press for more information.

She smirked. "Oh, did he now?" I sucked my lips in and her smile grew wider. "When did *Rahul* tell you?"

I let myself have the smile, let myself sink into the moment—just deep enough to enjoy it. Not deep enough to tell her more about Rahul. Not deep enough to let her find out that the person he liked was a lie. "Come on, I answered you, now you've gotta answer me. How does the cheating thing work?" Tabitha rolled her eyes at me, but it worked. It was just enough of a push to tip her away from small talk, into telling me about her work. About her life. About who she *was*.

If I'd understood any of what she was saying, I'm sure it would have been fascinating—she used the word "interweaving" a lot. I took the opportunity to watch her. I'd never seen her talk about her magic before, not like this. I'd always stormed out of the room or tuned out when she talked about it before. I'd always tried to send a very clear message: *I don't want to know about this.*

I realized now that when she talked about magic, her entire face lit up. She became animated. She grabbed saltshakers off neighboring tables to illustrate the ways that different bits of a spell interacted. She wandered down little side-paths of theorems and applications, then found her way back to what she'd been trying to say. "You see, Bressom thought that paper didn't have a memory, but then DeWitt decided to try a little experiment with *tree* memory . . ." and off she went, telling me about trees and how the bark remembers everything that's ever touched it.

"Do you think that has anything to do with the books in the library?" I interrupted, and she gave me a long look that I couldn't quite decipher.

Finally, she shook her head. "Nah." Then she went back to talking about Bressom and DeWitt, and their lifelong feud, and their dueling publication schedules.

"Okay, uncle!" I said, slapping my hand on the table. "I give up. Can you just give me the dummy version? The preschooler version?"

She chewed on her straw, a habit I remembered setting my teeth on edge when we were kids. "Um, sure. So, uh, the test looks into the contraliminal properties of the essay and compares them to the untegruous quality of the core subject matter, and—"

I dipped my fingers into my water and flicked them at her. "You know what? Never mind."

The water steamed off her skin in little puffs of vapor, and she bared her teeth at me in a hard grin. "So, how's the case going?"

"Good, I guess," I said with a shrug. "I mean . . . I've only been on the job for a week or so, but I think I've got some pretty good leads."

Tabitha raised her eyebrows at me. "Has it really only been a week?"

"Yeah, I know."

"So it's going well, then."

I shrugged again. "I don't know, Tab. This is my first murder case. I don't know if I'm supposed to have it wrapped up by now, or if I should just be scratching the surface." I fiddled with my straw. "I don't know if I'm actually any good at this."

She reached across the table and grabbed my hand. I almost drew away in surprise, but caught myself in time. Her fingers were cool and dry. I was reminded powerfully of the way my mother used to hold my hand, before I was old enough to cringe away and tell her I was too old for hand-holding. "Hey, of course you're good at this," she said. "You've been doing this for . . . um, how long have you been doing this for?"

"Fourteen years," I said. "Wow, holy shit, fourteen years. That's a long time."

"Damn." She grinned at me. "You've been doing this longer than I've been teaching, and I've got tenure. So you can't be all *that* bad at it, right?"

I gave her fingers a squeeze. "Well, okay, yes. I'm very good at following adulterous husbands and tracking down insurance scammers. But this is a whole different ball game."

"I have complete faith in you," she said. Her eyes were locked on mine. I realized I didn't mind the way she changed them with her magic. It wasn't so bad, if I just let go of the resentment I'd been clinging to for so long. If I did that, it felt less like looking into a flawed mirror, and more like looking at my sister. She bit her lip, then nodded, like she'd decided something. "I was wrong."

"What—?"

"I was wrong," she said again. "I should have introduced you to Sylvia. Back when we were together. She would have loved you." She picked at her fingernails without looking at them. "She was a lot like you, back before she was dying."

"She was dying?" I thought back to Sylvia's file and remembered that she'd taken a couple of days off right before she died. Tabitha's eyes went round for a moment, briefer than imagining.

"Before she died, I mean," Tabitha said it fast. I wondered if it was hard for her to get the words out, the way it was for me right after Mom died. "She was a lot like you, before she *died*. I think you two would have gotten along like gangbusters. And I know she would have agreed with me that you're a better detective than you give yourself credit for."

"Thanks," I said, and I meant a lot more than that but didn't know how to say it, so I decided to do what I'm best at. I decided to dodge. "Anyway, I might be good, but I haven't learned any magical tests to spot fraudulent insurance claims. Yet."

She ducked her head. "It's really a cool test. I, um." She glanced up at me, bashful. "I invented it."

I stared at her. "Tabitha. Now *you're* blushing."

"So?"

"So, you usually hide it from me when you blush. With . . ." I waved my hands at her face, making wiggly fingers that were intended to convey the contraliminal whatsit of whatever.

The tiniest smile I'd ever seen tucked itself into the very corners of her mouth. "Yeah, well. I thought maybe I'd try not hiding for a change." I didn't know what to say—it felt like she'd spotted my attempt to get out of the conversation and had used my own momentum to flip me onto my back. Fortunately, the waiter intervened by bringing us another round of drinks and popcorn. "Hang on!" I said, not quite grabbing his arm. "I know for sure we didn't order these!"

He flashed his teeth at me and winked. "They're on the house, kiddo."

As he walked away, Tabitha and I clutched at each other across the table.

"Oh my god," she whispered, her eyes wide and delighted.

"Oh my *god*," I whispered back, and we both failed to keep our laughter silent.

"You should go for it," she said. I shook my head and traced my finger through the condensation on our table. "Come on! He's cute, and I bet it's been awhi— Ow!" She rubbed her shin under the table.

"No," I said in an even tone, "I think I'm all set."

"Are things that serious with Rahul?" I flicked more water at her, and she cackled at me, not giving ground.

"Things aren't serious, I don't know. I like him. There's something there."

"Ooooh, *something*," Tabitha teased. "Come on, you've gotta give me better details than that. When did he tell you about the cheat-detection spell?"

The thought *you probably shouldn't tell her about this* wandered through my mind and smashed into *you're pretty drunk* and *fuck it*. Only *fuck it* survived the collision.

"He mentioned it earlier today. Before we made out." We did some more giggling, and it occurred to me that neither of us was the giggling kind. This was a performance we were putting on for each other. It was a shadow play of female camaraderie. I found that I didn't mind so much, as long as we were both pretending together.

"What were you talking about that made my little test come up?" she asked.

"Oh, he was telling me about Alexandria DeCambray," I said.

Tabitha raised her eyebrows at me over her straw. "Is she a suspect?" She was still trying to keep up the performance, but her voice was a shade too sharp.

I shrugged. "Who knows? I mean, she's just a kid. But he was telling me about this thing that happened with her last year." I told her the story he'd shared with me—about Alexandria's ambition, and her threat. When I mentioned Rahul's shattered car, Tabitha's face went grave. "What? What's that face for?" She shook her head, but I pressed her. "C'mon, tell me."

"It's nothing," she said.

"Tabby," I said, a little sad. "You can tell me. Honest." I wanted her to confide in me so badly just then. I wanted us to share something, some secret, like the time in second grade I'd helped her bury the shards of Mom's favorite mug in the backyard. We'd both spit in the dirt to make it a forever-pact, because we were both too chicken to do a blood-pact. I wanted that again; I wanted us to be *together* in whatever it was that she knew.

"It's just . . . well. It's just something Sylvia told me about Alexandria."

I leaned forward in my chair. The room tilted a bit, and I leaned back again. *I should drink some water,* I thought as I took another sip of my cocktail. "What is it?"

"I hesitate to bring it up, because it's from right befor—" she said. "Sylvia said that she was . . . worried."

"Worried?" I said. "Or scared?"

Tabitha made a scrunch-mouthed face. "Well, I guess Alexandria needed something. A potion." She looked around, making sure no one could hear. She was reminding me of someone, but I couldn't place who. She leaned in, sotto voce: "She needed an *abortion* potion."

I nodded and answered, my voice too loud, "Yeah, I know. It wasn't for her."

Tabitha frowned, then nudged my water glass toward me. I drained it, thinking, *What a good sister.* It was the first time I'd ever thought that about her.

"Right, okay. So, then you know that she didn't get it."

I chewed on a piece of ice. "Yeah?"

"Yeah," Tabitha continued. "She didn't get it, because her friend was too far gone for the potion to work. Ten weeks. Sylvia said no. She told Alexandria that the potion wouldn't work after ten weeks."

"Oh, shit," I said, remembering Mrs. Webb's finger prodding my shoulder. *That's surgical.*

"Anyway, I guess Alexandria wanted the potion. She thought Sylvia was saying no because of some moral objection. Sylvia told me that Alexandria showed up in her office and started making threats, saying that she was going to tell everyone that she'd seen us together if Sylvia didn't hand over the potion." Tabitha looked uncomfortable, glanced around again. A brief image of Courtney doing the same thing in the library flashed through my mind, too fast for me to hold on to. "Osthorne has a strict policy about staff fraternization. We would both have gotten fired. I would have lost my tenure and my professional reputation. Sylvia probably wouldn't have been able to work in a school ever again."

"I think . . . I think I knew that," I said, squinting at my empty water glass. Tabitha stuck her finger into her own glass before pushing it across the table. I downed it before checking to see what color she'd turned it. It was clear, but just a little bitter. Too much gin fuzzing my taste buds.

"But Sylvia still said no," Tabitha continued, as if I hadn't interrupted her. "She said that it was just plain too late in the pregnancy. She said that it would endanger the pregnant student to take the potion. Alexandria insisted. She can be . . . forceful, but I guess Sylvia told her she absolutely wouldn't budge. We were getting ready to tell Torres about our relationship—but then." My sister didn't fill in the rest of the sentence.

"So Sylvia said there was no way she was going to hand over the potion?" Something about this wasn't fitting right, but I

couldn't quite remember. All of the interviews I'd done ran together, muddy in my drunk memory.

"Sylvia would never do anything to endanger a student, even
if it meant risking both of our careers," Tabitha said. "So, yeah,
she said *absolutely not* about the potion. I thought of it right away
when you told me about what happened with Rahul. It's just
that . . . well, it's probably nothing," Tabitha said, and I frowned
at her. "Okay, fine! Fine. I just didn't know about the last part of
the Rahul thing, and it seems." Eyebrows. "Well. Strange. That
the last time Alexandria DeCambray blackmailed a teacher and
didn't get her way, she got aggressive. And then she tried to blackmail Sylvia and didn't get her way, and now . . . Sylvia's dead."

The words sent a snap of clarity through my mind. "Say that
again?"

"I said, it seems strange that the last time Alexandria De-
Cambray blackmailed a teacher and didn't get her way, *she got
aggressive.*" Her voice seemed to echo, and I realized that I was
leaning across the table, staring into her eyes. I shook my head.

"I'm sorry, Tabby, I think I have to call it a night. I didn't mean
to get this drunk." I didn't feel woozy anymore, but I felt caught
in the strangest sensation. It was like I'd been hearing double.
Tabitha just patted my hand.

"No worries, kiddo. I've got an early morning tomorrow
anyway."

I pressed against my temples with both palms—my head was
ringing. Not my ears—my whole head. Like a tuning fork. *How
much did I have to drink?* "That's right, it's Wednesday." The word
"Wednesday" seemed to have so many syllables in it, and I wasn't
sure I'd gotten them in the right order. My mouth was full of

cotton. "Wensdenay. *Wesndesnay.* Oh my god, wait, it's *Wesndes-day!* Are you going to be okay tomorrow?"

"I'll be fine," she said, tapping her glass. It suddenly refilled with water. She stirred it with her finger, and I thought I saw two glasses separate and then merge. *Shit,* I thought, *I'm wasted.* "I have a high tolerance," she continued, then drank her water with what felt like superhuman speed. "Let's get you in a cab, huh? And remember: cheeseburger, liter of Gatorade." She winked at me as she pulled out her phone. "Works like magic."

The cab ride back to Osthorne was strange. I told the driver I had a migraine—it was the closest thing to the truth I could find. I didn't feel properly drunk, but something in my head felt . . . wrong. *Did that waiter slip me something?* I wondered. I thought back to high school, senior year, when I'd snuck out of the house to attend a concert and wound up getting rescued by the bouncer. He'd seen someone drop something into my drink, and so he'd put me into a cab with one of my female friends. She'd told me later that she had spent the night taking care of me, shaking at the thought of what could have happened to me. I couldn't remember how it had felt—couldn't remember anything until the next morning, waking up on her bedroom floor with a raging headache and a wide, blank swath cut through my memory. *Had it been like this?* My head felt clear, but it was like a swarm of hornets was humming inside my skull.

I was so thankful that Tabitha was there for me this time. So thankful that it didn't occur to me to wonder why she didn't share the cab with me, where she'd gone—all that mattered was that she had been there, taking care of me, handing me water.

I got back to the school, paid the cab driver. Overtipped him because I couldn't focus on counting out the bills properly. I stumbled across the grounds, missed the keyhole of my apartment door three times. My pants tangled around my ankles as I stripped on my way to the couch. I lay in the dark, staring at the ceiling and wondering if I was okay. Sleep wouldn't come. My brain felt swollen, itchy.

Finally, I got up off the couch, letting the duvet fall to the floor. I wandered into the bedroom, my feet feeling very far from my legs. I sat on the floor, my back against the mattress, and opened the journal.

I'm so close. I'm almost there. But with the news, it feels like there's no time. I have to work harder. If I just work hard enough, I can do it. I can save her.

I sat up drinking glasses of water, then tea; as the sun began to lighten the sky, I switched over to coffee. The journal entries went from coherent to intense to manic. They focused on the same spell, the same equations over and over. They were desperate. *I feel like I can bend my own feelings about this if I just apply the right angle of Theoretical Alkalinity, or maybe I should apply something closer to a clouds-in-water method? If I can just remove the emotional aspect I know I can eliminate fatigue, and if I can do that then I can work hard enough, I just need to work hard enough how can I work hard enough*

I pulled my notebook out of my bag and started taking notes, scrawling interlocking circles and drawing lines between names and dates. I scribbled page after page, trying to capture everything that Rahul and Alexandria and Courtney and Mrs. Webb and Tabitha had told me—everything I knew about Osthorne, everything I knew about the case, everything I knew about Sylvia. But it didn't scratch the itch.

I don't know when I started writing on the wall. Not the wall itself, of course—that would be crazy. I wasn't going crazy. I was still fine. But the letters—I annotated them, marking down the connections I suddenly understood. The connections that now made sense. I tore pages out of my notebook and added them to the margins of the letters, drew lines from my notes to parts of the diary. It was coming together. It was really coming together. I mapped the connections between everyone, drawing a spider-web that spread across multiple walls. In the center of the web was that single bold phrase: *It was positive.*

In the space above and below those words, I marked the center of the spiderweb—the names of the two people who this whole case came down to: Dylan and Alexandria DeCambray.

As soon as I finished writing their names down, the ringing sensation in my skull faded away. It left exhaustion in its wake.

I stared at the pages strewn across my coffee table, flinching as the seven o'clock wake-up alarm on my phone went off. I turned the alarm off. It was over—whatever scrabbling creature had climbed into my brain was dead, and a steady wave of fatigue bloomed around its corpse. I turned my phone off and climbed onto the mattress, curling up in the center of it with the journal clasped to my chest. Sleep steamrolled me, and I sank into the dark like drowning.

CHAPTER

TWENTY-ONE

WHEN I WOKE LATE THAT morning, the sense of clarity I'd had the night before started to slip. I felt off-center. Something had slid out of alignment in the night. I looked at my notes on the wall, the connections I'd drawn, the notes and marginalia. It made sense in the same way that the whispers in the library made sense—there was something there, just out of the corner of my eye, that I knew would tie it all together. My memories of the frenzied hours of note-taking were slipping away from me like sand eroding out from under my feet at the beach, every hour a lapping wave that eased the details away grain by grain. By noon, all that was left was a masturbatory sense of shame and urgency. The clarity was gone.

I had to get it back.

I needed to be out of that bedroom, away from the wall. Away from the bare mattress. Away from the journal and the letters. Especially those. I felt certain that if I could get away from them for just a little while, I could find the thing I'd had a hold on the night before.

I ordered takeout, then spread out all of the case-related files on the living room floor. I spent the afternoon eating mediocre pad thai and reviewing everyone's stories, even though I already knew them like a tongue knows the backsides of teeth. I reread my notes on my interview with Mrs. Webb, with Dylan. I wrote the words "WHY THE LIBRARY" in capital letters at the top of a notepad, and then failed to write anything else after that. I stared at the pictures of Sylvia's body until I saw her whenever I closed my eyes. I couldn't reconcile her staff photo with the journal with the crime scene pictures—she was so smiling and ethereal in the photo, so obsessive in her words, so heavy in death. It was as though she'd suddenly solidified, and in doing so, died.

I realized that I didn't know anything about her. Not really. She was secondary to the case. I wondered if murder cases were always like that. Whenever I was tracking down an adulterer or following a dad who was behind on his child support payments, the person at the center of the case was also the one I spent all my time thinking about. But this was different. I hadn't thought about Sylvia nearly as much as I'd thought about Courtney, and Dylan, and Mrs. Webb.

I grabbed Courtney's school file, which Mrs. Webb had given me a few days before with strict instructions not to lose, damage, or copy any part of it. It was totally unremarkable. Everything there lined up well enough with what I would have expected of an upper-middle-class private-school girl—a couple of infractions for sneaking out, suspected drinking, fraternization with boys, decent grades. There was a referral from a guidance counselor, who recommended her for the same are-you-eating monitoring that Brea got; there was a letter from Courtney's mother stapled to it, saying that she didn't need the monitoring.

Dylan's file, obtained the same way, was much thicker. It was full of reprimands and detentions and notes from his teachers on how promising-yet-troubled he was. There was an essay, flagged for administrative review, that briefly mentioned thoughts of self-harm. There were no notes on follow-up. There were his notes from the same guidance counselor, who was concerned about his "self-aggrandizing fantasies of a widespread conspiracy" and his obsession with the Prophecy. It was nothing special, nothing surprising. He was a Jell-O mold of a teenage boy, and he had tried to fill himself up with purpose but it just wouldn't *set*.

If I'd been in high school at the same time as Dylan, I thought, I would have adored him. I would have thought he was way ahead of me. I had been lost too, and I would have been drawn to his intensity like a wasp to a spilled puddle of Coke. Did it say something about the person I'd become that I felt something between pity and disgust when I looked through his file? Did it mean I'd grown?

I wondered what they would have thought of high school Ivy. Would I have been friends with any of these kids, or would I have floated along alone, forming only the briefest of alliances and counting down the days until I could escape everyone? If I'd been magic, if I'd gone to Osthorne, or even to Headley with Tabitha, would things have been different? Would I have been able to deal with my mother's death the same way Tabitha had?

I sighed, rubbing my eyes, and tossed Dylan's file down. It had been the last in the pile. I grabbed the stack of papers and flipped it upside down, so Mrs. Webb's file was back on top. I picked it up, flipped it open, and started again from the beginning.

—

I woke up to the sound of my phone buzzing a few inches away from my ear. I startled, then slapped at my face. A Post-it note fell off—it had gotten stuck there while I was sleeping, curled up on the floor of the living room in the middle of a nest of notes and files. I had no idea what time it was, but it was already dark outside. *Jesus, Ivy,* I thought, *you're a mess.* I resolved to go to sleep at a decent hour that night. And to take a shower. And to eat something other than slowly congealing takeout Thai.

I splashed water on my face in the little bathroom, squinting at the thin sunlight that streamed through the tiny casement window. I stared at myself hard in the mirror. I looked old, but I wasn't sure if I looked older than I had at the start of this case, or if I just looked older than the high school version of myself I'd been dreaming about. In my dream, I'd been trying to talk to Alexandria DeCambray. She'd been taking pictures of me as I tried to tell her that I was in love with Sylvia, that she had to stop threatening her. Alexandria had been laughing and showing me the pictures; in the dream, my eyes were rimmed with the fat black crayon-eyeliner I'd worn throughout eleventh grade.

"Okay," I said aloud, gearing up to give myself a pep talk—but then I stopped, feeling weird about talking to myself. I stared into the sink for a minute or two, taking deep breaths, avoiding the mirror. "Okay," I said again, and that time it felt like all I needed to say.

When I walked back out into the living room, my phone was buzzing again. There were six text messages waiting for me. One was from my dad—he'd seen a comic strip in the paper that morning featuring a penguin who was dressed as a detective, and he'd sent me a blurry picture of it.

The other five were from Rahul.

Hey, how's i

Lol sorry, I hit send by accident. Hows it going

Okay well now the casual thing isn't going to work the way I thought it would but anyway I was wondering if we're still on for dynamite

*dinner tonight?

The last one included his unit number, just in case. I nearly choked when I saw the timestamp: 6:30 p.m. *Shit.*

I ran a hand through my hair, and it came away greasy. I was suddenly very aware that I could smell my own breath, and it smelled a lot like the cold, day-old fried tofu I'd eaten for dinner. I needed a shower, and I needed to sleep for the rest of the day, and I needed to eat some vegetables. I composed five different text messages turning him down, deleting each one before it was finished. Finally, swearing at myself, I hit SEND.

I can't wait for those scallops. See you at seven?

I went back into the bathroom to shower, dodging the mirror again. The Ivy I was—the half-feral detective with the perpetual hangover, covered in ink smudges, devoid of magic—that wasn't the Ivy Rahul deserved. That wasn't an Ivy anyone could want. And that wasn't the Ivy I was going to be tonight.

I was going to bring him someone different. Someone worthwhile. I cranked the water as hot as it would go and waited for the steam to turn me into the person I was supposed to be.

No, NO, NO WAY!" I laughed loudly enough that Rahul's enormous gray cat, Alphabet, jumped off my lap. I stretched my legs—she'd been ensconced on my thighs for well over an hour, ever since we'd finished eating and moved to the couch. My feet had both gone tingly.

"I swear to God," Rahul said, "I couldn't make it up."

"What did you do?"

He tucked his shoulders up around his ears, his eyes wide. "What was I supposed to do? I gave him the bathroom pass and told him to tie his sweater around his waist."

Alphabet rubbed her head against his ankles, and Rahul leaned down absently to scratch her behind the ears. His shirt rode up over his side, and my mouth went dry at the stretch of skin that was revealed.

"I'm so glad I'm not interviewing *that* kid," I said, tracing the seams on the couch so I wouldn't reach out and touch the place where the taut skin of his stomach disappeared into his jeans. "I wouldn't be able to look him in the eye."

"Ah, he's alright," Rahul said, stirring an unconscionable amount of sugar into his after-dinner coffee. "He's just, you know. A teenage boy. Not that I was ever like that, but you know. Lots of boys are. Probably." He took a sip of coffee, grimaced, and added more sugar. "So, can you tell me who you *are* interviewing? Or is that like . . . confidential?"

I was more than a little intoxicated by the way he leaned toward me from the opposite end of his couch, watching me with rapt attention. It wasn't an I'm-going-to-kiss-you-now lean; it was an I-can't-wait-to-hear-what-you-think lean. *This is what it feels like to do work that people want to hear about,* I thought.

I was used to people asking uncomfortable questions about my job. Everyone always wanted to know whether I had naked photos of politicians, whether I had ever touched a dead body. Whether I had secret cameras and microphones. They were the kinds of questions that were never really about the work—the kinds of questions that told me way too much about the people who asked them. The questions Rahul was asking about this murder case were more . . . wholesome, somehow. I finally had something going on that wasn't just seedy—it was intriguing, captivating. *This is what it feels like to be a* real *detective.*

So I barely hesitated. "Well, technically I probably shouldn't tell you, but—"

He held up a hand. "Then don't tell me. I can't keep a secret to save my life." He smiled at me, and I hated how badly I wanted to tell him which students I was looking at most closely. How much I would have told him, even though I knew it was a bad idea. "Is there anything you could tell me that wouldn't be ethically weird?"

I flipped through the case in my mind—it was all right there at the surface, the result of my two-day case data binge. "Um . . . shoot. I don't think so. There's a lot of information, but it's all in play right now. I don't know what's going to turn out to be important, you know?"

"Too bad." He winked at me and refilled my wineglass, which was only about half-empty.

"Are you trying to get me drunk?" I said, trying to be twinkly and charming so he knew I didn't mean it.

He still frowned. "I would never," he said gravely.

"I know," I whispered with a wink that didn't belong to me. "I'm making fun of you."

"Oh, thank God," he laughed. "I'm sorry. I know I get too serious sometimes, I just. You know. I'm not that kind of guy, and . . . I'd hope that would be a deal-breaker for you. Not that it has to be—oh, god, I'm overthinking this so much, aren't I?"

We both laughed, and I felt a flutter of excitement. A deal-breaker, he'd said, which meant there was a deal. We were a deal. It had been an embarrassingly long time since I'd felt like I was going to be a deal with someone. I couldn't remember the last time that anyone had made me feel so *excited* about being a deal.

It was that excitement that had stopped me from flaking on the dinner date, even though there hadn't been nearly enough time for me to polish the tarnish off myself. I'd arrived late, my hair still wet, feeling uncertain that I'd know how to pass as a sane person. He'd greeted me with a cold glass of crisp white wine and asked if I minded taking my shoes off. Then he'd given me the smallest, sweetest, chin-cuppingest kiss in the four seconds before a timer started going off in the kitchen. He'd shouted for me to watch out for Alphabet before disappearing around a corner, leaving me to meet the giant gray cat and take my shoes off and touch my lips with the tips of my fingers, wondering if this was for real.

It almost felt like it was for real.

Dinner had been perfect. The scallops had been fresh and buttery, and I'd made a sound when I ate the first one that had made Rahul turn very red. When I'd expressed amazement at the fact that they hadn't spoiled at all in the three days since he'd bought them, he'd looked bashful. "Actually," he'd said, "I got Tabitha to cast an entropy-delay cosper on them. Don't tell anyone—I think those are pretty strictly regulated. I'm not totally up on cosper law, though—"

"I promise not to tell anyone," I'd laughed. "But only if you promise to make me these scallops again every day for the rest of my life."

He'd bitten his lip, and I'd turned very red myself, which made us even.

After dinner, he'd cleared our plates, and I'd followed Alphabet to the living room. It was tidy, but not spare—not bachelor-y. There were pictures of him and people who looked like his family scattered among the half-dead potted plants; I'd inspected them as I kneaded my toes down into a huge knotty woven rug in a dozen different colors. In one picture there was an older woman with Rahul's nose and eyes, and a young woman with his smile laughing at both of them. Mom and sister, maybe. Another picture with someone who he told me was his ex-boyfriend, now his best friend, an amicable breakup that had turned into something like brotherhood. I wondered when I'd get to meet them, then scolded myself for assuming I'd get to meet them, then allowed myself a sweet wafer of hope—it could happen. *This might happen, Ivy.*

I'd also explored Rahul's bookshelves, crammed with books of every genre and profoundly disorganized. I had leaned my ear up against the shelf to see if the books had anything to tell me about Rahul, but the only thing I'd heard was Alphabet, yowling from the couch until I sat down and relented to her inspection. By the time Rahul had joined me, I was blanketed in cat hair and my fillings were rattling with the intensity of the purring.

It wasn't until Alphabet finally got *off* my lap that I realized how long Rahul and I been sitting there, just talking. He was still looking at me with that I-can't-wait-to-hear-you glow in his eyes, and I wanted to tell him everything, and I wanted to kiss him, and I wanted to wrap my legs around his waist and trap him against me until the sky turned gray at dawn.

But then Alphabet returned to my lap and started kneading my legs, and her tail brushed under my nose, and when I looked back up at Rahul he was laughing at me.

I rolled my eyes, *what can you do*, and started petting Alphabet, who was butting her head against my hands and purring like an outboard motor. She settled her considerable bulk onto my legs, and I gave up all hope of getting blood back into my toes. "You know, I can't tell you anything, but I *would* love to get your insights on something," I said. "For the case, I mean. It would be really helpful."

"Ohmygod, anything," he said, delight sparking in his eyes. "Does this make me a consultant? An *expert witness*? I feel so important."

"Oh, definitely. An expert consultant. Very important." I scratched the spot where Alphabet's tail met her back. "So, here's what you can help me with: what do you know about emotional manipulation magic?"

"What?"

"You know, like . . . spells that make people want to do what you tell them to do, or that make them feel scared when you're mad. Like if you were yelling at someone, and you could make them feel like you were the scariest thing on earth, but with magic . . . ? What?" He was looking at me like I'd asked him if he had a recipe for preschooler casserole.

"Are you talking about theoretical dynamism?"

"Uh, sure."

He stirred his coffee, his spoon scraping against the bottom of the cup. "I don't know much about that. I only took the theoretical magic prerequisites so I could get my degree—I didn't do any advanced courses or anything. Tabitha could probably tell you more about the theory than I could." He was looking everywhere but at me.

"I guess I could ask her," I said, sipping my wine. "I just thought you might know, since you're interested in these things. And shoot, you probably know more than I do, at any rate."

"Why do you want to know?" he said, the words taut. I'd said something wrong, I could taste it. For a few seconds, Alphabet's purring was the only sound in the room.

"I just want to understand it before I take it into consideration when I'm looking at the case." He looked at me blankly and I realized I'd forgotten that I needed to explain. "Oh, wait—I got ahead of myself, sorry. I do that sometimes. I'm thinking that the magical emotional manipulation thing might be a factor in the case because I think one of the students at Osthorne is doing it. To everyone."

Rahul let out a staccato burst of laughter. It didn't suit him—it was too sharp, somehow. "Oh, well, I can tell you for sure that *that's* not the case."

"How do you figure?"

"Oh, man, theoretical dynamism is—it's pure theory, Ivy," he said, crinkling his nose. "God, I'm sorry, I just—I thought you were asking if I knew *how* to do it." He reached across the couch and took my hand, looking at me with a relieved smile. "And that's not something I would ever want to know how to do. I wouldn't even really want to think about how to do it. That's like, hyper-advanced pseudo-theoretical stuff, and even if it *was* possible, it's illegal. And even if it wasn't illegal—it's *wrong*, you know? Like, morally wrong." He worked his fingers between mine and gave my thumb a tap. "I mean, I might be the bad boy of the physical magic education world, but . . ."

"Wait," I said, swallowing my own heartbeat as his thumb idly bothered at a callus on my knuckle. "If it's pseudo-theoretical, how can it be illegal? That doesn't make any sense."

His brow creased. "It's just like anything. It's just like . . ." He tapped my finger again as he thought. "It's like electromagnetic pulse manipulation. Just because nobody can do it doesn't mean it's allowed."

"I don't understand," I said. "Isn't that like outlawing unicorn breeding? What's the point of making something impossible illegal?"

Rahul tilted his head. He squinted at me like we were speaking two different but peripheral languages. "What? How do you not know about this? It's like . . . the first thing they teach you in Intro to Theory, when you're learning about Cautious Exploration. It's first-day-of-school stuff." He said "Cautious Exploration" like it was a principle, like the scientific method or gravity. Like I should know it inside and out.

My heartbeat stuttered again, but in the wrong direction. This was it—this was the other shoe, and it was dropping right on my head. I rubbed Alphabet between the ears as I tried to figure out a solution. It was just because he'd never asked if I was magic. That's all. It was just so *easy.*

And it felt so good.

I'd never wanted Tabitha's powers—I'd always been too angry to envy her, too bitter to want to eat off her plate. I didn't want to be magic. But I'd been tasting the life I could have had if I had been born equal to Tabitha. If I were magic, I could laugh with people. I could talk to them as if I were on their level. If I were magic, I could eat scallops here every night with Rahul.

I did what I do best: I scrambled for a diversion. "So it's really impossible? Theoretical dynamism?" I pawed through my memory, frantic. *Not yet, not yet, not yet.* "Is that anything like theoretical alkalinity, or is it closer to a more clouds-in-water method?"

"Uh, kind of, yeah," he said slowly. "More fists-of-sand than clouds-in-water, though, or at least that's my understanding? To do it, you'd have to be able to trace a person's emotional state to the exact source, and then trigger a response. No one can do that. No one knows where emotions come from, not for sure, right? I mean, there are ideas and psychology and everything, but none of it is concrete." He was picking up speed, getting into the subject. I held my breath: *Maybe he'll forget what he was about to figure out. Maybe we can just have one more date. Just one more before I have to tell him, please, please, please.* "In order to manipulate someone's emotional state, you'd have to have an intrinsic, molecular understanding of how emotions are created and executed, but we don't even have a basic concept of that right now. A couple of people have been accused throughout history, but everyone's pretty sure they were just, like . . . *super*-charismatic. To do something like that, you'd have to be the most powerful mage in the history of magic. Seriously, it's just not possible. And the ethical implications are—" With his free hand, the one that wasn't still holding mine, he puckered his fingers at his temple and then exploded them outward. *Mind-blowing.*

Everything seemed to zoom together: lead filings drawn to the magnet of a suspect. "So if someone *could* do that—the dynamism thing—they'd be like. Power coming out of their ears." I shifted under Alphabet's weight as I considered the possibilities, and Alphabet stood up with a grumpy *mrrrrg* noise. She paced in a circle before sitting on the cushion between Rahul and me with her paws tucked underneath her chest.

"Oh, for sure. In more ways than one," Rahul said. "They'd already have power—like, intrinsic power—but the kind of person who could change the emotional states of other people at will? They'd rule the world. Seriously, you never did this as an ethics-of-theoretical-research debate? I thought everyone did that, like reading *Catcher in the Rye* in English class."

"I never read *Catcher in the Rye*," I said absently. "So if a student could do that, the dynamism thing, they'd be more powerful than anyone else in the world," I continued with a dawning sense of horror. "They could do anything, right? They could do *anything.*"

Rahul ducked his head, catching my eye. "Ivy?" His hand tightened around mine, and I shook my head, trying to get my bearings.

"Sorry, sorry, I just—you just helped me realize something huge about the case."

"I'm really glad," he said, and his eyes crinkled like he meant it. "I don't know what I helped you figure out, because you sound kind of crazy right now, but I bet it all makes sense from the inside, huh?"

"Yeah," I laughed, "and it would all make sense from the outside if you knew who I was talking about. Oh my god. It all works." I felt giddy. I felt high. I'd figured it out, I had it, it was all coming together. I was going to solve a *murder.*

Rahul squeezed my hand again and bit his lip. "That's so great. Ivy, where did you go to school?"

"Andrew Jackson Memorial in Woodland," I answered automatically. "God, it all fits. She *does* have the power, she just doesn't know it yet. Or maybe she *does* know it, and—" My eyes landed on Rahul's face. He looked stunned. I realized too late what I'd said. "Oh."

He blinked at me, and I saw the understanding dawning there. Still, he gave me another chance. "I haven't heard of Andrew Jackson Memorial before," he said slowly. "Is it a charter or something? Out of the national districting program?" When I hesitated, he clarified for me. "The national districting program that encompasses all twelve magical secondary schools in the United States? The national districting program run by the MDOE?"

I swallowed hard, and tried to map a memory of his hand on mine, knowing it was the last time I'd feel it. "You wouldn't have clarified that if you didn't already know, Rahul," I whispered. I set my wineglass down on the coffee table, bracing myself for the way things would land after they fell apart.

He sat back against the throw pillow behind him. His face was very still, caught in the instant of falling-down shock when he'd realized that he didn't really know who I was. The air was cold on my hand, on the places where his fingers weren't. "I guess not," he murmured. "So . . . so you're . . ."

"I'm not magic," I said. I hadn't felt the injury of those words so deeply since Tabitha had left me behind. It knocked the air out of my lungs, and I had to catch my breath. It had been coming, and I'd hoped I could hold it off, but I'd been fooling myself. I didn't just like Rahul for his looks. He was smart. Too smart to be drawn in by my incompetent attempt at playing pretend. *Deal-breaker,* I thought. I clenched my jaw and prepared to cauterize the wound. "I'm not magic. I'm not special."

"But you're—"

"I'm just a regular old person. No powers. No anything."

I spread my hands open so he could see how incapable they were of doing all the easy things he taught fourteen-year-olds to do. Rahul was staring into his empty coffee cup, and slowly, his eyes found their way to my hands, then to my face. He stared at me like he wasn't totally certain who I was, or who he was. I didn't want him to be looking for differences between Tabitha's face and mine, but then he said it: "But your sister—"

Hot, thick shame crawled up my throat. *Why not me?* "Yep. My sister. Tabitha got it all, I guess. She's the special one. Sorry I tricked you into thinking I was special too." I cleared my throat. "I'm not. You picked the wrong sister. Guess it's better for you to find that out now."

"Ivy, I don't . . . I mean, it's not . . . I don't understand."

"What's to understand?"

"I don't understand why you lied." He took my hand and looked at me with a compassion that scalded me. "Why would you pretend?"

I swallowed a laugh. Really? It felt so obvious.

But then I let myself look into his eyes and hear the thing he was trying to say to me: that I didn't need to pretend. Not for him. It almost sounded like he thought it was true.

"I guess I needed—" I started, and his brow furrowed. I tried again. "I . . . it's not easy for me, being here. Seeing Tabitha, and all the magic, and everything. And I realized that I could kind of step into a different life for a little while. A life where I'm . . . better." I swallowed hard, tried to figure out a way to turn this thing around so I wouldn't have to reveal more underbelly, but he was staring at me hard and I was helpless to stop the words from coming out. "I started telling a story, and the story was about who I could have been if I was like Tabitha instead of like me, and then you were there, and I figured out that I could maybe have you be part of the story too, and—"

Rahul let go of my hand and rubbed his face with both of his palms. "So this was, what? An experiment?"

"No, I just—"

"I'm not a character in a story you're telling yourself, Ivy," Rahul said, and he dropped his hands from his face and looked at me with something halfway between anger and pity. "I'm a person. I'm a real person who really liked you. I thought you liked me, too."

"I do really like you," I whispered.

He shook his head. "No. You liked lying to me, and you liked your story. That's different."

"No, Rahul, I really—"

"I think you should go." He looked at Alphabet instead of at me. "I think you should go, Ivy. And I don't think you should call me again until you're ready to see me as a real person instead of as a . . . a piece in whatever game you're playing right now."

I couldn't see him through the tears that blurred my vision, and I was grateful not to have to see his anger. His disappointment. "Sorry. I didn't mean to—I'm so sorry."

"Me too," he murmured.

I turned around, tripping over the cat on my way to the door. "Sorry," I said again, and it was too loud, and I was jamming my shoes onto the wrong feet, and it was all falling apart. Just like always. I screwed it up, and it fell apart, and now I was losing the one good thing I'd finally started to think I could have.

He didn't get up to see me to the door. I closed it behind me, and I walked out into the place I always seemed to end up: alone in the night, walking away from yet another mistake.

CHAPTER

TWENTY-THREE

IVY! WHERE HAVE YOU BEEN? I was trying to reach you all weekend!" Tabitha was jogging up behind me in the hall. I had pretended not to hear her the first few times she'd called my name, but then her hand was on my elbow, and I couldn't escape. All I wanted was to get to Headmaster Torres's office, to tell her that I thought I'd solved the case, to get it all wrapped up—and then to go home and sit alone in the dark with a bottle of wine, like I had the day before. Like I would tomorrow, and the day after. And the day after that, until I felt better.

"My phone's been dead. And I lost the charger." I said. This wasn't exactly false—my phone was, in fact, dead. I hadn't lost the charger, though—I'd just decided I didn't want it charged. And the screen was badly cracked. It had fallen. At high velocity. Toward a wall. My grip on it had slipped somehow after the twentieth time I'd checked my messages to see that Rahul hadn't called.

The half truth came out just smoothly enough for a stranger to swallow. She didn't know any better. Not yet, at least. But maybe in a year or so, when we'd been getting drinks together and maybe brunch sometimes and when we'd been on a road trip together, when we were friends, when we were *sisters* again—if I didn't manage to screw that up too and drive her away—maybe then she'd be able to call me out on little lies like that one. It would be nice, to have someone who could do that.

"Oh, here, give it to me. I'll take care of it." She held out her hand for the phone, and when I gave it to her, she gave it a hard squeeze. There was a high ringing in my ears—then the screen flashed a full-battery symbol.

"Do you want me to leave your screen cracked? You could ask *Rahul* to fix it," she teased. She moved to nudge me with her elbow, but I flinched away, knocking into a big gray trash can. "Oh! Are you okay?"

No.

"It's fine," I said, trying to sound breezy. "I think I'm just going to get a new one. My phone, I mean. It's time for an upgrade anyway."

"Are you sure? Rahul can fix a cracked screen like—"

"It's fine," I snapped, snatching the phone back. A flash of cool surprise crossed her face. I felt something balanced between us start to tip, a high-wire walker in a stiff wind. "It's fine," I said again, softer this time. "Sorry. I'm kind of tired today. Lots going on with the case. Actually, I was just on my way to see you."

The thing that had been about to tip—the hopeful promise of our rebuilt relationship—steadied. "What's up?" Tabitha said with a too-bright smile that meant we could move past the tension. Then her eyes slid past me, and her entire bearing changed. She seemed to get an inch taller, a year older. Nothing I would have been able to put my finger on—but whatever she'd done, she radiated authority. "Alexandria," she called. "Shouldn't you be in class?"

I turned so fast that a muscle in my neck filed a grievance. Alexandria DeCambray was halfway down the hall behind us, her hand resting on the handle of the door to the library.

"I'm studying," she said, her voice sweet. I waited—and yes, there it was, the wave of *don't worry about it* and *move along* and *isn't she responsible?*

I shoved aside the anger and the loss and the ache of broken potential and everything with Rahul. I crammed it into the oubliette along with everything else. *Time to work, Ivy. Time to prove that you're not so worthless after all.*

I rested a hand on Tabitha's arm and she looked at me. I flicked my eyes toward her classroom, just across the hall from the library.

A breath. A pause. Then: "Alright, sorry to bother you." Tabitha's voice was steady, and when I looked closely, she seemed to be her normal self again. Or, at the very least, she was back to whatever she usually showed me. The girl passed into the library without looking back at us.

"I need to talk to you," I muttered. "I think I caught a big break in the case. I think . . . no. I *know* who killed Sylvia."

Her lips went pale. "Really?"

"I need to ask you a few questions," I said, and she pulled me into her classroom. Her face was taut. She had grabbed me hard by the arm—it would bruise, I was sure of it. She closed the door behind me.

"What do you need to know?" Tabitha said. I looked out

through the hallway-facing windows of her classroom—the door to the library was closed, and I couldn't see Alexandria through the glass window set into the door. I would have bet money that she wasn't at a study table. *Returning to the scene of the crime?*

"Did you feel it?" I asked, breathless with excitement.

Tabitha stared at me. "What?"

"Did you feel it, when Alexandria—just now, in the hallway? You felt that, right?" Oh, god, was I just a lunatic? Was I imagining the way Alexandria projected emotions onto everyone around her?

Tabitha leaned back against a lab table. "Oh. Oh, that. Yes. It's—"

"I know, I know, theoretical dynamism!" I interrupted, so excited that I thought I was going to leap right out of my shoes. "Yes, I knew it, I knew that's what she was doing! But it's impossible, right? It's supposed to be impossible!"

Tabitha cocked her head. Her hair shifted against itself, shush-shushing in the silence of the empty classroom. The sound reminded me powerfully of the books in the Theoretical Magic section. "Impossible is a strong word," she said. "But I don't think it's theoretical dynamism. Alexandria isn't focused enough to perform such a complex operation, Ivy. She's . . . well. She's just kind of a mean girl. You're just getting a taste of what it's like to be bullied."

I was about to say something unkind about knowing what it's like to be treated like crap by someone for no reason when something in the hallway caught my eye. I looked up, and there she was again—Alexandria, slipping out of the library, looking down the hall in both directions. "Hang on," I said to Tabitha. I burst into the hallway just as Alexandria was about to round the corner.

"Alex!" I called. She whipped around, her spun-gold hair flashing. The light that poured through the bank of windows nearby shifted impossibly, framing her in its glow.

"It's *Alexandria*," she hissed, and I braced myself. *Stupid stupid wrong get it right next time don't ever forget stupid wrong apologize.*

"I need to talk to you," I said through clenched teeth. Alexandria hesitated, debating whether to obey or dismiss me. Which girl would she be today? Was she the PI's best source, the cooperative young achiever who just wants to help in the pursuit of justice? Or was she the queen of this school, not to be trifled with, answerable to no one?

She chose something neatly between the two. It was a lucky thing for me: I didn't think I could stand another wave of disdain. I held the door to Tabitha's classroom open for her, and she sat at a lab table before I could tell her to take a seat.

"Tabitha, do you mind if we use your classroom? This shouldn't take long," I said, and Tabitha pursed her lips.

"I'd like to stay, if you don't mind," she said, looking between me and Alexandria.

"Fine," I said, shrugging. Trying to be as casual as possible. "No worries. Alexandria, you're not in any trouble."

She fake-pouted at me, honey-sweet. "Why would I be in trouble?"

I sat across the table from her and reached into my bag, pulling out a file folder brimming with papers. Almost all of them were related to this case, and at least half of them were relevant. While my hand was in my bag, I bumped the RECORD button on my little digital recorder, praying that it wasn't full yet. "Like I said, you're not in trouble. Certainly not for helping your friend," I said, dropping the files on the lab table. Alexandria startled, her eyes on the top file. I looked down.

A picture of Sylvia's body had slipped about halfway out of the folder. Her bare calf, just a trickle of blood caught in the creases along the back of her knee. No shoes. No stockings. I hurried to tuck it back into the folder—let Alexandria see me hurry. She pressed her lips together and stared at me with hard, wary eyes.

"I'm sorry," I said. "That must have been very disturbing to see."

"It's fine."

"I'd like to talk about Courtney." I slid it into the conversation as gently as a fillet knife between two ribs. Alexandria blinked, then lifted her shoulders in a cool shrug.

"What about her?" She didn't sound confused at all. No, she wanted to know what I knew. She wasn't about to give anything up for free.

"The abortion," I said. I thought I heard something—a low swear, from the far corner near the window—but when I looked, no one was there. I glanced over at Tabitha, but she didn't appear to have heard anything.

"I wouldn't know anything about an abortion." I returned my attention to Alexandria, and fought back a smile. I had her. She was playing hardball, but she was playing—I could see it in the set of her face, the raised eyebrows and the who-cares angle of her neck. She was putting on a display, something she'd seen on television a thousand times: *You won't crack me.* She wanted me to make her talk. To weasel it out of her.

She wanted to feel like she'd almost gotten away with it.

"Oh, come on, Alexandria," I said, flipping idly through the file folder. I dripped with honey, luring her out. "You know *everything* that goes on around here. Don't tell me you didn't even know about your best friend's secret pregnancy. Or about the abortion potions she got from Sylvia?"

Another noise from the far corner. I looked out of the corner of my eye—something flickered there, but when I turned my whole head, it was just a poster falling from the wall. Tabitha cleared her throat.

"I don't know if this is strictly—"

"Fine," Alexandria snapped, and again I looked back to her. She was glancing at the far corner too, trying to see what had pulled my attention away from her. "So maybe I knew Courtney was pregnant. So what?"

"So, she's not anymore, is she?" I said smoothly. "You helped her with that. You're *such* a good friend. She's lucky to have you."

Alexandria let out a short, sharp laugh and folded her arms. "Laying it on a little thick, aren't you?"

I shrugged at her, leaned back in my chair. "You caught me. Sorry. Should I just get to the point?"

She leaned back in her own chair, mirroring me. She tilted her head too. Considering. I waited, and finally, *finally,* she nodded.

"Okay," I said, keeping my voice steady. "I know what you did, Alexandria. I know all about it."

"And what exactly is it that I supposedly did?" She asked it in the same even, low tone that I'd taken on. I couldn't tell if she was trapped, or if she was playing with me.

That probably means she's playing with you, a voice whispered from somewhere near the base of my skull. I wondered if the voice was mine or hers.

"You helped your friend," I repeated. I had my eyes locked onto hers, and the rest of the room dimmed in my peripheral vision. "Courtney needed the abortion. She was scared. There are no clinics around here, none where she could trust that a visit wouldn't get back to her father. But you knew where to go, because you know *everything* that goes on around here." I kept the syrup out of my voice this time—I said it like a fact, the same way I might have told the president that he was in charge of the executive branch. Alexandria nodded, once, not confirming anything but not denying it, either. "You sent her to Sylvia for an abortion potion. But Sylvia wouldn't give it to her." Alexandria's eyes flicked to Tabitha, then back to me. I continued, keeping my voice low and even. "So you went to take it from her. And in the end, you got it, didn't you?"

The silence in the classroom thickened around us. The only sound was the clock on the wall, ticking down the minutes until third period ended, and Alexandria swallowing hard. She glanced at Tabitha. "I'm kind of thirsty," she said. "Could I have a glass of water?"

Tabitha pointed to her backpack. "You've got a bottle sticking out of your bag, there," she said. She was almost whispering. Trying so hard, I thought, not to scare the girl.

I didn't know if I could have been so kind to the person who'd murdered my girlfriend. *My sister is a better woman than I am.* As Alexandria uncapped her water bottle to take a sip, I thought I saw her hands tremble. But as soon as I noticed it, the tremor was gone.

Alexandria shifted in her chair, settling herself, and put the un-capped water bottle on the table in front of her. In the corner of the room, another poster fluttered to the floor. Alexandria fidg-eted with the bottle cap, her composure slowly washing away. "So, what? You think I stole it?"

"I don't think you wanted to," I said, giving her an encouraging shake of my head. "I don't think you *meant* to. I think you asked her for it nicely. Maybe you begged her for it. Maybe not, maybe you wouldn't stoop to begging. And then . . ." I spread my hands. "Then you blackmailed her for it."

Alexandria's eyes flashed up to meet mine, and I rocked back in my chair. *Wrongwrongwrongwrong she didn't do that you're wrong look somewhere else look somewhere else.* Out of the corner of my eye, I saw Tabitha flinch. It was the first time I'd seen someone else react to what Alexandria did—the emotional manipulation that her friends described as power and that the staff described as charisma, because they couldn't imagine that it was anything more than that.

I took a deep breath. "You blackmailed her for it, and maybe you tried *that* little trick, too."

Alexandria's brow knit, and triumph burned in my chest. Her confusion wasn't of the *What are you talking about?* variety. No—that face was *How do you know?*

I went on, relishing the moment—I was about to solve a *mur-der.* "And then, when she still didn't give in? When she still said the potion was too dangerous for Courtney to take that late in her pregnancy? What did you do then, Alexandria?"

Alexandria's eyes flicked again to Tabitha, to the posters in the far corner of the room that were outweighing the tape holding them to the wall. She took a long sip of water. She was calculating. *How are you going to get out of this one?*

"I didn't do anything," she whispered. She looked incredibly small. The room was thick with her manipulation; my head buzzed with *no no no no no no no no no look away go away*. "I didn't do anything. I didn't do *anything*."

I leaned my elbows on the table and ducked my head to catch her eye. "I don't think that's true," I whispered back. "I think you killed her."

Alexandria dropped the water bottle, spilling most of the contents. Tabitha picked it up, then flicked a hand at the puddle. It hissed away into steam. She was looking at Alexandria like she'd never seen the girl before.

"What?" Alexandria was shaking her head, hard. "I didn't kill her. What? I wouldn't—I couldn't even—how would I—"

"Come on, Alexandria," I said. "You can play like you *didn't*, but don't try to pretend that you *couldn't*."

Alexandria laughed desperately. "She was cut in *half*! I wouldn't even begin to know how to do that! Are you crazy?"

I stared at her. "Let's not play this game," I said. "You may have everyone else here fooled, but not me."

"What are you talking about?" She said it loud, not quite yelling, but close to it.

"You're not just a queen bee, are you, Alexandria? You're not just a master manipulator or a mean girl, oh no. You're more than that. You're more than any of them realize." I was talking fast, too fast. "How did you keep them all from noticing? Is that what the hair is for? The makeup? Does it make them underestimate you? How do you make them see you the way you want

MAGIC FOR LIARS   287

them to?" She opened her mouth to say something, but I didn't
let her. I couldn't let her. "You're the most powerful mage here,
aren't you? You're more powerful than any of them. They all
think that theoretical dynism—"

"Dynamism," Tabitha murmured, her eyes locked on Alexandria.

"—Dynamism," I continued, "right, they all think it's impossible. But it's *not,* not for you. You're bigger than any of them
know. You could probably cut someone in half with your eyes
closed."

Alexandria had her head in her hands. I realized that I'd been
yelling too. "What the *fuck*," she growled, "is theoretical dynism?"

"Dynamism," I said. "And don't try to pretend that you don't
know. Don't try to pretend that you're not playing all of these
people for fools, pushing them around with your powers." I was
standing now, pressing both hands against the cool surface of
the lab table and leaning toward her. "Don't try to pretend that
you don't know you're the Chosen—"

"*No!*"

We all jumped out of our skins as Dylan DeCambray appeared
in the far corner of the room. He stood on top of one of the fallen
posters, half-invisible, waving his hands in front of his face like
he was clearing away cobwebs. With every swipe of his long fingers, more of him emerged from thin air.

"She is *not* the Chosen One," he choked. His face was pink,
blotchy; there were wet streaks running down his cheeks. His
chin buckled as he stalked toward us, still fighting through tears.
"She is *not,* she's just a popular *bitch!*" He punched the surface
of the lab table with all the force his high-school-boy rage could

generate. The tendons in his neck stood out as he pointed a finger at her. "She might be able to keep everyone scared of her. She might be able to terrify Courtney into keeping us a secret, but that doesn't mean—she's not *worthy* of the Prophecy!"

"What do you mean, keep you a secret?" Alexandria said. "Wait—were you—"

"Dylan," Tabitha said, holding her hands out toward him, "let's calm down—"

"*I will not calm down,*" he shouted, pacing back and forth with long, loping steps, and the windows rattled with the force of his voice and his fury. "The Prophecy says that the Chosen One will be the most powerful mage of our time, and it's *not her*! The Chosen One wouldn't waste his power on hair and makeup and keeping people who are in love from being together!"

Alexandria laughed. "In love? What are you talking about?"

He wheeled around, his praying-mantis elbows swinging. "We were in *love,* Alexandria. Courtney and I were *in love!*" A fleck of spittle flew from his mouth—he was literally frothing. His eyes were wild and white. "And you *ruined it!*"

"What are you even talking about?" Alexandria had gone half-shrill. I couldn't tell if she was afraid or not. I certainly was. "When did you two even date? Wait—no way." There was a hysterical edge to her laughter. "Was it you? *You* were the father?"

"I was the father," he said, and he almost sounded calm. But then Alexandria laughed again, and rage exploded out of him.

"I've worked my entire *life* for this! She's not the Chosen One! It's not her! It can't be *her!*"

He crossed the room in a few long strides. None of us could have known what he was going to do to Alexandria when he got to her—none of us could have predicted what his intentions were—but his face was dark with rage. I stood up, knocking my chair over, and took a step toward him. Next to me, Tabitha's hands flared with electricity, making the hair on the backs of my arms stand on end. Alexandria stumbled backward over her chair, landing on the floor with her hands up, trying to protect herself from the rage and violence that was barreling toward her.

But it was too late.

Dylan had already exploded.

CHAPTER
TWENTY-FOUR

MY EARS RANG WITH PANIC. I'd closed my eyes, bracing myself for an arc of blood to catch me across the face, but the hot wet splash never came. I opened my eyes and uncurled my hunched body.

Like the volume being turned up on a radio, Alexandria's scream appeared on the horizon of my awareness. It was a long, sustained, movie-star shriek. She was staring at the nebula of flesh that was suspended in front of her.

It spun slowly, a long pink streak of mist and foam and jellyfish-like hunks. I swallowed bile as I stood up and walked in a wide arc around the Dylan-cloud. There were a few recognizable spots. A toenail floated like a translucent seashell caught up in the froth of a wave. An eyeball dangled, ripe and whole, in the center of a fog of blood. I made my way to Alexandria and put a hand on her shoulder.

She stopped screaming, and in the vacuum left by the absence of her scream, I heard the slam of doors up and down the hall outside.

"Alexandria?" I whispered. "Alexandria. Hey."

She turned her head toward me without taking her eyes off the tendrils of Dylan that hovered nearest her face. "Y—yeah?" Her voice was shaking.

"You need to put him back together, Alexandria. Can you do that? Please?" Some distant corner of my mind congratulated itself on the steadiness of my voice.

She shook her head, and tears spilled from both her eyes. She didn't seem to notice them. "I don't—I didn't—what?"

I gestured to the exploded boy. He took up most of the center of the classroom. "It's okay. You're not in trouble." That probably wasn't true, but this wasn't the time for honesty. "I just need you to put him back together, and everything will be okay. Okay?"

She shook her head hard, kept shaking it for too long. She started rocking back and forth. I gently cupped a hand along the back of her head, and she went still. She whispered, "I didn't do this, I don't know how to do this, I couldn't—Miss Gamble, she—can you do it?"

Voices in the hall. Footsteps. Far, but not far enough.

Can you do it?

But of course, I couldn't. I tried for less than a second, the way I always had, the way I'd always told myself I wasn't trying—I tried to reach out with something that wasn't my mind, with that something that Tabitha and Alexandria and Rahul and everyone here but me seemed to know how to access. It was a habit that I pretended not to have, and yet I did it then. I tried to reach out, and I failed like always. I couldn't do it. I would never be able to do it.

I snapped my fingers next to Alexandria's face. *"Hey,"* I said, my voice sharp. "This one's on you. Put him *back*. Come on. We don't have much time, now."

She finally turned to look at me, turned all the way, and I caught my breath. All of the magic was gone from her face. Her hair was still blond, but next to her scalp was an inch of dark brown roots. Her eyes were smaller, closer together, and she had a pimple on her chin. I would have been willing to bet that when she opened her mouth, I'd see crooked eyeteeth.

She didn't look all that different, though. Other than the stark terror in her eyes. "I don't know how," she pleaded, and I believed her.

"Okay," I said. "Okay, let's just . . . let's try." She grabbed my hand, gripping it so hard I felt the bones grind together. "Let's try this. Imagine . . ." I scanned my memory for something, anything from the journal, but there was nothing. All of that was so abstract and recursive and self-referential—but then I landed on a memory of Tabitha, nine years old, trying to help me understand how she'd made a daisy grow super-fast. How she'd explained it. "Imagine that your magic is a swimming pool, okay? Now hold your breath." Alexandria nodded, her eyes locked on mine, and took a deep breath. She didn't exhale. "Okay," I said. "Now . . . now freeze the water, and then dive in."

It hadn't made any sense at all when Tabitha said it that day in our parents' backyard. She'd said that, and I'd been so frustrated, so furious, that I'd stomped on the daisy and run inside. I'd locked myself in the bathroom and filled up the sink and spent an hour staring at the water, willing it to ice over.

It still didn't make any sense to me, but Alexandria's face grew determined. Her eyes unfocused, the same way Tabitha's had the time she'd turned all the salt in Mom's saltcellar to quartz.

The Dylan-cloud began to spin faster. The toenail and the eye drifted close to each other, and I had a wild urge to shout *Don't scratch yourself.* I held my breath as the pink fog picked up speed, whirling—not into a funnel, although I kept watching the bottom of the cloud, expecting it to narrow. Rahul's voice echoed in my memory: *Alexandria always seems to be right in the eye of the hurricane, though. Which I guess would make Dylan the hurricane.* And yet, the cloud didn't tighten at the bottom as it spun; instead it drew into itself, thickening in places. As I watched—as Alexandria stood beside me, as still as a cat—the cloud formed a tight sphere. Mountains formed on the surface, then separated themselves away from the loose planet of flesh, revealing their substance. I fought down bile as a long spool of intestine spun out into a Saturnine ring. Three flat planes of dark purple rested like lakes before tremoring and sliding together into a beating heart, which hovered like a spasmodic moon. It clenched and unclenched around nothing for the space of a minute before a fine flow of red and yellowish motes fizzed up from the surface of the sphere and began to flow through it, pulsing in time with the movements of the heart and sketching a wide ellipse.

"Oh my god," I whispered.

Bones formed, marrow first. Half of a brain branched backward from each of the eyes. Two crystalline networks of nerves, fine as spiderwebs, sketched the shape of a body in two pieces. Long meaty muscles began to group themselves together, looking disconcertingly like pork hanging in a butcher-shop window. I wondered if Alexandria would be able to assemble it all, or if Dylan would fall to the ground in pieces. The spinning slowed, and I let out a little of the breath I'd been holding, in an attempt to lessen my dizziness.

I tore my eyes away from Dylan's liver to look at his sister. She was sweating profusely—her hair had gone limp and wet, and she was reaching up to wipe at her eyes. Her lips were white.

"Alexandria," I whispered, not knowing what I would say, not sure if I should put a hand on her shoulder or if touching her would ruin all of this, would leave Dylan dead. She shook her head without taking her eyes from her work, and bit her lip so hard that I saw a thin line of blood appear under her tooth.

I looked back to Dylan just in time to see skin sheathing each half of his body. His eyes had eyelids now, and they were closed, but I could see his heart beating in the left half of his chest. It was worse, somehow, seeing him almost put together—it was harder than it had been to see him in pieces. The two halves drifted toward each other, spinning as slowly as the mobile over a baby's crib. They pressed against each other, and the seam in his skin began to heal over. It was like watching a sped-up video of a flower blooming—his skin formed a scab, and then a scar, and then it was smooth, and then I wouldn't have known that there had ever been a fissure there at all.

Alexandria made a small sound from the back of her throat, a sound like a weightlifter gripping a school bus by the bumper, and then Dylan began to float across the room. He drifted down to a lab table on the other side of the room, landing as gently as a leaf falling from one of the black oak trees that lined the school campus.

She collapsed, then retched. I didn't look back at Alexandria as I ran to Dylan, weaving between chairs. He was unconscious, but breathing. I pressed two fingers to his throat and felt the strong, rapid thud of his heartbeat pushing back. A sound exploded out of me without my permission—half sob, half laughter.

"He's alive," I said.

Someone in the hall outside the classroom let out a ragged scream. I looked up from Dylan just in time to see Courtney shove her way through a crowd of students that had gathered outside of the classroom to watch through the windows. She burst into the room, still screaming.

"Dylan! OhmygodDylan!" She ran toward the spot where I stood over Dylan's still body. She ran through a fine blue-gray powder that littered the floor—the remains of Dylan's clothes, if I had to guess. Her foot slid through the thick dust, and she tripped, sprawling headlong across the front of the classroom. There was a thick, wet crunch when her face hit the linoleum.

"Oh, Jesus," I said, looking frantically around for Tabitha—I couldn't handle this on my own anymore, there was just too *much*. But my sister was nowhere to be seen, so I went to Courtney and helped her up. Blood poured from her rapidly swelling nose.

"Fuck, fuck, fuck," I muttered, freezing up with my hands six inches from Courtney's shoulders—until Alexandria appeared in my periphery. I turned to look at her. She still wasn't wearing her magical enhancements, but she looked steadier than she had just a moment before.

"I think I can help?" She said it like a question, and before I'd taken even a split second to think it through, I was nodding. She reached out and took Courtney's hand, threading their fingers together. Courtney flinched away, but Alexandria held fast to it, biting her lip.

"Imagine your magic is a tree," she murmured, and I could picture fourteen-year-old Tabitha clear as day, trying to help me understand how she made a feather levitate. *It's like if magic is a tree, but all the leaves are made of taffy, and you just . . . pull it.*

Courtney cried out, and there was a smell in the air like strawberry lemonade, and then we all looked at her nose. It was still swollen, but it had stopped bleeding. Courtney backed slowly away from Alexandria. Her foot slipped in the blood that had dripped onto the floor. She was shaking hard, too hard to call it trembling.

I glanced at the window that looked out into the hallway. There was a massive crowd out there, just . . . watching. Silent. I had never seen so many eyes before, so many stunned faces.

The clock above Tabitha's desk ticked five times. It felt like hours.

The door to the classroom burst open, and Rahul ran in, followed closely by Torres. Mrs. Webb eased in a few steps behind them, then waved her hand at the windows. They went dark, but the afterimage of all those faces burned in my vision. From outside, I could hear voices—Toff and another teacher, trying to break up the crowd.

"What is going on in here?" Torres said in a voice that felt inappropriately calm. I tried to figure out where to start, but before I could say anything, Courtney interrupted.

"She did what she did to me, she did it, she did what Miss Gamble did, and I—she did it to him, is he dead? Did he die? What did you *do?*" With this last word, she lunged toward Alexandria.

Rahul caught her by the shoulders and held her in place even as she kicked and screamed nonsense panic-sounds like a cat trapped under a fallen branch.

"Mrs. Webb?" Torres said sharply, and Mrs. Webb stepped forward. She placed her palm against Courtney's forehead, and the girl slumped over, unconscious. "Thank you."

Rahul scooped the girl up and gently placed her on Tabitha's desk. He hadn't looked at me once since he came into the room.

"Now, Ms. Gamble," Torres said, leveling a cool stare at me. "What exactly happened in here? And why," she added crisply, "is there so much *blood* everywhere?"

"Excuse me, um, sorry," Alexandria said, and it didn't sound like her at all. She was quiet—almost timid. "I'm sorry to interrupt, but . . . Miss Gamble. I mean, Ivy. She didn't do anything."

Torres looked at her with the same removed stare, evaluating, then nodded. "What did happen, then?"

"Well," Alexandria started, stammering, "we were talking. Ivy—can I just call her Ivy instead of Miss Gamble? It's confusing because there's like, two of them? Okay, well, Ivy was, was asking me some questions. And then it, um, it turned out Dylan had snuck in and was doing his invisible thing to spy on us." Torres sighed, then nodded: this was an everyday occurrence. "He was really upset because, um." She flushed. "Because Ivy said I was the Chosen One. And then my hands got hot and then Dylan . . . exploded."

Mrs. Webb went very still. "Go on," she said quietly.

"I think I blew him up," Alexandria said in a quavering voice, and tears started to stream down her cheeks again. "I think I blew him up, and then Ivy came and she told me how to put him back together, and then Courtney came in and she tripped and broke her nose and that's why there's so much blood." Her chest shook as she held back sobs.

"You can't have blown him up," Mrs. Webb said, peering at Alexandria like she was some exotic new species of jellyfish, dredged up from the uncharted depths of the ocean for study. "You can't have. It takes years of . . . but then, your hands . . ." The old woman walked to Dylan, still on the lab table. The heat of his skin fogged the sealed black surface of the table. She flicked her wrist, and a long Osthorne-blue sheet billowed over Dylan, covering him from the chest down. She pressed a hand to his forehead, and I wondered if she was performing some magical evaluation I would never be able to understand, but it looked for all the world like she was a grandmother checking a child for a fever. She shook her head. "This isn't possible. This isn't something that happens by *accident*."

"Please," Alexandria whispered. "I'm sorry. I don't know how I did it, I didn't mean to—"

"That's alright," Torres said, laying a hand on Alexandria's shoulder. "It's okay. We'll talk about it in my office, alright? You're not in trouble."

Alexandria nodded. "Okay." Then she turned to me. "I'm sorry. Thank you. I didn't— I didn't do what you think I did."

I nodded at her. "I believe you."

I didn't know for sure if I was telling the truth, but her face forced the words out of me—and not with a body slam of emotion. It was the change in her. She looked completely haunted. She looked afraid. She looked terribly, terribly young.

I thought about the story she'd been building for herself—a

girl, a *young woman* in charge of her world. Unstoppable. Fearless. But that girl had never encountered anything this *frightening* before. She'd encountered drama with her friends and her parents and boys and grades. Maybe she'd seen bullying, intimidation, violence. But in all this time, she'd never encountered anything so frightening as her own power.

"Let's go to my office, Alexandria." Torres put an arm around Alexandria's shoulder, and started guiding her toward the door. "Mr. Chaudhary, please come with us. I'll need your assistance. Mrs. Webb? Would you mind waking the other two, and they can join us?"

Mrs. Webb nodded, and Torres, Alexandria, and Rahul walked out. I didn't see if Rahul turned to catch my eye as he left the room. I couldn't stand to look, in case he didn't. It was just me and Mrs. Webb. I realized I had no idea what her first name was.

She rested her hand on Dylan's forehead again, and something about the position of her fingers was different, but it was nothing I could have described in a report. He took a deep breath, a gasping, choking breath, and sat up.

"What—what happened?" He looked at Mrs. Webb like a drowning man might look at the shadow of a whale shark. "Oh my god, I was—what *happened*?"

Mrs. Webb peered into his eyes, but didn't see what she was either worried about or hoping for. "You aren't the Chosen One, my boy," she said. She didn't say it gently, but she wasn't cruel, either—she was ripping off a Band-Aid, and must have known that wasting time would only make it hurt more.

Dylan heaved an immense sigh. "Okay," he said. He nodded to himself, then to Mrs. Webb. "Okay. I'm not the Chosen One."

He laughed softly, still nodding. Something seemed wrong—the boy who had been ready to tear Alexandria apart was gone.

"It's your half sister," Mrs. Webb said. "I'm sorry. I know you two don't get along—no, now, don't try to deny it. But it's her. She's more powerful than anyone you've ever heard of. And she's going to need a friend in the next few years, when the Prophecy is fulfilled."

Dylan pushed himself off the edge of the counter. "It's funny," he said to Mrs. Webb—neither of them seemed to remember that I was still in the room—"it's funny, but I'm not so worried about it anymore." He looked like he was going to say more, but he interrupted himself with a retch. He doubled over, clutching the sheet to himself, and gave three long, hacking coughs. He held his hand to his mouth and spat something into it, something that clicked against his teeth.

"What is it?" Mrs. Webb asked sharply. "What did you find?"

Dylan pulled out a tiny blue marble—smaller than a regular marble, but bigger than a ball bearing—and handed it to her. "I don't know. This isn't mine? I, um. I don't feel so well."

She rolled it between her fingers. "Hm. Go along to Ms. Torres's office, Dylan. I'll be there shortly."

He walked out of the classroom with the sheet wrapped around him, sparing me the barest of glances as he passed, lingering for a moment next to Courtney's still-unconscious form. I started to raise my hand in a wave, but he was already gone.

Mrs. Webb walked to the front of the room. I drew up beside her.

"What is that?" I asked, gesturing to the little ball in her hand. She touched it to her tongue before dropping it into my palm.

"If I had to guess? I'd say it's his obsession."

I stared at the little ball. No mysteries swirled within its depths. It didn't feel warm, it didn't vibrate, it didn't glitter. It looked like a funny little marble, like something a grandpa would have in a cigar box tucked away on a shelf somewhere.

"Is that something you can do? Mages, I mean—you can just take something out of someone like this?"

"Of course not," Mrs. Webb murmured. "I was a healer for longer than you've been alive. This is impossible. But then, that's a Prophecy for you." She shook her head. "Young Miss DeCambray is probably only just starting to show us what can be done when magic is applied the right way. Or rather, when magic is applied *her* way."

"What do we do with it?" I asked.

"You dispose of it," she answered. "It's medical waste."

"Really? That seems . . . I don't know. Wrong, somehow."

"Does it?" she asked. "If you had your gallbladder removed, would you want to save it just because it pained you for a decade?"

I considered the little marble, then set it on one of the lab tables. "I guess not."

"Hmph." Mrs. Webb picked it up and hucked it. It smacked into the trash can near the door with a loud, satisfying *ping*. She approached Courtney and pressed a hand to the girl's forehead, then jumped backward as Courtney sprang off the table.

"Oh my god oh my god oh my god Dylan I can't believe she did it to *Dylan* you have to *stop her*—"

Mrs. Webb looked at me, apologetic, and then slapped Courtney smartly across the face. Courtney's mouth shut with a little *pop*.

"I'm sorry, young lady," Mrs. Webb said, and she sounded like she meant it. "You're panicking, and you have to stop. You're safe. Nothing bad is happening to you."

"But *Dylan*—"

"Dylan is safe too," Mrs. Webb said. "Everything is fine. Now, we're all going to go to the front office, and you're going to talk about whatever you need to discuss."

Courtney looked between Mrs. Webb and me. She shook her head. "No," she said slowly. "I don't need to talk to anyone."

"Are you sure about that?" I asked. "You seem pretty, uh. Traumatized."

"I'm sure," she said, looking away from both of us.

"Alright," Mrs. Webb said. She turned, walking toward the door. I looked between the two of them, trying to figure out what to do, then dashed out the door after Mrs. Webb, leaving Courtney in the classroom alone.

"Wait," I called, and Mrs. Webb paused in her brisk walk down the hall. "Wait, don't you think she needs, like . . . counseling or something? She seems really freaked out."

"She just saw her secret boyfriend explode," Mrs. Webb said, dry as kindling. "Courtney will be fine. She might be a little panicky for a few days, but then they'll *make out* and she'll have a big personal revelation about true love, and then she'll be back in school next Monday with new bangs." Mrs. Webb patted at her immaculate hair. "I've seen it a thousand times. Always a crisis, with these girls."

I didn't know what to say. It seemed wrong—it didn't seem like enough. But I didn't know how to say that to someone who clearly thought it was so much *more* than enough, so I watched her head down the hall away from me, slow and stately. Something didn't fit. I stood in the hall by myself, uncertain—where could I go from here? But before I could decide, Courtney eased the door to Tabitha's classroom open behind me.

"Oh, Courtney," I said, reaching for her automatically. She looked up and down the hall, then slowly sank to the floor, sobbing. "Oh, god, uh, oh man. What—what are you—" I stood there, not knowing what to do with my hands. She was sobbing harder than I'd ever seen anyone cry. Worse than Tabitha on my couch a few days ago. Worse even than my dad, sitting on the edge of the empty hospital bed in our living room so many years ago. It was a kind of sobbing that seemed to come from below her lungs, from the deep aching roots of her. Finally, desperate, I grabbed her under the arms and half pulled, half carried her across the hall and into the empty library. I steered her to a chair and she sank into it, folding her arms on the table and sinking her face into her elbows.

"Hey, shhh, hey," I said, over and over, rubbing her back in small circles. I've never been good at comforting people—never really known what they might need. But the low drone of my voice seemed to help, and after a while her sobs diminished, and became hiccups.

She lifted her head, and her eyes locked on mine. "Oh, god," she moaned. "Oh, god, I can't believe—I can't believe it happened to him, too."

CHAPTER

TWENTY-FIVE

ICE WATER RUSHED THROUGH MY belly. "What did you say?"

She gulped. "It happened to him, too. What happened to me. It's so awful—he's going to have nightmares for weeks."

I sat in a chair across from her and digested this. Alexandria had played me. She had played us all. "I don't know how I did it," she'd said—but she'd done the same thing to Courtney? When? How many times? How many people had she put at risk? *This girl is a monster,* I thought, and then I thought of all of the people alone in an office with her right now. Dylan. Torres. Mrs. Webb. *Rahul.*

I cursed myself for not grabbing my recorder out of my bag before I left Tabitha's classroom, but I had to know. I had to ask her. I had to be my own witness. "What did she do to you?"

She sniffed hard. "She did *that.* What she did to Dylan. Oh my god, Dylan—"

"Can you tell me about it? From the beginning?"

Courtney wiped at her eyes, and a long streak of mascara smeared from her eyelid to her temple. "Okay," she said, "okay I—I think I can tell you. Because, I mean. Alexandria's going to tell everyone anyway, probably." A bead of sweat traced its way down my spine. *Would Alexandria tell everyone? Or would she show everyone?* "It was when I needed the abortion. Ms. Capley, she didn't want to—she wouldn't give me the potion. She, um, she said I was too pregnant for it. I thought I was just eight weeks, but she said it was probably closer to like ten or twelve? And so she said, um, she said the potion wouldn't work." She sniffed every few words. "So then Alexandria told her to give me the other kind of abortion."

"The surgical kind?" I whispered, but Courtney flinched as if I'd spit at her.

"Yeah," she said. "The surgical kind. But then Ms. Capley was like, 'No, you have to go to the doctor for that, it's not safe to do it here,' and I was like, 'Okay but I *can't*,' and she was all, 'I'll make it happen'—"

"Wait, who?"

She shook her head. "Alexandria. She said she'd make Ms. Capley give me the surgery. And Alexandria tried to make her do it, but she just wouldn't. And so then I went to Mrs. Webb, but she was like, 'No, it's too dangerous to do this outside of a clinic' and she tried to give me a referral but like she just totally *didn't get it*—" She took a deep, ragged breath. "Anyway, so, then Alexandria was like, 'Don't worry about it,' and she got Ms. Gamble to do it."

I shook my head. "Slow down, Courtney. You're talking too fast, you're getting mixed up. So, Alexandria was like, 'Don't worry about it' and then she did it? She, uh . . ." I made a blowing-up motion with my hands. "Alexandria did the surgery?"

Courtney shook her head, her brow furrowed. "No," she said,

wiping her nose on her sleeve. "No, she threatened Ms. Gamble. Alexandria had some kind of . . . I don't know, some kind of leverage over her or whatever. So she made Ms. Gamble do it."

The sweat that had dripped down my spine froze into an icicle of horror. "Ms. Gamble, as in, your theoretical magic teacher? She performed your abortion?"

"*Yeah*," she said, drawing out the word as if she thought I might be a little slow.

I rubbed my eyes. "Walk me through it. What *exactly* happened?"

Courtney looked like she was going to throw up, but I had to be sure. I *had to.*

"Well," she said, "she, um. We went into her classroom, and she had me lie down on the lab table. And then she, um." Her voice had gotten so soft I had to lean in to hear her. "She kind of rubbed her hands together, and she kept saying 'okay, okay, okay,' like she was hyping herself up? And then she said, 'Here we go, deep breath,' and then I was kind of . . . I was . . . everywhere." A tear rolled down her cheek. "I could see all of myself? Like I was floating above my body, I think? I was—I mean, my body was in a big cloud, and I couldn't feel myself, and I could see this little, um. This little blob, kind of toward the middle of me? And then Ms. Gamble, she reached out with her finger and just sort of . . ." She made a plucking motion in midair with her thumb and forefinger. "And I could see myself but I couldn't see myself, and I was just in this big cloud? And then she said, 'Oh, wait,' and then she was focusing *really* hard, and then, um, I came back." The tears were flowing freely now, but Courtney was staring unblinking at her hands, seemingly unaware of the fact that she was steadily crying. I thought of Dylan's heart, grasping at empty air. "I came back, and it didn't hurt at all or anything, but . . . I don't know, I don't know, I saw all of my *insides* like *spooling back in* and—"

She started to hyperventilate, and I jumped up to rub her back again. "Okay," I said, "let's just take slow breaths. Slow, slow breaths. Here, put your hand on your belly like this, okay? Now take a deep breath. Hold it, hold your breath, there you go—" It didn't feel like I knew what I was doing, but something in all of that worked well enough to keep her from passing out or vomiting.

"I don't feel well," she said in a soft, high voice, like a little girl.

"That's okay," I said. "Let's get you to the office, okay?" I thought back to what Mrs. Webb had told me about surgical magical abortions. *It's perfectly safe if it's done by a medical professional in a sterile environment. The girl gets a sedative so it's not too traumatic.* If what Courtney was telling me was true, then Tabitha had performed an abortion on one of those lab tables—classroom desks with gum barnacling their underbellies. She'd performed an abortion with no sedative, no painkillers, nothing. She'd done the magical equivalent of a bathtub appendectomy performed with a rusty screwdriver and a watch strap to bite down on.

No wonder Courtney was freaking out, after seeing Dylan go through the exact same thing.

I towed Courtney down to the front office. I kept up a steady wash of soothing phrases—it'll all be okay, you'll be fine, you're safe now. I had no idea if any of it was true. If I'd been betting on it, I'd have said none of it was going to be okay. But it kept her calm enough to put one foot in front of the other.

"Wait," she whispered when we got to the front office. My

hand was an inch from the doorknob, but I stopped and looked at her. She was staring at her feet.

"What is it, Courtney?" I kept my voice soft.

"I just, um. Before I go in there. Because they're probably gonna call my dad and then I won't probably talk to you again." She sniffed, pulled at her blazer. "I just wanted to say I'm sorry if my texts freaked you out or whatever."

I shook my head. "What texts?"

She pulled out her phone and scrolled through a string of messages. They were all addressed to me. The picture of me and Tabitha outside the bar; the shot of Tabitha breaking into my house. *Are you safe?*

I looked between her and the phone. "Why?"

"I didn't want anything bad to happen," she said, hunching her shoulders. "I saw you talking to Ms. Gamble and then Dylan told me about the note he left you, and I just thought . . . I thought maybe I could help."

"But you were too scared to say anything directly," I murmured, trying to keep the words from stinging her the way they would have stung me.

She nodded. "I'm ready now," she said. "I just wanted to say . . . to say sorry."

"Okay," I said, feeling awkward. "Thanks, then. I think I understand what you were trying to do."

When I opened the door to the front office, Mrs. Webb was making a harried phone call. "Yes, well, young man, I'm a mandated reporter," she said in a voice that made me want to snap to attention. "And I'm telling you that I've got a Prophetic Fulfillment over here, and I need official attention paid to it. So, who will you be sending over?"

She saw us waiting and held up one long, knobbly finger. I guided Courtney onto one of the benches where truants and cheaters sat. I waited near Mrs. Webb's desk, watching Courtney shiver out of the corner of my eye. She looked small and exhausted there.

"Excellent. I'm very glad to hear it," Mrs. Webb said with grim satisfaction. "I'll expect your agent here within the hour. If it takes longer than that, I will be calling again. Is that understood?"

I imagined the person on the other end of the phone sitting up a little straighter in their desk chair. As Mrs. Webb hung up, I glanced between her and Courtney, unsure of how I should begin.

"Mrs. Webb?" I said. "Do you remember our conversation? In the teachers' lounge?"

She fixed me with an X-ray gaze. "Of course I do, Ms. Gamble. I'm not senile yet, you know."

I crossed and uncrossed my fingers, a nervous tic that I hadn't lost myself in since grade school. "Well, Courtney had a surgical abortion performed on her on school grounds, and I think someone should take a look at her to make sure she's . . . okay."

I had thought that Mrs. Webb was sitting stiffly before, but her posture then was nothing compared to the deep-rooted stillness that overcame her upon hearing about Courtney. I felt like the entire room was looking at us, listening. "When did this take place?" she asked. I glanced over at Courtney, who was staring at her feet as though she'd never seen them before.

Without looking up, Courtney whispered, "It was the third day of school."

Mrs. Webb narrowed her eyes, deepening the network of creases that branched from the corners of her eyelids. She stood from her desk, walked to where Courtney sat, and looked down at the girl. "Who did this?"

Courtney looked at me. I looked back at her, not understanding until suddenly I did understand. She wasn't sure if she could say it. She wasn't sure that it was allowed.

"She doesn't remember," I said, startling myself. I hadn't known I was going to lie until the words had already left my mouth.

Courtney nodded, tears filling her eyes, and I wondered what extra damage I'd done by implicitly demanding that she pretend she didn't know who had performed the dangerous, illegal procedure. "Yeah," she said softly. "I don't remember. I can remember needing it done, but when I think about it, it's just." Her eyes were glassy. "It's too much, you know?"

Mrs. Webb lowered herself into a stiff crouch in front of the girl. Courtney's eyes went round, and I'm sure mine did too—it was strange to watch the normally stern woman fold herself down into such a comforting position, like seeing a bird do a push-up. Mrs. Webb took both of Courtney's hands and spoke to her softly. "Did you see it? Or did the person who did this to you give you some medicine before the procedure, so you wouldn't have to see?" Courtney started breathing hard and fast, and Mrs. Webb placed a hand over the girl's chest. "It's okay," Mrs. Webb said, "I'm just slowing down your heart rate and your breathing a little bit, so you don't hyperventilate." Her voice was low and soothing, super-calm, as if she were trying to hypnotize Courtney.

Courtney took a few deep, slow breaths, then nodded at Mrs. Webb, who hesitated for a threadbare second before removing her hand from Courtney's chest. Courtney took two more slow breaths unassisted before she answered.

"I didn't get any medicine," she said. "It just kind of happened. I saw it all. I saw, um. I saw all of it." Her voice trembled halfway through her answer, but she maintained steady eye contact with Mrs. Webb.

"Have you talked to anyone about this?" Mrs. Webb asked in that same low, steady voice. Courtney shook her head, and Mrs. Webb nodded. "Okay. I'm going to find you someone to talk to—no, I'm sorry, but you will have to talk to someone, Courtney. What you went through is highly traumatic. It's illegal, and the person who did that to you didn't take the proper steps to protect you. Do you understand?" Courtney didn't quite nod, but she blinked a few times, and that seemed to be enough for Mrs. Webb. "You're a very strong girl," she murmured, squeezing Courtney's hands. "It takes a lot to go through what you went through. But you're not alone anymore." She straightened abruptly, and looked at me with a ferocity that Dylan would have envied. "Ms. Gamble, a moment, please." She walked into the hallway without waiting for me. Before I turned to follow, I caught Courtney's eye. She looked at me warily, and I'm sure she was wondering in that moment if I was an ally or a threat.

I wasn't sure what the answer was.

When I stepped out into the hallway, Mrs. Webb was waiting for me, and I could tell that she wasn't waiting to congratulate me on a student well counseled.

"Well, Ms. Gamble," she said, arms crossed. She only came up to my chin, but she was still towering over me. My stomach twisted in that familiar principal's-office way. "You've got some answers for me, I trust?"

I blinked, then wondered if I was blinking too much, then wondered if *not* blinking would be more suspicious. "What answers are you looking for?" I said, trying to speak in a super-normal voice.

"Who performed a back-alley abortion on this student at my school?" she said, and although her voice didn't carry the same wave of obey-me manipulation that I would have expected from Alexandria, I felt compelled by the sheer power of her disapproval to tell her everything.

But I couldn't. I couldn't throw Tabitha under the bus like that, not without knowing *why*. Not without knowing what had happened with her and Sylvia. Not without answers.

It was not lost on me that I'd been fully prepared to shove Alexandria headfirst under the bus I was now attempting to save my sister from. It was not lost on me that I was giving the benefit of the doubt to a woman who had performed a procedure for which she was absolutely unqualified, endangering the life and well-being of this young girl.

But I couldn't bring myself to tell Mrs. Webb the truth.

"I don't know," I said. "She doesn't remember. I think she was too traumatized. Maybe with time, and therapy—"

Mrs. Webb shook her head at me. "Try again, Ms. Gamble," she said, and my heart was pounding but I dug a nonchalant shrug out of the very bottom of my well of fortitude.

"I wish I could tell you," I said. "Are you going to be able to take care of her? I mean, is Courtney going to be okay?"

"I don't know," Mrs. Webb answered, her eyes still narrowed, still locked on my face. "I certainly hope so. But there's a reason that surgery isn't usually performed in high school classrooms, Ms. Gamble. I told Alexandria DeCambray so, and I told your sister so, and I told Sylvia Capley so. There's a reason that sedatives and anaesthetics and sterile environments are a critical aspect of patient care. Whatever happened to young Courtney— and I highly doubt that what happened to her was anything approaching the isolated, proper procedure that would have been performed in a clinic environment—it will have left scars. Lasting ones."

I didn't bite my lip, and I didn't look away, and I didn't clear my throat. I kept my eyes steady on hers. I nodded. "If I find out who did it, I'll tell you," I said, and the lie fell between us like blood dripping onto a white silk blouse.

"I'm sure you will," she said, and I felt two inches tall as she walked back into the front office without another word.

Something she'd said was stuck like a splinter under my tongue. As I tried to get a firm grasp on it, my feet carried me toward the library of their own volition. I walked in and closed the library door behind me, leaning against it, drumming my fingers against the doorframe.

It was too much. It was too much, and I couldn't do it by myself. I was alone with this impossible thing. I wasn't Tabitha. I wasn't smart enough for this.

Mrs. Webb said that she told Alexandria that surgeries shouldn't be performed outside of medical facilities. She said that she'd told Tabitha the same thing. And she said that she'd told Sylvia that, too.

"Be smarter," I hissed to myself, squeezing my eyes shut. There was something I was missing. They all went to Webb to see if she could perform the abortion. That already made sense, that fit together fine—

But then, it didn't. Because Sylvia already knew that it was too dangerous. So what was she going to Mrs. Webb for?

That was it, that was the thing. That was the thread I needed to pull on. I tried to get a good grasp on it, but the books in the Theoretical Magic section where whispering so loudly, and things got slippery. It was hard to remember what I was supposed to be thinking about.

The books were getting louder.

I dug my fingernails into my palms and tried not to pay attention to them, to the place I was in, to the way that everything here constantly reminded me that I wasn't magic. I just needed to pull on that thread, just needed to let myself see the shape of the thing that Sylvia asking Mrs. Webb to help was about. I just needed to be as smart as Tabitha, but I wasn't magic, I wasn't brilliant, I was ordinary, I wasn't Tabitha, I was nothing but *Ivy*—

Ivy. I heard it again. *Ivy*. And again, and again, layered over itself—*IvyIvyIvyIvyIvyvyIIvIvIvy*.

I whipped around, but there was no one behind me. I was awash in my own name, spinning, trying not to panic.

Then, just as the whispers stopped and silence fell over the library, I realized that I knew exactly where to find the end of the thread, the one that started with Sylvia asking for help. I didn't know what would be waiting for me there, but for once, I knew exactly where to go.

CHAPTER
TWENTY-SIX

BY THE TIME I'D MADE it to the Theoretical Magic section of the library, the whispering had started again. This time, they were back to being incomprehensible—a susurrant tide of words that sounded like they should have made sense, but which didn't fit together to form phrases I could recognize. I stood outside the aisle, trying to look in, but I felt the same dizziness as I had the first time I'd visited the library with Mrs. Webb.

"Tabitha?" I called, and I could only just hear myself over the whispering of the books. "Tabitha, are you there? It's Ivy." I felt like an idiot, yelling into the end of the shelf that divided Theoretical Magic from Poison. There was no answer, and I wondered if I was totally wrong. If she wasn't there—if she wasn't at the scene of the murder—I would still have to find her to ask the questions about Sylvia and Courtney that I didn't really want answers to. If she was there . . . well. Why would she be here, hiding, if she hadn't done anything? "Tabitha?" I called again. "I just want to talk." I hesitated. "I'm alone."

As soon as I said it, I knew that I'd said the right thing, and I knew that I'd already decided my sister was a murderer. I'd already decided she was guilty. Maybe that's why my gut didn't clench when the blurred section solidified and my sister appeared in front of me. She was sitting on the floor between the two massive bloodstains that marred the carpet, resting her palms on each one.

"Come on in," she said in a dull monotone. She didn't look at me when she said it. I walked between the shelves, and immediately heard a crackle behind me. When I turned around, the blurred barrier was back, closing us in.

"I set it up," she said, still staring at the books beside her, which were shaking with the force of their whispering. "There's always been a little baby barrier here, but it's never been so harsh. So . . . active. The day after Sylvia died, Torres called me to her office, and I was sure that she knew. But she didn't know—she just wanted me to set up a stronger barrier, something the students couldn't get past, so they couldn't contaminate the crime scene. She needed something that would keep them from taking pictures of the blood. And then, after we got back the official 'miz report that said it had been an accident, she told me to leave it up so the private investigator could take a look too." She huffed out a breathy little laugh. "I remember thinking that there was no private investigator in the world that I would be worried about. I figured there was no one who could possibly figure out what happened. I had totally forgotten that you lived in the area. Isn't that weird?"

I sank to the floor beside her, trying not to touch the bloodstains. "It's not so weird," I said. "I forgot that your school was so close to where I live."

"It's weird," she insisted. "It's *weird* that we're twins, but I didn't think about you. I didn't think about you at all. I never do."

I reached for her hand, and she gently—but firmly—pulled it away. Something in me whispered "But we were supposed to . . ." and I realized that I didn't know how to finish the sentence.

"Tabby," I said. "I think you need to tell me what happened. Why did you kill her?"

Her eyes were wide, dry, staring. "What did you say?"

"What happened? Did she cheat on you?" I was talking too fast. "Was there a fight? Why did you kill Sylvia?" I tried to keep my voice as gentle as possible, but it was hard to find a way to soften those words.

"I never thought of it that way," she said, stroking the blood-stains. "I never . . . you think that's what happened? I was trying to *save* Sylvia." I watched my sister and wondered if maybe this was worse than I'd thought. Maybe she was actually just plain *crazy.*

"How did you try to save her?" I said, but Tabitha shook her head. I tried again. "What did you do?"

"I miss Mom," my sister murmured. "I know you think I don't, but I do. I really do. I wish I could have saved her." My vision went white as I considered what she meant. "I wanted to, you know," Tabitha said. "I wanted to help her, but the doctors I talked to—the magic ones—they said she was too far gone. They said it was *impossible.*" Her lip curled. "*Impossible,* as if they can't reverse the polarity of magnets and grow a tree in a day and make wine out of milk."

I leaned back against the bookshelf nearest me, then flinched forward again as the books buzzed like hornets against my spine. I tried again. "Tabitha, what happened?"

"I went into theory," she said, answering an entirely different "what happened." "I decided that they wouldn't be the ones to tell me what's *impossible*." She finally looked at me, and her eyes were like the long-abandoned mine shafts that my friends and I had smoked in when we were in high school. We'd loved the entrances to the old silver mines because they were almost impossible to find if you didn't know where you were looking. The mines had been abandoned when they were no longer productive; all the treasure had been scraped away, leaving only holes behind. "Do you know what I learned?" Tabitha had a smile playing around the edges of her lips. "I learned that everything they think is impossible is a lie. The boundaries"—she gestured with her hands, describing a shape I couldn't have identified if my life depended on it—"they're imaginary."

She twitched her fingers, and sparks danced between them. I felt the tiny hairs on the backs of my arms rise and hum as my sister watched the electricity she'd called out of the air.

"Are you afraid of me?" she said to the sparks, and it took me a few seconds to realize that she was actually asking me.

"Of course not," I lied, hoping the strain in my voice didn't give me away. "I could never be afraid of you, Tabby. You're my sister." I was using her name too much, but I couldn't stop. I couldn't stop saying it—trying to remind her of who we were to each other. Who we'd almost had a chance to become. She kept watching the sparks, and the books hissed all around us, and I decided to ask her one more time. "Tabby? What did you do to Sylvia? Can you tell me?" She didn't answer. "Please?"

She opened her mouth, then closed it again without speaking. She shook her head. "It'll make me sad."

I thought of Tabitha's eyes in the picture Courtney had sent me. I thought of her on my couch, in the dark, waiting for me to come home. "You're already sad," I said.

My sister began to cry. Her head was bowed, and her tears fell straight down, splashing onto the dried blood, soaking the crusted carpet with salt.

"I miss Mom," she said again, and then again, and then I was holding her tight as she gasped and choked, mourning the mother I'd thought she'd forgotten. "I miss Mom, and I miss *Dad*."

I knew what she meant. Our father hadn't been the same since Mom died. He was functional—of course he was; after all these years, he'd have to be—but he was a husk of the father we'd both grown up worshipping. He'd been hollowed out by the loss of our mother, and he'd never really succeeded in filling the space where she'd fit into his life. He'd been searching for a hobby for sixteen years. Even then, we'd had to push him into trying new things. He'd spent the year after Mom's death eating cold ravioli out of the can and watching the History Channel for eleven hours a day. I wasn't even sure if he had friends back then.

"I miss Dad, and I don't want to see him," Tabitha said. "I don't ever want to see him again, because I'm pretty sure I'm becoming him."

"What do you mean?" I asked, rubbing my hand across her back in small circles.

"I mean, Sylvia's *dead*," she spat. "Just like Mom. She's *gone*."

"Tabby," I said carefully. "Mom died of cancer. Sylvia was murdered."

Tabitha shook her head at me, wiping her eyes with her thumbs and then drying her thumbs on the carpet. "No," she said. "Sylvia died of cancer too."

I stared at Tabitha, waiting for what she'd just said to make sense. "I'm . . . not sure what you mean." My eyes flicked to the two massive bloodstains. The one on the left was peppered with dark spots where Tabitha's tears had fallen.

My sister took a deep breath. "Sylvia was sick, Ivy. She started getting tired—just tired—and then she was tired all the time, and then she wasn't hungry, and then her joints started to hurt." My mouth went dry. This sounded familiar. So familiar. "So she went to the doctor, and they found—"

"Cancer," I finished for Tabitha. She didn't nod, but she met my eyes and I regretted finishing the sentence for her. I shouldn't have taken that from her. She should have been the one to say it.

"Everywhere," she breathed. "It was *everywhere*. It was in her *eyes*. It was in her bones and, and, and in her brain, and her *heart*." She stared at me with deep intensity, like she was willing me to understand. "They said they couldn't help her. They said she had a month. Less, even."

A slow, uncomfortable heat was building under my skin. This was all so familiar. My mother had died seventeen years before, but I wasn't ready for this. I wasn't ready to hear it again. I couldn't imagine how it had felt for Tabitha, when cancer came back to take away someone else she loved.

"So you decided to help her," I said.

"No," she replied, shaking her head. "No, not right away. I told the doctors that they had to try, and they said that they couldn't. And then I went to Mrs. Webb, and I asked her to try, and she said—she said it was *impossible*." Tabitha spat the word like it was poison she'd sucked from a snakebite. "*Impossible. She said it couldn't be *done*. And then it was the first week of school, and Alexandria DeCambray was in my office saying that if I didn't do surgery on her little friend, she'd get me fired, and that's when I had the idea." My sister's eyes were bright, feverish. I wanted to back away, but I wasn't sure what would happen if I did. I sat there, frozen in place like she wouldn't see me if I didn't move.

"So you did the surgery on Courtney," I said quietly. "You did it to see if you could do it."

"And it *worked*. It worked! I did it, and it went great, and she's fine! Nothing went wrong!"

"You realize that you didn't sedate her?" I said, and I couldn't keep the anger out of my voice as I remembered Courtney sobbing in the hall outside Tabitha's classroom. I also remembered Alexandria's face as she'd asked for a glass of water earlier—she'd been trying to get Tabitha out of the room so she could tell me the truth. I'd thought she had been afraid of confessing what she'd done, but I'd had it all wrong. She had been terrified of Tabitha. Terrified of my sister, who could take a person apart with a *thought*. But Tabitha just waved a hand as if I'd criticized the plaque that hung beside a masterpiece.

"She was fine," Tabitha said. "It took me a couple of hours to do the whole thing—longer than it's supposed to take, I think, but then I probably took her apart way more than I needed to. But it *worked*, Ivy! I reached right in and plucked the pregnancy away. It was gone." She smiled, proud of herself. "All those years I spent trying to figure out how I could have done it for Mom, and I finally had it."

Something solidified. "You'd been trying to figure that out all this time?"

"God, for years. Since the day she died. I worked so hard, Ivy. I worked and I worked and I worked and I just thought—"

"You thought that if you worked hard enough," I finished for her, "you could do it. You could save her."

Tabitha nodded, her eyes shining. She didn't seem to realize that I was quoting her. "Yes, exactly, exactly!"

"If you could just remove the emotional aspect," I continued, "you could eliminate fatigue. Right, Tabby?"

She frowned. "Wait, what are you talking about?" I reached into my bag and pulled out the journal. Her face whitened. "Where did you find that?"

"It was in my apartment," I said. "I thought it was Sylvia's, but it's yours, isn't it? How often did you go there before I moved in? Were you using it to experiment?"

She shook her head. "I was there all the time, Ivy. I was there every other day. But that was back before it was vacant. When . . . when it was still Sylvia's place."

I stared at her as it all fell together. That's why she was there, crying on my couch the night of my date with Rahul. She wasn't there to see me. She hadn't wanted to have an emotional sister-moment. She wasn't coming to me for comfort or looking to bond. No: she was there to remember Sylvia. To remember their relationship. To remember the love she'd had there.

I had intruded on her grief. Because it wasn't supposed to be my apartment at all. It wasn't supposed to be my life. It was sup-posed to be hers.

"Tell me the rest," I said, my voice breaking. "Tell me about what you did."

She took a deep breath. "Well, everything worked out great with Courtney. So I told Sylvia I could do it to her, too."

I shook my head. "But, Tabby—"

"And I did it," she said, continuing as if I hadn't said anything. "I set up the Theoretical Magic aisle so that nobody would ever know we were there. I had to set up extra wards on either end of the aisle—a little sign about reorganization, just in case, and black-out glamours, and soundproofing. She trusted me to take care of it. I don't think anyone even came by, though—they never do, not that early in the year."

"Why *here*?" I asked, incredulous. My voice was getting shrill and loud; the books fluttered to match me. "Why not, I don't know. At home? At your apartment, or hers? Why would you do this at the *school*?"

"I needed the books," Tabitha said simply. "We can't take them out of the aisle, and there are texts in here . . ." She reached out a fingertip to stroke the spine of a book with no title on the binding, which looked like it was made of water. "There are texts in here that I could never buy without attracting attention." She smiled at me, her gaze distant, as her hand slowly sank into the spine of the book.

"Tabitha?" I said her name sharply, and she blinked a few times before snatching her hand back. I tore my gaze away from the rippling book, although I couldn't stop myself from looking back at it every few seconds. "So, alright, you—you set up the aisle? You sterilized it?"

"Of course I sterilized it," she huffed. "I'm incredibly good at planning, *Ivy*. I set up the aisle in a *day*. And then I had to get a substitute for my classes, and I had to give a couple of other teachers food poisoning so it wouldn't look suspicious that Sylvia and I were both missing."

"You poisoned people?" I said, but she didn't seem to hear me.

"It took three days, uninterrupted. I couldn't sleep. I couldn't stop to eat. There was so much cancer, Ivy, and it was . . . it was *everywhere*. It was like trying to sort oats from rice. But I did it. I got it all. I took all the cancer out. I *saved her*." She glowed star-bright with triumph.

"That's impossible," I whispered. Tabitha's lip curled.

"Is it?" she snapped. She reached into the air in front of her chest and tugged a piece of paper out of it. "Is it *impossible*? Read the coroner's report, then. Tell me if it says *cancer* anywhere." Her voice had grown sharp, impatient.

I took the paper, brushing my thumb over the torn corner where she'd pulled it off the missing coroner's report. I didn't read it. It didn't feel important anymore. "Why did you take this?" I asked. My sister bit her lip, looking away from me.

"I thought you'd figure it out if you saw the report," she said. "I thought that if you saw that she had the same kind of cancer as Mom, you'd realize . . ."

I nodded. I didn't want to hear more. "So what happened, then? Why did you . . . why did she die? Did you two have a fight?" I tried to keep my words gentle again, tried to sound like I wouldn't judge her for murdering someone in the middle of a high school library. "Did she say something, when you put her back together?" Tabitha's eyes welled with tears again, and she covered her mouth with both hands, shaking her head. I pressed harder. "What happened, Tabitha? You have to tell me what happened."

She shuddered. "I fell asleep," she whispered, and the tears broke over the edges of her eyelids. "I tried so hard to stay awake, but it was three days, Ivy. It was three *days*, and the whole time I had to hold every part of her all together, and I couldn't put her back until it was finished because then the cancer might have spread more, you know?" She let out a hysterical laugh as tears streamed down her face, along her jaw, beading on the end of her chin. "I was so tired, and I was almost done putting her back together. And I thought I *was* done, I thought I had performed the final reunification, but . . . but I was so tired, and I had been working so hard, and I just couldn't do *enough*. I closed my eyes, just for a second." She looked at me, pleading. "Just for a *second*, and then when I opened them again, she was . . ." She gestured to the bloodstains. "I tried to put her back, but I couldn't do it. Every time I tried, something else fell out, and I couldn't—" She pushed at the air with her hands, a sculptor trying to push clay back into the shape of a vase. "I couldn't do it."

I didn't hold my sister as she sobbed into her hands. I didn't lay a comforting palm on her shoulder. Instead, I stared at the bloodstains on the carpet, listening to her cry over the woman who'd left them there. As her gasping sobs began to slow—How long had it been? Twenty minutes? Thirty?—I realized that the books were silent.

She'd fallen asleep. That was all. She'd saved her girlfriend from the cancer that had eaten our mother alive, and then, in the last few minutes—she'd fallen asleep. I didn't know anything about how magical surgeries normally went, but if they were anything like nonmagical surgeries, the doctor would have had a huge team of people working beside them, scrubbing in and out, providing relief. Making sure that the doctor was well rested and alert.

My sister hadn't just done something impossible. She'd done the impossible thing *by herself.* And she could never tell anyone.

"Tabitha?" I said. "I think you have to tell someone."

She looked up at me. "You mean *you* have to tell someone, right?"

I shook my head. "No, I think *you* have to tell someone. I think . . . I think you have to talk to someone about this. And I think you should stop working at Osthorne."

She wiped the back of a shaky hand across her eyes. "I don't understand," she said.

"Well," I said, picking up speed, "I mean, Tabitha. I think that what you did to Courtney left her really scared, and maybe really *hurt.* And she's not going to tell anyone that it was you who did it, not now, anyway. But the longer you're here, the more likely it is that she *will* tell someone. And who knows how long Alex will keep quiet. If this gets out . . . they'll put it together, just like I did."

She stared at me, her brow furrowed. "You're not going to tell anyone?"

I stood up, brushing myself off. There wasn't anything on my clothes, but it felt like there was something clinging to me. I didn't know if I'd ever be able to get rid of it. "I'm not going to tell anyone," I confirmed.

"But . . . why?" Tabitha was still sitting on the floor, looking up at me, and I saw my sister there, but I also saw a stranger.

I had wanted so badly for us to come back together, sisters and friends again after all those years. I had wanted her to turn out to be just like me in all the right ways. I had wanted her to be *mine* again. I had wanted us to exist in a world where that was possible.

But it would never be possible. She wasn't the same girl who had held my hand in an incubator, who had caught frogs with me, who had helped me smear on my mother's forbidden lipstick under a fort made of bedsheets. She wasn't anyone I really knew. And as I thought about it, I realized that everything I'd thought I knew about her—every little gift of laughter and relationship she'd given me over the past week—it was all fogged over by the fact that I had been trying to solve a murder she'd committed.

She was my sister. And that was all she would ever be.

"It won't bring justice to anything," I said, and as I said it I felt a steady rain of exhaustion begin to saturate me. I couldn't look at her. "But you did something horrible to Courtney. You know that, right?" She bit her lip hard, but didn't look away. "You did something that could have hurt her so badly, even more than it did, and you didn't protect her the way she needed to be protected. So . . . look." I rubbed my eyes. I was so *tired*. "Go find a research lab somewhere, or something like that. Work there. You can't teach here anymore, okay? That's the deal. You leave Osthorne—hell, leave the country. I won't tell anyone what you did. But . . . but you can't come back."

Tabitha watched me warily. "What are you going to tell Torres?"

"I'll tell her the truth," I said. "I'll tell her that the 'miz had it right. This was theoretical magic gone wrong. Sylvia reached into a black box, and it had a cobra in it." I didn't add that the cobra was named Tabitha Gamble. I didn't think she'd understand, if I did say it.

She stood up and made to hug me, but I stepped back out of her reach. She stood there, awkward and puffy-faced, as I avoided her eyes. I stepped away, dodging her, and the edge of my foot landed on one of the long arms of a bloodstain.

"I'm sorry," she said. I started to answer her—to say "It's okay," even though none of it was—but she didn't let me get a word in. "I'm sorry that I manipulated you."

"What do you mean?"

She gave me a rueful half smile. "I got you drunk. I added a compound to your water—something to loosen your consciousness—and then I tried to plant it in your mind that Alexandria DeCambray should be a suspect. I thought it would throw you off. I even . . . I even tried to do a little bit of theoretical dynamism."

A memory flashed—Tabitha sitting across from me, saying that *it seems strange that the last time Alexandria DeCambray blackmailed a teacher and didn't get her way, she got aggressive.* Her half smile held, as if she were telling me about a prank she'd pulled when we were kids.

"Well, it worked," I said, a muscle in my jaw spasming as it crystallized: *She was the one who drugged me.* "I suspected Alexandria. I was sure, actually. I was totally certain that she killed Sylvia. She's just a kid with more power than she understands— but you understood exactly how much power she had, didn't you?" The half smile had congealed on my sister's face. "The funny thing is, you're the exact person who would have been able to guide her through these next few years. She's about to have a really intense time, and you two are . . . God," I said, running a hand through my hair. A crazed laugh bubbled up through my chest. "You're *exactly* alike. She might not have been manipulating anyone on purpose, but she was still willing to make people afraid in order to get what she wanted, wasn't she?" I was getting loud, but I didn't care. "She was still willing to fuck with people's heads, just like you. Do you know, I've spent half the time I've been on this case wondering if I was going *crazy?*" I shook my head, and let fatigue snuff out the anger that had started to spark in my belly. It wasn't worth it. "She really could have used a mentor like you," I muttered. "If only as a cautionary fucking tale."

Before I left my sister behind in the Theoretical Magic section of the library, I reached out to brush the spines of the books on the nearest shelf with my fingertips. They were still and silent, like dead things, and my eyes grew suddenly hot with tears over the loss of their whispering. I let the tears flow as I left the silence behind.

CHAPTER
TWENTY-SEVEN

I WALKED OUT TO THE Osthorne staff quarters with the weight of seventeen years of estrangement—and many more to come—resting heavy on my shoulders. I wasn't sure if I could carry it. Not because I'd just spent a little over a week being drugged and lied to and manipulated in every way that these goddamned *mages* could think of. It wasn't that I was angry and hurt and exhausted. It wasn't that.

It was that I didn't know what to do next. How to keep going. I told myself that nothing had really changed: I was the exact same amount of alone as I'd been when I took the case. I'd never had anything, not really. Not with Rahul, and not with Tabitha. Both of those relationships had been fledgling at best. Rahul was a guy I had been excited about, sure; infatuated with, definitely; turned on by, no question. But I hadn't developed a real *relationship* with him yet. I didn't even know his middle name. And Tabitha—it had been nice to imagine becoming friends with her, rekindling that sisterhood we'd lost. I'd been like a kid playing house. I'd been living a ridiculous daydream where I was something more, where

I *had* something more. But it had only been a week, and I had logged more hours in dreams of future closeness than actual interactions with her.

I pictured myself going home and lying on the floor in the dark of my living room, staying there until my bones dissolved into the carpet. That, at least, felt like a worthwhile daydream.

Before I could do that, I needed to pack up the Osthorne apartment where I'd been staying. I opened the door and froze.

At first, I thought I'd walked into the wrong place. But then I realized that I was seeing the apartment through the eyes of a stranger—of a civilian. It hit me like a blow. My chest ached as I took in how far I'd let things go. The story the place told wasn't a good one. Files carpeted the floor. Horrible photos of Sylvia's body were taped to the walls next to notes about the particular arrangement of the corpse. Empty bottles lined the kitchen counter: rum, gin, wine, wine, wine, wine. A trail of papers led down the hall.

The bedroom was down the hall.

My knees felt loose. I walked across the living room on faraway feet, shoved a pile of half-crumpled notebook paper off the couch, and let myself collapse into the cushions. I needed to leave. I needed to clean the place up and get out.

I needed to go home.

I started sobbing, and I couldn't stop, and I didn't *want* to stop, because stopping would mean trying to find a way to comprehend all of the things I'd learned, and all the things I'd seen, and the broken place that my mind had become over the course of the past few weeks. It would mean looking ahead, to the drive home, to the flat-pack furniture in my empty apartment, to the bar where my favorite bartender pretended to give a shit about where I'd been and why I hadn't come around for a while.

And then a laugh bubbled up out of me, because maybe the bartender really *did* give a shit, and God, I actually felt a pang of *guilt* at the idea of disappearing. At the idea of making him worry. I was feeling guilty about the way I'd been neglecting the most important person in my life, the person who knew me best. A person I tipped for his time.

People don't stick, I thought, that old bruise I couldn't stop pressing. But pressing that bruise didn't give me the same sense of satisfied, aching relief that it was supposed to.

Because it wasn't *people* who didn't stick.

It was me.

It had always been me. I had always slipped away unnoticed, a guest leaving the wedding before anyone can ask her to make a toast. People didn't stick because I was made of fucking Teflon. I'd always told myself that it was better that way, that being alone was easier. That I wasn't a coward for easing my way out of friendships before they could really start.

I closed my eyes so I wouldn't have to look at the mess I'd made. I sat in the dark, and I waited for the worst of it to be over. I'd been alone for years. I'd been cleaning things up on my own for as long as I could remember.

This was nothing new.

I waited for it to pass.

It wouldn't stick.

The next night, I came back.

I had a bottle of wine in one hand, and a bag of takeout pho in the other.

I passed by the door to my apartment—no, not mine. Sylvia's. I'd stayed there, but it wasn't *mine*. It never had been. I reminded myself, and it didn't sting as badly as I thought it would. Already, it was less raw. Soon it would turn into a new bruise to press, a bone-deep ache that would throb every time I remembered the place that had never been my home.

I passed by the door to that apartment, which was empty now.

I passed by the door and kept on going, around the courtyard, to the door I wanted. I tucked the wine under one arm and knocked.

Rahul didn't answer. I knocked again. No sounds came from inside.

I sat down on the porch to wait for him, the bottle between my palms, the takeout hot against my thigh. He would come home from work, and I would find out if he was willing to hear an explanation. Maybe he wouldn't be interested—maybe I would leave, drive back up to my neighborhood. Check in with the bartender. Weave home later than I'd planned. Lie awake in the dark pressing on bruises.

But maybe he would be willing to hear an apology. Maybe he would be willing to let me try.

I watched as the late-afternoon light went gold, then gray. I waited.

Maybe this time, I would stick. Maybe this time I would tell the truth.

Maybe this time would be different.

ACKNOWLEDGMENTS

To DongWon Song, my agent and friend, who knew I could do this, and who I would follow to the bottom of the sea;

To Miriam Weinberg, my editor, whose brilliance astonishes me, and who I can trust to ask me for more until there's no more left to demand;

To my critique and thought partners, Sarah Hollowell and Sharon Hsu, without whom my soul and brain can't function;

To Mom and Dad and Rachel and Katie and Scott and Mathew and Becca and Amy;

To Ryan and Christina, who hold my heart together;

To Jonathan, who has known every good version of me and some of the bad ones;

To Meg, who paints the sky and makes my brain go quiet;

To Dominik, who can see the person I'm becoming and who doesn't let me hide from the truth;

To Minerva and Aaron, for being kind and for loving my dogs;

To every iteration of the cabin retreat crew—Mark Oshiro,

Camden Tayler, Jeeyon Shim, Stacey Matthews, Adam Winn, and of course, our neighbor Dick;

To my early readers, including Hilary Bisenieks, Kate Lechler, Mara Hampson, Sarah Hollowell, Ashley Stauber, Sharon Hsu, Angela Hines, Matt White, Aidan Moher, JY Yang, and Ace Tilton Ratcliff;

To Sarah Williamson, for walking me through the way things work;

To my queer community, for finding me when I so desperately needed you, and for loving me as I find my way;

To the MurderFriends, to the coven, to PQ, to the group text;

To Team DongWon—we're taking over the world, and I'm so lucky to be along for the ride with all of you;

To Hank and Pepper Jack, who are best friends with each other first, and who loved me even when I postponed walks to finish revisions;

To everyone who helped me get through the chapter of my life when everything changed, including the entirety of this book— to everyone who helped me pack, who took me in, who put me up, who watched me cry, who kept me safe, who bought me drinks, who believed me and gave me the gift of patience while I tried (and sometimes failed) to keep it together;

To everyone who has ever loved any of the versions of me that I've been;

To those versions of me, who were growing and searching and scared and brave:

Thank you.